*The terrorist war has come home . . . again.*

*And the future of America*

*will be determined in the air . . .*

*and in the shadows.*

Resounding praise for the new master
of explosive adventure,
*New York Times* bestselling author
# JAMES W. HUSTON

## Also by James W. Huston

BALANCE OF POWER
THE PRICE OF POWER
FLASH POINT
FALLOUT

*Available in hardcover*

SECRET JUSTICE

# JAMES W. HUSTON

# THE SHADOWS OF POWER

**AVON BOOKS**
*An Imprint of HarperCollinsPublishers*

This is a work of fiction. Names, characters, places, and incidents are products of the author's imagination or are used fictitiously and are not to be construed as real. Any resemblance to actual events, locales, organizations, or persons, living or dead, is entirely coincidental.

AVON BOOKS
*An Imprint of* HarperCollins*Publishers*
10 East 53rd Street
New York, New York 10022-5299

Copyright © 2002 by James W. Huston
Excerpt from *Secret Justice* copyright © 2003 by James W. Huston
ISBN: 0-06-000836-9
www.avonbooks.com

First Avon Books paperback printing: May 2003
First William Morrow hardcover printing: June 2002

Avon Trademark Reg. U.S. Pat. Off. and in Other Countries, Marca Registrada, Hecho en U.S.A.
HarperCollins® is a registered trademark of HarperCollins Publishers Inc.

Printed in the U.S.A.

10  9  8  7  6  5  4

*For Nita*

We sleep safe in our beds because rough men stand ready in the night to visit violence on those who would do us harm.

—George Orwell

# ACKNOWLEDGMENTS

First and foremost I would like to thank the Blue Angels—the Navy Flight Demonstration Squadron—who showed me great hospitality and friendship while I was with them. They continue to demonstrate the high professionalism and skill that has become their hallmark, but, more important, they are officers and sailors of integrity and honor who are an example to us all. It is an honor to have gotten to know them. I would particularly like to thank Commander Scott "Scooter" Moyer, USN, former slot pilot for the Blues, who gave me invaluable advice and guidance. In spite of his good advice I have taken editorial license with some of the Blues procedures and communications for which I hope he can forgive me. I would also like to thank Kevin Miller, my roommate in the Jolly Rogers and former Blue Angel who first introduced me to the inside of the Blue Angels many years ago.

I am grateful to my friend Balester Barthélemy who gave me great insight into French security. I would also like to thank my good friends Mike Johnson and Paul Singleton for their insight into special operations and computer security.

Lastly, I want to thank my agent, David Gernert, for his continued support and encouragement, and my editor, Henry Ferris, whose insight is invaluable to me.

# THE SHADOWS
# OF POWER

Lieutenant Ed Stovic stared at his name on the flight schedule in his squadron's ready room aboard the USS *Harry S. Truman*. He was listed as the wingman for Commander Pete Bruno, the squadron commanding officer. Stovic hardly ever flew on Bruno's wing. His eye quickly scanned over to the mission—covert escort of an EP-3. The big slow EP-3 was to fly down the Mediterranean coast of Algeria and "listen." Collect intelligence. There had been some talk that the Algerians were getting testy about the American battle group crossing into Algeria's newly claimed two-hundred-mile economic zone. It was just the sort of thing that might stimulate a response from the new Algerian government.

Stovic tried to contain his surprise as he looked around the ready room. All the other pilots were watching, some smiling, some giving him looks of feigned anger for having scored the only good hop on the schedule. He was to launch before the official first launch.

Stovic briefed with Bruno and manned up. The excitement was noticeable in the crisp movements of everyone involved in the special launch of the two fighters. It came off beautifully. The two F/A-18E Super Hornets rendezvoused with the tanker above the carrier to top off their fuel tanks. They pulled off the tanker and flew low and fast to their rendezvous point, a random latitude and longitude in the middle of a lonely section of the Mediterranean Sea where the EP-3 waited for them, orbiting a thousand feet over the sea.

The EP-3 wagged its wings on seeing the Hornets across the rendezvous circle. The Hornets closed on the EP-3 from the left and slightly behind. Stovic studied the ungainly plane. He had never seen an EP-3 close up. He had never wanted to see it close up. It wasn't a fighter, so he had never thought much about it. But now he noticed the bulges and antennas all over it, like body piercings defacing its otherwise clean body. Stovic watched Bruno carefully, waiting. Bruno glanced at him, raised his left hand above the canopy rail, then closed his fingers and thumb together, like grabbing a sandwich, to indicate he was about to open his speed brakes. Stovic moved his finger to the speed brake button. Twice, three times Bruno made the signal; then he moved his head forward and quickly back to signal execution. They deployed their speed brakes simultaneously, and their closure on the EP-3 slowed even more.

The EP-3 was flying at two hundred twenty knots, slow for the Hornets but manageable. Bruno moved up close to the EP-3, up to the cockpit where he could see the pilot, who waved at them. Bruno nodded. He looked over at Stovic, who was tucked comfortably under his left wing. Bruno backed off, dropped under the EP-3's left wing, kissed off Stovic, leaving him there, and crossed under the EP-3 to the right wing where he took up his own position. They tucked up close to the larger plane, now invisible to any radar that might be looking.

\* \* \*

Chakib Nezzar glanced ahead as his flight lead lifted off the runway. He pushed his throttles all the way forward. Brilliant flames roared out the back of the enormous engines of his MiG-25 Foxbat as the huge Russian-made fighter raced down the runway outside Algiers. Nezzar raised his landing gear and climbed after Hamid to join him as they headed out to surprise the American spy plane.

They climbed through fifteen thousand feet, careful not to use any of their electronic equipment. The American plane could detect any electronic signal they might make, and it almost certainly had Arabic linguists aboard listening to any radio communications. It was nearly impossible to surprise one of the U.S. Navy's EP-3 intelligence-gathering airplanes, but they were sure going to try.

Nezzar heard the first intercept transmissions. *"Bearing 350, distance 300."* It was in the blind, requiring no acknowledgment. He knew it was for him, and he was to add ninety degrees to whatever heading they transmitted and subtract one hundred fifty kilometers from any distance. So the American plane was 080 from them, one hundred fifty kilometers away.

They increased their speed, pushing through the sound barrier, through Mach 1.2, and headed directly for the unsuspecting American plane, which was ten thousand feet below them.

Kent Rathman used his new CIA badge to open the door to the Counter-Terrorism section on the first floor of the enormous office building in Langley, Virginia. He was surprised it actually worked. The first time was always iffy. He walked down the hallway, looking for Don Jacobs, the Director of Counter-Terrorism at the Agency. He spotted Jacobs's office across a large area full of cubicles and walked around to approach it from the side without the window so his approach couldn't be seen. He looked through the crack behind the door where it stood open and saw Jacobs still sitting at his desk checking his watch. Rathman stepped silently through the door. "Morning, sir," he said quietly.

Jacobs jumped, catching the expression on his face before it could fully develop into the shock he felt. "What are you doing in here? Are you Rathman?"

"Yes, sir."

"We're supposed to meet in a conference room. Didn't you get my message?"

"Yes, sir, but there wasn't anyone there. I thought I'd come find you and save you the walk."

"We're still going to the conference room." He started walking down the hall, then stopped. "We need to get one thing clear right away. I don't like games. If you like games, you're in the wrong place. You got that?"

Rathman tried not to smile. "Sorry, sir."

They reached the conference room. Jacobs grabbed a carafe and poured coffee from it. He held it up, asking Rathman if he wanted any.

Rathman took a cup gratefully. "Thanks."

"You come highly recommended."

Rathman said nothing.

"Have you met Carpenter?" Craig Carpenter was the Deputy Director of Operations, the number two in the DO, the Directorate of Operations. The Directorate of Operations consisted of several subdivisions, including the CAS, the Covert Action Staff for political and economic covert actions, the PM for paramilitary covert action, and the Special Operations Unit, for counterintelligence. Within the Special Operations Unit was the SAS, the Special Activities Staff.

"Yes sir. We've gotten to know each other pretty well."

"Why did he pick you to set up a new SAS team?"

"I think I was just available. He interviewed me, and thought I'd be a good liaison between the SAS and your people."

"So you're now a member of the SAS. At least temporarily."

Most people talked about the SAS in hushed tones. It was odd to hear Jacobs asking about it in full voice, not caring who was listening. "Yes, sir."

"What do you know about them?"

The SAS was one of the least well-known special operations units in the country. The Special Activities Staff—a nice vague name for a very pointed, deadly group—was responsible for covert action undertaken by the Agency. Rat had done his homework. He wasn't about to accept his current assignment without learning everything there was to know about the SAS. "I've gotten a lot of good information but would always like to know more."

"You have a lot of experience," Jacobs said watching Rathman's face. "You were involved with the French Special Forces in Bosnia. You nabbed several of the most wanted war criminals."

Rathman controlled his surprise. "Who told you that?"

"And after the World Trade Center, your Navy group, Dev Group, was given a pretty free hand. We heard you were personally involved in several missions."

Rathman paused. "I can't really talk about much of that."

"I've read all the op reports. You think I'd let you be the liaison with my counterterrorism people without checking up on you?"

"I assumed you had," Rathman said.

"One thing makes me wonder, though."

"What's that?" Rathman asked, sipping from his coffee but not taking his eyes off Jacobs.

"If you're so good, why did the Navy let you come on temporary duty to the SAS? Why would they let you go?" Jacobs didn't want to say what he thought, that the SAS hadn't done as well as had been expected in the War on Terrorism. This was a clear attempt on the part of the special warfare community to cross-pollinate those who had done spectacularly well into the CIA. Jacobs resented it.

"I was due to rotate, and my detailer was sending me back to BUDS." Basic Underwater Demolition/Seal training, in Coronado, California, was where all Navy SEALs were trained. "They were going to make an instructor out of me. My Dev Group CO thought that was a waste. He set this up." Dev Group, or DEVGRU, the Development Group, as it was known, was the Navy's counterterrorism SEAL team. The elite of the elite. The Navy didn't even acknowledge its existence. They would talk of a certain SEAL team, its predecessor, but not DEVGRU. The group was elusive, unidentifiable, able to work both under cover and overtly.

Jacobs stared at him. Too pat. "Nothing else?"

"No, sir."

"Sure?"

"Yes, sir."

"You haven't been sent here to 'show us how to do it' or something, have you?"

"Not at all. I asked for another operational billet, and they asked me if I'd be interested in going TAD to the SAS." That was mostly true. They had begged Rathman to go to the SAS. They needed more people operating at the highest levels. They needed to expand the American Special Forces capability wherever they could. And somebody had big plans for the SAS.

Jacobs smiled. "So have you been able to set up your corporation?"

"All set, sir. International Security Consultants, Inc. I've already got rental space in D.C., Virginia Beach, and New York and a whole bunch of employees. Even a few contracts. We even have a couple of weapons evaluation contracts from the U.S. government. Business is good."

"It had better be. This has to be a going concern. You have to actually get business and fulfill contracts."

"We're all set."

Jacobs drank from his cup as he looked over the top of it at Rathman, the one they called Rat. "I understand you're good with languages."

"Some. I can't do oriental languages, but I can handle a couple of others."

Jacobs stood. "Where'd you learn them?"

"Monterey." The Defense Language Institute was in Monterey, California. They could make someone speak like a native if they had him for long enough.

"Where will you spend most of your time?"

"Here in Washington. This will be my main office. The Virginia Beach office is a good second bet. I don't plan on going to New York much."

"How many people do you have working for you? I understand they're all part of the package." He said "package" with some sarcasm, as if he wasn't quite sure what was in the package that had just been handed to him. The SAS usually operated in teams of twelve, sometimes two teams together.

"Well, yes, sir. I thought your people interviewed and cleared all of them. At least that's what I was—"

"Yes, yes, we did. How many?"

"It's a flexible number, frankly. They have their own operations here and there, unrelated to whatever I'm doing, but in a push I could get probably twenty-four or so together for anything you needed."

Jacobs liked that answer. "I look forward to working with you, Rat." He said "Rat" with the vague distaste he felt for anyone who was just outside his grip. "By the way, why do they call you that?"

"Just a name thing. Based on my last name. Rathman—RAT-man. It started at Annapolis. I look forward to working with you too, sir." Rat meant it. He was stepping into a different world. Operating with DEVGRU had been his life, covert overseas operations, raids, kidnappings . . . other things . . . all in support of the longstanding, smoldering War on Terrorism. They had had success, but there was much still to be done. Rat was enthusiastic about going after terrorists from a totally different angle, with different tools and objectives. Whatever it took. It was a dirty war, but a war nonetheless. "I hope I can help you succeed."

Jacobs's face broke into a wrinkled, reluctant, ironic smile. "I need all the help I can get. I'll be in touch—"

A young man in a white shirt and tie and a CIA identification badge dangling from his neck rushed into the room. "Mr. Jacobs, you said you wanted to know if that Algerian thing got hot."

"What's up?" Jacobs asked, glancing at Rat.

"The Algerians have launched fighters and are going after the EP-3."

"How many?"

"Two."

"Did we do the escort?"

"Yes, sir. Two Navy F/A-18s are under the wings."

Jacobs put down his cup. "This could get interesting." He looked at Rat. "Come on. Let's see what the Algerians do when they find out our unarmed intelligence plane isn't so unarmed."

\* \* \*

The E-2C, operating two hundred miles away, broadcast through its encrypted radio to the two navy fighters: *"Gulf November 103 flight, you have two bogeys approaching from the west. Angels unknown, estimated speed, Mach 1.5."*

Stovic felt a rush of adrenaline as the transmission sank in. He ensured his radar was off, as was his radar altimeter and anything else that would send electronic signals out of his airplane. They hadn't said a word on their radios since starting their jets. As far as anyone else could tell, they weren't even there. Their radar signature would blend in with the EP-3 that flew five feet above their heads with its four large turboprop engines turning methodically.

Inside the EP-3 Chief Petty Officer Jerry Kenny pressed his earphones to his head. He squinted at the screen in front of him as he dialed the frequency in more carefully. He finally took his hands away, nodded to the linguist next to him, and pointed to the frequency. He started the tape. He switched the large screen display in front of him to the radar repeater mode and saw the two targets their air controller was watching. The two targets, *bogeys,* as they were being called, were fifty miles behind them.

The Chief, an Arabic linguist, looked at the radar return and compared it to the heading and distance information undoubtedly being transmitted to the fighters he was following on the screen. He watched the computer triangulate the GCI (Ground-Controlled Intercept) transmission he was listening to and confirmed it was coming from the Air Force base outside of Algiers that had launched the fighters thirty minutes ago.

Kenny nodded again and spoke through his lip mike, "They're sending their fighters range and bearing data but are adding ninety degrees to the bearing and subtracting a hundred and fifty from the range. Pretty basic. Everybody got the fighter channel?"

The three men to his right nodded. "Okay. Sprague, see if you can find any other traffic we haven't seen yet. Thompson, get on the HF and see if they're getting any help from anybody else. Amad, check the ground crew transmissions again. See if anyone else is turning on the ground."

They all nodded their agreement.

"Come on down," Kenny said to himself and smiled as he watched the two MiG-25 targets approaching them at an ever-increasing speed.

A similar picture was right in front of Stovic. The E-2C was transmitting its radar picture via data link to the airborne fighters. All Stovic and Bruno needed to see where the MiGs were was electrical power. Stovic's screen showed the symbols for two data link bogeys—inverted chevrons. He shook his head, moving his oxygen mask back and forth slightly. The MiGs were coming out to intimidate the unarmed EP-3 and probably thump it—fly underneath it, then pull up directly in front of it to startle and intimidate the Americans. Instead they were about to get a rude surprise of their own.

The American radios were deathly quiet now. Everything that needed to be known was being transmitted by UHF data link. And it was always transmitting. No one who was listening to the UHF transmission would be able to make any sense of it—it was all data and was all encrypted—and the volume of transmission didn't change if things got more interesting. There was simply no way to know what the Americans were looking at or whether they were even tracking the MiGs.

Suddenly Stovic's AN/ALR-67(V)3 radar warning receiver jumped to life. It was the unmistakable sound of a fighter radar. He tore his eyes away from his visual cues on the side of the EP-3 to glance at the display. MiG-25. Bigger than hell. He'd never seen this radar indication before. Few Americans had ever flown against the vaunted MiG-25. The Russians rarely sent them out, and the Algerians never did. It was the fastest jet fighter ever built. It was the gorilla of Russian fighters—big, fast, and mean.

Stovic watched the MiG radar. It was unusual for them to illuminate a target from forty miles away. They liked to sneak up on targets, illuminate late in the intercept, then be right on top of them. In this case, no doubt because they were confident the American surveillance plane was flying alone, they wanted the Americans to know they were coming, to be concerned and worried, and possibly do something they would never do if they kept their cool.

He ran through his combat checklist. His AIM-120 AMRAAMs were ready, as were the AIM-9 Sidewinders. His gun was fully loaded. He checked all his switches and held off only on the master arm switch, which would make his trigger hot as soon as he selected a weapon. Fifteen miles.

"Mr. President," Sarah St. John said softly.

The President put down the *New York Times*. His favorite thing to do every morning when he was at Camp David was to read the paper. He knew that his National Security Advisor wouldn't interrupt him lightly. "What is it?"

"They're all airborne. You said you wanted to know."

The President drank from his orange juice.

"The Algerians are coming out?"

"Yes, sir. MiG-25s."

"How many?"

"Just two."

"That's a pretty big fighter, isn't it?"

"Yes, sir. Biggest one they've got. Very fast. Capable of Mach 3."

President Kendrick sat back. "Think they know what we're up to?"

"We don't think so," she replied.

"You still having doubts?" the President asked.

"This decision has been made, sir. I just think if something happens, it will look like we set them up."

He rolled up the *Times*, tossed it to the middle of the table, and stood. "Get everybody. Let's go over this one more time. Could we still call off our fighters?"

She nodded. "They're escorting the EP-3, but nothing has happened yet. We've only got a few minutes, though."

"Get everybody into the conference room."

She hurried out of the room. It wouldn't take long, since they were all eating breakfast in the guest dining room in the next building. It was only his Chief of Staff, the Secretary of Defense, and Sarah St. John, the National Security Advisor. They gathered in the newly refurbished high-tech briefing room just next to the room where the President had been eating. The table he had been sitting at had been quickly taken away, and the room had been restored to a family room with a large brick fireplace.

They gave St. John curious looks as they entered the large room. What could have happened in the last thirty minutes since they had received the security brief?

President Kendrick stood against the wall in a loose-fitting polo shirt and khakis. "Go ahead, Sarah."

"We've talked about this. We agreed to send the *Truman* battle group into Algeria's new two-hundred-mile limit—"

"We *had* to, Sarah," Stuntz said. Howard Stuntz was the Secretary of Defense and was forever nipping at her heels, trying to impress her with his superiority. She had learned to deflect most of his comments. "We don't let countries just shut down international waters. And here, it's right by the Strait of Gibraltar."

"Of course," she replied. "But the EP-3, with fighter escort, could be seen as provocation. I just wanted to make sure we were all on the same page."

Stuntz rolled his eyes. "I hope it *does* provoke them. I mean really, a two-hundred-mile economic zone? No ships or airplanes allowed? It's ridiculous. What did they think we were going to do? Just say okay, close off the western Mediterranean? Libya did the same thing with their 'Line of Death.' Same deal. Same result. We sent in carrier battle groups until they made some stupid moves, lost some boats and airplanes and relented. The 'Line of Death,' " he said in a mocking tone, "suddenly went away."

She looked at the map of northern Africa that someone had called up on the huge projection screen in front of them. It had the positions of the forces in place, including the carrier battle group, the EP-3, and the F/A-18E Super Hornets with it. Approaching from the west were the two symbols representing the Algerian fighters. "I just don't want another China incident."

Stuntz grunted. "We've got to protect the EP-3—"

Kendrick interrupted. "Look, all that has happened is the Algerians have launched a couple of fighters. That's what we expected. There's nothing new. If they go out there and see the escort, they should turn around and tell all their friends maybe the American intelligence planes aren't such easy targets. Right?"

St. John replied, "Yes, sir. That's why we're doing this. I just wanted to keep the bigger picture in mind. The new regime in Algeria has been on the sidelines in the War on Terrorism, but they're sympathetic to the wrong people. They haven't done what we feared. I'm just concerned this could push them over the edge."

The Chief of Staff, Dennis Arlberg, a lifelong friend of the President, watched the President as the others spoke. Then he jumped in. "Look, the EP-3 is a national asset. The NSA and everybody else care a lot about what happens to it. This new regime in Algeria is borderline irrational. They come from people who used to kill civilian villagers in their own country for 'intimidation.' They don't come from the same kind of thinking we do. *They* are the ones who came up with the two-hundred-mile limit. Not us. And they had to know we always challenge restrictions on international waters. Always have, always will. No matter who is President.

"The only thing different about this is the escort. But if you think we should troll up and down the coast of Algeria in their new two-hundred-mile limit without protecting an unarmed, slow airplane, you're out of your mind. If they make something of it, it's at their peril, and we have a carrier battle group right there in case they do."

Kendrick asked, "Is the MiG-25 a problem for the Super Hornet?"

Stuntz shook his head. "Anything can happen, of course, but it shouldn't be any problem."

"Anything else?" Kendrick asked. No one responded. "Keep me posted."

Twelve miles behind Stovic and Bruno, Chakib Nezzar and Hamid, the lead pilot, accelerated to Mach 2. They stayed together, transmitting from their radars to ensure the EP-3 knew who was coming after them. They kept their noses below the horizon to get down to the Americans' altitude quickly. Chakib kept his left hand on his throttle and ran through his combat checklist. He knew there wasn't any chance of combat, but he had live missiles on board and needed to do everything by the book.

Eight miles. Chakib could now see their target. He squinted at the airplane, afraid his eyes were tricking him. He had seen photos of the EP-3 before. It looked like the antisubmarine P-3, only fatter, with odd antennas and bulges, clearly modified for the collection of intelligence. But he'd never realized just how fat it really was—bulbous, stubby, ungainly, unlike the photos he had seen. There was something odd, or wrong. The fuselage was moving from side to side as if it were made of unattached parts. Chakib leaned forward and squinted, wondering what exactly he was seeing.

As they closed on the EP-3 at fourteen hundred miles per hour, Chakib's heart went to his throat—he realized he was looking at four jet engine exhausts that didn't belong to the EP-3. Four afterburning exhausts. It had to be an illusion of some sort. Then he saw the other four wings and the other four tails, the ones attached to the four afterburning engines, the ones that defined the images his brain had refused to recognize—two American F/A-18s tucked under the wings of the EP-3, waiting for them. There was no way they could slow down. They were committed to flying below the EP-3 at twice the speed of sound, underneath two of her front-line fighters armed to the teeth, and would pull out directly in front of them.

Chakib cursed and quickly threw his master arm on. If the Americans were going to take the MiGs, it wouldn't be without a fight.

His lead quickly transmitted in a high-pitched voice in Arabic, *"American F-18s under the wings!"*

Chakib grimaced. He looked up and saw the EP-3 pass directly overhead a thousand feet above them.

They screamed past the Americans. The supersonic booms from the MiGs shook the EP-3 and the two Hornets violently. He saw the Hornets light their afterburners, begin to pull away from the EP-3, and accelerate to catch up with the MiGs. Chakib watched as his flight lead pulled up hard into a climb, as they had planned, but now they were climbing in front of two armed F/A-18s that could shoot them down any moment. Chakib held his breath against the hard G forces pushing him into his seat at six times the force of gravity. Their noses pointed up as they climbed away from the Americans. Good, he thought. Let's just go high and head back to Algiers. We have shown them they can't just fly down our coast without cost. But as they straightened out with their noses pointing directly away from the earth and his lead chattering on the radio to the ground controllers in Algiers, he saw his lead come out of afterburner. He frowned and pressed his lips together. No, he thought. Keep your speed up and head back.

As their speed dropped below Mach 1.5 and headed toward subsonic, Hamid pulled his MiG back toward the Americans. Don't do that, Chakib said to himself. But he knew better than to transmit on the radio such a disagreement with his leader. And he had heard the ground controller encourage Hamid to "continue investigating" the American spy plane.

He reduced his throttle and pulled the stick back to bring the nose of the Foxbat around toward the Americans, now a mile behind them in perfect missile firing position.

The two MiGs dropped below supersonic and began turning even more sharply.

"*Lock them up!*" Hamid commanded.

Chakib shook his head as he turned his fire control

radar back toward the American fighters and raced toward them.

Bruno was shocked to see the MiGs turning back. The MiG-25 had no hope of prevailing in a turning fight with an F/A-18. In a straight race, there was no contest; the MiG was much faster. But the contest was equally unbalanced—in the other direction—in a turning fight.

*"Combat checklist. Master arm on,"* Bruno transmitted.

*"Roger."* Stovic flipped up the switch just over his left knee. They watched as the MiG-25s came back down from altitude, heading directly toward them, or possibly back toward the EP-3 that was behind them.

Bruno transmitted to the controller on the ship for the first time on their encrypted channel. *"Pueblo, they're turning back into us."*

*"We've got them."*

*"Any instructions?"*

*"Intercept and escort."*

*"Roger,"* Bruno said, acknowledging the only order that was really possible. They had no indication the Algerians had anything in mind other than a little sporting flight, a quick flipping of the bird, then back to the officer's club to boast to their Algerian friends how they had shown up the Americans.

Stovic was on Bruno's left in combat spread—a mile off and slightly higher—watching the two MiGs turn back. He put the MiG on the left in the reticle in the middle of the HUD—the Heads-Up Display—on his windscreen and pressed the button on the throttle to focus his radar energy around that point. The radar immediately saw the reflected energy from the MiG-25 and locked it up. The symbology on the HUD changed to show he had a target locked up and an AMRAAM

(Advanced Medium-Range Air-to-Air Missile) selected, the AIM-120, a smart missile that had its own internal radar.

Stovic and Bruno were thinking alike. Without saying a word they kept their throttles at full military power—full speed without afterburner. They would stay subsonic and maneuverable, their place of best advantage against a MiG-25.

Chakib Nezzar was breathing harder than he wanted to. Hamid was still in the same hard turn down toward the earth, and Chakib was trying to follow. He transmitted, *"They have me locked up!"*

Hamid looked at his own receiver just in time to see and hear the energy from Bruno's F/A-18 radar battering the skin of his airplane. Hamid leveled off from his slashing downward turn and prepared to climb over the Americans, who were in front of them and below them, clear against the dark blue sea underneath.

Chakib leveled gratefully next to Hamid and waited for him to begin his inevitable climb. Hamid reset the autopilot switches, then returned his hand to the stick to begin the climb. His gloved hand reached too far and pushed the large handlelike trigger on the backside of the stick. The large AA-10 missile on his left wing dropped and fired, leaving a large trail of white smoke as it headed down toward the ocean, unguided. Hamid cursed and quickly turned off his radar to prevent any chance of the missile guiding, or hitting anyone.

Chakib's mouth flew open as he yelled into his oxygen mask, "No!"

Bruno began yelling at the same time. *"We're being fired on!"* He watched the missile go straight out from the Foxbat. *"Animal,"* he said. *"Check the—"*

Stovic's heart pounded as he heard Bruno on the radio. He kept his eye on his target as the huge radar-guided missile from the other Foxbat tore from the jet.

Everything proceeded in slow motion, as if he were watching a movie. He focused on the MiG-25 on the left, the wingman. As he watched the MiG that had fired turn hard away, the one that hadn't fired continued toward him. He found himself icily calm and acutely aware that he didn't feel any danger; there was a chance the missile that had come off the MiG had gone instantly stupid or had been a mistake. But he also knew the rules of engagement, and based on what had happened, he could fire with a free conscience. He might never have such an opportunity again.

Shooting down a MiG was a dream. Every Navy fighter pilot carried around a not-so-secret dream of shooting down an enemy fighter. But what had raced into Stovic's mind was more than just the glory that might come to his Navy career from being known as a MiG killer. It was how he might use that new reputation to accomplish his lifelong dream of becoming a Blue Angel, a member of the Navy's elite flight demonstration squadron. He found his dreams crowding out his judgment as he moved his finger up on the inboard throttle to the trigger, determined to shoot.

He looked at the base of the HUD, confirmed he had a good AIM-120 AMRAAM selected, and pulled the trigger before Bruno could finish his sentence.

The missile flew off in a rage and guided toward the Foxbat on the left, directly in front of him, accelerating to Mach 4. *"Fox one!"* Stovic transmitted, indicating to those on the carrier that he had fired a radar missile at the target. The frequency came alive with radio transmissions. Other fighters were racing to their aid, and the controllers were shocked and looking for the Admiral to get directly involved. The Hornet computer showed Stovic how long until impact on his HUD.

Bruno released his microphone button on the throttle. Never mind, he said to himself. Inadvertent or not, it was a shot, and Stovic was justified in returning fire. He selected an AMRAAM on his weapons selection panel and waited to see what came next. If the other MiG fired, he would fire instantly. Under any rules of engagement he was entitled to defend himself. But something made him hold his fire. He just couldn't believe the MiGs had come out to shoot somebody or that the presence of the Hornets so rattled them that they fired out of fear or panic. It just didn't make any sense. He reduced his throttle to keep his distance from the MiGs and watched the two missiles in front of him. The Algerian missile had gone straight down to the ocean, and Stovic's missile was heading straight for the wingman.

Chakib saw the missile come off the Hornet. Just what he had expected, and just what he would have done if he had been flying the Hornet. But the missile was coming at him. It flew straight toward him, leaving its thick white smoke trail behind it, like a flaming arrow flying through the sky directly at his heart. As the MiGs had started up, they were tempted to continue up, but they knew that as fast as they were, the AMRAAM was faster. They pulled hard away from each other and broke down toward the water. The AMRAAM had no problem distinguishing the MiG from the water.

Stovic kept waiting for the MiG to fire back, to attempt to shoot him down as the other MiG had already fired. He couldn't imagine what was going through the mind of the pilot as he tried to maneuver his heavy fighter away from the best air-to-air radar missile in the world. The AMRAAM came up from under the Foxbat and slammed into its left wing. The warhead exploded in a fraction of a second, sending its fragments into the Algerian fighter and severing the wing.

The Foxbat flipped into uncontrolled flight and

threw Chakib up against the canopy. He tried to reach the ejection handle but could only touch it with his fingertips. Chakib fought the panic that gripped his throat as his MiG tumbled out of control. Several fragments of the American missile had punctured the back of the airtight cockpit and wind noise shrieked in his ears through his helmet. He could hear Hamid screaming at him on the radio, but the sounds were drowned out by the dying sounds of the MiG engines coming apart and the wind. Chakib watched the sky and earth spin in front of him. He couldn't tell if he was right side up or upside down. He was spinning too fast. The G forces mounted, forcing him up higher against the canopy. He pushed himself down from the canopy with one hand and finally wrapped his fingers around the ejection handle. He pulled it with all his strength and felt it move up four inches. He waited for the canopy to come off the MiG. Nothing.

He pulled the handle again, then reached for the alternate handle. He pulled it. Still nothing. It was then he felt smoke in his eyes and smelled it through his oxygen mask. He began to panic. He reached for the emergency canopy jettison handle. He heard Hamid transmit on the radio, *"Chakib! Get out of the airplane! You are on fire!"*

*"I can't!"* he screamed. *"The ejection seat is not re—"* He pulled the canopy jettison handle, the canopy rails were blown off by explosive cord, and the canopy flew off the airplane. *"I got the canopy off!"*

Wind whistled around him, throwing him back against his seat, which was now free to burn in the open air. Fragments from the missile warhead had disabled the seat and punctured the rocket fuel that should have thrown the ejection seat clear of the airplane. It now burned intensely just behind Nezzar, through the entire back of the ejection seat and the parachute in it. It started burning the harnesses that kept him strapped in and the boots on his feet. *"There's fire!"* he cried. *"The seat is on fire!"*

Stovic watched as the Foxbat continued to spin toward the Mediterranean. He kept his radar locked on the second Foxbat, which was between him and the burning plane.

*"Animal, knock it off, knock it off,"* Bruno transmitted, using Stovic's call sign to make sure he heard him.

Chakib strained to get out of the cockpit and away from the fire. He saw with horror that the skin on the back of his hands was hanging off, drooping to the side as if made from putty. The pain on his feet was intolerable as he pushed himself up into the airstream, away from the seat. *"I'm on fire! I'm on fire!"* Chakib's screams were transmitted over and over again on his radio.

*"Get out!"* Hamid yelled.

Chakib's plane plummeted down in a perfect spiral trailing a long flame and black smoke behind it. He kept his microphone on the entire way down, crying out in pain, screaming that he was on fire, until he clearly couldn't take any more. He finally wrapped his wounded hand around the emergency release handle and pulled with everything he had left. He felt the pressure release from his harnesses, and he climbed out of the Foxbat cockpit to escape the fire. He jumped and flew up into the airstream. He was pulled out of the cockpit and just missed the two huge tails of the Foxbat as the airstream pulled him behind his falling jet. As the Foxbat spun below him, he reached up to his left shoulder with his right hand, the burned skin hanging down toward the sea, and pulled the ripcord to manually deploy the parachute. He felt the cord release and the back of the parachute open. The wind whipped it up, and he looked up over his head expectantly. The white silk parachute was a tattered mess with brown singed edges on large and small holes. The half of the parachute on his right was detached from the risers, spilling out all the air that might have slowed him. His parachute was burned, ruined, and there was no backup. Chakib looked down at the sea. He watched his Foxbat plunge in below him, throwing up a tower of white water. He looked up at the American fighter that had shot him down.

High above in the EP-3, the Arabic linguists put down their headsets solemnly. Their smiles had vanished.

*"Splash one Foxbat,"* Lieutenant Stovic transmitted to the controller on the *Truman* as he circled and followed the Foxbat down to the sea. He watched it hit with satisfaction, then looked at the pilot and realized the same thing the pilot had realized, that his parachute wasn't going to stop him. He was doomed.

*"Roger. Good shooting,"* the controller replied. *"Where's the second bogey?"*

Bruno watched the other MiG circle the white foamy remnant of his wingman far below them above the Mediterranean. *"He's on scene SAR."*

*"Should we send a helo?"*

*"Negative. His chute never opened."*

*"Roger that. Your signal is RTB."* Return to base.

He glanced over at Stovic, who had joined on his wing. *"Roger, RTB."*

## CHAPTER 2

The phone rang in the studio apartment in Georgetown with a loud, demanding ring that Ismael had grown to hate. Several weeks before, he had taken the phone apart, disarmed the bell, and installed a light instead. But he had quickly learned that he couldn't see the light all the time, especially when he was asleep. He had put the bell back in but had lined half of it with felt, so the ring sounded like a muffled, distant request. It hadn't been enough to wake him, so he had taken the felt off and restored it to its original state. Now it annoyed him again, but it was enough to wake him.

"Ismael!" his mother cried as soon as he answered the phone.

Ismael felt a chill of dread. His mother had not called him once since he had left Algeria three years before to come to Washington to study engineering. His father always called. *Always.* His mother would use most of the time to talk to her second son, but she never placed the call. "Mother, what is it? Why are you calling me in the middle of the night?" he replied in the comfortable Arabic they spoke in their home.

"Your brother!"

"What about him? What?"

"He is dead!" she shrieked, breaking down into uncontrollable sobs as soon as the declaration was out of her mouth.

Ismael could barely speak. "Dead? What happened?"

There was no reply, just the sound of his mother sobbing in a way that he had never heard before, the kind that told him her life had broken and was beyond repair. His father took the phone. "Ismael," he said in his deep, soothing voice.

"What *happened*? Is this true?"

"Yes. It is true—"

"But how? Was there an accident?"

"No. The Americans. They came to challenge the two-hundred-mile—"

"No!" he cried, his head falling. "I knew as soon as I saw that we were saying—"

"The Americans sent their aircraft carrier here to provoke us. They sent one of their spy planes to fly near our coast. We sent fighters out after it, and there was a battle. Your brother was shot down."

"No," Ismael moaned. "They shot him down?"

"Yes. I spoke with the pilot who was with him, in the other plane."

"Did he parachute out? Is he in the sea?"

His father hesitated. After some prodding he had gotten the entire story from the other pilot, including the fire and the desperate attempt to climb out of the jet. Ismael didn't need to know it all. It would just hurt more. "There was no parachute. The American missile hit right at the cockpit. He was killed instantly."

Ismael's mind was flooded with memories of his older brother. His hero. His brother was in nearly every memory he had of his entire life, and it all came back to him at once. The heaviness of the new emptiness in his life hit him like a fall onto his back from a fence that he recalled from Algiers. His brother had tried to break the fall but to no avail—he had landed flat on his back, the wind knocked out of him. He had lain motionless, staring up at his brother, wondering if he was dying. He felt the same thing now as he stared at the memory of his brother's face.

Neither of them had married, but they had looked forward to raising their children together. They had promised to live near each other in their favorite section of Algiers, near a small park where their sons could play soccer together. He fought back tears as he tried to talk. "I will leave today. Mother needs me."

"No, there is nothing you can do. We don't even have the body . . . It is so far—"

"There will be a funeral for him."

"Yes, but we don't know when."

"I will be there."

"I am sorry to have had to tell you this, Ismael." His father's lips quivered as he tried to retain his composure. He was a physician. He dealt with death every day. But he never expected to have to deal with the death of one of his sons. He desperately wanted to see his only remaining child, but he didn't want to look weak before him or his mother. He tried to sound calm as he replied, "Do come home, son. It would be good for your mother. For . . . all of us. Do you have enough money to get—"

"I have money."

"But your studies?"

"I have an exam in three days. I will leave that afternoon. I must be there."

"Thank you."

"Roll it!" Commander Bruno yelled at exactly 2000 hours on the night of the busiest day of his life. He sat in his gray steel and burgundy chair in the front of Ready Room 7, directly under the arresting gear aboard the USS *Harry S. Truman*. The Ragin' Bulls, VFA-37—Strike-Fighter Squadron 37—had a nightly tradition, which was common in Navy squadrons, of gathering in the ready room for an evening movie. The commanding officer would set the time, and the duty officer would ensure that the movie—a DVD actually—rolled at that time—to the *second*—and that it was framed on the screen and in focus. If he failed, he was subjected to endless ridicule, various objects were thrown at him, and he would receive an additional day of duty, where he might be able to redeem himself.

The evening had become a big party. Their squadron mate had shot down the first MiG a Navy pilot had shot down in years and the first MiG-25 ever. In a short time they would be headed home, out of the Mediterranean to Norfolk, Virginia. It was the perfect ending to a fabulous cruise in the Med.

Stovic tried to act as if nothing had happened. When he and Commander Bruno had landed after the shoot-down, the atmosphere aboard the carrier had been electric, particularly in their ready room. Everyone on the carrier from the Admiral down to the lowliest seaman apprentice knew that the MiGs had been after a defenseless EP-3, the slow, lumbering intelligence plane that some Air Forces liked to intimidate. The aggressors had gotten a rude surprise, and had paid dearly for it. The schoolyard bully had picked on the chubby kid again, but this time had discovered a big brother who wasn't afraid. The squadron wanted to hear every word of what had happened. Over and over again Stovic had been called on to recount the shoot-down.

The movie finally rolled, but it was a surprise. Bruno had made a copy of Stovic's gun camera tape. It was in the VCR waiting for the signal. When the duty officer rolled the tape, all the pilots expected *Terminator 3*, starring Arnold Schwarzenegger. Instead they got the gun camera film. They all recognized it instantly and roared their approval. They watched as the MiG-25s flew by them and pulled up; they listened to the radio comm between Bruno and Stovic; and they screamed enthusiastically as they saw the MiG-25 fire at Bruno. Stovic replied instantly by firing his own missile at the shooter's wingman.

There were cries for a rerun of the gun camera film, but Bruno shook his head. "Roll 'em!" he yelled again, and T-3 lit up the screen.

The start was perfect again. Commander Bruno grinned and gave his approving thumb's-up to the squadron duty officer, who relaxed for the first time in eighteen hours. The phone was still ringing off the wall. Grubby, a Lieutenant, junior grade, had been ordered by Bruno to protect him and Animal from all the curious callers who just wanted to hear the story of the shoot-down. They had told it enough. He knew Stovic needed to be with his family—his squadron mates—to feel normal and allow what had happened to settle in.

The phone rang again. Stovic sat on the far left side of the ready room in the second row, in his assigned chair, which had his name stitched into the seat cover. He glanced at Grubby as he tried to concentrate on Arnold. He saw Grubby look at him, raise his hand in assurance, and shake his head to whoever was on the phone. Grubby hung up and returned his own attention to the movie.

There was a knock on the door in the front of the ready room. Grubby jumped up from his chair, furious that someone would ignore the signs clearly hanging on the doors in the front and the back of the ready room that read DO NOT DISTURB! CLASSIFIED BRIEF UNDER WAY!

He pulled the door open, stepped out of the ready room, and closed the door behind him to keep the room dark. The red passageway lights illuminated the faces of two officers in khakis and flight jackets that he recognized immediately. Commander Rob Strauss, the ship's Intelligence Officer, and Lieutenant Commander Jennifer Harrow, the Air Wing Intelligence Officer. "Yes sir, ma'am?" Grubby said.

Strauss spoke. "We need to talk to Lieutenant Stovic."

Grubby grimaced. "Boy, he's about debriefed out. Didn't you guys already talk to him a couple of times?"

"We need to talk to him again. A few more questions have come up."

"I don't know." Grubby shook his head widely. "He's really beat. I'm not sure he even has any voice left."

"We'll write yes and no on a piece of paper, and he can point," Harrow added sarcastically.

"Can't it wait until tomorrow? Skipper told me not to let anyone interrupt him. He's in the middle of a debrief right now."

"You mean a movie?"

"I'm sure some of the pilots are watching the movie—"

"This is from CAG himself," Harrow said, invoking the Air Wing commander for the first time. His desires trumped those of any squadron commander.

"You sure this can't wait?"

"We're sure."

"All right. Wait here. I'll ask the Skipper, and if he says it's okay, I'll get Animal out of his debrief."

They nodded, and he slid back into the ready room, ducking under the huge image of Arnold brandishing some unrecognizable weapon. He crossed to Bruno and crouched beside his chair. "Ship's Intel and CAG Intel want to talk to Animal."

"Those guys never give up." He glanced over at

Stovic, who was deeply involved in the movie. "Okay, but we're going to rewind to this spot when he comes back."

"Yes, sir," Grubby said. He stood up to his full height so he blocked the movie, a move that was greeted instantly by catcalls and various missiles. He pointed to Stovic and motioned for him to come to the front of the room.

Stovic excused himself down the aisle and followed out the front door. The two Intelligence Officers were waiting for him. "What's up?"

"We had a couple more questions. We've sent off the initial message, and as you might expect, Washington has some questions."

"Shoot."

"Most can wait to later, but one can't," Harrow said.

Stovic felt his heart jump. "What?"

Harrow glanced at Strauss and asked, "How do you know the MiG that fired was firing at you?"

Stovic was surprised at the question. He narrowed his eyes as if he were answering a question that was so obvious it was all he could do to keep the sarcasm out of his voice. "It wasn't me, so much. I assumed he was firing at the Skipper. But when I saw the missile come off the rails I knew he was shooting at somebody. He might have been shooting at the EP-3, I guess, which was about five miles behind us. Could be. But that didn't really matter to me. Once he fired at us, the fight was on."

Strauss followed up. "How do you know it wasn't an inadvertent missile release? An accident?"

Stovic rolled his eyes. "Is that what this is about? They claiming it was an accident?"

Strauss and Harrow nodded.

"What a crock. If you fly up supersonic after three American planes—okay, so they thought it was one

plane—then pull a big turn back into them and fire a
missile, I don't really care whether they had an accident
or not. That's hostile, and I'm not going to sit around
and try to figure it out. Check the gun camera tape.
You can see the missile come off long before I shoot."

"We looked at it," Harrow said. "His missile never
guided."

Stovic was incredulous. "So what? So they've got a
stupid missile, or they don't keep their radars up to
snuff. So what?"

"Why didn't Commander Bruno fire?"

Stovic's face turned red. "I don't know. Why don't
you ask him?" He waited as the impact of his rhetori-
cal question was less than he had hoped. "Are we
done?"

"Not quite," they said, looking up and down the
small passageway leading to the main fore and aft passageway outside the ready room. "We've got the pilot
on tape," Harrow said in a near whisper.

"What?" Stovic asked.

"The EP-3 was listening to their ground control radio. As soon as the missile came off the rail, the lead
MiG broke radar lock. Did you notice that?"

"No," Stovic said defensively. "He didn't have me
locked up."

"Right. He had Commander Bruno locked up. And
then he shut his radar off and turned away." She
looked up into his eyes to make sure he was getting her
point. "To make sure his missile didn't guide. He transmitted to his ground controller that his missile came off
the rail in error. He squeezed the trigger when turning.
He said he was turning away to disengage when you
shot his wingman."

Stovic didn't know what to say. "You buy that? You
think his master arm switch just *happened* to be on?
Was that a mistake too?"

"Does the MiG-25 have a master arm switch?" she asked, making a note.

"Sure as hell," Stovic replied. "Sorry. I've got no sympathy. Anybody that goes into a fight—even an intercept with a fighter from another country—with his master arm on is taking the risk of an accidental shot. That's just too bad for him." He shrugged. "That's the way things go in the major leagues. When you throw at a batter's head, you might just get hit yourself. Even if the ball just got away from you." He turned to go back into the ready room. "The guy should've jumped out earlier."

"He couldn't," Harrow replied.

"Why not?" Stovic frowned. Suddenly hot, he rolled up the sleeves on his olive flight suit, the same one he had been wearing during the shoot-down.

"His seat failed. He was burning to death, so he jumped out. He hit the water right after his jet. They're trying to recover the body."

Stovic closed his eyes and nearly laughed. Unbelievable. Hero to goat in eight short hours. "Thanks for telling me. You really made my day."

"I thought you'd want to know what happened," Harrow said.

Stovic was about to say something he would regret. He held his tongue, walked quickly back into the ready room and down the row to his still warm seat. No one could see that his ears were red from embarrassment and humiliation.

"Rewind!" Bruno yelled to the duty officer, who was about to do just that when the ready room phone rang again. He answered it, argued with the person on the other line, then nodded vigorously as he looked at his luminous watch dial for the current time. He placed the receiver back on its cradle and stood at his duty desk. He yelled to Stovic, "Animal! CAG wants to see you!"

Stovic's blood went cold. "What for?" he asked weakly. The others laughed and slapped him as he made his way down the row again.

"Get this," Grubby said, getting everyone's attention as he turned down Arnold's carnage. "*Today* show sent a message. They want you on in two days, and CAG is flying you off to Rota, Spain, to head back to New York!"

"Whoa!" the officers yelled.

Bruno stood and shook his hand. "Hero for a day!" he said, smiling. "The Ragin' Bulls will be watching!"

# 3

Y ou were saying?" Kendrick said to St. John, who was running the meeting, much to the distress of Stuntz, the Secretary of Defense, and Woods, the Director of Central Intelligence.

"Yes, sir. We've been hearing loudly and directly from Algeria," she said, looking at Woods. "They are beyond furious. They are screaming we set them up, that we attacked after an inadvertent shot came off their plane, that they turned away and we took advantage of the situation to embarrass them. They say it is an act of war, a declaration of war on our part, and we had better be prepared for a response."

"Or what?" Stuntz interjected. "What are they going to do? Send more of their crack Air Force out after the carrier battle group? Let them send them all. I hope like hell they do. This is nothing a sound ass-kicking won't take care of, Mr. President. This new group of lunatics that has gotten control of the country needs to understand the penalty of playing recklessly with the big boys."

Kendrick tried not to laugh. Stuntz was a great Secretary of Defense. He got everything organized, running smoothly, and ran the budget like a Swiss railroad, but he was over the top in his belief that force could solve any problem. "What penalty did you have in mind?"

"Well, the National Security Advisor a minute ago—if I heard her right, and I may not have—just suggested we pull back outside the two-hundred-mile limit. I say the hell with that. We should go in to the *twelve*-mile limit, the only recognized international waters limit, which is really three anyway, but for—"

"Stewart, what are you hearing?"

Woods waited until there was complete quiet. "We have good information that they are planning a strike against the carrier battle group. Probably at first light. They're not much for flying at night anyway, but over the water? Never. We think they're going to come after the *Truman* first thing in the morning."

"What do they have that they could put in the air?"

"Some more MiG-25s, MiG-21s, MiG-23s, the usual Soviet fighters, but not that many of them."

"Could the *Truman* handle them?"

Stuntz wanted to answer that. "If you don't mind, Stewart?" Stuntz insisted.

Woods shook his head.

"Sir, the *Truman* almost certainly could handle it. With its battle group and antiair capability, they could take whatever Algeria wanted to bring. But there might be an American plane or two that would get lost, and there's always the risk of a kamikaze type of attack. There would be some risk."

"What is the other carrier relieving the *Truman*?"

"*Eisenhower*."

"Can they handle it between them?"

"Almost certainly. But I think we just let that come. If they want to attack two American battle groups with their old MiGs? Let them. What we need to decide is whether to pull them outside this bogus two-hundred-mile limit. I vote a big hell no. Move them in closer. Stick their stupid noses in it."

St. John was less sure. "There's no additional risk, and it could easily be seen as a desire to give no further provocation—"

"Further?" Stuntz asked.

"Yes. Further. I told you going inside that limit would set them off. Well, it did."

"So what?" Stuntz asked, amazed.

"So if we hadn't done that, we wouldn't be here now. The can of worms is open, but we don't know what's inside. These people have no track record. They could do anything."

"And if they hadn't set a silly, arbitrary limit, *we* wouldn't have had to test them, would we?" Stuntz asked her.

"In any case, Mr. President, as your National Security Advisor, it is my belief that there is substantial additional risk in leaving the Navy ships within that limit, and virtually no benefit. We've made our point. There is great benefit in pulling them back a little, and no additional risk. I think we should take both carrier battle groups outside two hundred miles. Then if the Algerians come out, our carriers will see them coming from a long way away and can take whatever action is appropriate."

"State?"

The Secretary of State, Richard Moore, thought for a while, then walked slowly to the front of the room and stood in front of the electronic chart. He was the oldest person there by at least ten years. "Mr. President, I think when teaching someone a lesson, it's best to confine the learning to one subject. One thing at a time. Otherwise there could be confusion. Right now they are angry. Humiliated and angry. That is a dangerous combination. And although it's not that big a lesson, it is a clear one. If that's the picture you want, you should pull back now. If on the other hand you want to start a war with Algeria, then you should keep the carriers where they are."

"How's the diplomatic community responding?"

"Officially? They are disappointed in our provocative moves. In private, the Europeans at least say they would have done the same thing."

"What about this idea that our pilot shot when he didn't have to?"

Stuntz turned his head toward the President, sitting at the end of the table opposite the Secretary of State, who was still standing in front of the electronic chart. "Sir, I've personally reviewed the gun camera tape. It was sent back from the carrier. Everyone on my staff agrees—under the pressure of the moment, our pilot was justified in shooting. It met the criteria as a hostile act under the rules of engagement they have been using. Anything else is just academic. He was justified, and he shot. Nobody can second-guess him now."

The President stood slowly. "I want hourly updates from intelligence and diplomatic traffic. This thing may heat up a lot, or it may cool down. If it heats up, it won't be because of anything we have done. I want the *Eisenhower* to steam through the Strait of Gibraltar and rendezvous with the *Truman*. And tell both the battle groups to stay two hundred miles away from Algeria to the extent they are able. Stewart, how are we for the ability to collect intelligence on Algeria?"

"We're in good shape, sir. Lots of things in place. Anything big coming, we should hear about it."

Kendrick looked calm. "Then we're right where we want to be," he said.

Rat checked his pulse as he stepped off the treadmill. He much preferred running outdoors, through woods or by streams, but he had wanted to check out this civilian gym in D.C., which had the reputation of being an outstanding gym without too many politicos. Not too many obsessive staffers and interns beginning their idealistic little political careers.

The gym was three floors high, with free weights on the ground floor, exercise equipment on the second floor, and a track on the third floor. It was sparkling new and overall was the best gym he had ever seen. Rat had spent most of his time in small, smelly Navy gyms or packed into some forgotten corner of an amphibious ship where a universal gym had been crammed. He kept a log book recording every workout. It helped him keep a balanced program and kept him honest on the rare days when he didn't feel like working out.

Rat rubbed the sweat off his arms with a small towel and saw the logo for a special report from Fox News emerge on the screen of the small television at the head of the treadmill. He quickly grabbed the light headphones and listened.

A man came on the screen. "We have a special report, an update on the shoot-down in the Med."

Nice to have something catchy to call it, Rat thought.

"The Algerian government continues to express its outrage at what it calls the aggressive and unlawful conduct of the United States. It has called for an emergency meeting of the UN Security Council to discuss sanctions against the United States for violating Algerian airspace and attacking Algerian aircraft within that airspace." The picture cut to a balding man standing before a blue curtain and a blue oval sign that said THE PENTAGON and had a drawing of the building. The man was from the Department of Defense and was obviously answering questions at a press conference. He said, "The United States continues to believe in freedom of navigation on the high seas and in international airspace. The fact that someone claims it as their own contravenes international law and threatens international commerce. It will not be tolerated. The shoot-down was an unfortunate incident, but American forces are entitled to defend themselves when fired upon."

The reporter continued. "There was rioting in the streets of Algeria tonight, with firebombs and bricks being thrown at the American embassy." Taped pictures showed an angry mob hurling things over the fence around the embassy. Rat watched the back of the crowd to see if the anger was universal or mostly the few in the front of the swelling mob. The fury looked authentic, deep, and widespread.

"The Marines at the embassy are on full alert and are prepared to defend the embassy. The President and his national security staff are at Camp David and following developments very closely. It is unknown whether President Kendrick intends to cut his working vacation short and return to Washington to deal with this developing crisis or stay in Camp David.

"One thing that may ease tensions somewhat is that, according to a source in the Department of Defense, the American carriers are being pulled back behind the claimed two-hundred-mile limit. But although moving out of the disputed area is expected to ease tensions, Algeria wants compensation for the family of the dead pilot, replacement of its MiG fighter, an apology from the United States for intruding into its sovereign airspace, and a promise never to intrude again into the two-hundred-mile limit without permission of the government of Algeria."

Rat had heard enough. He replaced the headphones on the treadmill and tossed his towel in a bin. Good old

Algeria. He had been there often enough to know they would use this for all it was worth.

The next morning at 7:20 A.M., Ismael stared at the *Today* show on the small television on the table in his studio apartment. He watched in horrified fascination as the immaculate Navy pilot in his white uniform narrated the gun camera film from his Super Hornet. Ismael watched his brother's MiG-25 turn back toward the Americans, do nothing aggressive at all, then get shot by the American pilot. He watched his brother spiral down to the water for what seemed like minutes. The Navy pilot spoke in a calm, clinical tone about what had happened. Ismael waited until he saw his brother's plane splash into the water. He put the banana he had just peeled back on the plate and sat back in his rickety chair. The American pilot feigned humility and had meekly tried to deflect being called a hero. Smoke curled up from the toaster behind Ismael as the small slice of bread from the baguette he had bought that morning started to burn. When he turned off the television, his hand was shaking. He looked at his watch.

He pulled out a scrap of paper and wrote: "Lieutenant Ed Stovic. Virginia Beach."

Sarah St. John was beginning to believe they had weathered the storm. As the sun prepared to rise over Washington, she sipped her coffee and reviewed the latest intelligence reports. Algeria continued to make threats and noise, continued to try to keep the attention of the international media focused on its claims of offense and violation, but it had been very careful to take no military steps at all; and in spite of the continuous mob presence outside the U.S. embassy, there had been no mob attack. Maybe Stuntz was right, she thought. Maybe the presence of the two battle groups during the hours and days right after the shoot-down was enough.

She glanced up as Brad Walker, a member of her staff, came in to give her the hard copies of the slides he planned to use for the morning's intelligence brief. "Morning," she said.

He sat down across from her in silence as she reviewed his presentation. He glanced at his watch. They didn't really have time for major changes. She was a perfectionist, and he knew it. Anything that wiggled, that didn't say what they thought, had to come out. Anything they couldn't *prove* had to say so clearly. She had made it clear since taking her job as National Security Advisor that there would be no half-assed briefs, no "close-enough" attitudes. She took her job very seriously, and although she had been regarded skeptically by the lifelong professionals when she came in, she had impressed them. She was willing to listen, and she took what they knew and expanded on it. She handed the slides back to him. "These look good." He began to get up, but she stopped him. "What's your conclusion?"

He smiled. "Ah, you noticed the last slide only says 'conclusion.'"

She returned his smile. "Exactly."

"Well, I think we've basically dodged the bullet. Algeria is now unable to do us harm. We're back to normal, and they've had their opportunities to tell the world what they think. So on we go."

"You think their shot was an accident?"

He nodded. "Yes. I do."

"Wouldn't that make it more likely that Algeria isn't going to just let this sit?"

"They don't have many options."

She shook her head. "It's the very sort of thing that

might make them throw in behind the terrorists. They've been on the sidelines. Now they may do something stupid."

"But we don't have anything to fill in the gap. To tell them what we think is likely to happen."

"No, we don't," she said, standing and putting on her suit coat. "But we'll mention it. Maybe it will start someone thinking."

"Stuntz will be on the opposite side."

"Of what?"

"Of whatever we say."

She smiled. "You noticed."

He stood to join her. "Oh yeah. I also noticed that you don't think much of him."

She didn't say anything.

"Seems to me that you think he's a dinosaur. You're the new regime, and he's old news. That about sum it up?"

"You are perceptive, aren't you. We see things differently, true. But I also don't trust his motives. He's into empire building, which I *despise*. I'm motivated by the truth. By doing what's best for the country." They stepped out the door of her office, and she got a glimpse of his skeptical face. "What?" she demanded.

He shook his head. "You think you should be Secretary of Defense, don't you?"

"I don't really have the experience."

They walked down the corridor together. "But you at least think the National Security Advisor should be a cabinet level position."

"It does seem that the Security Advisor would have more interesting things to say at a cabinet meeting than, say, the Secretary for Veterans' Affairs. I don't want to be harsh, but don't you think national security is more important than building the next VA hospital, or raising their benefits by exactly the cost of living?"

"Without a doubt. But if you could, you'd be SECDEF right now, wouldn't you?"

She walked ahead, faster than she had been walking. Walker hurried to catch up.

Ismael stepped off the Air France jet into the terminal in Algiers. He saw his father first, Dr. Mohammed Nezzar. He tried not to show any emotion, but he knew no homecoming would ever be the same now that Chakib, the great hope of the family, the Air Force pilot, was dead. He crossed to his father and embraced him. Only then did he see his mother standing behind her husband, unable even to look up, as if she were responsible for what had happened. Ismael knew she would never forgive herself for having encouraged Chakib to fly, to be one of the elite of Algerian society, one of the leaders in the Air Force. The fact that it had been a burning desire in him since he was a small boy gave her no comfort. In her mind, it was her fault.

Ismael moved behind his father and embraced his mother. "Mother, it is not your fault—"

"Ismael, I wish you could have been home, we needed you. Why Washington? It was all so horrible . . ." She began to cry uncontrollably.

Ismael held her small frame close to him and looked at his father.

The doctor looked at his wife sadly, then at Ismael. "Since it happened. She cannot stop crying."

"Why did this happen, Father?" Ismael asked. "Why Chakib?"

Dr. Nezzar grew thoughtful. "Let us go home. There we can discuss this freely."

Ismael looked around and nodded. He threw his bag over his shoulder and followed his father out to their car, a nice but old Mercedes-Benz. They drove in silence through the crowded streets and stopped in front of their two-story home, a stark white stucco house with a red tile roof like many others nearby, on a dirt street on the outskirts of the capital city. The houses were so close together that they looked like one continuous building.

Ismael walked quickly to the bedroom where he and Chakib had grown up. He dropped his bag and let the memories sweep over him. He was four years younger than Chakib and had always been the brunt of his older brother's pranks and early tests of manhood. They were always in competition, and Chakib always won, mostly because of his years. Ismael had closed the gap, gaining on his older brother every year. He had surpassed him in height three years before, when Ismael grew to be six feet tall and Chakib was only five feet ten. He had surpassed him in education, at least in one way, by gaining admission and a government scholarship to George Washington University in the United States.

But in his parents' eyes, he knew, he would always be the younger brother. The one who came after. The one from whom less was expected.

He surveyed the room where they had grown up together, the corner where they had sat and schemed, the bed frame they had broken when wrestling, the soccer ball on the shelf from the game where Chakib had scored the winning goal against another youth team from Tunisia.

Ismael rubbed the stubble on his cheeks. He was tired. He sat on the bed and closed his eyes.

"Ismael, come. Let's talk," the doctor called from downstairs.

Ismael left his bag on the floor. He went down to the tile-floored kitchen and sat heavily at the rough wooden table.

"Tired?" his father asked.

"Yes, a little."

"How is Washington this time?"

"The same. Noisy, dirty, full of crazy people."

"You should come home if you don't like it," his mother said in a tone of bitterness.

"I want to finish my engineering degree—"

"With those who killed your brother?" she asked.

"How did it happen?" he asked, finally ready to know.

The doctor spoke. "He was on duty. On alert. Ever since the government has reclaimed—"

"Claimed for the first time," Ismael corrected. "The *first* time, Father. Never before claimed."

"Long ago—"

"Okay, not since the invention of the airplane."

"The Americans came with their aircraft carriers. Their battle groups—"

"They said they would, Father. You cannot just claim ownership of international waters and not expect consequences!"

The doctor knew that. "So when they came, our . . . government," he said bitterly as he glanced at the door, "ordered our fighters out to defend our shores and our seas from the Americans. They were ordered to intercept an EP-3 spy plane."

"Why Chakib? He isn't senior enough to get a mission like that. They must have expected it to go badly. He was expendable, Father."

"I think it was innocent enough, just to escort a spy plane as it flew down our coast. No orders to attack."

"So they fired on the Americans?"

"Chakib's friends—other pilots—tell me they were ordered not to fire at all unless fired upon. We knew the Americans would have much more difficulty with an ambiguous situation than they would with us attacking them. They used to let the Russians fly right over their carriers in the Mediterranean. They would just escort them. After the EP-3, Chakib was to fly directly over the carrier and have the other fighter take pictures of him there, to show the world that they had gone into the lion's den and pulled his tail. But the missile . . . we are told it was an accident. The one in charge of the flight fired his missile accidentally. He tried to stop it—"

Ismael was stunned. "*Accidentally?* How do you do that?"

"That is what we have been told," his father answered, and then added quickly, "by the pilot, the one on the flight. I have spoken with him personally."

"The Americans say that we fired at them."

His face darkened. "I don't think so. But what difference does it make? Chakib is dead. He will never walk through that door again. He will never joke with us again," he said, his face fighting the irresistible contortions of grief. "Your mother," he began, unable to finish.

"I know," Ismael replied, glancing at his mother, who pressed her hands together in her lap and stared at the floor. "The funeral is the day after tomorrow?"

"Yes. Day after tomorrow."

"They never found the body?"

"Nothing. They found some wreckage. . . ."

Ismael wasn't sure whether to tell them. "I know who killed Chakib."

"What?" his father gasped. "How?"

"They had him on national television, telling everyone, smiling, laughing, about how he had killed my brother."

The doctor felt personally insulted. He was shocked. "Are you sure?"

Ismael reached into his pocket as he shifted his

weight in his sandals. He pulled out the slip of paper and put it on the table in front of his father.

The piece of paper just lay there, forming a weight greater than the paper on which it was written. A small gust of wind caught it and turned it slightly. No one reached for it. It was as if they were afraid to touch it. They both understood the implications of knowing the name of the American pilot that had shot down Chakib.

"Why did you bring his name into this house?" the doctor asked accusingly.

"Don't you want to know who did this to your son? Don't you care?"

"You soil this house by bringing the name of the murderer here and setting it on our table as if it's the name of a friend!"

"I thought someone might want to know who it was."

His father leaned back in disbelief. "Why would I want to know the name of the American that killed your brother? What good would that do me? It is like a *curse,* like an omen. . . ."

"Since when do you believe in curses and omens?" Ismael asked harshly.

"I'm concerned about your mother," the doctor hissed.

Ismael held his tongue. He knew he'd been trumped. He knew better than to say anything about his mother's unbearable grief. "I'm sorry," he said, picking up the piece of paper. He placed it in his pocket. "I shouldn't have brought it."

"The funeral has been set," the doctor continued, as if there had been no piece of paper.

"Yes."

"It will be a state funeral, for a martyr and a hero of

the state. They will do the ceremony at the mosque in the city center. They will have seats of honor for his family—for your mother and you and me—and thousands of others will attend. It is to honor him." He waited for Ismael to say something, then continued, "We will be ready to leave here at 10:00 A.M. The funeral is at noon. They think it will take over an hour for us to get there. They think the streets will be full of mourners, people expressing their love for your brother."

Ismael looked at the clock. "And until then?"

"We will just stay home."

"I need to take a walk," Ismael said, standing up as his father stared at him. "I need to see the old neighborhood."

His father stood again. "Yes. Go see some of your friends. Maybe they can come to the funeral too. To honor Chakib."

Ismael nodded and walked out of the house, glad to be free of the depressing atmosphere. It was harder than he had expected.

Ismael spent the next day and a half wandering through Algiers, seeing it as he had never seen it before. He compared it to the scenes of Washington, D.C., with its prostitutes, homeless people, and general self-centeredness.

The cleanliness of his city, or at least most of it, the modesty of the women, and the conforming influence of Islam made it as different from Washington as it could be. As he walked through the city where he grew up, watching the people on the streets and the small shopkeepers working with customers or smoking in the doorways, he realized he was beginning to feel like an outsider. He had been away from his country too long.

# CHAPTER
## 4

Lieutenant Ed Stovic and Karen, his wife, stood on the tarmac in front of VFA-37's hangar at Oceana Naval Air Station in Virginia Beach, Virginia. They looked up into the sky with the other squadron family members who anxiously awaited the squadron's fly-off from the carrier. It had been a fabulous cruise for the squadron. No accidents, no deaths, lots of good flying, and to cap it off, an aerial engagement with the Algerians that put one of their pilots on the *Today* show. They were already expecting the E award for excellence within the F/A-18 community and hoped they might even get the Jumpin' Joe Clifton award as the best fighter squadron in the Navy. The sky was the limit.

Stovic was floating. His appearance on television had caused friends, distant family, and acquaintances to come out of the woodwork with words of encouragement and praise. He had also heard another piece of news from one of his roommates in the JO Jungle—the Junior-Officer Jungle, as they named their stateroom. The rumor was that CAG, the Air Wing Commander, was going to put him in for a Silver Star. Pilots who shot down planes in Vietnam were routinely put in for

Silver Stars, and most received them. Since then it had been harder, but CAG was determined to try for it. He didn't think a Distinguished Flying Cross, or worse, an Air Medal, did it justice.

"There they are!" Karen shouted, pointing out toward the Atlantic Ocean.

Stovic's attention had wandered, but he immediately saw the squadron's F/A-18s in a large diamond formation heading toward Oceana Naval Air Station. It was a beautiful sight—fourteen Navy gray F/A-18s in tight formation against the clear blue sky. Stovic tried not to smile as broadly as he wanted to; he didn't want to look silly.

Bruno was leading the way. They came over the field at fifteen hundred feet in perfect formation and began a gentle left-hand turn toward the crowd. The wives and children were impressed by the show and the noise. Some of the visitors were fathers and mothers of the pilots and held grandchildren on their shoulders.

The F/A-18s circled around behind the hangar and broke up into groups of four to reenter the break and land. They came in perfectly and all taxied to their designated parking spots in front of the hangar. They hadn't landed their planes on steady ground for six months. Every landing on cruise was on the carrier, always shifting or rolling or angling in some indescribable way. It was a new feeling to actually roll out after landing, to stop without the arresting gear jerking the airplane to a grinding, concussive end. One of the lead briefing items for the fly-off had been "Keep your tailhooks up!" to avoid catching the single arresting cable on the runway at Oceana that was for emergency only.

After the Hornets were lined up in front of the hangar with their engines turning, on the Skipper's signal they all shut down their starboard engines, then their port engines, then opened their canopies at the same instant. They left their radios on and their helmets plugged in as their engines wound down, so they could hear Bruno transmit his last few orders: *"Safe seats! Lap belts, now! Shoulder harness, now!"* And then, *"Dismount, now!"*

And with that, all the pilots disconnected their helmets and oxygen masks, stood up, and threw a leg over the side to grab the first step of the ladder that ground crew had lowered from the port side of each aircraft.

They stood in front of their jets in their flight gear and quickly removed their helmets, survival vests, and G-suits. They put on their soft khaki hats and marched in formation to the front of the cordoned area, where people were screaming for them. The pilots smiled, unable to contain their joy at being home and back with their families.

The Command Master Chief unhooked the rope, and the children ran out to greet the pilots. The formation collapsed as no one could stand the separation anymore, and sheer joy filled the air as overhead the second F/A-18 squadron flew in their uniquely shaped formation to duplicate the ceremony with their families just down the tarmac at another hangar.

Inside the spotless Ragin' Bulls hangar, where the airplanes that needed maintenance would be pulled in just a few hours, there were red, white, and blue decorations all over and a huge cake in the middle. WELCOME HOME! was inscribed in large blue letters with big bulls in two corners of the enormous cake. Punch and food filled the long tables next to the cake.

Karen watched the families, the interaction between the wives and husbands, the glee of the young children, and the sullen attitudes of the few junior high children. She knew all the spouses from the spouses' club of the squadron and could see the joy on their faces.

Bruno came up to them. "Animal! Nice work on the *Today* show!"

Stovic wasn't quite sure what to say. "Did you catch it?"

"You kidding me? We recorded it. I required the SDO to show it every night before the movie. We threw popcorn and shit at your ugly face every night. There we were slaving away on the boat, steaming across the Atlantic, while you go become a national celebrity on TV, see your wife, go to the beach, and generally rub our noses in it."

Stovic smiled. "What can I say?"

"You can say, 'Thanks, Skipper, for giving me the duty tonight! Cause I'd love nothing better than to take care of the squadron here at the hangar while you hardworking go-to-sea Navy officers relax at home.' "

"Whatever you say," Stovic said, still smiling.

Bruno put a large piece of cake into his mouth. "Oh, that's sooooo good," he moaned. "I'd forgotten how good a simple white cake can be!" He looked at Karen. "Sorry, Karen, how have you been?" he said, rubbing enough cake off his lips to kiss her on the cheek.

"Pretty good," she replied. "Until Ed told me about his plans for his shore tour."

"What plans?" Bruno asked, feigning ignorance.

"He didn't tell you?" she asked skeptically.

"What did he tell you? Astronaut? Aide to the President of the United States? Military attaché to Paris? Which one?"

"The Blue Angels," she said.

"Yeah, we talked about that one a little too." He tried to read her face. "Perfect job for a national celebrity like him. Hey, Ricardo!" he exclaimed, waving to an old squadron mate who had come to welcome him back. Then to Karen again, "Tough job to get, but the guys who have done it loved it."

"Did you put him up to it?" she asked, the disappointment obvious in her voice.

"No way. You know he's always wanted to do it. He started talking about it as soon as he got to the squadron. Don't try to feign ignorance. You've known about it since before the squadron."

She knew he was right. But she always wanted that desire to be in the future, like the boat he was always talking about buying to sail up the Chesapeake. "I hoped you'd talk him out of it."

Bruno frowned in surprise. "Why would I do that?"

"It's like sea duty," she remarked.

He shrugged. "What's wrong with sea duty? But it's not like they go on cruise for six months at a time."

"Aren't they gone like three hundred days a year?"

Bruno knew the number was about that, but he wasn't going to step in front of that train. "What is it, Animal? You know?"

"Something like that."

She shook her head. "Don't worry about me. I'll just stay home like a good little wife and take care of the kids."

Bruno replied, "This sure is fun, but I gotta go shake some hands. I'll catch up with you two later."

She spoke to her husband. "Let's go get some punch."

"Sure," he said, biting his tongue. They walked to the end of the table, where Karen ladled punch into two plastic glasses. "You'd already talked to him about it?"

"The CO has to go along. You've got to get his endorsement on the application and then go on cross-countries to air shows."

"You've really looked into this," she said, looking into his eyes.

"Maybe we should talk about this later," he said,

looking around at his squadron mates and their families.

"When does all this start?"

He drank the entire glass of pink punch and put it down on the table. "Pretty much right away. It's like a fraternity rush. You've got to get the current Blue Angels to want you."

"So you just got back from cruise, and you'll be gone on weekends to air shows?"

He had blown it and he knew it. He had wanted her to be enthusiastic about it, but he had been so afraid she'd try to stop him, he had put it in motion without getting her okay. "Pretty much."

"When's the first one?"

"Day after tomorrow."

She was stunned. "You're going on a cross-country day after tomorrow?"

"Yeah."

"Where to?"

"Memphis."

"When were you going to tell me about it?"

"I don't know. Today. Look, I thought you supported the whole idea."

"I support *you*," she replied. "But I sure don't support you being gone for three hundred days a year."

His face looked strained. "Come here," he said, taking her by the arm and walking to stand in the shadow of one of the F/A-18s from another squadron. They were out of view of the rest of the people there for the fly-in. "I owe you an apology. I can't really explain it, but I think I was afraid you wouldn't let me do this. I was afraid you'd say no, and my dream would go up in smoke. Because if you said no, and I did it anyway, you'd hate me."

"What are you saying?"

"I'm saying that now is the time. We have to decide

together if this is what we want. If you want me to stop this process, now is the time. I haven't gone to any air shows, haven't really committed myself. We always said we could veto whatever the other one was doing. Well, here it is. Do you want to veto it?"

She looked up at him. "How bad do you want to do it?"

"Ever since I saw the Blues fly in Philadelphia at an air show. Since I was ten. It's what made me choose to fly in the Navy."

"What is it about it that's so attractive?"

"We've talked about this—"

"I want to hear it again."

"I don't know. It's sort of like the pinnacle of flying. Flying in the Navy is hard enough, but flying aerobatics in a supersonic jet eighteen inches from five other jets is awesome. It's just beautiful."

"Three hundred days a year?"

"Yeah. I know. Look, I probably won't get selected. Like a hundred guys apply."

"Right. You're a famous MiG killer and you're on the *Today* show and they'll turn you down?"

"Probably."

She walked out of the shadow and looked at the people. She thought about their future. She was tired of the Navy life and the strain it put on the family. "If it's what you really want to do. But frankly, I hope you're right. I hope you don't get chosen. But if you do, we'll just have to make the best of it."

"Thanks." Stovic couldn't believe it. "I don't really deserve you. I mean that."

"After it's over, we're going to have to talk about some other dreams in the family. Some that don't involve you going to sea or being gone all the time."

"Fair enough. You have my word."

\* \* \*

"Morning," Jacobs said to Rat.

"Morning, sir." Rat had been paged by Jacobs. Not a page from the SAS head that a mission was on or from the Directorate of Operations that it was time to lock the doors and begin emergency planning for an imminent mission—this was from Jacobs. Sort of a liaison emergency. His first. He was interested to see what Jacobs wanted. Others in the SAS had mentioned that Jacobs was considered an odd duck. He was acknowledged to be brilliant, but he didn't care much for U.S. law, international law, or general expectations that limited his ability to act against perceived terrorist threats. He was one who always wanted to fight fire with fire because he always knew he could start a bigger fire than any terrorist or organization could ever hope to put together. So Jacobs was admired, but Rat had been cautioned about working with Jacobs too closely. You could get singed.

This summons had ended in Jacobs's office, which was big enough for maybe three or, in a pinch, four people. There were six people in the office, including Rat.

"Since the shoot-down that we watched? We've been keeping an eye on developments in Algeria."

Rat waited.

"I assume you have too."

"Yes, sir."

"Others in Washington are beginning to wonder what the Algerians are up to. They can't imagine that there will be no response—militarily—to the shoot-down."

Rat looked at the others in the room. He didn't know any of them, and couldn't imagine why they were there, or why Jacobs hadn't introduced them.

"Some believe Algeria is looking for a different kind of response. You're familiar with the concept of asymmetric warfare?"

"Sure. You act differently than expected, and not in response to the direct threat. If they're coming in through the front door with their Army, you go through the back door with your Navy, or send guerrillas to their parents' house. Something unpredictable and effective."

"Exactly. The thought is that Algeria is unable to just let this go. They continue to scream in the media and in the UN—big surprise there—but they haven't done much other than that." Jacobs stopped and waited for Rat to respond.

"What does this have to do with me?"

"We're starting to get a little concerned that Algeria may go the terrorist route."

Rat nodded.

"That's where you come in. You've worked with French counterterrorism units before. Bosnia—" Jacobs stopped, seeing the warning flash in Rat's eyes. "And other places. Algeria used to be a French colony, obviously. I would wager that the French have much better information than we do, and you're just the guy to share it."

"They probably have some pretty good information. But I've been reading some of the reports from Algiers since the shoot-down." Two of the others in the room looked startled. Why would this operator be reading intelligence files when there was no mission? "I like keeping up with current events," he said, answering their unspoken question. "And we have some pretty good intelligence ourselves."

"Really. What have I missed?" Jacobs asked in an icy tone.

"We've seen a lot of activity in their foreign office. Not with officials but with some people who are known to have contacts with some very bad people."

"Right. So what?"

"So they're not going to take military action against us. They'd get slaughtered. You think at this point in this War on Terrorism, we wouldn't love some country to give us a nice focus for all our lingering anger?"

"Sure. We know all that."

"They are clearly going to do something that can't be traced back to the government. That's all. They're talking to people who can make that happen."

"And where do you think they're going to do that?"

"No way of knowing, based on what I read, but you guys know a lot more than I do."

"Are you ready to go to Algeria?"

"That's not the way to do this. I don't think it will be in Algeria."

"Where will it be?"

Rat was frustrated. He was just talking about things he'd been reading. He hadn't done any hard analysis. That was *their* job. "I really have no idea."

"You willing to get involved if we get an indication?"

Rat nodded. "Depending on what it is, sure. Of course."

"We'll call you."

The escort arrived at 10:00 A.M., just as Dr. Mohammed Nezzar had said, right after the muezzin cried
their musical prayers from the tops of the minarets
through the powerful speakers that projected over the
entire city. Ismael had donned traditional Algerian
clothing, leaving his Tommy jeans in his bedroom. The
Algerian dust and fine sand on his feet from wearing
sandals pleased him. He hadn't washed his feet since
returning home. It was how he wanted to be for his
brother's funeral, how he always was during his youth.

His father opened the front door of the house. More
than a hundred people waited in the street. A crowd
was building fast. They all wanted to show their sympathy and anger. It wasn't to be an escort so much as it
was a processional, a mass of support that would walk
from the dead pilot's home to the place of the funeral
to exemplify to the world the great loss they had all
suffered.

Ismael squinted as he stepped out into the sunny
street behind his mother, the official focus of grieving.
He saw for the first time several bearded young men
who were carrying a coffin over their heads, the coffin
that was going to be carried behind the grieving family

through the streets of Algiers. To Ismael the empty coffin renewed his pain over the idea of his brother's body somewhere at the bottom of the Mediterranean.

As they stepped into the street, the throng made way for the mullahs and the family to head the procession. The group behind them swelled as people poured out of every house and building to join them. They moved as one, a sea of grieving, suffering, wailing humanity, toward the mosque.

The men carrying the casket began shouting out for mercy, for justice, and for revenge. They shouted prayers and expressions of grief in Arabic, with a few crying out in French. Ismael balked as clerics grabbed each of his arms to walk with him, to escort him as part of the family. As his father had predicted, Chakib had become a symbol for all of Algeria.

The group became a mob, crying and yelling, turning on the United States as the focus of their grief. The numbers grew to a thousand, then ten thousand, as they rolled toward the city square, then fifty thousand. Thousands more walked parallel to them in the streets several blocks away. Whenever they came to an intersection, Ismael could see thousands more people in both directions heading the same way as the family and the casket.

The raw emotion of the event began to penetrate Ismael's hardened exterior as the sounds came from everywhere. He felt the buoyant strength of the thousands around him. It was a feeling he had never experienced. He felt as if they could do anything—tear down a building or overthrow the government. If the Americans were here, they would suffer the wrath of these Algerians for killing one of their sons. For the first time in a long time, Ismael was proud to be Algerian.

The clerics arrived at the mosque. As soon as they

were in place, the mullah began the amplified prayers of the funeral, familiar to all Muslims.

Ismael was moved. He fought back tears as the mullah explained life and death and how we control neither. He gave thanks to Allah for the life of Chakib Nezzar and all that he had been able to accomplish. He grieved for the family, for the entire city and country, and, to Ismael's surprise, for the wife and children Chakib would never have.

As he sniffed hard to fight his emotions, Ismael raised his head up and saw a television camera perched on the wall of a building to his left. Just under the camera was a small sign that said CNN. He was surprised they identified themselves at all. An American company was not welcome in Algeria. This crowd, raging over the shoot-down of his brother, could easily turn on whatever American symbol it could find to demonstrate the anger smoldering in the city over Chakib's death. But perhaps they wanted America to see how deeply they felt the loss of one of their sons. Ismael tried to get CNN out of his mind. He tried to get America out of his mind. He didn't want to think about it. He wanted only to listen to the prayers and think of his brother.

Later, as he stepped back into his parents' house, he couldn't even remember the rest of the funeral. It was all a dream, a flowing, noisy, confusing sea of moving people, sounds, and emotions. He recalled only finding himself back at his family's house surrounded by well-wishers, both those he knew and the hundreds he didn't know who stood outside the house in something like a vigil, watching for them, supporting them, praying for them, and offering to do anything for the family. It was a show of support he never expected.

The food flowed freely. Ismael sat on the steps to the

second floor of the house. His pain was deeper than he expected as he contemplated a future without his best friend. He was suddenly aware that someone was sitting next to him on the tile step. It was a pilot from Chakib's squadron. He was in the dress uniform he had worn to the funeral.

The pilot spoke to him. "I don't know if you remember me. My name is Raid Hamid Saadi—"

"I know," Ismael said, remembering him from the one time he had visited his brother's squadron. Hamid had made an impression on him as being full of bluster and self-importance, two personal qualities that caused Ismael to instantly dislike someone. He had a twisted ability to remember those he disliked.

"I speak for the rest of the pilots in the squadron when I tell you how sorry we are for the loss of your brother. We miss him terribly and want to extend to you our condolences. We pray that Allah gives you comfort, and that someday, Allah gives you vengeance."

Ismael looked at the pilot and didn't say anything.

Hamid leaned over slightly to look up at Ismael's face. "Did you hear what I said?"

"Yes, of course."

"Do you accept our condolences, for you and for your family?"

"Yes, I do. Thank you."

"Your brother thought very highly of you."

Ismael blinked and looked around the crowded room full of women preparing food and men eating it. "How do you know that?"

"He spoke of you often."

Ismael took a drink from the cup he was holding. "What was he doing over the Mediterranean?"

Hamid lowered his head, ashamed he had to tell the story again, and this time to the brother of his wingman. "We were just going to fly by the American spy plane, then fly over the carrier to take pictures—"

"Then why have missiles?"

"In case we were attacked!" the pilot said, biting the air, keeping his voice low to avoid the looks that would come their way if he didn't.

"You fired first," Ismael said softly.

"Why do you say such things?"

"I saw the film from the American jets."

"Ah, yes. I forgot. You are living in Washington, in America. You are still a student."

"I saw it."

"It was an error. The missile came off my plane as an accident. It is clear to anyone watching it carefully." The pilot hesitated. "And he is the one they shot down. If they thought I had fired at them, they would have fired at *me*. I would have gladly taken that missile for your brother."

Ismael could hear the guilt. Hamid had screwed up, and it had cost his brother his life.

"The Americans were waiting for us. They were going to attack us under some pretext. They were lying in wait for us, hidden under the wings of the spy plane that was flying in our airspace!"

Ismael didn't respond.

The pilot moved even closer to him. "I have said what I came to say. I am sorry that you are angry. I too am angry, angry at the United States and their Navy, which violates our airspace and our territorial waters. I am angry at their hair-trigger attack on us, and that your brother was killed." He stood up and walked down the three steps. His face was again level with Ismael's. "If I or anyone else at the squadron can do anything for you or your family, please let me know." He waited for a reply but quickly realized Ismael wasn't even going to look at him. He turned quickly and moved to a group of men who were standing near the kitchen. He smiled and joined their discussion seamlessly.

Ismael lifted his head and watched the group from above. He knew many of them, but they were obviously afraid to approach him. He guessed that the fury he felt in his heart was showing on his face. He needed to get out of the house, to the shade in the dirt street behind the house where he and Chakib had kicked a soccer ball to each other and against the back of the house in spite of their mother's complaining of the noise and damage to the wall.

He stepped out of the sweltering room full of mourners into the still sunny street. Two men who had been leaning on the side of the house watched him come outside. They looked at each other and watched carefully where he was going. He turned and headed down the side street in the shadow of his father's house. They followed him. He walked back and forth for two or three turns lost in thought, then felt their eyes on him. He stopped and turned toward them. They were leaning on the back of the house across the narrow alley. He knew them instantly. "Madani," he said, his tone revealing only recognition. "Khalida."

Madani spoke. "We share your grief for your brother."

"What are you doing here?"

"As I said—"

"We both know better," Ismael said.

"We have missed you," Khalida said menacingly.

"It has been, what?" Ismael said, looking at Khalida. "Three years?"

"Maybe four, or even five," he replied.

Madani smiled and pushed away from the building to walk closer to Ismael, who stood motionless in the middle of the dusty street. They stood two feet apart, close enough so that no one could hear their conversation. Madani's smile faded. "You were one of the best. You excelled at the training. Firearms, explosives, electronics, everything. You are a *natural*. We needed your skills. Of all of us, you were the brightest. The one who could make a difference. And you walked away."

"Yes, I did."

Madani was about to respond when he noticed two women in conversation coming down the alley carrying baskets of bread. He looked at them suspiciously. One of them glanced at him and, seeing that he was looking at her, quickly looked away. He waited until they were out of earshot and continued. "Why? Why not stay with us? Why leave us at such a critical time?"

Ismael spoke as he saw the women over Madani's shoulder. One of them turned her head to look at him, as if in wonder at why the conversation had stopped simply because of their presence. "I sickened of killing people with whom I had no quarrel," he hissed. "You killed randomly—"

"To sow fear throughout the country, as a warning!"

"I have no problem killing enemies. But I couldn't attack our own villages because someone believed they were not loyal to something they'd never heard of!"

"But what now? What *about* our enemies? Who is to defend Algeria? Even now the Americans provoke us, kill your brother. We cannot fight them on their terms."

Ismael turned away and headed back toward the house.

Madani grabbed his shirt and pulled him back. "You must listen."

"Why?"

"Because you don't know what I have to say yet."

"I've heard enough of what you have to say." Ismael was fighting the images that were flooding back into his head. In his youth he had been lured into a zealous Islamic group that fought for the overthrow of the secular state of Algeria. It had been his chance to express himself, to find himself, to use weapons and feel very powerful. His parents had no idea. He spent much of his free time training with them, learning weapons, tactics, electronics, explosives, everything, all for the day when they would challenge the rulers of the country. But Ismael had quit. Or at least those at Madani's level within the group thought he had quit. In fact, his intellectual abilities had been recognized, and it was quickly acknowledged that using him to attack people with a rifle was foolish. He needed to be trained and used at a much higher level. It was for that purpose that some had been able to maneuver him into a position, even in the old regime, to obtain a scholarship to attend college in the United States and study electrical engineering. He had been there for three years on a student visa, attending classes and acting like the student he was. Even with the new scrutiny on student visas under the American War on Terrorism, the Americans had left him alone.

Madani pleaded. "Your family has been wronged. Algeria has been wronged. All of Islam has been wronged by the United States."

"That won't bring my brother back."

"We are not here to talk about stupid ideas like bringing your brother back," Khalida said. "Do not utter such nonsense."

Ismael glared at him.

Madani continued. "You will be returning to the United States."

Ismael nodded.

"Do you have no *outrage* over what happened to your brother?"

"Yes," Ismael said. "I am outraged that Algeria sent my brother out against the Americans and that his incompetent section leader fired a missile without intending to."

Madani looked at Khalida, who returned his look of concern. "You are speaking in a way that could result in your—"

"And I am *outraged* that an American pilot gloated on the American television about killing my brother and showed the gun camera film of my brother's airplane crashing into the sea. And no parachute."

Madani nodded enthusiastically. "The Americans have humiliated our country in front of the entire world. They have slapped us in the face. And you, Ismael, my friend, have been put in a unique position to do something about it."

"I must go."

"We are here to offer help. We can give you money, weapons, assistance, whatever you need. We already have people in the United States."

"Then why don't they do it?"

"Because he was your brother," Madani answered. "It is your duty."

Ismael kicked at the dirt with his foot. He made no response.

"Think about it. And when you decide what to do, talk to us."

"How?"

"We have a chat room on the Internet. It can be used for communication, but you must be very careful."

Ismael shook his head. "No. Those rooms are being monitored."

"You have a better way?" Madani asked, perturbed.

Ismael nodded. "I have created an e-mail encryption software program. It has never been used. I developed it and never showed it to anyone. In America, when you do such a thing, you are required to give the back door key to the NSA, the agency that listens to your phone calls and tries to read your e-mail. I don't think they'll be able to break this one. I will give it to you."

Encryption had been a hobby of several of his EE class-mates at George Washington. They all theorized that the NSA could break anything. Maybe. Ismael doubted they'd break this, at least not fast enough. But he knew that if he went back to the States, he would need what-ever advantages he could muster. They would have some very smart people looking for him. "Can you get me another passport?"

Madani smiled. "Of course. As many as you want."

"I can't go back to my student apartment. They will be waiting for me." Ismael's mind was working. Plans were forming. "I need to get back to the United States immediately, before they start looking for me at the en-trance points." He thought. "A Moroccan passport. Can you do this?"

"Of course."

"I want to take a car or the train, something untrace-able, to Morocco and leave for the States from there."

"We will get you out of the country unseen. We promise."

"I will meet you tonight, behind the train station by the taxi stand at eight. I will bring you a disk with the e-mail encryption."

Madani nodded, then handed Ismael a small pack-age. "Here. Put this away."

"What is it?"

"American cash. You may be able to use it. If not, then you can return it someday."

Don Jacobs didn't like the initial reports at all, the videotape of the funeral, the anti-American attitude, activity, and agitation. He had grown accustomed to it in so many places—constant demonstrations, the tired anti-American rhetoric—but this one was different. It was from a specific event—the confrontation between

the American Navy fighters and the Algerian Air Force
MiG-25s. He leaned over his desk and reviewed the file
that had been hastily compiled. It was mostly specula-
tion and guesswork, but part of his job was picking the
good guesses from the bad. If you got enough of them
right through instinct, analysis, or intelligence, you
succeeded, and you got promoted. But if you got it
wrong, it could get ugly.

His office door opened and closed. "Sorry."

Jacobs looked up at him. "Come on in. See the file?"

"Yeah," Rat said.

"What do you think?"

Rat sat on the edge of the chair. "We've been watching those guys for years. They've never operated outside the country."

"You saw what they did in those villages."

"Yeah. Brutal, but that was before they got into
power."

Jacobs kept reading. He finally threw the file down
and dropped his reading glasses on top of it. "You
think they're *less* likely to do something when they're
in power?"

"No. They're worth keeping an eye on."

"What about the agent report we got about the funeral?"

"The meeting in the alley?"

"Yeah."

"That one got my attention," Rat said. It had gotten
his attention like gears clicking into place in a transmission. It was what he had learned to look for in
counterterrorism operations, when things start fitting
together, disparate things, things you might not even
regard as gears. He had learned they all came together
for a terrorist operation to occur, and the key was spotting the gears before the operation got under way.

"His brother was the pilot that was killed."

"Exactly. And he has an open ticket to return to the States. He's been a student here for three years. Before the World Trade Center even. And he got by the heightened scrutiny of student visas because he's a legitimate student. He's been attending classes regularly, doing well. He's on schedule to get his degree next year."

"An open ticket back to Washington. This could be a real problem."

"Not only a ticket, but he used to be one of them. I saw one of your analysts thinks his whole 'retirement' from the killing business when he was seventeen was bogus. That he was tapped by someone higher up for bigger things. They're running him without the old guard even knowing it. But he was just speculating."

Jacobs shook his head. "What are the chances of that? We whack some random pilot, and his brother is a student here."

"When you have five hundred thousand foreign students here, the odds aren't that bad."

"You think he'll come back?"

"No doubt in my mind."

"And do what? Study?"

"That's the question, isn't it. But I don't think he'd come back just to study. Not now."

Jacobs was thought of as one of the cleverest men in the Directorate. He didn't take unnecessary risks, or at least what were perceived after the fact to be unnecessary risks. That was, of course, the impossible standard to which all in the Agency were held. He got up early and stayed up late just to out-think his prey. "Why can't we just turn him back when he tries to get into the country?"

"We can. But if we're right, and he has something else in mind, you think he'll just show up at Dulles and say, 'Hi, I'm back'?"

Jacobs shook his head. "So what's your thinking?"

"I know what I would do if I were him."

"What?"

"Go after the symbol."

"What symbol?"

"The one who was on the *Today* show smiling about it as the gun camera film showed his brother getting killed."

"The *pilot*?" Jacobs asked, amazed at the thought.

"Exactly. The pilot. Lieutenant Ed Stovic."

Jacobs sat back and put his hands behind his head. It hadn't even occurred to him. "You think that's what Algeria has in mind? Not just him, but Algeria?"

"Maybe. They may have other things in mind as well, but I'll bet that's where he starts."

"Why do you think so?"

"Because people will see the symmetry. They may actually sympathize with him."

"And it's simple."

"Very."

"I'm used to our war being elsewhere. We have to give this to the FBI and the INS. We can't operate inside the U.S."

"You can't. But *I* can."

Jacobs stared at Rat, not sure whether to pursue the suggestion. "Meaning?"

"I have a company, remember? Security consultants. Weapons testing."

"But you work for us."

"That's what you think. I just work *with* you," Rat said. "I'm a private businessman. Anyone can hire me to do security inside the U.S. or outside."

Jacobs studied Rat. He was beginning to suspect something deeper than just an interest in the latest possible terrorist exposure. "Why do you care?"

"He's a Navy pilot."

"So?"

"And he went to the Naval Academy."

"That's it?"

"We were in the same company. Same class."

"Ah," Jacobs said, understanding now what he had been missing. "That explains a lot. It might be to his advantage for you to look out for him."

"You still need to tell the FBI and the INS. Maybe he will just walk off the airplane at Dulles."

"Maybe he will. I'll pass all this on to the FBI. They'll have primary responsibility."

"Give them my number. Tell them I'll be around, and to leave me alone. I'll have my team working on it. I'm also going to watch his apartment on the off chance he goes back. I doubt he will, but maybe there's something there he needs."

"I don't know about this. We should leave it to the FBI."

"You really believe that?"

"Sure. Why?"

"I've heard a lot about your opinions of the FBI since I've been around here."

Jacobs was taken aback. "Who?"

"Various people."

"Oh? And what did they say?"

"They said you melted down about Hanssen. Said you'd never trust the FBI with anything again."

Jacobs carefully considered his response. "How do *you* feel about the FBI?"

"I think they're swell."

Jacobs laughed out loud. "Right."

"So are you going to tell the FBI everything you have?"

"I'll tell them what I think they need to know."

"Tell them I'll be looking for this Algerian too. I'll stay out of their way, but I'm going to be around."

Jacobs got a very serious look on his face. "If anything comes of this, it's your ass, not mine. Even if they trace you back to whatever government position they trace you back to, you were moonlighting. Operating on your free time."

"My free time. Yes, sir."

"Just to make sure we understand each other, I'll deny I ever authorized you to do anything. Unless this goes overseas, in which case I'll give you whatever help you need."

"I understand."

"Stay in touch. Give me reports."

Rat had heard enough. *We have nothing to do with this, but give us reports.* "What if I find him?"

"That would depend on the circumstances. You'll just have to exercise your perfect judgment."

Ismael walked up the stairs to his room at the Motel 6. He was in Virginia overlooking the beltway, the circular freeway that ringed Washington, D.C., like a moat and protected Washington from reality. He closed the door behind him and sucked in the chilled air that he had grown to love. He kept the room as cold as he could make it to fight off the humidity. High temperatures didn't bother him. Algeria could get very hot. But the humidity in Washington in September was unbearable. He quickly crossed to his desk, turned on the television, pulled his laptop out of its carrying case, and plugged in the phone line. He logged on through his Internet provider and entered his PIN.

He went to a search engine and typed in "Lieutenant Ed Stovic." He stared at the screen as CNN blared behind him. Finally the blue bar was done and he had five pages of hits to go through. He quickly went by the ones that were from genealogies and other irrelevant information and came up with several hits from newspapers reporting on the shoot-down. He skipped those and scrolled down the page. Finally he saw what he wanted. "The Ragin' Bulls." He selected the page and found himself staring at the VFA-37 web page, proclaiming to the world how great the F/A-18 squadron was.

His face clouded as he read the latest "press release" from the Ragin' Bulls of their great victory in the Mediterranean, but he read every word on the web page that discussed the shoot-down until he finally found what he was looking for—the pictures of the pilots. He scrolled down the names on the list until he found Stovic. He clicked on it, and a picture of a naval officer came up on his screen, the smiling face of a dark-haired officer in a dress blue uniform with Navy wings and ribbons over his left breast. It was him. The same Navy pilot as on the *Today* show. Stovic's biography was summarized right next to his picture.

Ismael read it carefully, then copied the text and saved it to his hard disk. He right-clicked on the photo and printed it on his color printer. He put the photograph in a file folder and then printed every page of the squadron web page. He finally copied the page that gave the contact information for the squadron. Oceana Naval Air Station, Virginia Beach, Virginia. He could still hear this Stovic telling the interviewer on the television how fortunate he was that the shoot-down had occurred at the end of their cruise. He was heading home to be with his family. Ismael went to a locator web site. It compared every major city's phone book with other identification data. He entered Stovic's name. Up came Stovic's home address and phone number in Virginia Beach.

He leaned back in his chair and stared at the address. He exited out of the search engine and went to Hotmail. He checked to see if he had any e-mails. There was one. The return address was a list of numbers. He clicked on it to open it and saw nothing but gibberish. He frowned, then remembered the CD he had given Madani. He retrieved the CD from his backpack and slid it into the drawer. The computer automatically loaded it and walked him through the installation of what it called "E-Mail Helper." He waited as the blue bars ran from left to right and it was finally loaded. It asked him if he wanted to run the Helper software now, and he clicked on the "yes" box. It asked him to call up the e-mail, which he did. Suddenly the computer screen went dark, and countless combinations of numbers scrolled by faster than he could ever hope to read them. He stared at the screen, waiting. A completely different screen came up, and in the middle was the Hotmail e-mail. It was from Madani, written in the plainest language imaginable. He clearly didn't think anyone would be able to decode it:

Brother Ismael:

I know you want to operate alone. I know you will do what you are going to do without our help. For now, that is acceptable. But we have recently learned of some information that you need to know. The things that were originally told to us of your brother's death are not true. Your impressions of Hamid were apparently correct. Your brother did get out of his airplane. He died because his parachute was burned and unable to stop his descent. Recently a Liberian freighter stopped in our port to deliver your brother's body. It has been recovered. They took pictures of him on the day of his death. Those pictures are attached. We thought you would want to know what this American pilot did to your brother. Do not look at them if you do not want to see them. Let us know if we can help you. Madani.

He stared at Madani's words; the news worked its way down into his mind. He had already generated terrible images of his brother, but new ones were exploding in his head. He had to look at the photos. He had to know. His imagination would be worse than anything that might have actually happened.

He looked at the symbols for the three photographs. All he had to do was click on them. He moved the cursor arrow over the first one and stopped, his finger resting on the touch pad. Two touches was all it would take. He waited. His heart pounded. He could feel his pulse in the tips of his fingers on his laptop. He touched quickly twice, and the computer slowly opened the photograph. His brother lay on the deck of a ship still in his flight suit and harness. Ismael's eyes darted around the photo, drinking in the image too fast. He breathed rapidly.

The parachute with its brown edges lay in a heap around him. He could see several pairs of work boots and shoes in the photograph of the sailors standing in a circle around Chakib. His face was completely burned on one side all the way to his mouth, exposing his teeth back almost to his ear. His hands and arms were missing the skin, and the muscles and ligaments underneath were a white, fishlike color. He had been burned badly before he hit the water.

Ismael closed his eyes and looked down for several minutes. He finally closed the photograph and looked at the other two. They were from the same angle, only closer. He closed the photographs, then closed the e-mail and the encryption program. He pulled up a map web site and calculated the distance to Virginia Beach.

"How was your flight?" Karen asked.

"Great," he said embracing her. "2 v. 2 against Air Force F-16s."

Brandon and Carrie, two and five, jumped up from the table and rushed to greet him. He picked up Brandon and hugged Carrie to his leg. "How are you guys doing?"

"You haven't forgotten Carrie's ballet recital tonight, have you?" Karen interrupted, glancing at the clock.

"Nope," he answered.

"We need to leave in an hour."

"Roger that—" he said just as the doorbell rang. He looked at Karen. She shrugged and shook her head.

He put Brandon down and walked to the door. He jerked the front door open, hoping to startle whoever was standing on the other side.

The person wasn't startled at all and was intent on startling him. He charged in, grabbed Stovic behind his left knee and in one swift and deceptive movement threw Stovic to the ground on the woven rug by the door. He moved around on top of him and pinned him to the ground. "Give, Animal?" he growled.

"Rat!" Stovic exclaimed, with his shoulders on the rug and his legs and boots dangling in midair.

"Give?" Rat insisted.

"Yes!" he said, trying to get it out forcefully through his bent neck. "I'd have surrendered before you took me down! You don't need to bother pinning me!" Both knew that Stovic could have reversed the situation on Rat in two moves. Wrestling with Stovic was something Rat knew not to do. Stovic outweighed him by at least fifteen pounds, especially now that he wasn't wearing plastic jogging suits and throwing up in the locker room to get down to one eighty-five before weigh-ins. Stovic had grown accustomed to seeing his weight start with a two for some time.

At Annapolis they had carried on a four-year competition for the title Toughest Man in the Company. Stovic had been the Tennessee State wrestling champion and won more matches than he lost wrestling for the Naval Academy. But Stovic knew not to cross Rat in any form of personal combat other than wrestling. Rat had some hand-to-hand skills that he never talked about. He arrived at the Naval Academy with moves no one had ever seen before. He wouldn't acknowledge them as martial arts nor would he say where he had obtained such skills at eighteen years of age. But after some halfhearted challenges by various curious members of the battalion, word quickly spread not to mess with Rat. A broken wrist or elbow was likely to be the result. Everyone thought he was destined to be a SEAL.

Rat laughed and let Stovic out of his cradle hold. "How the hell you been?" he asked as they scrambled up and as Karen came from the kitchen to see what the commotion was.

"Great," Stovic replied. "What are you *doing* here?"

"Hey, Karen!" he said as he crossed to her, kissing her on the cheek.

"Rat! I thought you were off somewhere. You're always gone."

"I'm off all right," he replied. "I'm CIVLANT," he said smiling, using an acronym that was well recognized in the Navy for both mocking the Navy's obsession with acronyms and conveying his exact meaning. CIVLANT meant CIVilian, AtLANTic: out of the Navy and living on the East Coast.

"You got *out*?" Stovic asked, shocked.

"Bigger than hell," Rat said.

"But I saw you before cruise. You were in that supersecret DEV GROUP, or whatever."

"Shhhh," Rat said, putting his finger to his lips. "Whatever SEAL group I was in, I am now a business tycoon."

"We were just about to sit down for dinner. Can you join us?"

"Sure."

"I just can't believe you got out. Why didn't you tell me?" Stovic asked as they walked into the family room and toward the kitchen table. "You never even e-mailed me on cruise. Not once."

"Yes I did—"

"Oh yeah, yeah," Stovic said, recalling. "A video clip of some major league baseball game. The pitcher hit a bird with a fastball right over home plate—"

"That was a *cool* video," Rat laughed out loud, remembering the image of the bird's feathers exploding from the ball's impact. "But I couldn't tell you I was getting out. I knew you'd bust my balls, plus I'd owe you a hundred bucks."

"That's right!" Stovic remembered. "First one out gives the other one a hundred bucks. Pay up."

"Don't have the denarii with me. I'll get it to you."

"Like I figured. Not good for your bet. What a dog. So you didn't like being a SEAL? I thought you were the personification of a SEAL, except for being fat and all," Stovic joked.

"Yeah, I liked it. But what with my family . . . I didn't want to be on the road all the time."

Karen frowned. "Family? Is this new?"

"No. Just seeing if you're listening. I'm not surrendering my independence for anybody. And no kids. I hate kids. Too much complaining." He looked at their two kids. "Except yours, of course. They're perfect."

"Very funny," she said. In addition to telling anyone who would listen that he was going to be a SEAL, he always told everyone he wasn't going to marry. He didn't want to be hampered by having a family. Being a SEAL was going to be his life.

"I don't know," he said, taking a long drink. "I just got tired of being a superhero all the time."

"Right, so . . . what, you slept with the Admiral's daughter?"

"I'm saving myself for marriage."

Stovic rolled his eyes. "So what are you doing now,

and what brings you to our humble house unannounced?"

"I'll tell you about it, but first I've got to hear about this shoot-down thing! You're famous!"

Stovic smiled. "No big thing, really. The Algerians pulled a stunt that didn't work out. They shot at my CO, and I fired back. My missile guided, and theirs didn't."

"A MiG-25, no less."

"Believe that?"

"You going to get a Silver Star or something?"

"I don't know. The Skipper and the CAG are conspiring to do something."

"That's outstanding—"

"They now say they fired by accident."

"What else are they going to say? They intended to shoot you down but were too incompetent to pull it off? Anyway, you wanted to know what I'm doing. I've started a company. Security company. Lots of evil people out there scaring the shit out of a lot of good people who are willing to pay top dollar—actually, *above* top dollar—for high-quality security analysis and protection. We do mostly training and planning. It's a blast. I travel all over the place and do all kinds of fun things. I was just going out to eat, heading down to the beach to go to that shrimp place, and I said, hey, why pay for a good meal when you can mooch one from your friend and his wife instead?" He chuckled as they smiled at him. "Actually, I saw the *Truman* was back from cruise."

Stovic didn't believe him. He wasn't sure why, but in studying Rat's face he saw something more serious than just "dropping by," though he couldn't imagine what it was. And to hear that Rat had gotten out of the Navy was so surprising that it was unbelievable. Not even a letter or some angst-filled e-mail wondering whether he was doing the right thing? This just didn't fit. Stovic watched Rat's face as they sat down with the children opposite Rat at the table. They talked about friends, classmates, the Navy, and Ed's pursuit of the Blue Angels. Rat ate like a starved man. As he sat back he asked casually, "How's the neighborhood?"

Stovic looked at Karen, who gave him an immediate "what's up with him?" look. He replied, "Fine. Why? Thinking of moving in?"

"Actually, yeah. I've never owned a house. I lived in the BOQ for so long I forget what it's like to actually have a house. I lived in one room full of camouflage uniforms and greasepaint. A house would be cool," he said, examining the ceiling and floors.

"Where are you staying?"

"Friend's condo. He's deployed. I'm house-sitting."

Stovic nodded.

"It's great here. Quiet, pretty, very nice," Karen replied.

"Any weirdos?"

"Just us," Stovic replied.

"Any crime? Anybody look out of place, anything like that?"

"You're worried about criminals?" Stovic laughed. "I figured you'd love a little crime."

"I hate having to get up to pound some criminal." He was obviously probing. "Seriously, ever see anything that made you suspicious or anything?"

"Just today," Karen said casually.

Stovic looked at her. "What happened today?" he asked, suddenly concerned.

"What happened?" Rat asked, sitting forward.

"I was out in front of the house, and this guy drove by."

"What guy?" Stovic asked. "Why didn't you tell me?"

"Because it wasn't significant, and you'd only been

home about ten minutes when Rat got here."

Rat pressed. "What guy?"

"I don't know. Some loser."

"Just once?"

"No. Three times."

Rat was focused. "How do you know it was the same guy?"

"How many Ford Contours come down our street?"

"A Ford Contour?" Stovic asked. "Who the hell drives a Ford Contour? Maybe it was a real estate agent looking for houses to put up for sale. The market's hot—"

"Rental car," Rat said. "Did you see the driver?"

"Yeah."

"What did he look like?"

"Young—"

"You doing your security thing?" Stovic asked.

"Always practicing. Maybe you guys'll hire me. What did he look like?"

"Dark hair. Young. That's about all I saw."

"How do you know he was looking at you?"

"He seemed to be looking over the entire neighborhood. All the houses."

"Probably some burglar, casing all the houses. Seeing who's home during the day," Stovic said.

"No doubt," Rat said in agreement, but clearly not believing it. "See anything else like that?"

"No. Why?" Karen asked.

"I don't know. I'm a believer in vigilance." He looked at the two children. They weren't paying attention. "Ed, you guys got a weapon in the house?"

"Sort of," he replied. "I had a handgun, but when we had kids, I put a trigger lock on it and put it in the attic. I couldn't get to it in less than about fifteen minutes."

"What kind is it?"

"It's a .22 Magnum. I taught Karen to shoot it."

"Why are you asking about that?" Karen interjected, looking grave.

"No reason. Just security conscious. I'm a big believer in having a gun in every house."

"With small kids?"

He screwed up his mouth in understanding. "Makes it a lot tougher. A *lot* tougher. But if you're interested, I can give you something with a lot more horsepower. It'll stop a truck."

Stovic shook his head. "Nah. Chances of me having to whack some burglar with a large-caliber handgun are a lot less than me dropping it and blowing my toe off."

"Well, I wouldn't worry about it. I'm sure it was nothing."

They finished dinner in near silence. Stovic and Karen ate slowly, the rest of their conversation now tainted with the same lingering anxiety that had settled into their stomachs.

"Rat," Karen said for the second time. "Hello, Rat," she repeated.

"Yeah?"

"We've got to go to Carrie's ballet recital. Want to come?"

"Sure," he said. "Can I bring my camera?" he asked. "I've sort of gotten into photography. A new hobby."

"Sure," Karen said. She couldn't imagine why he would want to take pictures of Carrie's ballet recital. Until that moment and throughout their entire lives he had expressed exactly zero interest in what their children were doing. She wondered if he could even name them without prompting. "We need to get going in about ten minutes."

"No problem. I'll be right back," Rat said as he got up quickly from the table. As soon as he was in the living room he began peering through the windows from behind the blinds. It was nearly dark. He looked for any movement or signs of anything being disturbed. He walked quickly out the front door and stopped on the porch. He looked quickly around, taking everything in.

He went to his van, which was parked in the drive-way, and retrieved a small digital camera as well as two handguns that he put in their holsters, one on his hip under his baggy Surf Company T-shirt, the other on his ankle under his loose khaki pants. He turned on the two infrared cameras that pointed out from the front quarters of his van and were triggered by motion detectors. They would record anything that moved within a hundred feet. He grabbed what appeared to be an ordinary digital camcorder. He turned on one of the miniature cameras he was going to place under the eaves of their house. It transmitted a perfect signal of his face that showed up clearly on the small two-and-a-half-inch screen on the side of the camcorder. He closed the door of the camera, threw the strap over his shoulder, and said to his squad, through the microphone in the invisible earpiece he was wearing, "Groomer, you guys get all that?"

"Got it," came the quick response.

"I want cameras everywhere. As soon as we leave, install whatever you need. And I don't want any of it discovered. Got it?"

"We're set."

"And Groomer, don't get carried away with that new gun."

"Come on, Rat. Let me take out a couple of cats at least. The sound suppressor on this thing is *awesome*." Groomer, Ted Groome, worked for Rat. He had come to the SAS from DEVGRU with Rat.

"Check in with me every fifteen minutes. I'm getting

good images on this camcorder. We'll see how much range we have."

"Roger that. Robby said they'd work out to five clicks."

"I don't know where this ballet thing is. We'll see how it goes."

Ismael waited at the Navy Exchange parking lot outside the gates of Oceana Naval Air Station in his rental car. He had traded the white Contour in on a Red Taurus, claiming the Contour smelled funny. Karen had in fact seen him. He had seen her too. But no one had seen him that morning, including Lieutenant Ed Stovic, when he had followed Stovic to work in his green Explorer with the Ragin' Bulls sticker on the back window. He had followed Stovic from the quiet neighborhood all the way to the gate at Oceana, where Ismael had found the Navy Exchange parking lot a convenient place to turn in without having to show any identification whatsoever—no awkward moment at the gate of the air station.

Ismael had spent the night considering his plan. It was plain and direct, the kind that was most likely to succeed. He didn't want to die, but this direct action made his death almost sure. He was prepared to accept that to accomplish his goal. He had been waiting at the Navy Exchange parking lot for over an hour. If he sat in his car much longer he would draw attention. The lot was busy, and the street running toward the base was full of traffic leaving for the afternoon. It was 4:00 P.M., and most of the sailors were heading home. Ismael had noticed the day before that the pilots usually left later than many of the enlisted sailors, because they were flying later in the day.

He gripped the steering wheel tightly, reflexively, as a dark green Explorer drove in front of him past the gas station. He craned his neck to see if the Ragin' Bulls squadron sticker was in the lower left corner of the rear window. He glimpsed something but couldn't be sure. He pulled out of the lot into the traffic and kept his eye on the Explorer several cars ahead. They got to the end of the road and waited at the stoplight.

The light changed, and he turned left down the two-lane country road toward Virginia Beach. He maneuvered through the traffic, trying to get close to the Explorer. He was going to have an "accident" with Stovic, and when the Lieutenant got out to express his outrage at the carelessness of whoever'd hit him, Ismael would be waiting with the handgun that was jammed in his belt. It would make headlines, and everyone in the world would know about it by tomorrow.

The traffic opened slightly as they accelerated ahead. He was three cars behind Stovic. He followed, watching Stovic's Explorer as he turned down Virginia Beach Boulevard, a four-lane road with a large grass median. Ismael could now clearly see the squadron sticker on the rear window. He knew that if he was going to make his move it had to be on a larger road where his movements wouldn't be as obvious. The left lane was empty between him and Stovic. He pulled into it and accelerated to pass the three cars between them. He was closing on Stovic and would come up on him from his left, in his blind spot. He would turn into him at the last moment, as if he were driving too fast to change lanes. He accelerated toward Stovic as the light in front of them turned red.

"*You seeing that?*" Rat said forcefully on his radio from ten cars back.

"*I got it,*" Groomer replied from his.

"*If you let him hit our man—*"

"*Relax,*" Groomer said as he jammed the gearshift of his Toyota 4Runner down to second gear, glanced in his side mirror at Ismael's car, and slammed the accelerator to the floor. He was in the right lane, two cars behind Stovic. The lane to his left was clear. He threw his wheel to the left and headed into the other lane. His 4Runner careened directly in front of Ismael's car.

Ismael was focused on the Explorer. He never saw the Toyota coming. He slammed into Groomer's Toyota just over the left rear tire. The Toyota spun around violently and came to rest in the left lane facing the wrong way, blocking Ismael's Taurus.

Stovic heard the loud bang and looked in his rearview mirror as he glided through the intersection. Holy shit! he thought as he saw the Toyota spin around. The guy changed lanes right in front of that red car. What an idiot. He thought of stopping to help but saw that already five or six cars had stopped. He couldn't do anything they couldn't do. He drove on.

In the Taurus Ismael struggled to free himself from the shoulder harness and the deflating air bag. His face hurt from where he had plowed into the air bag, and his left shoulder felt numb from the shoulder harness. The entire inside of the car was covered with some kind of white dust, like talcum powder. He couldn't understand what had happened. Stovic had been *right* in front of him. Everything had been working *perfectly*.

Ismael looked at the instruments in front of him. The engine was still running. He looked for the Explorer but could see only the dark red Toyota against the right front of his car. He suddenly saw a large, burly, tough-looking man climb out of the Toyota in a state of obvious menace. The man was wearing leather gloves. He began to walk around Ismael's car toward the driver's door.

Ismael threw the gearshift into reverse, but there were two cars right behind him. He backed up slowly, not wanting to hit them. The man with the gloves was on him.

Groomer slammed his right fist into the driver's door window. It shattered, throwing glass onto Ismael. "What you doing hitting me, you dumbass! I'm going to pinch your damned head off, you punk!" Groomer reached in, trying to unlock the door and pull Ismael out, but Ismael wasn't having any of it. He threw the gearshift into forward, floored it, and accelerated around the Toyota onto the grass shoulder and around to the other side.

Groomer pulled his arm out of the window and jumped aside just in time. He ran back to his 4Runner and accelerated, but the left fender had been bent into the tire, making it impossible for him to move. He cursed and jammed the other large lever on the floorboard of his truck into four-wheel drive. He jammed the accelerator to the floor and felt the front wheels try to pull the truck out of whatever was dragging the left rear wheel. The Toyota shuddered and fought, but the fender was buried too deeply in the wheel. It wasn't moving. He grabbed the headset. *"I'm busted, Rat. Wheel's stuck."*

"Damn it!" Rat exclaimed, back in the pack of cars stopped behind the accident scene. He threw his van into gear and drove onto the grass and around the mess of traffic, glass, and confusion. He wheeled around Groomer and made the same right turn Ismael had made. He roared down the side street looking for Ismael. Nothing. No red Taurus with a smashed front. He accelerated to each intersection and looked both ways. Nothing. One intersection after another; no Taurus. Rat drove faster, his frustration growing. *"Robby, you still got the local law standing by?"*

"Yeah. They've got a helo airborne."

*"Tell them it's their baby. I'm not chasing this guy through residential streets in a van."*

*"I'll pass it on."*

Rat drove back to Groomer's Toyota and got out.

Groomer was examining his fender and the tire. A Virginia Beach policeman had stopped. Groomer was furiously pulling at the fender.

"You're going to have to tow that," the officer said.

"Shit!" Groomer said. "I had my hands on him!"

"The helicopter locate him yet?"

"Not yet," the officer said. "I'm sure they will, though. He can't have gone far."

Ismael had done the opposite of what anyone expected. Instead of heading for the airport, he had headed for the beach, a dead end where he would be obvious and trapped if anyone thought to look for him there. He drove up Pacific Avenue, north toward the end of Virginia Beach, until he was in the residential area away from the strip at the end of the road. He turned into a small dead-end street that was partially covered with sand and parked nose-in next to a bush that masked the damage to his car.

He had planned his escape carefully, selecting the quiet street and the very bush where he now sat. He saw no one, then heard a helicopter in the air. He dared not look up. He pulled out a sun cover to put underneath the windshield to reflect the sun but mostly to mask the existence of a deployed air bag. He took out a wet rag and wiped down all the surfaces he had touched in the car. The rental agency would be looking for the nonexistent Egyptian whose passport and credit card he had been given by Madani.

He pulled his shirt over his handgun and climbed out of the car in the swimming trunks he was wearing. He went to the trunk, opened it, and slipped on a large straw lifeguardlike hat and sunglasses. He grabbed a colorful towel, a folding chair, a bag with sunscreen, a book, and a wallet full of money that would pay for the cab ride back to the airport that evening. He walked away from the car to the beach.

# CHAPTER

## 7

**D**on Jacobs was furious. Rat hadn't known him for long, but long enough to know that he was furious. Perhaps it was the bulging veins on his forehead or the red complexion that gave it away. Rat sat in the hard chair across from Jacobs's desk, waiting to be asked something, to be able to defend himself, but Jacobs's silent pacing was driving him crazy. Jacobs looked like a bear in a zoo that checks both ends of the enclosure for possible escape routes twenty times a minute all day long. After several minutes Jacobs spoke. "So we were right. We smoked out his target. We were there in exactly the right position. We did everything right." He stopped. "Right?"

"Yes, sir."

"Good. Good." Pacing again. "Then where is Ismael Nezzar? Is he here? Is he somewhere I can interrogate him? Because we did everything right. You just said so."

"We had a problem—"

"A problem?"

"Yes, sir. Like it says in my written report—"

"Yes, I've read it. But it must be wrong, because you just said we did everything *right*."

"Maybe not everything . . ."

"All because a fender got stuck in a tire? Weren't you there? Didn't you have anyone else in the traffic? Didn't you anticipate he might make his move in public, in traffic?"

"Sure. But you said you didn't want us to have too high a profile. You said to coordinate with local police. We did. And they lost him."

Jacobs kicked his desk chair, which was on wheels. It went flying across the room and slammed into the bookcase. "I hate looking stupid. More than anything else, I *hate* looking stupid. *Especially* when it's by one punk student *asshole* who's too big for his britches. You know how hard it is to get within an arm's length of a terrorist?"

"Very well."

"We did it! You did it! And we have *nothing* to show for it!"

"I could have taken my whole team down there, but you said you didn't want that big a footprint."

Jacobs lowered his voice. "Do whatever you have to do, but get this son of a bitch. He's in *my* country, and I want him."

"Yes, sir. I'd like to coordinate with the FBI—"

"I've already told them. They've already sent people to watch Stovic, and they're looking all over for this Ismael Nezzar."

"But?" Rat asked. He could tell there was more to it.

"I don't trust them. I never tell them everything I know. I can't trust them with that kind of information."

"Still because of Hanssen?"

"That goes way deep with me."

"So what did you tell them?"

"That Stovic is a target of a terrorist, and the terrorist's name is Ismael Nezzar, and his location is un-

known. But I want *you* to get him. I don't want this
asshole arrested and defended by some ACLU smart-
ass. You understand?"

"Yes, sir," Rat said. He heard Jacobs loud and clear
but would do whatever he thought was appropriate,
regardless of what Jacobs said. Rat reported to a higher
authority.

"You were right on the money about Algeria," President Kendrick said to Sarah St. John. After every meeting with the National Security Council to go over
current events and whatever else she thought was worthy of his time, they would adjourn by themselves to
the Oval Office and debrief what had been said. It was
a tradition she had worked hard to protect. Cabinet
members, particularly Howard Stuntz, the Secretary of
Defense, and Stewart Woods, the Director of Central
Intelligence, were jealous of her private time with the
President.

But she understood the power of relationships, the
trust that could build up between people over thirty
years. She and President Kendrick had been classmates
in college and had shared a burning interest in international affairs. They had even dated for a short time, but
quickly learned they were too much alike to be truly
compatible.

They thought any international problem could be
solved by the sufficient application of brain power and
persuasion of those involved. She had pursued her pas-
sion to a doctorate, while Kendrick had chosen to go
into business. But they had stayed in touch, particularly about their favorite quirky professor in the school
of international relations, an odd duck who wore black
socks and sandals to class every day and hinted that he
had served in the CIA. He had crazy hair and came off
as unstable, but St. John and Kendrick had loved sit-

ting through his classes for the entertainment value alone. The professor had constantly warned about believing what you saw, especially if the government was involved. He implied that everything from the government was part of a massive disinformation campaign and to be doubted.

St. John had studied under him for her master's degree but had gone elsewhere for her doctorate. She had learned from him, especially about not always trusting the government and paying attention to rivalries between agencies. President Kendrick shared some of her concerns about internal government rivalries. Their private meetings were intended to solidify their trust of each other. Complete, unwavering trust and reliance. No games, no rivalries.

"There is the report of the attack on that Navy pilot. That might be from the government, or it may be the brother acting alone."

"It doesn't sound much like a government."

"True. But things don't work like they used to. They realize they can't take us on directly, so they're supporting or in some cases starting terrorist organizations, and they spend all their effort making them untraceable back to the country. Here, he's from Algeria. So the issue is whether he's working for them."

"Are we doing enough?"

"According to the FBI they're protecting his family now."

"But how did they stop him in Virginia?"

"Apparently with the help of the Agency."

Kendrick didn't like it. "They can't operate inside the United States."

"There are a very few things they can do, and so far they're okay. I checked."

"So are we doing enough?"

"I think so. If it's just one man."

"And if it's not?"

"I think we need to turn up the heat a lot."

Kendrick nodded. "Call Justice and get the FBI to put this high on their list."

"Rat, what are you doing here?" Stovic asked as Rat walked into his office at the squadron.

"I was looking for you," Rat said.

"How'd you get in here?"

"I sort of 'kept' my active duty Navy ID."

"Nice."

Rat smiled, looking around. "So you got selected for the Blues."

Stovic nodded vigorously. "How'd you hear that? I just got the call last night!"

"I have my sources."

"Can you believe it?"

"Foregone conclusion."

"Not if you'd seen the interview."

"Why?"

"Oden—that's the name of a Norwegian god—he was pretty tough on me. Wanted to know if Stovic was pronounced like Milosevic or with a hard *c* like Stowevick. So he looks at me like I'm some Serbian war criminal. I have to tell him all about my grandfather fleeing Communist Yugoslavia as a stowaway, so he lays off. Then one of the other guys wants to know all about the shoot-down, and whether it changed my life, and the whole *Today* show thing. It was amazing. And it only takes one vote against you, and you're out. I figured I was done, but I guess not. Pretty exciting. Oh, get this, as I was standing up to go into the interview, out comes this female Lieutenant in whites. I figure great, I have to compete against a woman who's trying to be the first female Blue Angel *ever*. She'll be a shoe-in. But then I notice she's a flight surgeon. She was interviewing for flight surgeon." Stovic looked at Rat. "You should meet her."

"I've sworn off women. They distract me from my mission." Rat smiled.

"Right." Stovic laughed.

Rat watched his friend's face closely. "You excited?"

"I can't even tell you." Stovic suddenly realized Rat wasn't wearing a uniform. He was wearing his usual casual wear, khaki pants, a T-shirt, and rubber-soled leather sandals that were sort of European looking. "But what brings you to the land of the Ragin' Bulls?"

"Have you accepted yet?"

"Accepted what?" Stovic asked, confused.

"The Blues. Did you tell them you would do it?"

"Of course. Right away. I didn't want them to change their mind."

Rat was focused. "There's something I need to tell you."

"Shoot."

"Somewhere we can go?"

Stovic looked at the work he had to do. It could wait. "We can walk down to the gedunk and get something to eat. That will get us outside."

"Great."

They walked out into the hangar, through the stairwell painted squadron colors, and out into the bright Virginia sunshine. They walked down along the hangar toward the snack shop. "What's up?" Stovic asked.

Rat stopped in the parking lot halfway to the gedunk, a little place where people bought microwave sandwiches, candy, and sodas. "You may want to reconsider."

"Reconsider what?"

"The Blue Angels."

Stovic was shocked. "Why would I reconsider the Blue Angels? Are you out of your mind?"

"Because of what I have to tell you. I'm starting to see this differently."

"Let's have it," Stovic said.

"Remember when you were driving home and there was a wreck behind you?"

"On Virginia Beach Boulevard? How do you know about that?"

"I was there."

"Where?"

"And that night when we went to Carrie's ballet recital? I had my guys put up a bunch of surveillance gear at your house. For your protection."

"From *what*?"

"Someone's trying to kill you. The guy in the car was trying to hit you. He was probably going to shoot you when you got out of the car."

"What?" Stovic asked, his voice rising in concern and pitch. "Who?"

"Ismael Nezzar."

"Who the hell is that?"

"The brother of the pilot you shot down in the Med."

Stovic stared for a moment, just long enough for the gears to fall into place, the same gears Rat was always looking for. "He's here?"

"He was a student at George Washington, studying electrical engineering."

Stovic rolled his head back in disbelief. "You've got to be shitting me."

"Nope. The guy who Karen saw drive by your house? Probably him."

"So now what?"

"So if you keep doing what you're doing, it will be about you and him. I think we can protect you."

"We who?"

"The government. I wasn't just a starving bachelor

when I stopped by your house. I'm still working, bro. I'm here to look out for you. Actually, to get Ismael, but part of that is looking out for you. The FBI is working it too, but they've been in the background. As of now, they're moving into the foreground. This is getting a lot of national attention now."

Stovic saw the implications, and he didn't like what he saw. "So if I join the Blue Angels, it gives him a better target, a much more important target, and a way for him to make a big statement, not just come after me."

"Exactly. So that's why I'm here. You may want to reconsider. You may be a lot better off flying anonymous jets out of Oceana. You're never in the same jet, right?"

"Pretty much. No one would ever know if I was in a particular airplane from off the base."

"But in the Blues, you'll be flying the blue jet with a big #6 on it every day. Right? Always you, always doing the same maneuver at the same time in one air show after another."

Stovic stared down at the parking lot and put his hands on his hips in anger and confusion. "What would you do?"

"I don't know. It's up to you."

"What are the chances of this guy trying something again?"

"Virtually certain, in my opinion, unless the FBI finds him first, before he has another chance, which in my opinion won't happen."

"I'll have to think about it. I'll talk to Karen. But I *hate* the idea of being intimidated by some murderer."

"Sometimes it makes a lot of sense to be intimidated by a murderer."

Stovic looked into his friend's eyes. "Think you can find him first?"

"That's what I'm going to try to do. But not by

scouring the country. That's the FBI's job. I'm just going to stay close to his target and wait for him to come to me."

"Target. Me."

"Exactly."

"What about my family?"

"I'll have several people watching Karen and the kids, as will the FBI. We'll be coordinating. But there aren't any guarantees."

"Shitty deal."

"Yep."

"What would you do?"

"Just what you're doing. It's just that you're going to have to go forward with your eyes wide open."

"You're going to look out for me?"

"Yeah."

"What about when the Blues go to El Centro in the California desert in January. You coming along for eight weeks?"

"Absolutely."

"How you going to pull that off?"

"The Blues will know. At least some of them. The CO and some others. For the rest, I'm a former Navy guy who is working desperately to get a book published. A coffee table picture book called *The Blue Angels*. I don't have a publisher yet, but the Navy's cooperating."

"That's your hobby. Photography."

"It actually is. I'm pretty good at it. This would be different, but I can pull it off."

"This guy sounds like bad news."

"He is."

"Then we've got to get him, don't we? Seems to me it's our duty to get him. It's part of what we need to do as Navy officers, or as one officer and one former officer."

"Two Navy officers."

"I thought you got out."

"I say that. But not really."

"So you're still in?"

Rat nodded.

"Maybe together we can get him. I'm sitting on the sidelines now in the War on Terrorism. Had the one thing in the Med, but other than that I haven't really contributed. It's time to hang my butt out a little."

"If you do, I'll do my best to make sure it doesn't get shot off."

"Let's do this," Stovic said finally.

Ismael leaned on his elbow as he stared at his computer screen after another long night of Internet research. He had grown accustomed to living out of motels two or three nights at a time. He couldn't go back to his apartment. Washington maybe, for the right reason, but not his apartment. Not a chance.

He thought of Stovic and how close he had been to him. That Toyota haunted him. The movement was too quick, too intentional to be just someone changing lanes. It was someone protecting Stovic, he was sure. But who? Who would be watching out for Stovic? Someone who knew that Ismael was after him. But how could anyone know? How could anyone even suspect him? Maybe all it took was for someone to put his name together with Chakib's.

He typed "Stovic" into the web browser again, for perhaps the hundredth time since he had learned the pilot's name, and hit "enter." He waited as the list of hits came up and scanned them one last time before shutting down his computer and getting some sleep. His weary eyes passed over the list, page after page, the same list he had seen before: the genealogies for the Stovic family from Wisconsin and in particular Dr.

Richard Stovic, who had found a cure for something or other, and the Stovic who was a star on his high school hockey team in Minnesota and had decided he needed his own web site to publicize the inevitability of his future status as an NHL celebrity.

Ismael was about to shut down his computer when he saw a new hit from the Department of the Navy, a public relations press release. He frowned and clicked on the hyperlink. The text-only document came up on his screen. It was dated that day and released just thirty minutes before. It was a list of assignments, transfers, changes of command, and other irrelevancies. He didn't see Stovic's name anywhere. He clicked on "find" and typed in Stovic's name. It immediately highlighted his name under a paragraph that was headed with the phrase "U.S. Navy Blue Angels flight demonstration squadron announces selections."

He had never heard of a flight demonstration squadron and wasn't even sure what it was. He read through the brief paragraph, which told of Stovic's assignment to the Blue Angels effective in October.

He typed "Blue Angels" into the browser and, after reading several articles, was directed to their home page. He clicked through pages of photographs, biographies, and finally, an air show schedule. These were the Navy's elite, a team that existed to be in the public eye, to show what great, courageous, skillful pilots they were. They flew inches apart at hundreds of miles an hour just feet off the ground. *Graceful, beautiful,* and *awe-inspiring* were just some of the adjectives used in every article and description he found.

Ismael couldn't believe it. Stovic had applied to become a Blue Angel after killing his brother. No doubt he used the shoot-down to work himself into the position of being considered by this elite team. They probably saw him on the *Today* show too. Ismael clenched his jaw as he thought of his brother's death helping the very pilot who killed him take the next step up the career ladder.

He slammed his laptop closed and got up from the chair. He poured tap water into the coffee pot in the bathroom and waited for it to get hot so he could have a cup of tea. His mind raced, flush with the possibilities of the Blue Angels. After some time, after Stovic became a Blue Angel, he would strike. At Stovic himself but also at the Blue Angels, the famous team that represented the Navy. He would take Stovic's life for the entire world to see, to be played over and over again on CNN around the world. People would gasp and shudder, wondering how it could have happened.

He took the tea bag out of his tea, dropped it into the empty metal waste basket with a thump, and crossed back to his computer. He had waited too long and been automatically logged out. He logged back in and examined the Blue Angel air show schedule again. According to the press release, the new team was to report to the Blue Angels on October 6. He checked the schedule. San Francisco. Fleet Week.

# CHAPTER

# 8

Stovic and Pete Walters—the other new Blue Angel, whom they called Link—climbed into the rental cars under the watchful eye of Larry McKnight, #7. The Blue Angels' wives, various VIPs, and other support personnel were already in the caravan. The cars were lined up in front of the large hotel by Union Square in downtown San Francisco. The curbside was crowded with anxious San Francisco police officers on their Kawasaki and Harley motorcycles, who would lead the caravan through the city.

McKnight signaled to the lead police officer. They roared off with their lights leading the way, blocking traffic from the cross streets down to the waterfront. Residents and tourists stopped and stared, wondering who could be in the ten-car motorcade.

The cars were so close to each other as they raced through the streets of San Francisco that the Navy drivers—some pilots, some enlisted maintenance men—stuck their left hands out the windows to give the pilot's signal for "speed brakes"—a sort of lobster claw opening and closing—to warn the driver behind when they were about to slow down. They raced over and down the hills in single file. The police blocking the intersections leapfrogged from one to the next until the group drove through a small army fort down one last hill to the mouth of a long concrete pier that curved to form a sail bay directly in front of Ghirardelli Square. The police gathered around the cars as the Blue Angel group climbed out and stood around trying not to notice how much they were being watched by the audience that had gathered to see the air show. Rat scanned the crowd carefully. Others from his company were already there, already part of the growing crowd.

Those attendees straining at the barrier took particular notice of the beautiful women who were obviously wives of the Blue Angels. They wore jackets like ski jackets in Navy blue, gold, and white that had BLUE ANGELS embroidered in script across the back and the number of their husband pilot on the front left side. In the front of the group was a tall, striking blond woman who wore #4. The women stopped to talk to each other about whether this would be a good time to walk over and do some quick San Francisco shopping, as the Blues wouldn't fly for another two hours.

First they received the wristbands that would allow them instant access to the secure pier and to the reserved seats for the Blue Angel VIPs. McKnight wrapped them around each wife's wrist and clipped them expertly.

Stovic took in the beauty of what lay before them, the prettiest city in the country, the bay, the airplanes, and the excitement. He smiled slightly, then remembered Rat and why he was there. "You think we're okay here?"

Rat checked the back of his digital camera, then glanced up. "I never assume anything."

"Why would he be here?" Stovic asked, deflated.

"I didn't say he would be. It's unlikely, but possible."

Stovic zipped up his new Blue Angels jacket against

the cool breeze but also just to feel the new jacket in his hands. "Why would he come here? I'm not even flying yet."

"Intelligence. Strictly intelligence."

"You really think he's here?"

"No."

"Well, I'm going to assume he's not. I can't live like some paranoid lunatic."

"You won't mind if I do."

"Nope," Stovic said.

Rat was surprised at the number of people waiting by the waterfront for the Blue Angels to fly. About two hundred thousand were crowded onto the buildings, balconies, and boats, anxiously waiting for the air show to begin over the water between them and Alcatraz. The sun was dazzling, and the bay was a choppy, inky blue.

A few hundred feet behind Rat, Ismael watched carefully from a grassy area next to the pier by a booth where they were selling Thai chicken sticks. He watched those who had driven down to the concrete pier with the Blue Angels walk toward the guard at the rope line.

Ismael had arrived in San Francisco two days before the Blue Angels. He realized that the way to look completely inconspicuous was to look extremely odd. He allowed his hair to go wild and his beard to look greasy. He found some clothes at a thrift shop that were much worse than the oldest clothes he owned. He put them on the day he arrived, and he hadn't changed out of them since. He had slept in them. He had rubbed some foul-smelling dark substance he had found in the gutter onto his threadbare denim jacket. No one would look at him from less than five feet away.

He ate his chicken on a stick as if it was the first meal

he'd had in a week. He moved behind the Thai chicken booth toward the water and watched the Blue Angel VIP procession. He tried to look past them, toward the airplanes conducting the air show over the water. The woman pilot who was talking to the crowd on the radio was flying so low that no one could see her unless they were up and away from the rest of the crowd. Her wings couldn't be more than a foot off the waves.

Four of the Blue Angels' wives walked by him toward the shops. Two others headed toward the pier through the security cordon. He wanted to test the security. He hurried to walk immediately behind them, looking down at the ground as if he were half crazed. The wives casually exposed their wrists under their Blue Angel jackets and were waved in by the security guards. Ismael had been careful not to look at any of the VIPs in the Blue Angel party.

He tried not to look startled as he realized suddenly that he was walking directly behind the wives and right next to Lieutenant Stovic in his new Blue Angel jacket. He hadn't recognized him in his uniform with a gabardine hat and sunglasses on. Ismael tried not to stare. He immediately drank in the information his eyes provided him. Stovic was of medium height, slightly shorter than he was, probably six feet tall, with a thick frame and black hair. He looked very content. Ismael noticed a man who wore a photographer's vest full of film and odd bulges walking next to Stovic with a camera. He was filming everything. Ismael ducked quickly and picked up an abandoned Thai chicken stick off the pavement. He began licking it. He couldn't allow himself to be photographed.

He stayed down and scoured the area for cigarette butts on the concrete leading to the pier. He waited until Stovic and the photographer had passed. He followed the wives' group toward the pier. He tried to pass by the security check behind one of the VIPs but was stopped by the security guard. "You got a wristband, scumbag?"

He looked at the guard confused. "What?"

"Wristband. You got one?" the guard asked impatiently, knowing there was no way in hell this smelly homeless guy had a wristband to the VIP section.

"No. What is it for?"

"This is for VIPs only. You have to have a wristband."

"I just want to go on the pier."

"No wristband, no pier."

Ismael shrugged. "That is discrimination," he muttered as he turned away. He walked past the food booths and smoking sausage grills toward Ghirardelli Square. Behind him, the Red Baron squadron had begun its air show, flying four white Stearman biplanes. He noticed how loud their propeller engines were over the beautiful San Francisco Bay.

He moved to the left along the waterfront and down by the water. He waited as the biplanes finished their air show, and listened as the Blue Angel announcer began speaking.

He could hear the enthusiastic announcer quite clearly. He turned and sat by the sail bay to watch the air show more carefully, to see how and where the airplanes flew. He looked back over his shoulder and saw people everywhere. He took particular note of a tall apartment building on the hill behind the shopping center. Not only were the balconies of each apartment filled with excited onlookers, but people were on the roof of the building, hanging over the edge in anticipation of the Blue Angels, who they knew would soon come streaking in over the bay. It was an amazing sight. It would be quite an audience for a dramatic act of revenge.

The loudspeakers suddenly burst into life as the Blue Angel narrator said in a distinctive, enthusiastic tone of voice, "Goooood afternoon, ladies and gentlemen! Welcome to today's performance of the Navy flight demonstration squadron, the Blue Angels. . . ."

The C-130 Hercules cargo plane, flown by Marines, came humming across San Francisco Bay at a low altitude from directly behind them and pulled almost straight up in front of them. After making a couple of passes, the cargo plane disappeared, and suddenly, from his right, appeared the Navy Blue Angel diamond formation. Ismael tried not to be impressed. He tried to force himself to hate the entire production and the beauty of the spectacle in front of him. The sky was clear and crisp with a hint of fog still lingering to their left just across the Golden Gate Bridge.

He watched the diamond formation pull up into a high loop over the bay. The blue and gold airplanes appeared to be welded together. Ismael had never seen such skill demonstrated in the air. He had been to his brother's Air Force base many times and had seen numerous demonstrations of fighter prowess, but always by single airplanes going fast or performing difficult maneuvers, never by a group of airplanes performing the maneuvers together.

He watched the two solos drop down over the water, one from his left, over the Golden Gate Bridge, the other from a point far to his right. They flew directly at each other and, just before hitting, rolled into knife-edge passes to miss each other by mere feet as they screamed past in opposite directions, fifty feet off the water.

Ismael tried to pull back from the enjoyment of the

show to evaluate whether the show was vulnerable. The Blue Angel aircraft were unarmed. He was confident they expected nothing difficult out of an air show other than the flying.

As the solos completed another blistering pass, then pulled up into high G turns above the crowd, Ismael glanced back at the apartment building. He thought of how the Concorde was brought down in Paris by a small piece of metal on the runway that caused the tire to come apart, fouling the engine. He realized how little it took to bring down a jet. He looked at the solos as they passed over the water again, then back at the apartment building.

He watched every move of the entire Blue Angel routine. He sat until they were finished, until the crowd started to disperse. He pulled his feet back to avoid being stepped on. He listened to the comments of admiration and awe. He fell in with the moving crowd and walked toward the apartment building and up the hill. He stopped at the point near Ghirardelli Square where men pulled the cable cars around a rotating platform to head back uphill. Tourists waited in line for forty-five minutes, a captive audience for the musicians and beggars who were there every day asserting their turf rights against others who might want to move in. He walked to his seedy hotel room on the edge of Chinatown. It had bars on the windows on the ground floor and puddles of urine on either side of the front door where homeless men slept every night. He went into his room, turned on the television, and pulled his laptop out from behind the curtain where he had placed it in a silly attempt to hide it. He disconnected the room phone from the wall jack and plugged in his computer. He dialed in and quickly went to the Internet and his e-mail account. He called up the encryption software and sent a note to those in Algeria. He had decided on a course of action, a course that was bigger than a handgun and a car wreck.

Groomer slipped his headphones over his head and swiveled in his chair to face the screen in the back of the white van.

The door opened, and Rat stepped in and closed the door behind him. "Anything?"

Groomer shook his head. "Nothing. Pretty place, though."

"Everybody in place?"

"Sure."

Rat didn't like the tone. "Don't get complacent on me."

"Never," Groomer replied. He slipped his headphones off and flipped the switch that turned on the speakers in the van so he could hear any phone calls made at the Stovic residence without using his headphones.

"You hear anything from Washington?"

"Yeah. Robby says the guy's not going anywhere near his apartment. Not a chance. He may be in Washington, but he's not going to his apartment."

Rat nodded. "That's my take too. State says he hasn't even come back into the country."

"So he must not be here at all, and that guy that stove in my Toyota must be somebody else, just some random asshole."

"Exactly. Or *maybe* he has a fake passport. But we know *that* can't be."

"Why?" Groomer asked.

Rat frowned at him. "That would be *illegal*."

Groomer chuckled, a deep rolling chuckle, then got serious. "Can I ask you something?"

Rat nodded, looking at him.

"Why hasn't Stovic told his wife what the hell we're doing?"

"She'd just get spooked. If this Ismael guy sees any of that, he'll know someone's onto him."

"That's what I'm missing. So what if he knows we're onto him? He'll just go away, and that will be the end of it."

Rat shook his head. "If he knows someone's waiting for him, he won't go away, he'll go deeper underground or get more help. It'll make it much harder. When you turn the light on, do the cockroaches give up, or do they just get smarter?"

Groomer chuckled. His massive shoulders were exposed in the Surf Company tank top he was wearing. He was amazingly strong, and had a bushy goatee. His hair was cut in a buzz. His status as a member of Dev Group would not be obvious to anyone. "They get smarter."

"You've got to be smarter than the cockroaches, Groomer. See, I don't turn the lights on at all. I use night vision goggles when I'm hunting cockroaches." He watched an image on one of the remote cameras. "FBI guys check in with you yet?"

"Yeah. I gave them our entire layout. They're impressed, which is good, because they'd better be. But they think they're in charge—"

"They are," Rat interrupted.

Groomer looked over his shoulder at him. "Then what the hell are we doing here? We're going to be tripping all over each other. Shouldn't have two people doing the same thing."

"They're watching out for the family. That's their job. Stovic is our job, and they know it. They don't like it, and think we're outside our jurisdiction, but this is coming down from way on top. So they can't complain."

Groomer shrugged. Whatever.

"You get us a house in El Centro yet? Farmhouse? Somewhere way out of the way?"

"Yep. We've all got to pretend like we speak Spanish, though."

"No problem. I'm going to go check on Stovic."

"How's he taking this?" Groomer asked.

Rat stopped on his way out of the van. "Lightly."

"Why?"

"I don't know. You ever hear of Blue Armor?"

"Huh-uh."

"These guys that get selected as Blue Angels think they're invincible. They'll deny it all day long, but they think they can fly faster, lower, tighter, better than anyone. I think our boy Ed may be thinking that applies to everything else too; he isn't bound by the same rules the rest of us operate under."

"You'd better get him out of that."

"That's part of my job," Rat said as he stepped out of the van and closed the door silently behind him. When he turned to walk away, a woman was waiting for him. Rat stopped.

"You Rathman?" she asked.

"Yeah. Who are you?"

She shook his hand. "Terri. FBI."

"What can I do for you?"

"You're in charge of this . . . whatever . . . this group? The guys in this van and around?"

"Yeah."

"They've got to understand we don't need them. We're here to do a job, and we don't want them in the way."

"They won't be in the way."

"The fact that they're here at all makes them in the way."

"Well, you don't need to worry about them. They're pros. They're here for Ismael Nezzar. You're here to protect the family, right?"

"Seems to me we're here for the same reason. I'm going to try to get them moved. We don't need them."

"Well, you go ahead and get them moved. But in the meantime, you've got the family, right?"

"Don't worry about that. We've got them covered."

Rat didn't want to hear whatever else she had to say. He walked away toward his car. "You let me know when you get us moved. Okay, Terri?"

Brad Walker sat heavily in the chair in Sarah St. John's White House office just down the hall from the President's. He sighed and closed his eyes momentarily.

"You okay?" she inquired.

"Yeah. Yes, ma'am. Just tired."

She nodded and leaned back. She looked him over carefully. He looked disheveled. "What's up? You wanted to see me."

"I've been getting some inquiries from other agencies. People at my level. But it's clear they're being prodded to ask—these aren't their questions. I know most of them. We're friends. But these questions are coming from the top."

"Meaning?"

"Meaning that the Secretary of Defense is onto this, and probably the Attorney General."

"Onto what?"

"The fact that I'm getting encrypted e-mails with an encryption that isn't recognized by the people who do the recognizing. They hate that."

"What are they asking you?"

"These odd questions like how I communicate with

you, and with people outside the NSA. Whether I use special encryption to do top secret e-mails, that sort of thing, just enough to let me know they know I have software that isn't the usual."

"Well, you do. But there's nothing illegal about that."

"Right, but the NSA is supposed to have the code to all encryption software."

"They do. But they're also forbidden from snooping on American citizens."

"Unless they're communicating with a foreign national."

"Yes, well, let them do what they want, and we'll do what we want. As long as we stay within the law, I have no concerns. Do you?"

"Yeah, sort of. I feel like I've got to start looking over my shoulder."

"Why?"

"Because people are suspecting that we're doing something wrong."

"But we're not."

He sat and stared straight ahead. He finally asked, "So just keep going?"

"Yes." She turned her back on him and reviewed a report she had received from another NSC staffer.

Karen moved two boxes from a window seat onto the floor so she could open the bench. She brushed back her hair, noticing again the shocking impact of the saturated air, more humidity than she ever felt in Virginia. The two children climbed over the boxes, undoing most of the organization Karen was trying to bring to the house. They shrieked with excitement. The beautiful old house sat on stilts on the beach directly west of Pensacola. It was a battered gray with white trim, a big, drafty three-story house. It was more than she could ever have hoped to find in Pensacola. She was trying to make the most of a difficult situation and was thankful to have found a home that she could pour herself into. It was the kind of house that she would love to own even after they moved away from Pensacola. They could rent it out while they were based elsewhere and maybe one day move back to the peaceful beach, or if he stayed in the Navy for a career—something she still couldn't completely accept as inevitable—they could retire and live on the beach, go for walks, watch the sunsets, and grow old together. She found herself smiling. She allowed herself to at least consider that perhaps their time in Pensacola wouldn't be as bad as she had thought.

The screen door in the front of the house slammed, and Stovic walked in. "Wilma, I'm home!"

The two children ran to greet him as Karen stood up from the window seat. She smiled at him as he came into the large family room and looked out the large windows at the vista of the beautiful Gulf of Mexico with the sun setting to his right.

"This is gorgeous," he commented. "I can't believe we found this place."

"It really is pretty. Thanks for putting up with my whining in the moving process."

"You didn't whine, you just . . . expressed yourself."

"Yeah, that's it," she smiled. "Maybe it was celebrating Christmas in the Holiday Inn that got to me."

Stovic nodded. "We should have gone to your folks' house."

"We had to finish moving."

She was right. He was just trying to make her feel better.

Karen looked around. She didn't want to ask the next question, but she had to know. "Did you find out when you leave?"

"Yeah. It's like we thought, 0800 tomorrow. One stop, then land at El Centro in the afternoon."

"Make sure I've got the number of where you're staying."

"It's a hotel. Desert something. I've given you the number a couple of times."

"Are you going to be able to get back at all?"

"We'll be flying twice a day six days a week for all eight weeks. Only day off is Sunday."

Karen took a deep breath and sat down heavily on the bench. She felt bad for the kids. She looked at them. "And we're not welcome."

"They tried it in the past, but it didn't work out. We'll be so focused, no time to do anything, really."

"When will we see you?" she asked, watching their children.

"After the opening air show in El Centro we've got one show in Arizona, near Phoenix—Mesa, I think—then we fly back here. I think we arrive on March thirteenth or something."

"So nine weeks."

"Pretty much." He stood there awkwardly, not quite knowing what to say. He needed to finish packing his gear so he could take it to the hangar in the morning to be loaded aboard Fat Albert, the Blue Angels' C-130 Hercules, which would be carrying everyone's gear to El Centro, the winter home of the Blues. Then he'd climb into jet #6 and take off with the rest of the team to California. He looked at the side of her face. It showed sadness. "I'd better go finish packing. I'll take the kids with me."

"Yeah," Karen said standing, recovering, controlling any emotions that made it all the way to her face. "Dinner will be in about an hour."

"I feel like I should apologize for something. Like I've done something wrong."

She looked at the floor, trying to decide whether to say what she was thinking. "It's just going to be hard," she began. "You know, Ed, the Navy will eat you up. They'll use you as much as you'll let them for as long as you let them. But someday they won't need you anymore. And when you look around for your family to go fishing and play in the sand, they'll be grown and gone. And you will have missed it."

"I know."

"I know you do. Just don't let yourself get dazzled by all the admiration. The worship. People *worship* the Blue Angels. Other wives have told me about it. It goes to your head. Then, at the end, you feel like you owe the Navy something. Just don't get like that. We have to go after our dreams, but all our dreams. The whole family. Right?"

"Right," he said, distracted.

"What?" she asked. "What are you thinking?"

"Karen, look, there's something I should tell you, but they asked me not to."

"Who's they?"

"The federal government."

She didn't say anything. She just waited.

"Sit down," he said. "I'm not sure how to say this. . . . You know Rat?"

"Sure . . ."

"He's actually around to protect me. His whole photographer thing is a cover."

She frowned and her mouth went dry. "Protect you from what?"

"You know the Algerian fighter I shot down? Well, the pilot who was killed had a brother. And he's in the States and may be trying to get back at me—"

"Get back at you?"

"Yeah. That wreck I told you about on Virginia Beach Boulevard?"

"Yeah."

"It was him. He was trying to smash into me, then jump out and shoot me."

"What? Why didn't he?"

"Rat stopped him."

"Is he still around?"

"They don't know where he is. Rat thinks he's going to try to get me during an air show or something. He's not sure. But sometime when I'm with the Blues."

"How?"

"They have no idea. Could be anything."

"So why are you still doing this? It's already dangerous enough. Now some guy is trying to kill you? This is crazy!"

"Well, we're not sure—"

"Rat's here to pro*tect* you?"

"And the FBI, they're all around, you just can't see them. I think we'll see more of them soon. They're discussing how to do it. I don't really understand."

"Maybe this is a sign. Maybe you just aren't supposed to be a Blue Angel."

"A sign? From who? God?"

"Maybe. How do I know? But maybe you should consider quitting. I mean wouldn't you be safer just flying out of Oceana?"

"Probably."

"Maybe it's time to back away. Doesn't it make the hair stand up on the back of your neck to know somebody is going to try to *kill* you?"

"Sort of. But we can't let terrorists control our lives."

"I sure can. If it's safer to do something else, then maybe we should. Am I safe?"

"I haven't heard anyone say you're not, but I guess they'd really have no way of knowing."

Karen leaned back against the window. The sun had

set behind her, and they hadn't turned on the lights inside the room. Her face was almost imperceptible backed by the last remnants of the day's light. "Will you at least consider quitting? For us?"

"When we're in El Centro, I'll think about it. But I really don't think it will change anything."

"Think about it, Ed, for me." She touched his face.

He nodded.

Ismael returned to the Quality Courts Motel where he had moved after three days at his last motel—never more than three days in any one place—and dumped the magazines on the table. He had to have a Stinger missile to be confident of success, and *anything* you wanted was for sale in America. He had read an article about the Russian Mafia in Brighton Beach, New York. They could get anything and would sell anything to anyone. He read of Russian military helicopters and a Foxtrot submarine that had been sold to a Colombian drug cartel by the Russian Mafia.

He scoured the advertisements in the weapons magazines, the ones for international soldiers that will fight anyone for pay, the ones for those obsessing about handguns, or shotguns, or assault weapons, or armies and navies, or tanks, or military history, or arms of the future. Every kind of weapon had its adherents and its own magazine. As much as Ismael already knew about weapons from the early training he had received in the Algerian desert, he was shocked at the detail in the publications, details from manufacturers, from those who used and sold the weapons, and sometimes details about where one could get such weapons, occasionally illegally.

Many of the ads directed those who were interested to post office boxes, but a few had phone numbers. He noticed one ad in particular: "Any weapon, anytime, any caliber, anything you need, for anywhere in the world, I can get it for you. Competitive prices, everything confidential." There was a telephone number with a Washington area code. Ismael had an irresistible urge to call. His instincts were warning him against it, against violating one of the fundamental precepts taught to him years ago—never deal with someone you don't know. But he knew there were only two ways to get a Stinger—the black market or dealing with the people who had the few left over from America's support of the mujahideen in Afghanistan in the eighties. Not many had made it out of Afghanistan during the War on Terrorism, but he knew that a few had. He didn't want to play that card, though. The price would be too high.

He picked up *Weaponeer Magazine,* the one with the ad he had seen, rolled it into a scroll, and jammed it in his back pocket. He walked to a pay phone six blocks away, a phone he had never used before and would never use again, and dialed the number. He listened carefully as the phone rang, and finally a man with a gruff voice picked up the receiver. "Yeah."

Ismael hesitated. He fought to speak, then hesitated still more.

"Somebody there?" the man asked.

"Yes," Ismael said quickly. He tried to make his voice sound lower. "I'm calling about the ad."

"Which one?" the man asked impatiently.

"The one in *Weaponeer.*"

"Sure. What do you want?"

"You say you can get anything."

"Sure. I'm a licensed gun dealer. Also broker. I'm licensed to ship interstate and sell anything that's legal."

"I don't know if what I want is legal."

"What is it?" the man asked directly.

"I'm not sure."

"Sounds interesting. I have access to a lot of things. Maybe we should meet."

"No," Ismael said, startled at the thought of meeting face-to-face with this man.

"Then I can't help you. If you won't tell me on the phone, and you won't meet with me, then forget about it."

"Perhaps I could write to you or something."

"Bullshit. I don't play games. You want something, you tell me. You don't wanna tell me on the phone? Fine, but we don't do business. That's the way I operate. If you like that, then talk to me. I don't really give a shit."

"Fine."

The man hesitated. "Fine what?"

"Fine, we meet."

"All right. How about tomorrow, 9:00 A.M.? You come over to my—"

"No. I will call you at this number tomorrow at 8:30 A.M. and tell you where we can meet."

"Why the games?"

"Because I don't know you."

"Where you calling from?"

"Doesn't matter."

"It does if you're in California. If we're going to meet tomorrow, we both have to be able to get there. Right?"

"Yes."

"Okay. From where you are, can you reach southeast D.C. in half an hour?"

"Yes."

"Good. Me too."

"I'll call this number, 8:30 A.M. tomorrow morning."

"Fine." The man hung up.

Ismael placed the receiver back on the cradle. He was breathing heavily, excited and anxious at the same time.

* * *

The six Blue Angels flew over the runway at El Centro. Stovic had flown into El Centro several times in the past, mostly on weapons detachments with his squadron and their F/A-18s to the Chocolate Mountains. It had always been one of his favorite places to fly—the control of the air over El Centro was relaxed—an informal encouragement of creative and fast flying, unlike nearly all the other towers in the Navy system, where radar guns and speed control were the order of the day.

Stovic was trying to keep his place in the tight formation. He was like a boy with a new fishing pole, but he also felt a little like an imposter. He was flying with probably the most skilled and finely trained aviators in the world. He also knew he and Link, the other new pilot, would be the subject of intense scrutiny as the only ones on the team who didn't know what they were doing. Every debrief, every review of the videotape would concentrate on their performances.

The desert sky was beautiful, and the Chocolate Mountains were clearly visible in the distance. He was the last of the six to enter the break, and pulled sharply to the left and into the break with a six-G turn to impress anyone who was watching. It was an odd feeling for Stovic to think of people on the ground watching his every move, expecting him now to be perfect. The G forces felt fresher and newer in his blue jet. He was ready to learn how to fly like a Blue Angel.

He turned downwind, lowered his flaps and landing gear, turned onto the base leg of his approach, and landed uneventfully. He taxied toward the Blue Angel hangar. His plane captain was waiting for him and directed him to his parking spot. Everything was done precisely, to form habits, so that when it mattered, when half a million people were watching at an air show, it would be automatic. The pilots joined the other Blue Angels near the hangar and walked through it to the ready room, where they would brief and debrief every flight until they left El Centro.

Oden walked next to Stovic. "So, Animal, how does it feel to be in a blue jet?"

"Good. Really good. How about for you? Is it all old hat now?"

"Never old hat. Never routine. Always a thrill."

"What do we do now?"

"Quick debrief, then off to the hotel."

"What about tomorrow?"

"You and me—first day of learning the routine. Brief, fly, debrief, do all that twice, then dinner, bed, and get up and do it again the next day. And the one after that, and the one after that. We'll pull so many Gs, your balls will be sagging down around your ankles." He laughed. "It's quite a workout, but our first air show is in two months."

Ismael called the dealer at exactly 8:30 A.M. from yet another pay phone. "It's me," he said.

"So what will it be?"

"Coffee shop, the Sunnyside coffee shop on—"

"I know where it is. Nine."

"What do you look like?"

"Fifty. Big. Burly. Wearing a brace." The line went dead.

Ismael started for the coffee shop immediately, only a three-minute walk from the telephone he had used, and began to watch the restaurant. He didn't want any unpleasant surprises. He wondered what kind of brace the man would be wearing. The man had said he was "burly." Ismael wasn't quite sure what that meant, but he thought it meant heavy.

He stood outside the restaurant for twenty-five minutes. He saw nothing unusual or suspicious. At 9:00 A.M. exactly, a large man in a cheap green nylon jacket and a leather cap tried to get by him into the door. "You the guy?" Ismael asked the man.

The man stopped and looked at him. He was wearing a metal neck brace that came up from his chest, inside his jacket. It looked like a brace for someone who had broken his neck, and held the man's head at an awkward height above his shoulders. It was obviously uncomfortable. His chin spilled over the brace in front. "Yeah. What's your name?"

"Doesn't matter," Ismael replied.

"We going to do business or play games?"

"That's up to you."

"Let's cut the cloak-and-dagger bullshit. If you need what I got, then you need it."

"What's *your* name?"

"Dick. You?"

"Bill."

The man gave a curt smile. "Bill."

Ismael nodded.

"Fine, *Bill*. Let's go inside and see if we have anything to talk about."

They went inside the restaurant and asked for a table for two toward the back. They sat down, and Dick took off his hat. Ismael thought he looked amazingly strong. He had rough fingers. He was someone who worked with his hands or at least spent much of his time outdoors.

"So," Ismael said. "You can get anything?"

Dick shrugged. "That's more of a marketing thing. I can get a lot. What you lookin' for?"

"I have many needs. Maybe you could give me an idea of the kinds of things you have or can get," Ismael said clearly.

Dick shook his head. "No. I'm not doing a list." He

took a long drink from his coffee. "Tell me what the hell you need."

"Where would they be delivered?"

"The bigger the item, the more scrutiny we're likely to get, the more likely it is the delivery will be somewhere different. Say you wanted a .50-caliber machine gun, not that you would. And if I were inclined to get it for you, not that I would be, then I might want that to be delivered somewhere outside of Washington, in, say, Maryland. Maybe some secure building somewhere." He grabbed his coffee cup without using the handle.

Ismael asked, "What about for a handgun?"

"A handgun? Shit, you don't need me for a handgun. You can buy those in a thousand different places. I could get one for you, sure. Pretty much anything you want. But is that what this is about?"

"No, but I would need one anyway. Personal security. Home security, I think it is called here."

Dick studied his face. "When you say here, you mean the U.S."

"Sure."

"Where you from if you're not from here?"

"Doesn't matter. Why do you care?"

"I don't. I just thought it was an unusual thing you said. I like to know who I'm dealing with. You from here?"

"Maybe. Maybe not. You can get handguns?"

"Of course. But what else do you need?"

Ismael hesitated. He was starting to get a bad feeling. Or perhaps it was just his inexperience. "I'd rather not say."

Dick sat back in frustration. He reached for his cup again. "Then what the hell are we doing here? If you're not going to tell me what you want, I don't think I'm going to be able to tell you whether I can get it. Unless you can help me figure out how to read your mind, I think we're about done."

"Perhaps I will tell you then."

"Let's hear it."

Ismael sat silently, then said, "What happened to your neck?"

"Don't worry about it."

Ismael stared down at the table.

Dick finally tried to stimulate him. "Look, what's your target?"

Ismael felt as if he was slipping into a moving river against his will and his head was about to be pulled under the water. "It's aviation related."

Dick squinted. "What the hell does that mean? You trying to shoot down an airplane? Is that it? You want some sort of shoulder-fired SAM, don't you?" Dick looked around at the other people in the restaurant. "Are you shitting me? You know how hard those are to get?"

"I didn't say that's what I want. I said it was aviation related. I didn't say the weapon was aviation related. I could be talking about jet fuel."

"Then tell me more."

Ismael stood up. "Excuse me for just one minute. I have to use the rest room."

Dick nodded and adjusted the neck brace.

Ismael went to the bathroom. The door opened, and a man came out. Ismael pulled the door closed behind him and locked it. He stared at himself in the mirror, controlling his breathing. His instincts were screaming at him to flee, but he had to get a missile. He had learned a long time ago, though, to trust his instincts. He had to get out of there. He stepped out of the bathroom and looked around for another door. Nothing. He'd have to go out the same door he came in.

He turned his head away from Dick and walked

briskly toward the front of the restaurant and out the
door. The traffic was loud as soon as he opened the
door onto the street. He glanced quickly up and down
the street, trying to remember the location of the closest
Metro stop. He saw several trucks and vans parked and
moving along the street. Each one of them in his now
panicking mind held five or ten federal agents who were
there to grab him. He tried not to run, but he was so an-
imated he jumped into a run every third or fourth step,
when he would catch himself and start walking again.
He could almost hear the hum of camera shutters in his
head. He was sure he had been photographed.

How stupid could he have been? He reached the
Metro stop, ran down the stairs, bought a token, and
rammed it into the gate. He jumped on the first subway
that arrived, planning to ride the trains for an hour in
innumerable and inconsistent directions. He settled
back into the seat next to a glass window etched with
graffiti.

Back at the restaurant, Dick had begun to wonder
what had happened to Ismael. He got up, went to the
bathroom, and found it empty. He stepped into the
bathroom and locked the door behind him. He took an
earpiece out of his pocket and placed it in his ear. "*Shit.
I think he's made us. He's not in the restaurant. You
guys see him?*"

"Yeah. He bolted," a woman answered. "He
walked out of the restaurant about three minutes ago.
He headed down into the subway. We've got two guys
trying to track him, but we can't reach them right
now."

"Damn it!" Dick shouted as he punched the paper
towel holder, causing the bottom door to open and all
the paper towels to fall out onto the floor. He didn't
even notice. "You get his picture?"

"Lots," she replied.

"Let's get back to the office. We've got to start working this one right away. I don't like what he said."

"Where do you think he's from?"

"Don't know. Middle East, northern Africa somewhere. Young. He must be desperate. Nobody's called that phone number in six months."

Rear Admiral Don Hooker walked down the passageway of the Pentagon. Even though it was a hallway, all the Navy officers called it a passageway. That's what it would be on a ship, so that's what it must be on shore as well. Ceilings were overheads, walls were bulkheads, drinking fountains were scuttlebutts, the usual nautical words. But Admiral Hooker wasn't feeling very nautical right now. He had been summoned by Vice Admiral Robert Girardi, the Admiral in charge of preparing the final Navy budget to be submitted to the CNO, the Chief of Naval Operations. It was in its final stages of preparation. Hooker knew that if he was being summoned, it wasn't to congratulate him because they had found a pile of extra money in the budget and were wondering if he needed any of it.

He walked into the reception area of Girardi's office and greeted Senior Chief Helen Johnson, who sat there. She was annoyingly efficient and humorless. "Morning, Chief. Is he ready to see me?"

"Yes, sir. He's been waiting."

Hooker looked at his watch. He was right on time. To the minute. He walked in, and Admiral Girardi looked at him. "Don, how are you?"

"Good, Admiral. What can I do for you?"

"Let's not rush into this. I have something I want to talk to you about, but I can't really get my throat going this early without a cup of decent coffee. Senior Chief!" he yelled.

"Yes, sir?" she replied.

"Get us two cups of coffee. Black."

"Yes, sir," she answered, jumping up.

Girardi closed the file on his computer that represented the latest work on the budget.

The coffee came, and they drank from the heavy mugs. "Well," Girardi said, "we need to talk about something. Like I said. But before we do, tell me how things are going for you."

"Really good, sir. This is a great job," he lied. He would rather be at sea. Naval officers belonged at sea. He had already commanded an air wing and a nuclear carrier. He had been on the fast track to Admiral and was selected before almost anyone else in his year group. All was well. But now, instead of taking over a battle group, he had ended up in the Pentagon. He still wasn't sure how it had happened, or why, or really what the career implications were, but he knew he would be watched.

"Well, you're one of our best. But I've got some unpleasant news for you."

Hooker waited.

Girardi drank deeply from the coffee and put the cup down on the corner of his desk. "The Blue Angels are under you."

"Yes, sir." Hooker smiled. He loved the Blue Angels and everything about them. They flew F/A-18s, the same plane he had flown for the last ten years in his squadron tours. "Why?"

"We need to talk about them."

"Yes, sir."

"How much do they cost the taxpayers every year?"

"I don't really know, sir. They're not broken out as a separate item in the budget—"

"Let me save you the trouble," Girardi said putting his hand up, stopping Hooker. "I had one of our whiz kids go through and figure out how much it costs to keep the Blues flying every year. We amortized the airplanes, the buildings, all the capital assets, threw in the personnel costs, the fuel costs, travel, maintenance, everything that you would calculate if you were flying the Blue Angels in the private sector. It was quite an interesting exercise—"

Hooker could see where this was going. "You could do the same for a destroyer—"

"Except a destroyer is a combatant, not a circus act."

"That's not fair, sir. The Blues are inspirational. I'll bet eighty percent of the Navy pilots that have worn the uniform since 1946 saw the Blues perform before signing up. Maybe more."

"Well then, let's put them in the recruiting budget. Problem is that would be more than the entire recruiting budget put *together*."

"It would not," Hooker replied.

"You get the point."

"Sir, are you implying what I think you are?"

The Vice Admiral played with one of the sugar packets that had come on the silver tray. He hesitated. "We've got to make some hard decisions, Don. The JSF program is in some trouble. They're looking for money. Congress isn't going to bleed out one more cent. They're funding the War on Terrorism, which is a black hole of spending, and trying to support the new procurement and personnel concerns. Either we get it done with what we've already been allocated, or something else happens, like canceling the Joint Strike Fighter for the Navy." He toyed with the sugar pack. "We can't let that happen. We don't have any medium bomber capability anymore, not since the A-6 went away. That was early Vietnam technology. Then we pissed all over ourselves with the A-12, and it got canceled. So we've had to do it with strings and mirrors ever since. The new Super Hornet gets us part of the way there, but we need the JSF. And we don't *need* the Blue Angels. At least not to fight a war."

Hooker was furious. This kind of decision represented everything that was stupid about Washington. Decisions made by accountants or armchair warriors, with no feel for the fleet or what motivated the people in it. "Sir, I think this is a *huge* mistake—"

"We all love the Blue Angels. They're great. But sometimes we have to make hard decisions."

Hooker put his coffee cup down on the desk untouched. "I have to go on record as disagreeing with this one, Admiral. I think we're doing the Navy a disservice."

"Where would *you* get the money from? We've got to keep the JSF alive!"

"I don't know, sir. If you want me to go through the entire budget and come up with alternatives, I could do that, maybe like building fewer day care centers or not refueling one of our nuclear submarines—"

"The decision has been made. I have to get on with other things. Sorry. And you have to go tell the Blue Angels. Where are they right now anyway?"

"El Centro. Winter training."

"You'd better get out there. No sense putting off the inevitable."

Hooker stood. "Sir, when was the last time you saw the Blue Angels?"

"What the hell does that have to do with it?" he asked, annoyed.

"Do you remember?"

"I don't know. Probably ten years ago."

"When was the last time you were in the cockpit?"

"Two or three years before that. Why?"

"I don't think you would have made that decision if you'd seen them recently. They're an inspiration—"

"What the hell does that have to do with anything? Are you going to ask me when was the last time I rode a merry-go-round?" He paused. "Do you want me to get someone else to go out to El Centro?"

"No, sir. I'll go. I just wanted you to know that you're making a big mistake."

"You've said that, and I don't want to hear it again."

Hooker stood, nodded, and walked out of Girardi's office.

Stovic sat in the cockpit of #6 on the runway with the throttles full forward in military power. He wore his new Blue Angels helmet and a lip mike that reached around from the side attachment to his helmet and touched his lips. No oxygen mask. Didn't need it. And no G-suit. He had never flown a jet without an oxygen mask and a G-suit. It felt naughty, like driving your car without a seat belt.

He scanned his instruments, looked to his left and right to see that the flight controls of the airplane were moving correctly, checked the rearview mirror for good rudder, and released his brakes. He moved the throttles into full afterburner and raced down the runway with his two jet engines screaming and tearing up the air. This was his first chance to practice the first maneuver he would do during the air show, the low transition, where as soon as he got airborne he would pull his landing gear up, settle the airplane down to fifteen or twenty feet off the runway, accelerate down the entire length of the runway, then pull the stick back hard and climb away from the crowd like a rocket. It was an amazingly impressive maneuver, one that left onlookers shocked with its daring and power. The four jets that made up the Blue Angel diamond, the ones that flew around as if they were welded together, had already taken off and were lining up for their first maneuver. Oden, #5, had just taken off and was waiting for Stovic to get airborne so they could line up their first solo maneuvers. Every aspect of the flight, every move was being videotaped for a later debrief.

Standing out in the desert by the runway was the video team and Andrea Ash, the new flight surgeon, the one Stovic had met in the hall at his interview. Much to his surprise, the Blues wanted the input of a layman, someone who didn't know the intimate details of the formations and the maneuvers. She had been selected. She was to watch every flight and sit in on every debrief to tell them what she thought. Stovic's F/A-18 rolled quickly down the runway and accelerated.

He watched the airspeed indicator run up to one hundred knots very quickly. His Hornet was clean and fast. The Blue Angel mechanics were the best in the Navy and kept airplanes tuned like sewing machines. He saw his airspeed pass through one hundred thirty knots and rotated the airplane off the runway. As soon as he was airborne, he raised his landing gear and lowered the nose so that he was flying straight above the runway, accelerating rapidly. He felt the gear and flaps clunk into place and the gear doors close over the wheels. He passed through two hundred fifty knots, then three hundred knots and was approaching four hundred knots by the time he reached the end of the runway. He lowered the nose of the aircraft as he reached the end, to make his pass extremely low. It was intoxicating to be able to do maneuvers that were typically forbidden. This was the kind of thing that would get you written up for a flight violation if you were an ordinary Navy pilot flying something other than a blue jet. He timed his pullback carefully, waited until he reached the end of the runway, and jerked back on the stick as the G forces loaded onto the airplane instantaneously. The Hornet's nose pointed quickly into the sky and continued to rise. He looked in his rearview mirror, saw the exhaust of his jet kick up sand at the end of the runway, and smiled. His F/A-18 was rocketing into the sky when suddenly his fantasy flight was interrupted by reality. *"Blue Angel Six, tower."*

*"Six, go ahead,"* he replied, not wanting to know what they wanted. The tower wasn't supposed to say anything unless something had happened that was out of the ordinary. He knew all the other Blues were listening.

*"Yes, sir, got a report from the Blue Angel maintenance chief at the end of the runway that on your rotation you may have hit a runway threshold light. You may have damaged your engine exhaust. He requested you return immediately and land for inspection."*

*"Roger,"* Stovic said, suddenly feeling sick. He relaxed the pressure on the stick and reduced the throttle as he rolled over and descended to break altitude. *"El Centro tower, Blue Angel Six, request entry to the pattern for the break from the west."*

*"Roger, Blue Angel Six, cleared, you're number one in the pattern. Break when ready."*

*"Roger."* Stovic flew into the break, executed a low G roll with an easy turn, and landed. He taxied back to the Blue Angel hangar. As he prepared to shut down his Hornet, Stovic saw Oden come screaming into the break—barely subsonic—and pull his aircraft into a 7.5-G break turn, clearly furious. He could hear Oden now. Stovic shut down his airplane and climbed down to the tarmac. His maintenance crew chief was already

examining the back of the aircraft. Stovic walked around behind the airplane. Now three or four people were stooped underneath the Hornet looking up at the exhaust nozzles. "Check this out," his plane captain said as he pointed at some scrape marks.

"Right here, sir," the maintenance chief said as he pointed to the same spot.

Stovic rushed down and looked up at the tail. The markings were clear. The steel threshold light had gouged the engine exhaust. Stovic felt horrible. "What you think, chief? Do you need to do anything right now?"

"Yes, sir, we're going to have to change those out." They covered their ears as Oden taxied his number five jet back to the line and shut it down next to Stovic's. Before Stovic could even say anything, Oden was out of his jet, crouching next to him underneath Stovic's #6. He looked up at the gouge marks, then at Stovic. Without saying a thing, he indicated with his head that they were going to walk over to Oden's jet and have a chat.

Stovic felt the way he had when he was being escorted into his father's den for a thrashing. Oden walked around to the far side of #5 and waited by the ladder. Stovic followed him. Oden looked at him with blazing, violent eyes. "What the hell were you doing?"

"Low transition, Oden. First time I tried it."

"You realize what you hit?"

"Runway threshold light, I guess. The ones at the far end of the runway."

"You know how far those lights stick up from the ground?"

"Not really, but not very far."

Oden nodded. "Try twelve inches. You realize you took your thirty-million-dollar jet and your ten-cent, piece-of-shit body and placed them within a foot of hard ground going four hundred knots?"

Stovic nodded penitently.

"You know what happens when you actually touch them to the ground at four hundred knots?"

"Yep. Sorry."

"Let me explain to you what you apparently did not get. When you rotate this airplane in a hard pull, the tail actually goes *down*. It rotates on the axis that runs through the middle of the airplane. You don't see it when you're away from the ground, but if you watch close to the ground, you'll see that any hard pull actually rotates at the axis point, which is just behind the wings. The tail goes *down*," he said slowly. "You cannot start your pull-up any lower than about fifteen or twenty feet. And right now, I want you to start that pull-up about *fifty feet* until I tell you to get lower. Clear?"

"Yep. Very."

"Didn't we have this conversation before during the brief? Didn't I tell you to do it at fifty feet?"

"Yes."

"Then why were you at ten feet?" He waited while Stovic took a deep breath without answering. "Listen, I think you're going to be okay. But you're pushing it too hard too fast. We're not trying to set any records here. We're just trying to put together a good show. If you goon it up, then we're in a mess. Got it?"

"It won't happen again."

"Go get in #7. Let's try it again."

Patricia Branigan hurried down the hall to show Lew the photographs. They were high-quality color. She burst into his office. "Lew," she said in her always too loud voice.

He looked up at her malevolently as he sat trying to eat his sandwich with a knife and fork through a mouth held almost closed by the infuriating neck brace. "Or should I say Dick," she said, recalling the name Lew had used with Ismael as they walked into the restaurant.

"Very funny," Lew said. They were not a team exactly, not partners, but their styles so complemented each other that they often found themselves working on the same investigations. They worked out of FBI headquarters in Washington, in counterterrorism.

"I got the photos," she said, handing him an envelope.

He extended his right hand as his left swept his frustrating sandwich aside.

She spoke while he pulled out the prints. "Young guy, clearly Middle Eastern or North African"—he looked up—"like you said. Probably not a professional."

Lew nodded. He replied as he looked at the photographs, "How old you guess this guy is? Younger than you?"

"Up yours, Lew. I'm *thirty*. You're too old to even remember thirty." She glanced down at the picture lying on Lew's desk. "He can't be more than twenty-five. I'd guess younger than that. Maybe twenty-one."

Lew nodded. "We gotta start running this guy. Immigration, visa applications, CIA, everybody. I have no idea what he's up to. But it ain't happenin' on my watch. You and Foley need to start digging."

He handed the photographs back to Patricia. "Give copies of these to everybody. Make sure they get to the counterterrorism task force at the Agency. You know the routine."

She nodded as she gathered them up.

"He didn't really say much." Lew pondered. "What's

your take on this? You getting the same feelings I'm getting, or am I off base?"

"We all know and respect your feelings, Lew—" she said sarcastically.

"No bullshit. Seriously. What's your take?"

"On one hand, he's clearly an amateur. Still, even a kid with a loaded gun can cause a lot of problems. And he wants more than a gun. He wants something big. So big he couldn't even say it. But the only hint we got before he spooked was when he said it was 'aviation related.'"

"When I started talking about shoulder-fired SAMs, he didn't stop me. He didn't say I was way off."

"So what the hell could he have been talking about?"

Patricia stared at Ismael's face in the photographs, then looked at Lew. "I have absolutely no idea."

"Neither do I. But he's moved way up on my list. I'm going to find him and find out what the hell he has in mind. Let's just hope it isn't much."

She turned to go. "Whoa, whoa," she said, grabbing her head. "Are you on the internal database? The one that lists nationwide warnings?"

He shook his head, then turned to his computer to access the site. "Now what?"

"We got a warning recently that a team had been assigned to some Navy pilot. A security detail. Big deal, some other agency is playing, and it isn't all kosher. Anyway, they named the guy they were after. He had already made an attempt on this pilot's life. Car thing. Remember?"

"Yeah, go on," he said listening.

"So the guy was the brother of that downed pilot from Algeria. Remember? And he was here on a student visa? An actual legit student visa."

"Right."

"Maybe he's looking for a new weapon."

"Son of a bitch. You may be right," he said. "Do they have his picture?"

"It was attached to the e-mail. It's posted on the bulletin board."

He went to it and called it up. He found the notice, read the warning, and opened the photo.

He sat back in amazement. "You're amazing." He motioned for her. She stood behind him and looked at the screen. "Ismael Nezzar. Bigger than shit. That's our boy. Call the head of that security detail. We're now on it."

Secretary of Defense Howard Stuntz sat in his burgundy leather chair in his plush office at the Pentagon waiting. Melissa, a new member of his staff, finally came in and closed the door. Stuntz sat forward quickly, the bottom of his chair thumping against the stops. "Well?"

"Good morning, sir," she said, forcing back a smile at his eagerness.

"Well?"

Melissa sat in the chair across from his desk. "Nothing, sir. Nothing really."

"That's impossible!" he exploded. "She's into something. I guarantee it. She's sure as hell doing something."

"Sir, at your request, and probably against good sense and maybe the law—"

He was frustrated. He wanted answers, solutions. "If someone in her position is compromised, how the hell are we going to find out?"

"The FBI—"

"The FBI? Are you serious? They're in her pocket! She knows what they're doing before the damned Attorney General knows! Can you explain that to me?

She is compromising this entire administration, all for her little Machiavellian schemes. She has delusions of power or control. Somehow she's inside everything."

"Well, sir, anyway, we've had people look at everything. Her e-mail, her phone usage, cell phone, U.S. mail, we've put a worm in her computer at home and at work to follow her on the Internet and into any anonymous e-mail accounts, and nothing. Clean as a whistle."

"What else is there? How is she communicating?"

"With whom do you believe she is communicating?"

"I don't have any idea. Someone. Someone who is outside regular channels, that's for sure," he grumbled. "So what do you have? Nothing? You've got nothing?"

"We also checked her staff. Everyone who reports to her."

"And? And?"

"Well, there is one person who seems to be playing with some things he shouldn't."

"What? Who?"

"Brad Walker, sir. The one who often gives the briefs on behalf of the National Security Council?"

"Sure, I know him. Young guy. Confident."

"That's him."

"What about him? What's he doing?"

"He has encryption software on his personal laptop and an anonymous e-mail account at Hotmail. He's been sending encrypted e-mails."

"Hmmm. Now that's interesting. Is that illegal?"

"Maybe. You're supposed to tender keys to all encryption software to the NSA. They don't have that one. They're very interested in it because they can't break this one without a lot of effort."

"Can't you steal it off his computer?"

"It's his personal laptop. He never leaves it anywhere. All we get is the data going out when he plugs in. He has a cable modem at home, and we're on the cable. But all we see is the encrypted data going by. We can't get inside his computer."

"Can't yet. Keep trying."

"Yes, sir."

"How do you know he's not messing around with someone's wife and sending her secret e-mails on where to meet?"

"That's possible, but based on the data going out, the instructions for the rendezvous must be pretty complex."

Stuntz nodded. He leaned forward more, magnifying his paranoia and his poor posture. "What else? Is that it?"

"Pretty much."

An idea suddenly occurred to him. "Is it possible he's just taking his computer to her place so she can type a message, then encrypt it on his computer? Maybe she's giving him a disk!"

"That's possible," Melissa nodded.

"Get inside her home computer. Get onto her hard drive and see if she's composing messages she's giving to this Brad person."

"Yes, sir. Will do."


Stovic heard the knock and went to open his hotel room door. Lieutenant Andrea Ash was standing there in her Blue Angel flight suit. Not that she flew much. All the Blue Angel officers—even those who didn't fly at all—wore flight suits as their uniform.

"Hey, Animal," she smiled. "You ready?"

"Yeah. Where's Bean? He was going to stop by." Stovic had grown close to Bean. He appreciated his humor and humility. Bean had accepted him into the team immediately. As far as Bean was concerned, Stovic had nothing to prove. A member of the team was just that, a team member. As #4, Bean had the second most important position on the team. He made sure everyone was where they needed to be in the formation. And he did it brilliantly.

"He's in the parking lot. I just thought I'd come pick you up."

Stovic nodded and closed the door behind him. He put his cover on and walked behind Andrea toward the parking lot. "What's this all about tonight, anyway?"

"Command performance. Boss wants everyone at Hernandez's Cocina tonight. Rendezvous is at 1830."

"What for?"

"Don't know. Oden thinks it's something big. Something either really good or really bad. He doesn't know which."

"I guess we'll find out."

They drove to the restaurant. Andrea sat between Stovic and Bean. Oden and Hoop were in the backseat. No one knew what was going on, but none of them had confidence it was going to be good. Bean didn't notice Rat's car behind them, and none of them thought much about the four men unloading from a King Cab pickup in the restaurant parking lot as they arrived. It was Groomer with one of their sections. He had already been to the restaurant and dropped off two others who had taken up strategic positions. They had been doing it every night at every place Stovic had eaten. He hadn't noticed once. He would have to be very attentive, though, to recognize someone he only saw every third or fourth evening, a cowboy or a businessman or a truck driver, one of the sixteen men Rat had brought with him to El Centro, wired for communication like the Secret Service and armed.

Stovic, Bean, and Andrea met the other members of the team at the Cocina, a large busy Mexican restaurant on the outskirts of El Centro. The local residents knew the Blue Angels. They saw them there every year and respected their privacy. The Blues got waves and nods but none of the smothering autograph seeking and endless discussions that became the norm during the air show season everywhere they went. They had a large table in the back corner. They immediately noticed a man in his fifties sitting next to the Boss. The quick exchange of looks made it quite clear that no one knew who he was.

The Boss ordered pitchers of beer. They ordered their food and devoured the chips and salsa while they waited. After fifteen minutes of the usual chatter about flying, families, and the show schedule, the Boss got everyone's attention. "All right, guys. Couple of things I want to tell you. First, I'd like to introduce Admiral Don Hooker. He's our boss in Washington." Hooker raised a hand in acknowledgment. "He called me and said he had something to tell us, so I asked him along to tonight's dinner. We'll find out together what he has in mind. But right now, I'd like to ask Animal to come over here."

Stovic was caught off guard. He pushed his chair back and walked around to stand next to the Boss's chair. He pulled his stomach in, trying to look as trim as he could without showing any effort. The Boss stood next to him in the corner of the restaurant. He put his arm on Stovic's shoulder. "Now Animal here, for those of you who don't know him, is our new opposing solo pilot. He is intent on flying his airplane very fast, very low. He in fact is already an expert on flying low. Tonight we'd like to recognize one of his accomplishments. He has flown the lowest pass in the recorded history of the Blue Angels that did not actually touch the ground." The Boss reached under the table and pulled out a large, heavy plaque. The broken runway threshold light was bolted to the plaque and stuck out like a microphone from the thirties. The Boss handed it to Stovic, who held it in front of him as the other pilots clapped and hooted. The Boss spoke. "I'd like to present this plaque to Lieutenant Ed Stovic, the Blue Angel to have flown the lowest ever pass and *survived*. We would like to thank you for giving us all one great thrill, and we all hereby ask you not to give us any more such thrills."

Stovic spoke. "Thank you, Boss." He waved to the others and nodded as if receiving a truly great reward. He held up his hand to quiet the praise and applause. He nodded and continued holding up his hand until it was quiet. Rat took a flash photograph from the table next to the Blue Angels. "Thank you. Thank you," Stovic said. "First, I'd like to thank my mother for having given birth to me. I'd like to thank the kids who taught me to go sledding, which made me very comfortable four or five inches off the ground. And I'd like to thank all the pelicans of the world that I have observed who fly one or two inches off the water and inspired my low flying. I yearn to fly like them." He glanced at the Boss. "All seriousness aside, Boss, I hear you loud and clear. It won't happen again."

The Boss spoke again as Stovic made his way to his seat with his plaque. "It is my personal objective to insult everyone on the team at least once this year. I just couldn't resist starting with you." He stared at Stovic. "If you do that again—"

Stovic shook his head as he sat down and raised his hand in surrender.

Two waiters came in and quickly delivered the steaming hot Mexican food on plates too hot to touch. The Blues waited for the Boss to continue speaking as he appeared intent on doing. They were starved, and weren't going to give him much time before they dug in. He saw their distress. "Eat up, please," he said. They did.

"While you're eating, let me tell you the real reason I wanted to get together briefly tonight. First, I think everything's coming along fine. Everybody's making good progress. We're about where we should be at this point. Other than our little brush with threshold lights," he said glancing at Stovic, "I haven't seen anything that has given me great concern. We need to keep working, sure, and continue making progress, but I'm pleased with where we are." The pilots nodded their agreement as they ate hungrily.

The Boss looked around the restaurant. Their table was away from the others by a good distance. It was as if they were in a private room. "So maybe this would be a good time to ask Admiral Hooker to talk to us for just a moment. Admiral . . ."

Hooker stood reluctantly and looked at each of the people seated around the table. Boy was this going to be unpleasant, he thought. "Good evening," he said. "I'm Admiral Don Hooker, and I'm here from the Pentagon. I can't tell you how much nicer it is to be in El Centro than in Washington. I prefer the actual desert to the moral desert that calls itself Washington."

"I'll drink to that!" Bean said.

Hooker smiled. "What I've come here to tell you I wanted to tell you to your face—to your faces. It's not good news and is probably irrevocable. I'll never give up, but I wanted you to know what is happening."

The pilots looked at each other with concern.

Hooker continued. "Each year we have to justify our existence—your existence, the Blue Angels—with the Navy. The budget. There's always a discussion, and at the end, they always approve it. Well, this year they cut you out. They don't think they can keep the Joint Strike

Fighter program going without a significant infusion of cash from the Navy budget. They're scrounging around the whole budget looking for ways to move money, and someone took a look at your budget and decided you were expendable. So I regret to tell you—you have no idea how much I regret it—that this will be the last season for the Blue Angels."

"What?" Oden exclaimed angrily. "How can they do that? That's *crazy.*"

The Boss shook his head. He'd been blindsided. If Hooker had told him, he would have moved mountains, called every Admiral in the Navy who wears wings, called every Blue Angel from the past, and made a move to get the decision changed. Now it was a done deal, and Hooker was announcing it to the team. The Boss felt betrayed. He tried not to show it. The Boss spoke to the team. "Don't worry, I'll push back through whatever avenues I can identify. I'm not going to go down without a fight."

Hooker glanced at the Boss. "Feel free. You have my blessing. I tried, but discovered pretty quickly that the JSF is more important to Washington than the Blue Angels. Sorry, but that's what I've found. I've shown them the benefits, I've shown them the number of people whose lives have been touched by seeing the Blue Angels fly—not only those who become Navy pilots, but all the people across the country who have seen you fly. I've given them graphs showing how many millions of people have seen the Blues. They all think it is very impressive and that it will be too bad to lose that impact."

"Why the budget crunch? What's happened?" Hoop asked.

"When the Joint Strike Fighter was finishing its carrier suitability tests, they found some structural changes they needed to make before it gets cleared for carrier use. No money was in the budget for that.

Turned out the amount they needed was about what your annual budget is."

The pilots stared ahead, not looking at each other. Animal finally spoke. "Do we get to finish the season?"

"Yes," Hooker replied. "This is all about next year's budget. We're okay for this year, but after this, . . . well . . . you'll have to find something else. You're going to have to get real jobs."

Stovic sat silently. His first year on the Blues would also be his last. He couldn't believe they were getting shut down. It was like shutting down Christmas. You just didn't do that. The Blues were an institution.

All the Blues had stopped eating and drinking.

The Boss spoke. "I don't like this either, but we've just got to do the best we can this year. I want us to go out with the reputation of being the best Blue Angel team ever to fly. I want us to be able to ride into the sunset proud of what we've done. I want us to leave a legacy so when people look back they'll regret the Blue Angels aren't around anymore. Maybe one day they'll bring the Blues back." The Boss sat down.

"Sorry to drop this on you," Admiral Hooker said. He reached down, picked up his glass, and raised it. "To the Blue Angels."

The pilots felt pride and anger coming together inside them like a chemical reaction. They stood slowly, fighting their feelings. They muttered, "To the Blues."

"Well," President Kendrick asked Sarah St. John as they flew back to Washington from the Armed Forces Staff College, "what did you think of my speech?"

"Perfect," she said. "I assumed the students would all think alike. You obviously talked about what they wanted to hear. They couldn't get enough."

She crossed to the other side of Air Force One. She grabbed a can of soda out of the refrigerator and sat down across from the President with a small lacquered table between them.

"Had any more thoughts about the War on Terrorism? You said you were going to think about it."

"We talk about this a lot, don't we?"

"It's important. Any ideas?"

"It's not what you want to hear."

"Try me."

"We need to take more chances. More chances politically, economically, militarily, and with our Special Forces. Greater risk can mean greater reward."

"Or greater failure."

She sipped from the soda can. "That's the risk side."

"You have anything particular in mind?"

"I'm getting there."

"How?"

"By opening up certain . . . communication channels. Sometimes the chain of command means keeping new ideas down. I like listening to those who will actually have to execute them instead of planning with people who only have vague recollections of actually doing things. I believe the key is listening to the operators."

Kendrick frowned as he looked up at a young man who was delivering the iced tea he had requested. He nodded at the waiter and returned his attention to his National Security Advisor. "Meaning what, exactly?"

"Shortening the chains of command."

"You mean going *around* the chains of command."

"Maybe . . . maybe to some degree. But I want to see things get done. We have to be creative and take some risks."

"And they'll be my risks. Not yours."

"I appreciate that."

"You have something up your sleeve?"

"Not really. I've got a few things I'm working on, but I won't do anything without your okay."

"You promise?"

"Absolutely."

Kendrick rubbed his eyes. He was beyond tired. He was starting to show how fatigued he felt. People were starting to look at him as if to say, "You okay?"

"Sarah, we go way back. Don't we?"

"Yes, sir."

"One of the reasons I have you here, other than the fact that you're incredibly smart—"

"Mr. President—"

"No false humility, none of that. But one of the reasons you're here is because I trust you." He watched her face. "But this job isn't mine. I work for the country. If it turns out you're someone I can't trust, if you let me down, or lie to me, or go behind my back, or do something without my approval that you know I would have wanted to know about, I'll fire you so fast they won't know where to forward your mail."

She was taken aback. He had never spoken to her like that. "There is absolutely nothing for you to worry about, Mr. President. You have my word."

"No agenda at work we haven't talked about?"

St. John felt cornered. She hadn't wanted to discuss it openly, but she would rather do that than deny it. "You may be right."

Kendrick was surprised. "About what?"

"Maybe I do have an agenda."

"Oh, and what might that be?"

"I think you've got the wrong guy as your Secretary of Defense."

"Stuntz?"

"He's impulsive, unthinking. He believes the best idea is the one that occurs to him first. Mr. President, his approach is dangerous. He—"

Kendrick smiled slightly. "You want his job, don't you?"

"I think I could do a better job. It's critically important to your administration. You don't need a cowboy in that job."

"I think you're critically important to my administration as the National Security Advisor. That's where I want you to stay."

"That's fine, sir. I am content. I just don't want you to get undercut."

Kendrick nodded and put his head back on the soft leather. He was asleep in seconds.


Rat stood next to Andrea Ash who was setting up the professional quality camera that recorded every practice maneuver on videotape. They stood at the end of a dirt road in the desert near the El Centro Naval Air Facility. Rat had ingratiated himself with the squadron. They knew he was around, that his book project had been blessed by whoever needed to bless it, and that they would see him everywhere. They didn't mind. His status as a former SEAL was known but not discussed. His presence was simply accepted.

The diamond sat on the runway prepared to take off. The morning was cool, and the sky was turning from pink to light blue. The sun was just now over the horizon. The temperature would climb steadily to the high eighties, but the air would feel wonderful even at the hottest point in the day.

Rat examined the large containers of gear that sat on portable tables. They were bleached from their constant exposure to the sun.

"Morning," Rat said to Andrea.

She was adjusting the radio equipment and watching a sailor prepare the video camera to start recording. It stood on a large wooden tripod with a long neck to allow it to shoot up at very high angles. The sailor was ready.

"Morning," Andrea replied. She took a long drink from a travel mug full of coffee. She looked tanned and content. "What brings you out here?"

"I heard about this whole videotape thing. Animal was telling me about how you film every practice, then debrief."

"We do."

"How did you get the job of critiquing the pilots? I mean you're the one who gives comments at the debrief, right?"

"True," she smiled. "Kind of counterintuitive, isn't it?"

"I just didn't think the pilots would listen to nonpilots."

"They wouldn't if I said, 'You need to ease up on the stick at the top of the loop,' but they listen to me if I say, 'Number four looked out of place as you started up. He seemed to start up later.' Then it's just an observation of asymmetry, as opposed to how to fly your airplane."

Rat nodded.

"Want some coffee?"

"Sure," he said gratefully. The video operator heard her offer and went to pour Rat a cup from the large thermos in a Blue Angel mug. "Thanks."

"So you're a flight surgeon specializing in asymmetry."

She laughed. "That about sums me up. Asymmetry. Always on the lookout for asymmetry. You find it in the most unlikely places."

"I'd like to take a couple of shots out here, if you don't mind. I'd like to have a picture of you guys standing around watching practice, giving objective input to the pilots."

She shrugged as the Blues roared to afterburner and rolled down the runway. "Samuels, you got the camera going?"

"All over it, ma'am."

"That okay?" Rat asked.

"Sure," Andrea said, her attention now fixed on the Blues instead of him.

The Blue Angels were beginning to fly as a team. The pilots in the diamond were closing the distance every day, flying closer and closer together. The two solos were flying passes much faster and closer than they had been. Stovic's confidence was building, and Oden's precision was getting more remarkable. During an air show the solos flew either at each other or with each other. On the passes—for which the solos were famous—they were to pass as closely together as possible and then flip on their sides in parallel knife-edged passes to look as if they were flying right into each other. Crowds always gasped and brought their hands to their mouths until the solos passed each other and pulled up intact.

The Boss was like a caller at a square dance but calling a ballet instead. It was smooth and lyrical, unrushed, calm, and beautiful. He would call out the next maneuver—like the diamond loop—and the other three diamond pilots would respond with their call signs in less than a second: "Loop, Link, Beaner!" They would say them so quickly that no one who wasn't clued in would know what was happening. They would hear, "LpLnkBeaner!" Bean would always take advantage of being last by drawing out his call sign and saying it with energy, even adding another syllable, "Beaner!"

The Boss would then put the tight diamond in the perfect position to start the maneuver, taking into consideration the wind, the clouds, the crowd, and their speed, and start them in his singsong command with slightly rising pitch on each word, "Up . . . we . . . go. . . ." The pilots would start pulling back on their sticks on the *g* of "go." And the boss would continue, "*A . . . lit-tle . . . more . . . pull . . . ,*" with a distinctive *p* to be heard clearly over the radio. The pilots would increase the G forces on their airplanes by pulling back harder on the stick with the first sound of that *p* in "pull," the diamond pilots' eyes riveted on the Boss's airplane to know *exactly* how much to pull, or how much power to put on.

The Boss would then tell the diamond where they were—they couldn't even grab a glance in front of them when they were in their tight formation—"*Exiting area crowd right . . .*" and they would slip out just slightly to ease up on the demand of the formation flying, with the wings of the other blue jets twenty or thirty inches from the other canopies during the maneuvers in front of the crowd.

And as the diamond exited, the solos would be lined up for their next pass, the next amazing feat of precision flying that would wow the crowd and make those who wanted to fly jealous that someone else could be having so much fun in an airplane, flying around just below the speed of sound fifty feet off the ground, pulling on the stick like a maniac and ripping the air as if they owned it.

Twice during the air show Stovic and Oden joined the diamond. They then formed the Blue Angel delta. Even Stovic was impressed that they could do it, forming a six-plane delta formation, nearly as close together as the four-plane diamond. They would do the maneuvers, "*Up . . . we . . . go . . .*" and break off with the others for the fleur-de-lis that took them to all points of the compass, where each Blue Angel would reverse his airplane and come racing back toward the center point at the other five jets, all trying to arrive at the same point at the same time, separated only by one hundred feet in altitude.

They were growing in confidence and it was show-ing. They were almost ready to let the public see their work of art.

Rat reached into his camera bag and pulled out a long cylindrical device. He looked through it at the Blues as they lifted off the runway.

"What's that?" Andrea asked glancing over her shoulder.

He was surprised by her question. "Laser range finder. Helps me focus my camera on them."

She frowned. "Laser range finders transmit. There's no room in that thing for a battery. And your camera should be focused to infinity at this distance." She looked into his eyes, waiting for a response.

He smiled and put the device back up to his eye. He watched the indicator in the eyepiece tell him the in-frared signature of the airplane, the temperature range that was coming from the F/A-18s, the heat a missile would see if it were looking.

"You're not going to answer me?"

"You didn't ask me a question."

"Okay," she grinned. "What the hell is it that you have in your hand that you just looked through?"

"Laser range finder," he repeated.

"Not going to tell me, huh?"

"Just did."

"Whatever."

He pressed the button on the top of the sight, in-serted it into a base in the camera bag, and recorded the information. He took out his Nikon digital camera and took a couple of shots of the Blues as they pulled up into a loop. He then stood back and began taking pic-tures of the desert way station where they were stand-ing. He took several photographs of Andrea. She tried to ignore him, then couldn't. "What did you do in the Navy again?"

"I was a SEAL."

"And you got out?"

"I wanted to start my own company."

"Did you?"

"Yes. Security company." He took a step closer and took another picture of her. "Would you like to get together sometime? Go out and do something?" He looked around at the desert terrain. "I'm not sure what there is to do around here, maybe go out in the middle of nowhere and shoot cans." He laughed.

She made a quick note on her clipboard and spoke to him without looking. "Why not? If you promise we can actually shoot cans."

"Seriously?"

"Sure. Why not?"

"How about tonight? After dinner?"

"Do I have to bring my own gun?"

He was surprised. "You have a gun?"

"No, but I could go get one."

"Nope. Ten-day waiting period in California."

"Too bad. Do you have one I can borrow?"

"I'll see what I can do."

"Sorry, they're taking off. I have to pay attention."

**S**o, Bradley," the Secretary of Defense said. Stuntz sat in his leather chair and leaned back slightly, having gotten Walker's attention. He touched the fingers of one hand against the other in an annoying, attention-getting way. "Thank you for coming over here. It's not every day I get to talk to a member of the National Security Council staff."

Right, Walker thought. Just the National Security Advisor herself. "Sure," he said guardedly.

"I'm sure you're curious about why I've asked you to come here."

"Yes, sir."

"I have a large staff of my own, you've reminded yourself. What could I possibly want with you?"

"Exactly," he said.

"What would you do if you found out that somebody was leaking classified information out of the National Security Council?"

"What would I do?"

"Right. What would you do?"

"Well, I don't know. It would depend on how I found out, who was doing it, and who else knew. But I'd probably tell the FBI."

Stuntz pressed. "It is my belief that someone is operating within the National Security Council in a way that is contrary to usual practice. Contrary to norms. You know, against the national interests."

Walker was baffled. "In what way?"

"By communicating with someone or someones, if that's a word, outside the circle of people cleared to know what the NSC knows."

"How?" Walker asked, seeing where this was going.

"Through the use of computer encryption software that is not on the NSA list. To which they . . . we . . . don't have the key."

"Truly?"

"Yes."

"Who?" Walker asked.

"We're not sure. We thought you might be able to tell us."

"How would I know?"

"Because the communications have always occurred when you were in the building. I had them check the log-in sheets."

"Me?"

"Yes."

"Must have been someone else there as well."

"Yes. There were a few others. That's why we don't know who it was. You see, it may not actually be illegal. But it gives me great pause."

"Yes, sir."

"Would you keep your eyes open?"

"Yes, sir. Absolutely."

Stuntz sat forward. "I'm turning this over to the FBI as well. I wanted you to know that. They'll be doing an *investigation*," he said, drawing it out for emphasis, "and seeing if anything classified has been lost."

"Well, I hope they find out whatever is going on."

"Yes, so do I. And Brad," he said in a falsely friendly

tone, "if you become aware of anything, would you let me know personally?"

"Sure, Mr. Secretary. Happy to." Over my dead body, Walker thought, disgusted by the Secretary of Defense and his love of machinations. He worshiped Sarah St. John and would do anything for her. She was straight-ahead, honest, and skeptical. Incredibly competent yet doubted from many sides, for reasons Brad couldn't quite figure out. "Happy to."

Rat and Andrea drove out one of the many two-lane country roads in Imperial County. It was dark, but there was a nice moon high up on the horizon. Rat watched the road and occasionally glanced down at the portable GPS—Global Positioning System—receiver sitting on the seat between them.

Andrea was watching him with bemusement. "Do you actually know where we're going?"

"Sure."

"Where are we going?"

"To the desert."

"We're surrounded by the desert, in case you hadn't noticed."

"We're going to a particular *place* in the desert."

"Have you been to this particular place before?"

"No."

"Hence the GPS receiver."

"Exactly."

She picked it up and examined it. "You're just Inspector Gadget, aren't you?"

"Absolutely. Happiness through technology and gadgets."

"So what is this for? Don't you have a map?"

"The guy gave me the turnoff as coordinates. He said we'd never find it in the dark in a million years without a GPS fix. How much farther?"

"Four hundred meters."

He slowed, staring at the opposite side of the road, looking for the dirt road turnoff. "There it is," he exclaimed as he wheeled quickly off the road and onto the narrow, rutted dirt road that climbed away from the country road up a hill.

Andrea grabbed the door handle as they flew along the dirt road, up and down through several turns, then to the top of a small hill.

The rented Cherokee climbed the dirt hill effortlessly and leveled off at the top. Rat brought it to a quick stop, waited until the dust settled, and climbed out enthusiastically. Andrea climbed out and stood next to Rat, who was looking around the hilltop.

"This is perfect," he said.

"For what?"

He went to the driver's door and pulled out a night scope. He closed the door and held it to his eye. He scanned the entire area slowly.

"What are you doing?" she asked.

"Making sure we're alone."

"Aw," she said smiling. "How sweet. You want to be alone with me."

"I sure do if we're going to be shooting guns." He put the night vision scope back in its sleeve and looked at the sky. "It's sure pretty out here tonight."

She nodded. "It's so peaceful. It's sort of sacrilegious to break up this peacefulness with gunfire."

He looked down at her. "You chickening out on me?"

"No," she said. "But don't you like the peace? The quiet?"

"Absolutely," he said. "So you ready?"

"For what?"

"To shoot."

She shook her head and shrugged ironically. "I guess."

"Great," he said. He walked to the back of the Cherokee and opened the doors. There were several cases. "What do you want to shoot first?"

"I don't care. If you just want to talk, that's fine with me. I don't feel any great need to shoot if you don't want to."

"No, it's no problem." He took several cans and threw them out onto the rocky, sandy terrain thirty yards away. "Targets." He opened a small box and took out a black semiautomatic handgun. "Best handgun in the world. Para Ordnance 14.45 LDA. You'll love it. It's like a classic 1911—" He looked at her face. "You have no idea what I'm talking about."

"I'm listening."

"Well this one carries fourteen rounds of .45 ACP ammo. Very powerful, but still not much bigger than the standard .45 auto. The kind the military carried from 1911 through some time in the nineties when they went with the 9-millimeter Beretta instead. This one you can carry with the hammer down, totally safe, and then when you pull the trigger, it's double action. Don't need to cock it at all. Just pull the trigger."

"Okay."

He pulled a clip of ammo out and rammed it into the handle, releasing the slide. "Ready." With no warning, he turned and fired at the four cans in rapid succession and hit them all. They leaped into the air and clattered back down to the desert in protest.

"How can you even see those cans?" she remarked, amazed.

"Look for the labels. Here you go," he said, handing the handgun to her.

She took it gingerly. "It's heavy."

"Not really. Only forty ounces. Pretty light, really. Have you fired a handgun before?"

"Sure. I qualified with the 9-millimeter."

"Go for it."

She pointed the gun toward the cans, looked carefully through the sights, and fired. The gun jumped in her hand, and a can rose up into the sky.

"Shit hot!" Rat exclaimed. "Keep at it."

She turned back and handed it to him. "That's enough for me."

"One shot?"

"Yeah."

He wasn't quite sure what to do. "What now, rifle? M-16? I have an automatic. Ever fired an automatic before?"

"No, thanks."

He looked disappointed, then smiled. "Want to see something that will really water your eyes?"

"I don't know. Depends what you have in mind."

"A gun. Rifle, actually."

"Is it legal?"

"It is, actually. Largest rifle that can be privately owned in the United States." Without waiting, he pulled out a long case that extended under the backseat and touched the driver's seat. He opened it, assembled it, and stood up with it. He held it across his chest and pointed it away from them.

"What is *that*?" she asked, truly frightened.

"My favorite weapon. The Barrett M82A1.50 caliber semiautomatic rifle."

Andrea took a step backward. "It's enormous!"

"Five feet long and thirty pounds," Rat said. "During Desert Storm, a Marine shot one of these rifles at an Iraqi armored personnel carrier from a mile away. It exploded in a fireball. All the Iraqis climbed out thinking they'd been hit by a missile. But it was just one bullet from this rifle."

Andrea was standing with her arms folded. "What do you have it for?"

Rat realized he had gone too far. He had no possible reason as a private citizen to own his favorite sniper rifle. It just wouldn't do to tell her it was the best for long-distance sniping. "For my security company. Sometimes we're called on to set up a defense, and what's coming may be heavily armed, or a helicopter."

"You some kind of gun-nut *psycho*?" she asked, half joking.

He tried to laugh it off. "Yeah, that's me. Psycho."

"Would you mind putting it away?"

"Not at all," he said, putting it back into its case and then into the Cherokee. He pulled out two light nylon bags and quickly assembled two camping chairs. "You weren't really up for blasting this peaceful night away anyway, were you?"

"I was, but then I got here, and it was just so pretty and quiet. Thanks for getting out the chairs."

"No problem. Would you like something to drink? I brought a cooler."

"What do you have?"

"Beer, wine, soda."

"Any water?"

"Sure," he said. He gave her a bottle of spring water. She drank it quickly. "Can I ask you something?"

"Uh-huh." He took a bottle of Dos Equis out of the cooler and opened it.

"I don't believe you, about the whole photographer thing. You're no photographer. Maybe as a hobby, but not to make a book."

Rat sighed and smiled. "Maybe you're right. I may be here for something else too. And you're bound to find out fairly soon, when the Boss tells everyone else, which, according to what he and the FBI have told me,

will be before the first air show in Arizona this Saturday."

"So tell me now."

"I have several men here to protect Ed Stovic. The
FBI is here too, but they'll have a lot more people in
Arizona."

She touched his arm in alarm. "From what?"

"An Algerian is trying to kill him. The brother of the
pilot he shot down."

"Are you sure?"

"We're sure."

"And the government has hired you?"

"More or less."

"So you're not some psycho."

He smiled. "I may be, but this gear is here for a purpose. I shouldn't have shown you the Barrett. It's kind
of intimidating."

"Anything I can do to help?"

He pondered her offer. She might be useful. "Not
right now. But maybe. I'll let you know. You have to
keep this to yourself."

She nodded and put her head on his shoulder. He
leaned down and kissed her. She kissed him back gently.

"Should we be getting back?" he asked.

"Not unless you want to. I'd just like to watch these
amazing stars awhile longer."


The Blue Angels flew in loose formation across the California desert, past Yuma, Arizona, and across Arizona
to Mesa on the eastern side of Phoenix. They taxied to
the parking spots that had been set aside for them on
the tarmac and shut down their jets. Dozens of smiling
people from the air show organization were waiting for
them, thrilled even to be near the Blue Angels. The pilots went straight to their luxury hotel in Scottsdale

where they had already been checked in. The perfectly manicured golf course across the street beckoned to several of them who tried to play whenever they could, but they knew they wouldn't have time that afternoon because of the "commit" they had, a little earlier than usual.

Rat had beaten them to the hotel. He had left Groomer in El Centro with the other half of his group. The rest of his squad, as he liked to call them, had left early with him to get to Scottsdale and check into their hotel. By the time the Blue Angels arrived he had been to where they had to go that evening and been over every foot of the hotel in which they were staying.

He was waiting in the lobby for them when they arrived. Andrea was quietly telling all the pilots they just had time for a workout and giving them a map of the hotel that showed where the cavernous fitness room was. They all nodded and headed toward their rooms.

Rat changed into his gear in the room next to Stovic's and watched his small TV monitors as Stovic changed. As soon as Stovic was ready to leave his room, Rat stepped into the hallway, where they met.

"Nice timing. You coming to work out?" Stovic asked.

"Wouldn't miss it."

"You've probably already worked out ten times today," he said as they walked down the thickly carpeted hallway.

"Just once."

"You'll waste away, only working out twice a day." He looked at Rat's heavy gym bag. "What's in the bag?"

"Camera gear," Rat said, telling part of the truth.

"Still doing the camera thing."

"You bet. Got to get some pictures of the Blues lifting weights. Part of who you are."

"True enough."

They walked to the hotel spa. Stovic was speechless. He had never seen a weight room like it in his life. It looked like something you might see in an NFL training room. A really nice NFL training room. A hundred people could work out there at once. The other Blue Angel pilots were arriving. They looked at each other, nodded at Rat, and stared. They were standing just inside the glass doors, and the few people who were there stared back at them.

Their shorts and T-shirts gave no indication they were the Blue Angels. The others stole glances at them, wondering who they were. They had to be *someone*. No business group would have good-looking men in their twenties or thirties, all of whom were in perfect shape, wore their hair in various conservative cuts, and traded barbs with each other like brothers. They spread out quickly and began lifting as pairs, trading off, watching each other, spotting for each other. Three of them had brought gloves and weight belts.

Stovic and Rat worked around the free weights with each other, talking and laughing about nothing in particular. But all the Blue Angels stopped to watch when Rat slid under the bar and started doing bench presses with so many forty-five–pound weights on the bar that it bent as he pushed it away from his chest. Stovic was spotting for him. "Geez, Rat, don't kill yourself. How much do you have on there?"

He struggled to lower the sagging bar back to its cradle, exhaled, and said, "Two ninety."

Stovic was impressed. "You're a stud," he said.

"Just steady. You work out enough, keep adding weight, you build up. That's all." Rat lay on the bench, preparing for his next lift.

Stovic leaned down to him so no one else could hear. "There's some weird contraption in the corner of my room. Where the ceiling meets the two walls. It looks like a camera or a motion detector. You know anything about that?"

Rat hesitated, looked at him, and reached for the bar suspended over his face. He lifted it and pressed it again, grunting against the huge weight, then put the steel back in its cradle with a loud clang. He sat up. He reached for one of the bottles of water nearby and looked at his friend. "It's mine," he said quietly.

Stovic looked concerned. "What is it?"

"Camera. Video camera. Wireless. Same kind I put in your house in Virginia Beach."

"What for?"

"Why do you think?"

"He could have come to El Centro too. You didn't have anything in that room."

Rat stood up and took two forty-five–pound weights off the bar. "You sure about that?"

"You had cameras in my *hotel* room?" Stovic cried.

"This guy is serious. So am I." He sat down on the bench again across from Stovic. "But I think he's likely to use a SAM. I don't think it's just about you and him anymore. It's about him and the U.S., him and the Blue Angels."

"To shoot us down?"

Rat didn't want to give him too much. "Maybe. And if you were going to do that, to make a point, where would you do it?"

"At an air show. In front of a million people."

Rat watched his friend's face. He was sorry he had to ruin his tour with the Blues, to fill it full of concern and fear, regardless of whether or not Stovic allowed it to show.

Stovic stood in front of the air vent and let the cold air blow over him. He was angry, but it had stopped building. He realized he was angry at the wrong person. "So now what?" he said to the wall.

"Now we up the ante. We're going to have cowboys all over the place. FBI, NCIS, local police. And at some point, the Boss is going to tell the rest of the team. Probably tonight."

Stovic nodded. Stovic's eyes grew even more intense. "This guy won't stop if I run away and hide."

"He might. He might disappear and regroup and think of an entirely different plan that we would *hope* to discover before he got close. You know how rare it is to be onto a guy like this *before* he pulls the trigger?"

"So if I stay in the team, he'll come after us. As long as the Boss is okay with that . . ."

"But it's about you, Animal. He's going to try to kill *you*. You'd better be *sure*," Rat said.

"I'll be fine. Don't worry."

"No. You won't be. You'll feel like you're under attack even when you're not. And he might take months to get his weapons, set up, maybe even recruit some other men."

"From where?"

"Wherever. It's not hard. The people he was dealing with in Algeria are hard-core."

Rat watched Stovic continue to relax into a fighter's mentality, someone who now recognized the threat and was evaluating how to deal with it.

"If I stay in the Blues and keep flying, hang my ass out, you think we can get this guy?"

"I do."

"You don't think he'll go after Karen, do you? Or the kids."

Rat didn't want to speak too quickly. "You never know. We've got a lot of people there. It'd be hard for him, but it's possible. He does get his motivation from a death in his family. . . ."

Stovic thought about all the possibilities. He only

knew he couldn't run away. "I say we keep right on going."

"It may not turn out like you think it will."

"I know."

"You sure about this?"

"I'm sure. Come on. We've got a commit to go to tonight."

Rat and Stovic showered quickly and joined the others in the lobby, Stovic in his invincible superhero blue flight suit and Rat in his casual photographer's gear and a large bag that was loaded with camera equipment and several nonphotographic items. A number of FBI special agents had flown to Phoenix as well as the Navy's NCIS agents, the Navy Criminal Investigation Service, formerly the NIS. They had been told that the Blue Angels had a commitment that night away from their hotel and would be heading off in a caravan as soon as they arrived. Lew and Patricia had arrived in Phoenix late and had rushed over to the hotel to be part of that caravan.

Lew had called the Phoenix office of the FBI, and they were sending a dozen special agents to the public appearance and more to the hotel. The air show would receive as much coverage by as many special agents as they could put together from the western United States. Ismael's pictures—his student visa, his passport, and the photos Patricia had taken in Washington—had been circulated to everyone concerned.

Lew wheeled their rental car into the driveway of the ornate hotel. Lined up next to them, as if a race were about to start, were several identical red Pontiacs with stickers on them announcing their Blue Angel numbers. Lew, Patricia, and two special agents from the Phoenix office jumped out and looked for the commanding officer of the Blue Angels. John Grundig, the administrative officer of the Blue Angels, and the one to whom Lew had spoken when they were finally connected to the team, recognized the four as likely federal officers and jogged to where they stood in a cluster. "Hi. I'm Lieutenant Grundig."

"Lew Savage, FBI. We spoke."

"Yes, sir."

"Where's the Boss?"

Grundig looked around. "He's right over there. Next to the car with the number one on it."

They walked over to the Boss's car. The other Blue Angels and support people looked on with curiosity. It was not unusual for people outside of the squadron to be in the caravan, but it was unusual to see four people wearing suits approaching the Boss at a time like this.

The admin officer tapped the Boss on the shoulder. "Boss, these are the people—"

The Boss stopped getting into his car and stood up. He looked at them. He smiled. "Hi. Steve McMahon." They all shook his hand. "I don't really have time to talk right now. Can we do this after?"

"Up to you. But we'd like to go along tonight, if you don't mind."

Boss nodded. "My one request is that I decide when to tell the rest of the team. I have to think about how it will play into the preparation for the air show. Understand?"

"Completely." Lew nodded.

"John, anyone have any extra seats?"

"Yes, sir, Boss. There are two seats in Oden's car and two more in mine."

"There you go. See you there." Without waiting for a response, the Boss climbed into his car and started the engine. The others followed his example.

"Come with me," the admin officer said. He pointed Lew and Patricia to the car Oden was driving, with Stovic in the passenger seat, and told the NCIS agents to ride with him. Lew struggled into the backseat on the passenger side, and Patricia sat behind Oden. They shook hands with Oden and Stovic, smiling, and Oden started the engine.

Oden looked in the rearview mirror. "Who are you guys with?"

Lew glanced at Patricia, then at Stovic. "We're from Washington—"

"And we're here to help you," Stovic said.

Lew tried to smile. "Yeah, that's it. We're with the Bureau."

"Of what?"

"FBI," Lew said.

"Oh," Oden frowned, confused.

Less than a minute later, on the Boss's signal, the police lights were activated and the two lead motorcycles led the caravan out of the driveway and onto the wide streets of Scottsdale. After a fifteen-minute drive through the flat, scenic outskirts of Phoenix, they arrived at their destination, a single-story sprawling, luxurious hotel that reeked of class and sophistication. They climbed out of their cars in the huge circular drive in front of the hotel and walked into the wide open lobby. In the back of the hotel they could see the crowd-filled patio and grass around the enormous pool, with torches burning all around and a Hawaiian-shirt–Blue-Angel theme present everywhere. The pool wasn't just large, it was the size of a small continent. You could swim from one pool to another through caverns and moving waterways, down slides and into hot

Jacuzzis. The pools were acres large, deep blue, and glistened in the late desert sunshine. The air was warm but not hot the way it would be in three months. It was the perfect time to be in the desert.

The Blue Angels lined up inside the lobby at the top of the stairs that led down to the lawn area and the pools. Stovic was sixth in line. On the signal, the Boss led them down the stairs and onto the landing for the first flight of stairs, with a balcony in front of it. They stood six or eight feet above the crowd. They were surprised by the large number of people there to see them. Many wore Blue Angels shirts and hats, others wore airplane logos and squadron insignias. They smiled and strained to see the pilots.

A short, rotund air show organizer stood by them on the landing. He had a portable microphone and a large PA system set up to point down. He spoke at length about the air show that they were all excited about seeing the next day, the largest air show in the history of Arizona, the largest static display of airplanes *anywhere,* the largest display of war birds—airplanes restored to their World War II greatness—and of course, the most exciting aerial demonstration ever, capped on Saturday and Sunday by the Blue Angels. He beamed as the crowd burst into thunderous applause.

The Blues stood quietly, their hands crossed behind them in a casual parade rest, and waited for their turn. The chairman of the air show committee, at the zenith of attention of his short-lived appointment, introduced the Boss: "Now, ladies and gentlemen," he grinned, "it is my great pleasure to introduce to you the commanding officer of the Blue Angels, Captain Steve McMahon!"

The Boss stepped forward and took the portable microphone casually. He smiled as he waited for the applause to die down. He finally greeted the crowd and conveyed to them what a great pleasure it was for the Blue Angels to be able to fly at the air show in Arizona. He continued to smile as the cameras flashed in the darkening evening. He went on to introduce the team.

As he went down the line, Stovic waited with great anticipation as his name was finally called. He stepped forward to receive the adulation of the crowd as the opposing solo, the cowboy of the team, the one who flew the fastest and lowest and gave the show its zip. He was amazed at how much he loved the applause, the adoring looks, and the respect he was receiving. He let it all wash over him. He knew you weren't supposed to *love* it, but he found it hard not to. As he stood there looking over the crowd with Rat to his right and just behind him, he also realized how vulnerable he was. He found himself studying the faces of the people in front of him for hostility and weapons, thoughts he had never had before.

After the presentation and questions, the Blue Angel teams stepped into the throng of people and spread out so they wouldn't crowd each other. They signed T-shirts, posters, or programs, whatever was offered to sign. He always signed the same—"Lt. Ed Stovic, #6." He relished the attention, the status as some kind of a star, and the fact that he always had to carry a Sharpie permanent marker to sign autographs. He was all smiles and encouragement, with occasional quick glances up at those standing in line to see if anyone was about to kill him.

"Here's the latest e-mail," Brad said handing an innocent-looking notebook to Sarah St. John.

"Thank you," she said placing the flat NSC notebook into her soft leather briefcase. "Any problems?"

"No. But ever since Stuntz 'invited' me to his office, I've been gun-shy. They're trying to break this."

"No doubt. Probably illegally. We may have to look into that."

"Maybe they're reading them."

"Maybe so. Wouldn't change what I'm doing."

"It would save me a hell of a lot of trouble."

"Don't lose your nerve now," she said smiling. "I've been thinking about the last few e-mails. Pretty clear what's going on. But seems to me, we may have an opportunity to get creative here. To do something different, sort of dissonant. Something they wouldn't expect at all."

"Like what?"

"I'm not sure yet. But now that they're going to eliminate the Blue Angels from the budget next year, we need to use that to our advantage."

"How?"

"Did you see the report from the CIA?"

"Yes."

"They think this Algerian is wired into the very highest echelons of the Algerian government. He's considered by some to be their brightest star. Yet they play this student, out of touch game with him. And he was in fact studying—"

"That doesn't mean anything. The head of Hamas got his Ph.D. in the U.S. and lived openly."

She nodded. "Anyway, I'm sure they have a plan that's much bigger than just having their man ram his car into Stovic. It makes me wonder what really happened there. What were they actually trying to accomplish? How did he just disappear? Why show himself, then disappear? I don't get it. Anyway, they want a big show. So we may just give them one."

"Is our friend on board?"

"I'll find out as soon as I read what you just gave me. Did you read it?"

"You asked me not to read those e-mails."

"I know I asked."

"I do what I'm told."

"Good for you. Do you think Stuntz suspects you're the one who has the encrypted e-mails?"

"Sure. Why else would he have invited *me* to his office? As if I matter."

"Now you see why we're doing it through you. I've always wanted to drive Mr. Stuntz crazy. If this helps, even a little, it will be a nice bonus."

"Easy for you to say."

"Don't get weak-kneed on me, Brad. Hang in there. It's just about to get interesting. I'm thinking of a plan. Do you know Admiral Hooker at the Pentagon?"

"No."

"Look him up. Tell him I want to talk to him."

The day had dawned beautiful and clear, and the community was anxiously awaiting the show. Several hundred thousand people made their way to the airport long before the Blue Angels were to fly. The aerial demonstrations started at 10:00 A.M., with the Blue Angels scheduled to fly at 2:00 P.M. as always.

The stands were packed with the usual array of children, parents, and air show aficionados. The spectators' eyes raced back and forth through the empty sky, trying to see what would happen next. They shielded their eyes from the blazing sun as the Navy Leap Frog Parachute Team prepared to jump from a CH-46 helicopter hovering thousands of feet above the runway. Patricia walked along in front of the stands holding a small digital camcorder aimed at the runway. What the small screen showed her was not obvious from her posture. The camera in fact had two lenses: a large one that looked like a normal camcorder and a smaller one that blended in with the body of the camera and actually pointed in the opposite direction, allowing Patricia to film things directly behind her in which she had no apparent interest. As she pointed toward the runway, she was in fact studying the faces in the crowd and recording them all digitally, later to be enlarged and examined. She tried to find some indication that would direct her to his face—a beard, perhaps, or an unusual haircut that looked new—but she didn't see anything obvious. She zoomed in and back on several men, but none was Ismael. She moved down toward the other end of the stands, closer to where the Blue Angel VIPs were sitting. She had been invited to sit with them. She didn't want to miss any of the actual air show.

Behind the stands, Ismael walked from one booth to another, examining the Blue Angel paraphernalia, the military recruiting trailers, and the airplanes that were on static display. He had trimmed his thick beard and hair so that now it was short stubble. He wore a hat that had a Lawrence of Arabia look—a long white cloth hanging around the sides and back to protect the neck from the sun. Ismael used it to protect his face, to make sure no one would recognize him. He had also bought gaudy sunglasses for a dollar that made him look silly and superficial. He was sure they were looking for him. He was well aware of the enormous chance he was taking by even being there. But he had to get the information he needed. It was worth whatever risk he had to take to get it. He didn't think they'd really expect him to show up at an air show in Mesa. He wore a T-shirt with an airplane on it, and running shoes, apparently the American uniform for attending an air show.

He stopped as he noticed one particular booth that seemed to specialize in the Blue Angels. He scanned the offerings: hats, T-shirts, photograph books, videotapes, calendars, and plastic airplanes. He bought three different videotapes of the Blue Angels and four books about the team. He made his way to the viewing stands and took a seat in the middle of the stands, surrounded by a mob of people. He watched the air show out of the corner of his eye while he began reading one of the books about the Blue Angels. He wanted to know everything about them, their history, their traditions, their air show routine, and whether it was the same at every show. In other words, whether it was predictable. Targetable.

Ismael paid no attention whatsoever as one airplane after another took to the runway to put on the next demonstration. He had no interest in them. He read the book, flipped through the program, and waited for the Blue Angels.

Ismael sat up quickly when the Blue Angels' narrator, #7, Larry McKnight, as Ismael now knew—said loudly over the public address system, "Goooood afternoon, ladies and gentlemen!"

McKnight continued his memorized lines with his back to the runway, never actually looking at the Blue Angels or what was happening. He was like a conductor who always faced the audience.

In San Francisco Ismael hadn't been able to see the Blue Angel pilots prepare for the air show. They had flown out of Oakland airport, and the show took place over the water. Here, as in most other venues, their shiny blue jets were parked right in front of the crowd.

The Blue Angel pilots were lined up at attention, their blue flight suits matching their immaculate jets. They wore their Navy officer hats and aviator sunglasses. Ismael watched every step. Stovic was on the left, closest to the airplanes. He looked strong. Very good military bearing. The pilots formed into a line, shoulder to shoulder, and marched down the line in front of their airplanes. As each pilot reached his airplane, he would execute a smart right turn and go di-

rectly to the ladder the plane captain had already lowered from the shoulder of the Hornet. The Boss was the
first to his airplane. His plane captain saluted him
crisply and climbed up the ladder after him to help him
strap in.

The others followed and were quickly seated in their
jets. Dazzlingly bright yellow helmets covered their
heads, and gold-mirrored visors covered their eyes.
They adjusted their lip mikes to touch their lips for
easy talking on the radios. The canopies came down simultaneously, and they started their engines. On a radio signal from the Boss they tested their smoke
together, blanketing the runway and grass behind them
with dusty white smoke. Off it went, and they were
ready to taxi.

The Boss was the first out, with #2 joining on his
wing immediately, just inches away. They taxied in
three pairs toward the short hold area of the runway.
Then the four that made up the diamond taxied onto
the runway itself. Ismael raised his eyebrows as he realized for the first time that they were going to take off in
a formation of four airplanes. They ran up their engines and rolled smoothly down the runway in a deafening roar, inches apart.

They were airborne in seconds, and #4 quickly slid
into place in the slot forming the diamond as they
raised their landing gear. Inside their airplanes the Boss
came over the radio: *"Up . . . we . . . go . . . a lit-tle
more . . . pull. . . ."* They all pulled back harder on the
stick on the *p* of "pull."

Ismael started the stopwatch on his new digital
watch.

Johannson—Oden—taxied onto the runway. He
went to full afterburner without hesitation and began
his takeoff roll. He watched his airspeed carefully, and
as soon as he had enough speed he lifted off the ground

and continued pulling his nose up, leaving his gear and flaps down. With the nose twenty degrees above the horizon and barely enough airspeed to keep flying, he rolled the Hornet over on its back in a dirty roll, a move that looked for all the world like an airplane trying desperately to fall out of the sky. Oden continued the roll all the way around and back upright until his extended landing gear was pointed back at the runway a mere twenty feet below him. He raised his gear and flaps and flew away. The excited crowd sighed in relief.

Stovic had already taxied into position on the runway while the crowd watched Oden do his dirty roll. As soon as Oden raised his gear, he went to afterburner and guided his Hornet down the runway. He waited until he had enough speed to fly . . . longer . . . a little longer still, holding it on the deck . . . now. He pulled back on the stick sharply and the Hornet jumped off the runway. He pushed the nose back down for the plane to settle into level flight just feet off the runway. He held the throttles full forward, throwing raw fuel into the engine exhaust—the afterburner—to generate as much power as the plane had. He kept accelerating, holding the jet down near the ground, until he reached the end of the runway. The pavement stopped and the dirt began and he pulled back hard on the Hornet. It pivoted, pointed its nose up, and rocketed away from the earth. In the VIP section Patricia filmed the entire air show with her reverse lens engaged, checking every face in the crowd that she could see. She didn't see anyone that gave her concern.

Ismael, sitting high in the stands fifty yards away from Patricia, was amazed at how low Stovic had stayed over the runway. He tried not to be impressed, to pay no attention to how aggressive and courageous the pilots were. He wondered whether his brother could have made it flying in such a formation, then quickly dismissed such heretical thoughts from his mind.

He checked the time and wrote it down in the top right corner of the small sketchpad that had been under the book in his lap. He began diagramming the entire routine for the aircraft with the number six on its tail. He watched the diamond come and go and the solo passes and climbs. As the air show progressed, he drew a series of small boxes on the page, each box representing a maneuver in which number six was involved—every climb, every dive, every pass with the lead solo in which they flashed by each other mere feet away from complete destruction—and noted the exact elapsed time over center point since Stovic's takeoff. He then put two numbers next to each box, the time to the second when the maneuver crossed the center point of the airfield, and a ranking from one to ten of how vulnerable number six was in each maneuver; which would cause the most damage to the team, the crowd, and American pride.

The routine went off beautifully. The Blues were thrilled with their second show of the season. A long season lay ahead of them, but if they could build on the precision they had shown today, it would be a great year.

After the show the Blue Angels walked into the debriefing room to view the videotape and conduct the confidential no-holds-barred debrief. The Boss walked next to Stovic, then stopped him. "I think we owe it to the team to tell them what's going on."

"Yes, sir. I agree."

"Tonight."

"Yes, sir."

They went in to the confidential debrief. Everyone from outside the team was excluded. The pilots ran through the videotape of the show and went around the table with comments. They first criticized themselves, then mentioned "safeties," things that could be done better to improve the safety of the show. It could be a brutal, painful process. No one held back, and each said exactly what he thought. But it was constructive and allowed the team to build a better show each time they went out. At the end, when each of them was done with whatever he had to say, he would say what every Blue Angel pilot said at the end of his portion of the debrief, the phrase that each of them meant: "Glad to be here, Boss."

Stovic had never meant it more.

The Blue Angels had changed into jeans and polo shirts and were standing around small tables in the bar of their hotel in Scottsdale. Stovic didn't have his usual enthusiasm. All he had been able to think about during the air show was whether someone was targeting him. It was his first air show after leaving El Centro, the beginning of their official air show season, and he should have been concentrating on flying as well as he could. He had done that, but all under the dark cloud of being a target. He didn't know if he could take an entire season of being a target. The Boss walked in with a grim look on his face. Whoever saw him first got the attention of the others at the table. The Boss gave one short jerk of his head toward the door. The Blue Angels tossed money on the tables and walked out with him. "My room," the Boss said heading for the elevators. The others looked at each other with confusion, but followed. They went into the Boss's room and sat around the edges of the bed and in the two chairs against the picture window. The room felt crowded and tense. Waiting for them were Lew, Pat, and the two officers from the NCIS. Andrea sat on the floor next to

Rat, who was leaning against the loud air conditioner in the corner. Everyone noticed.

The Boss spoke. "I learned something recently that I haven't told you about. I didn't want to spook you or change the way you flew. But sometimes being overly cautious in our business can be more dangerous than not. I think it's time for you to know what's going on. I probably should have told you about it before the show today. I'm sorry, but now I'm going to rectify that."

He looked at the FBI agents, then back at the team. "You may have seen these people around before. They're with the FBI. They're here to talk to us, but the bottom line is . . ." he hesitated. He didn't know what effect it would have on the team, but he couldn't just let it go anymore. "Somebody's out to get us." He searched for the right words to tell them, something accurate and comforting at the same time. Nothing came. "Tell you what, rather than just flail around here, I'm going to turn it over to Special Agent Lew Savage of the FBI."

Lew stood with some difficulty and adjusted his brace for maximum comfort. "Evening. I'm Special Agent Lew Savage, and this is Special Agent Patricia Branigan. We're with FBI Counter-Terrorism. One of the little things I do is I leave a phone number in a lot of magazines for people looking for things they shouldn't be looking for. It's sort of an ongoing sting operation. Anybody stupid enough to call it is usually up to no good. A few weeks ago, I got a call. I met with a guy who was looking for weapons. 'Aviation related,' he said. For some reason I haven't yet figured out, he spooked before we got close to the deal. I don't even know exactly what he was looking for. So he skipped out. But we got his photo, and we got his voice on tape.

We've traced him down. He's an Algerian student studying electrical engineering in Washington."

"It's me he wants," Stovic blurted.

Lew replied, "That's our guess. The Algerian pilot who was killed in the shoot-down that Lieutenant Stovic here was involved in? That was our man's brother."

Others shifted nervously on the bed. The springs protested. The air conditioner by the window kicked on noisily in the silence.

Lew continued. "It's not just that he wants to get Mr. Stovic. We think he's trying to shoot down the Blue Angels. The team. Or whatever of it he can."

The pilots grew increasingly uncomfortable. "How the hell is he going to do that?" Hoop asked.

"That's what we wondered. I think when he contacted me he was looking for a shoulder-fired surface-to-air missile. Maybe even a Stinger."

"A Stinger? Is that even possible? Are they available on the black market?"

"Very hard to come by and very expensive. But if someone is dedicated to getting one, yes, it can be done."

"Well, shit," Oden exclaimed. "Think he got one?"

"He called me out of an ad in *Weaponeer,* for God's sake. He's an amateur. He's probably heard of Stingers but wouldn't recognize one if he saw it."

"So there's nothing to worry about, really. Right?" Bean asked.

"I think he probably called us first, before he knew what the hell he was doing. Since then either he quit— which I don't believe for a second—or he's getting smart or getting help."

"We're not sure," Patricia added.

"Why not?" Oden pressed.

"We haven't seen him since Washington. So this may

be a lot of worry about nothing. He may have gone home when he found he couldn't get a missile."

Lew continued, "But I don't want to paint it too rosy either. This started in Algeria. He was seen with some men from a particularly vicious group in Algeria. They're well connected."

The Boss interjected, "So now what?"

"It is our belief that he *will* be able to get shoulder-fired missiles."

Stovic pushed him. "And do what? Smuggle them into the United States?"

"Maybe. That's hard. But maybe. Or maybe he'll try something completely different. We just don't know. We do know that you're going to have to look out for yourselves too. We're here and will be at every air show. And we're going to do everything we can to track this guy down before he has the chance to do anything. But we've got a hard job too. If he's truly working alone, it makes it even harder.

"So you have to be vigilant and look out for yourselves. But we might be wrong. He may decide to go after Lieutenant Stovic all alone or do something else crazy that we haven't yet thought of. Keep your eyes peeled. By the way, here's his picture," Lew said holding up an eight-and-a-half-by-eleven copy of the photograph Patricia had taken with her telephoto lens. "I've got copies for each of you. Keep this to yourselves. If you start advertising to the air show organizers that there's some lunatic after you, they'll either cancel or you'll be playing to empty stands."

The pilots sat silently and stared at the photos. No one wanted to say anything. No one knew what to say. Finally the Boss broke the silence. He stood and looked at Lew. "Thanks for coming. We'll let you know if we see anything, but until then, we're going to keep right on going as if nothing has happened."

Lew and Patricia looked at the NCIS agents and motioned for them all to leave. The Blue Angels needed to talk alone.

The door closed behind them, and the pilots and others sat silently.

The Boss spoke again. "I also want to introduce Kent Rathman." He pointed to Rat. "You have already met him. But he isn't a photographer. He's a former SEAL who is on special assignment from the government to protect Animal."

Bean interrupted. "Looks to me like he's protecting Andrea a hell of a lot better than Animal."

The pilots laughed. Rat smiled.

The Boss continued. "So if he asks you to do anything, please cooperate."

Rat stood. "If anyone sees anything unusual at all? Please let me know. I'll be here every step of the way until this is over, one way or the other."

Stovic spoke. "If you guys want me to resign, to leave the Blues so maybe he won't come after you guys, I'll do that. It's not fair to bring this to you."

Oden, the one who had been the closest to voting against Stovic after his interview in Pensacola, spoke quickly. "It isn't you, Animal. It could have been any one of us. They're targeting you because you did what you were supposed to do as a Navy pilot. You didn't sleep with his sister. You didn't attack his family at night in their house. He's trying to divide us. To make us think it's personal so we'll turn on each other. Well, as for me, I'm going to keep flying the lead solo, and the only guy I want as the opposing solo is you. This is the last year for the Blues. We've got to make it a good one. We're off to a good start, and I say we just keep right on going. If this guy sticks his head up, he's going to get it shot off."

\* \* \*

Rat's chartered jet landed at Ronald Reagan airport in Washington, and one of his men picked him up in his BMW. They drove to their office in D.C. where the team heads were to meet at 0700. Rat noticed the traffic was already heavy at 0600, not that it surprised him. The traffic around Washington was horrendous and getting worse.

They wheeled into the underground parking garage and took the elevator to their offices on the fourth floor overlooking Arlington.

Rat was the last one to arrive, even though he was thirty minutes early. He looked around the conference room at his friends, now his "employees."

"Morning, men," he said.

"Morning, sir," most responded.

"Thanks for coming. I know it's not easy for you to get away from your teams, but I wanted to tell you the latest developments and our plan. Anybody have any trouble getting here?"

"Nope," they replied, downing their Starbucks coffee by the pint.

"Good. Well, it's out of the bag. Everybody knows what's going on. The Blues know Nezzar is after them." He poured a cup of coffee for himself. He had been up all night revising his plans and thinking through the problem, and was starting to feel that tug of fatigue. "Let's start with Washington. Robby, how are things going?"

Robby nodded his head slowly. He was black and wore his hair in dirty dreadlocks. He wore some kind of African or Jamaican shirt and black-framed sunglasses with yellow lenses. His baggy pants hung down over his flip-flops. "Good, Rat. Nothing—"

"You're looking pretty good, Robby," Rat smiled.

"My supersecret ultraconvincing look. The one that gets me no second looks in Washington City, bro." Robby smiled.

"Nothing happening?"

"Nothing. It's boring. I guarantee you he's not coming back to his apartment—"

"How much did you have to give away to get the apartment next door anyway?"

"Five large. She almost choked when I told her I wanted to sublease *that* piece-of-shit apartment. She wondered why, but not for long, not once she saw the cash."

"You got all you wanted through the walls?"

Robby nodded. "No problem. Phone lines, cameras, motion detectors, everything. Only activity has been the FBI, who come about once every couple of weeks to see if their secret dust on the floor has been disturbed or if there are any other signs of life. They're always disappointed."

"You still need to be there?"

"Nah, I need some more excitement. I'm a social animal, Rat, I need some companionship. I'm sick of watching an empty apartment."

"Good. I need you on the air show detail. I want you with me."

"That's what I'm talking about," Robby said nodding, sending his shoulder length dreads wagging as he gave the man sitting next to him some kind of made-up incomprehensible handshake.

"The feds getting anything?" Robby asked.

"No. They're still playing catch-up. They don't have anything we don't already know."

"Well, if they paid attention to what they had, they might get better."

"Meaning?"

"That digital video you sent me—the one the Fibbies took of the crowd at the air show in Mesa?"

"Sure."

"I ran it through our face recognition software. Instead of trying to get it to match a database of known terrorists, I pulled the photos we have of Nezzar, made a composite, and put that in the software. I ran their tape through just against that composite. Check this out." He pressed some buttons on the small remote he had been playing with, and a projector hanging from the ceiling threw a large bright image on the white wall at the end of the conference room. "Here's the video of the air show. You can hear the jets in the background. It's when the Blue Angels are flying. She zooms in on a couple of people, and I expect they ran those faces. But I bet they didn't run the others in the frame. It's a high-resolution camcorder. We got some good data. Check it right . . . here." He froze the image. "She's checking out the guy in the blue baseball cap with the USS *Enterprise* on it? See the scrambled eggs on the brim? But look down to the left. See the guy with the Lawrence of Arabia look?"

He pulled up the face recognition software display window and showed the computer comparison of the air show man and Nezzar. "It's not perfect. Enough of his face is hidden by the hat, the shadow, and the sunglasses that the software can't get as many reference points on the face as it would like, but it gave us an eighty percent likely on the ID."

Rat stared at the face. "Groomer? What do you think?"

Groomer studied the images. "Can't say for sure, but it sure looks like him."

"He's very bold. For him to come into an air show with obvious security, FBI all over the place, and knowing he's been seen in person in Virginia Beach *and* in D.C."

"And to pull it off," Robby said. "We were there too, don't forget. We didn't see him."

"A lot of people at an air show." Rat wondered where Ismael was. He had become invisible. "Groomer, what about Pensacola? Seen anything suspicious?"

"No, sir, but the FBI don't want us there. They don't understand why we're there, and resent it, frankly. They think we're much more likely to get in the way than help."

"They're primary on the family. That's clear. Our job is to get Nezzar. Their job is to protect Stovic's family. You think you'll recognize him if he shows up?"

"He might recognize *me* from when I tried to rip his head off in Virginia Beach. Which raises an interesting point. Are we cleared to slot this guy if he shows up?"

"No. We're not. Just take him down. They would love nothing better than to interrogate him."

"What if he makes an aggressive move?"

"Well, if called to respond, we can't help that, now can we? But you've seen nothing?"

"Feds are going to put at least one special agent inside the house. Pretty good idea, I think, but we have to take care of where this guy is *likely* to show up."

"The air shows," Rat said, nodding

"He's smart. They think he's stupid because he called their sting number. Granted it wasn't the smartest move, but I'm beginning to wonder if he wanted them to know he was out there."

Rat thought for a moment. He looked around the table at some of the most experienced and talented counterterrorism operatives in the world. And they couldn't find one man. "Groucho, what about at the Agency?"

Groucho looked around the conference room, then

remembered it was actually a SCIF—a Specially Compartmentalized Information Facility—a place where they could keep top secret information and discuss it freely. "They're working some angles in Algeria and even working with the FBI on some American Algerian angles. But so far they got no location on this guy at all."

"All right," Rat said finally. "The real change now is that I had to tell Stovic and the team what's happening. Everything will be different. He's going to show that he knows. He won't mean to, but he'll show it. And then his wife will start to show it. She'll be looking around when she goes to the grocery store, and she won't take the kids to the park anymore, or go to the beach. I know that's what she'll do, sure as shit. So if our target is watching, he'll know we're waiting for him.

"We're going to shift every available person to the air show section. With me. We can't miss anything. The next show is in New Orleans. I'll be going there with the team, and I'll expect the rest of you to be there already. Let's be real smart in this because if we fail, we will have failed a lot of people.

"Clear any new developments through me right away. And if you locate this guy, don't close on him unless you have to. If you have time, call me."

The Blue Angel pilots sat in the leather chairs in the ready room in Pensacola waiting for the Boss to appear with his "guest." He had called an emergency all-officer meeting and was being very coy about the content. The pilots were all convinced it was good news based on the sparkle in the Boss's eyes and his efforts to suppress the smile that was struggling to get out.

Stovic had no idea what it was about and thought that speculating about it was ridiculous. "Just wait about five minutes and then you'll know," he said to

Bean, who had come up with the latest new rumor, that the brass were going to cancel two air shows and let them all stay home with their families. Not that Bean believed that. He just thought it would be nice. In fact, Bean had made it up completely and was trying to sell it as a rumor that he had heard from someone else. So far he had no takers.

Stovic sipped from his #6 coffee mug and wondered if perhaps the announcement had something to do with him.

Bean leaned over to him. "How you handling everything?"

"I look in my rearview mirror a lot."

"What about Karen? How's she doing?"

"Not that great. She had figured out how to handle the regular danger—accidents, flying into the water, night carrier ops, you know. Now she feels violated. Especially when she remembered seeing this guy drive by our house in Virginia Beach. She's spooked."

Bean nodded sympathetically. "Let me know if you need anything from me."

Stovic stood up to get some more coffee as the Boss came into the ready room with an Admiral in tropical whites behind him. "Attention on deck!" the Boss roared.

The command caught so many of them off guard that several nearly pulled muscles struggling to their feet with unexpected haste.

"As you were," the Admiral said.

As Stovic's heart recovered its regular beat, he sat down and looked at the Admiral's uniform. He was tall and distinguished looking, with gold Navy pilot's wings over his left breast. He had several ribbons, none of which was for a medal of any note. The only combat ribbons were "been there" ribbons. Nothing for valor, no air medals, no Silver Stars or Distinguished Flying

Crosses. He looked at the Admiral's face. It was the same Admiral they'd seen in El Centro in civilian clothes, the one who had told them they were being cut from the budget. Great, Stovic thought. More bad news.

The Boss spoke. "This is Rear Admiral Don Hooker. I'm sure you remember him from El Centro." The Boss gave his pilots a cautious look. "I know what you're thinking—this is the guy who cut us out of the budget. True enough, except most of you have been in the Navy long enough to know that when a request comes from uphill—from your superior—there's only one right answer. The request to cancel the Blue Angels didn't come from Admiral Hooker but from his superior. But he's not here to talk about that. He's here to talk about something else. I'll let him explain." He pointed to the Admiral. "Sir," he said, turning the floor over to him.

The Admiral cleared his throat as if he were about to address Congress through a microphone sitting on a table with green felt. "Good morning, gentlemen. It's a pleasure for me to be here." He paused.

They nodded at him, waiting.

"I fought to keep the Blues alive for next year, and I'm sorry that I was unsuccessful."

They stared.

"Something has occurred to me, though, that might give us a chance to bring the Blues back. Something rather different." He fought back a smile. "I came down here to discuss it with Captain McMahon. When we were done, he asked if I would be willing to discuss it with you. Or at least tell you about it.

"The reason the Blues lost their line in the budget is because of the shortfall on the Joint Strike Fighter. . . ." He hesitated. "Especially considering the problems they've been having with carrier suitability, they've had to do some major shifting around of money to keep the program on schedule. I don't have to acquaint you with the problems. They've been in the press.

"The Admirals who are the cheerleaders for the JSF thought it needed to be showcased, to show what a great airplane it is and how it will be the savior of the Western world of aviation. They've arranged for the JSF to fly in an air show coming up in two weeks. All the Admirals will be there in their best uniforms to cheer on the JSF." He waited until they were all looking at him. "The same Admirals who took your money.

"Those Admirals haven't seen you fly—haven't seen the Blue Angels fly—in ten or twenty years. They still remember fondly when the Blue Angels were flying A-4s!" He laughed.

They smiled and kept listening.

"Those Admirals need to be reminded of what naval aviation is all about, what the Blue Angels are—the representatives of everyday Navy pilots. They need to see you fly again. I'm here to ask the Boss if you would be willing to cancel the air show that's currently on the schedule and add this one in its place."

The Blue Angels frowned. Big deal. Another air show. One show or the other didn't really matter to them. Must be D.C. so they can wheel all the geezer Admirals to it.

Oden was typically skeptical. "Why would we cancel one air show for another? Wouldn't it be a lot easier just to fly the Admirals in for one of our other shows? Say, Annapolis?"

Admiral Hooker smiled. "Normally, yes. But I haven't told you where the air show is that I have in mind."

"Go ahead," the Boss said, sitting hard on his enthusiasm.

"Paris."

The pilots sat up and tried not to gape. "As in the Paris Air Show? The one in Paris, France?"

"Exactly."

"Seriously?" Oden asked.

"Seriously. And as it turns out, the *Truman* is heading across the pond next week for a two-week NATO exercise in which the French are—miraculously—going to actually participate. She could carry you close enough to France to fly off and arrive three days prior to the air show. Long enough to get over the time change and have a little fun. You could stay over a couple of days too, maybe even bring your wives—at your own expense, of course—if you want. What do you say?"

"And the idea is that we would actually fly a show in Paris?"

"Exactly. Now I tell you the why. It's the biggest air show in the world. It's only held every other year. The Blue Angels have never flown in the Paris Air Show, and I think it's about time they did. The air show is going to be used by the DOD to showcase the Joint Strike Fighter, the very plane that has stolen your budget for next year. Well, I thought you guys could return the favor—steal a little of the JSF's thunder. It will fly at the Paris Air Show to try to encourage some other countries that are considering signing on to the program— particularly Norway, Belgium, and England. We need their participation to buy more fighters. It brings down the per unit cost—well, you don't need to hear about that. The JSF will be flying, but more importantly, the Admirals that cut your funding will be there to cheer on their baby. Maybe if you fly in front of them, stir their loins a little about flying for the Navy, maybe you can turn them around. Who knows, maybe if those other countries sign on, they can restore your funding for next year. And if not, well, may as well go out in a blaze of glory."

"Shee-it hot!" Hoop yelled.

Stovic immediately saw a chance to bring some good news to Karen. Finally he could do something for her. They had never been to Paris. They had always wanted to go. When they got married, they had the fantasy of her chasing the carrier, flying to ports in Europe and the Mediterranean and meeting him when the ship pulled in. They had a dream that he would take leave from an Italian port and go to Paris, or vacation in Greece or Italy. But she had gotten pregnant, once, then twice, and their dream had never materialized. But now the children were old enough to stay with her parents in Charleston. The two of them could spend a couple of days together in Paris.

The Boss stepped to the front, the reason for his excitement now evident. "We'd have a lot to do, but I've already told the Admiral we're game. Anybody disagree?"

They were unanimous. "Can we tell our wives about it? Can we fly them over?"

"Sure," the Boss said. "I called the organizer of the Paris Air Show this afternoon, just to see if it was even possible this late in the game. When I told him who I was and what I wanted to do, he said we could fly anytime we wanted, and they were willing to move whatever was in the way. He was thinking one show on Sunday afternoon, the last day of the air show. So why not?"

Oden spoke up. "Boss, look, if they're going to cancel us, they're going to cancel us. We're not going to change their minds by flying in front of a bunch of Admirals. You're just trying to get us a good deal as part of our last year. I for one want to tell you we appreciate it. I don't really care whether we convince them. I just want to go to Paris. Thanks for looking out for us!"

* * *

Ismael waited by the side of the road in the dark coun-
tryside of Tennessee just outside Knoxville. It was just
after midnight. His rented Toyota was suspended on a
jack. The left rear wheel projected a little more than
was comfortable into the narrow mountain road. He
had spent the day confirming what he already knew—
where the man lived, where he worked, and how he got
to work.

A car was coming. Ismael looked to be working a
little harder than he actually was, as if one of the lug
nuts was frozen on his flat tire. As the headlights
caught him, he dropped the tire iron in apparent disgust. He held a rag in his right hand. The car slowed.
Ismael shielded his eyes to see who was coming to his
aid. It was him. If he didn't stop to help, he would run
over the tack strip lying across the road thirty feet
ahead.

The white Jeep slowed to a stop behind him with its
lights on. The man who climbed out was a young man,
twenty-four according to Ismael's information, a large
man, perhaps six feet two inches tall and well over two
hundred pounds. "Need any help?" he asked kindly.

Ismael looked embarrassed. "I can't get the wheel
off. I have a flat tire. I have to get on my way. I have a
spare, but I can't get this one off!"

The man nodded knowingly. "Maybe I can get it. I
can be pretty mean to a tire iron!" He smiled, walking
toward Ismael.

Ismael stepped back, nodding eagerly, as the man
bent over to look at the wheel. Just as he was ready to
pick up the tire iron and have a try at freeing the wheel,
Ismael spoke to him. "How do you like working at the
Coca-Cola bottling plant?"

The man looked at him curiously. "It's okay. I like it.
I'd rather not work at night, but it's steady. I'm in line
to be an assistant manager in a couple of years."

Ismael leaned toward him. "Does it provide well for you and Mrs. Stovic?"

The man turned back quickly. "How do you know my name?"

"You are Rick Stovic, aren't you?"

Rick frowned. The tire iron lay on the pavement. "I asked you a question. How do you know my name?"

"Because I came here to find you."

"Do I know you?"

"No, I'm a friend of your brother's."

Rick wasn't buying it. "How do you know him?"

"He did something very special for me," Ismael said, his voice getting louder as he recalled everything.

"What?"

"He changed my life forever."

Rick had seen and heard enough. "I've got to get going. Hope you can get that tire off."

"No, wait," Ismael said before Rick could move a step. "I have come to you to return the favor. I need to give you what your brother gave me. It's like a pact."

"What did he do for you?"

"My brother was Chakib Nezzar."

Rick frowned, looking up and down the road for traffic. "Who is that?"

"The Algerian pilot. Your brother killed—"

Rick knew what was coming, and before Ismael could finish his sentence Rick rushed him.

But Ismael had more in his hand than a rag. He lifted his right arm and fired. The bullet slammed into Stovic's chest and dropped him to the ground. He looked up at Ismael as he lay on the road. His chest gurgled as air escaped from his punctured lung.

"He killed my brother!" He fired again into Stovic's chest, into his heart, killing him instantly.

He put the gun in his belt, lowered his car to the ground, put the tire iron and the jack into the trunk, pulled up the tack strip, and climbed into the Corolla to drive back to Washington.

"Hello," Stovic said, grabbing the ringing phone while climbing out of the vivid dream that had been dominating his unconsciousness. "Hello?" he repeated, unsure of whether he had already said it.

"Who is it?" Karen asked, concerned, sitting up in the bed next to him. She reached for the lamp on her side of the bed and looked at her luminescent alarm clock. It was 3:00 A.M. She was the lighter sleeper and was instantly awake. She didn't have to clear the cobwebs.

"Eddie!" a woman's voice cried. "Eddie!"

The plea was like a shot of adrenaline to Stovic. His heart raced. He knew the voice. "Debbie?"

" Eddie, oh God!"

"Debbie, what is it? Is Rick okay?"

She broke down. She couldn't say anything. She sobbed on the phone.

"Who is it?" Karen asked again.

Stovic put his hand over the receiver. "It's Debbie. She's out of control." He moved his hand. "Debbie, what is it? What happened?"

"Rick . . . was working at night. At the bottling plant. He was coming home. They found him on the side of the road—"

"Was he in a wreck?"

"No, he was shot!" she blubbered.

"Shot? Is he all right? Is he in the hospital? I'll be right there. Are you okay?"

"You don't understand," she cried. "He's dead!"

"Dead? Rick's dead?"

Suddenly the FBI agent in the house ran into the Stovic's bedroom. He had heard the phone ringing followed by the commotion. His hand was on his hip where his gun was. "Everything okay, Mr. Stovic?" he asked.

Stovic shook his head. "My brother's been shot."

"Where?" the agent asked, wincing.

"Knoxville, Tennessee."

The agent ran out of the room and down the stairs.

"Debbie, I'll be there tomorrow."

"No, you don't need to. There's . . . nothing, you can't . . ."

"I'll take care of everything. I'll be there tomorrow. I'm sorry. I'm really sorry. He loved you so much." Stovic remembered. "You were such a good wife to him. God, I'm sorry, Debbie."

"Come tomorrow," she begged. "I need you, Eddie."

"I'll be there. Get some sleep."

"Okay."

"Do they know who did this?"

"No. He was shot twice in the chest. They found him lying on the road."

"Where was his Jeep?"

"Right behind him."

"Broken down?"

"No. It was fine."

"All right. I'll be there tomorrow."

"Thank you."

Stovic hung up and looked at Karen. He felt as if he'd been hit with a sledgehammer. "Rick's dead. He was shot twice. They don't have any idea who it was."

"Oh, Ed," she said. She grabbed his head and pulled it to her shoulder. "I'm so sorry."

Stovic fought back the tears that had raced to his eyes.

A block away Rat stood up as tall as he could in the van. He slammed down the headphones in which he had been listening to the phone conversation and yelled at Groomer, who was sitting at the console next to him.

"Shit!" He punched the metal wall next to the console. "How could they have been so *stupid*? They didn't cover his brother?"

Groomer threw his headphones down. "We've been blindsided."

Rat threw his head back and grabbed his face. He tried to think of what the next step should be, and how he was going to explain this. "I'm going to get this guy if it's the last thing I do, even if I have to go to Algeria to do it."

"He's smart," Groomer remarked.

"So are we."

# CHAPTER

# 15

Carl, Sarah."

Carl Dirks, the Attorney General, was taken aback. He didn't think the National Security Advisor had ever called him, and certainly not at home as he was stepping into the shower at 5:00 A.M. "Hello, Sarah. What's the matter?" he asked, quite aware of the hour.

"You need to get with the Director of the FBI immediately. The brother of the Navy pilot—"

"Whoa," he objected. "What are you talking about?"

"Early this morning, last night, actually, the brother of the Navy pilot who was involved in the Algerian shoot-down—"

"What about him?"

"His brother was murdered in Tennessee. On a highway. It looks like it was a trap, an ambush. I'm convinced it's the terrorist we've been looking for, the brother of the Algerian pilot who was killed."

"Okay. So why are you calling me?"

"You need to get the FBI to close the airports, all borders everything. We have to keep this guy from escaping. He might flee the country. He may try anything, but—"

"Look, Sarah. How do you know this?" he said,

switching on his bedroom television in the dark, to the moaning protests of his wife, who rolled over and pulled the covers over her head. "I haven't heard a word about it. What makes you think this has happened? And if they think this Algerian did it, it would be the FBI who would have concluded that, and they haven't told me a thing about it."

She was quiet for a moment, then, "It fits. It's exactly the kind of thing he would do."

He watched CNN to see if it had made it to the national news yet. "This is a law enforcement matter. The FBI can handle it, I'm sure."

"Are you going to call?"

"Sure, I'll call," he said reluctantly.

"Okay," she said. "I have to do a few other things. I'll talk to you later in the day."

"Okay, Sarah. Bye." He hung up the phone and climbed into the shower.

Ismael tried not to look over his shoulder as he walked through the Miami airport. He had asked for a seat in the back of the airplane so he could board right after those in first class. He didn't think U.S. agents would wander onto airplanes randomly looking for him, but they might have alerted security forces at all major airports. He sat waiting for the boarding to begin and pretended to read a paperback novel he had bought in the airport bookstore. His attention drifted from the book to the television hanging from a column. It was tuned to CNN. Nothing unusual at all. No mention of Knoxville, no mention of the murder, or the Blue Angels, or him.

Ismael opened the book to a third of the way through. He tried to read it, and tried even harder not to look around or even up. He feigned boredom and annoyance at how long it was taking to get out of Miami.

He had the unshakable feeling that everyone in the airport was looking at him. He was grateful that he was in Miami, where every second person was non-Caucasian.

"May I have your attention, please," the gate attendant said over the PA system. "Avianca Airlines would like to announce the boarding of Flight 251 to Caracas. We would like our first-class passengers to board first, please, then rows twenty-five and higher. First class only, please, to gate twenty-three."

The passengers started shuffling toward the gate, allowing small passageways between them for the few first-class passengers. They waited for a minute, then, "Rows twenty-five and higher, please."

Ismael handed the attendant his boarding pass and walked onto the jet.

Rat stood waiting for Stovic and Karen as they arrived at the Knoxville Airport. He stood just inside the security barrier, watching carefully. He had his whole team in Knoxville.

He greeted Stovic with a nod of his head. He walked to him and hugged him, the first time he had hugged a man since he could remember. He hugged Karen and kissed her on the side of her head. He looked over at Stovic. "I'm sorry. I never thought he would do this. I should have—"

"It's not your fault, Rat. This guy is a murderer, and he's after me. It's my fight."

"No. It's our fight."

Stovic nodded. "Come on, Carrie, you need to keep up."

She put up her arms, insisting he carry her. He swept her up quickly, as Karen lifted Brandon onto her hip and wrestled with her carry-on bag.

Rat put his foot up on the side of the baggage claim carousel. "How you doing?" he said to Stovic.

Stovic looked at his children. They weren't watching. "I didn't need to pull that trigger, Rat. If I had just held off for a couple more seconds, it would—"

"Don't start down that road. It's a dead end. You did what you should have done."

"No, I didn't, Rat. You don't know," he replied. "I was looking out for myself." He rubbed red eyes and picked Carrie up again. "You okay?" he asked.

She shook her head and put it down on his shoulder to rest. She was exhausted, and very sad. She loved Uncle Rick. He always played with her, ran around his small yard chasing her and making her squeal in fun and terror. He always told her that when he had a little girl, he wanted her to be just like Carrie, and then everything would be perfect—he would have two Carries, one as a daughter and one as a niece. He told her he was going to name his daughter Carrie, so she could be just like her. She protested that nobody else could be Carrie because she was, but he always insisted, laughing, that one Carrie wasn't enough, that he had to have two. He sent her small presents three or four times a year. She loved him. She squeezed the neck of her father tighter. She knew somehow that whatever had happened involved her father too. She didn't know how, just that her parents were afraid.

Their bags arrived, and they pointed them out. Rat pulled them off the carousel easily and set them on the floor. "I've got a car. Want to ride with me?"

Karen nodded. "Have you been to Rick's house?"

Rat shook his head. "I drove by. I've got some people there, but I wanted to wait for you."

Karen looked at her husband. "We've got to go straight there. We've got to take care of Debbie and the baby."

Stovic nodded. "And Rick's . . . funeral." He could hardly say it.

Karen put her arm through his free arm. "It's not your fault."

"Yes, it is."

Rat interrupted. "Come on. My car's out front."

Ismael stepped off the airplane in Algiers and felt instantly refreshed. The dry desert air was like a cleansing bath after the humidity of Miami and Venezuela. He had forgotten how much the smells of the desert and the city blended together where North Africa met the Mediterranean. Still, he realized that his optimism might be based on the knowledge that he was relatively safe. The FBI wasn't here, and they wouldn't be coming. The CIA was another matter—they knew exactly who he was, and might do something here, although he doubted it. In Algiers it was a different equation. There were many more people willing to do anything to help him than there were those who could be after him.

Perhaps the Americans would assume he had finished what he had planned on doing, that killing Stovic's brother was sufficient. Ismael carried his bag out of the terminal, climbed into a taxi, and headed to a place he had never been before. He had heard about it, he had even been with people who had been there and refused to talk about it, but he had never experienced it. He knew he would be received with respect. He had proved himself, as was reflected in the encrypted e-mail he had picked up from his numerical Hotmail account at Simon Bolivar Airport in Caracas.

He knew he *should* go home to see his mother. To comfort her. But he couldn't. *He* wasn't in Algeria. Only his new identity with his new passport was here. The Americans would probably track him anyway, but he couldn't go to his home or see his family. Not until he had done what he had left to do. The taxi dropped him off in the middle of a busy market. He made his way to an alley full of shops selling copper pots. He passed a coffee house and a large shop where several men sat smoking. He turned down a nondescript walkway between the two shops. The incessant market activity ensured his anonymity. At the end of the walkway was a small wooden door that opened quickly as he approached. It closed behind him just as quickly, just as he had been told in the e-mail.

In the dim light behind the door a man pushed him against a stone wall and thrust his feet apart. He quickly searched Ismael for weapons, then escorted him up some stairs into a large, airy room. It had a beautiful rug on the stone floor. There were four men in the room talking. Ismael recognized Madani and Khalida. "It is good to see you," he said, almost meaning it.

Madani crossed to him and they kissed each other. "We received your e-mail. Thank you. You have returned safely after a bold stroke. We didn't think you would make it. You were too exposed. Tell us about what you have done."

"I accomplished one small thing."

"You have shown well for yourself, and you made it out of the country." He walked to the window and looked out over the rooftop next door. "So I take it from your e-mail you are not done. You have something else in mind. Yet you were unclear on what that might be."

Ismael felt he had done enough now that he didn't need to explain himself. "I hesitate to disclose my thoughts, other than to those who will be helping."

"Ah." Madani smiled. "Now you need help."

Ismael stood motionless. "Yes. The question is, From whom do I need the help? I don't know if you're the one, or whoever it is that you report to. But whoever is in charge, whoever has access to a lot of money, a lot of assets, and people who will die for the right cause, that is who I need to talk to." He glanced at Khalida, then stared at Madani.

"What is it you have in mind?"

"Something even more bold and daring than what I already did."

Madani hesitated. "I will take you to the person you need to see. He knows you are here. He wanted to meet you, to welcome you back to the fold—"

"If he wants to work with me on this, then our paths are parallel for a time; that is all. I am not back in anyone's fold." His eyes darkened. "If we can help each other and work together for a short time, then good. If not, I will find other means."

Madani scoffed. "How will you do that? What other means do you have at your disposal?"

Ismael stared at both of them. "More than you will ever know. Don't underestimate me. Let's go."

St. John read the latest encrypted e-mail and put it deep in the pile of documents in her office that were scheduled for shredding. She rubbed her forehead and noticed the wrinkles that seemed to be getting deeper. She glanced at the crystal clock on her desk. The President had asked to see her at 9:00 A.M.

She walked down the hall to the Oval Office and opened the door. "Good morning, Mr.—" She stopped. President Kendrick was sitting with Dennis Arlberg, his Chief of Staff, Stuntz, Stewart Woods, the Director of Central Intelligence, and Attorney General Carl Dirks. "Well. Good morning to you all," she said, recovering smoothly. "To what do I owe the honor of an unscheduled meeting with such an august group?"

"Surprised?" Stuntz smiled.

"Yes, I am," she said, crossing to the silver coffee pot that always had fresh coffee in it. She was more than surprised. She was annoyed. *So much for the Presi-*

*dent's trust.* "Someone want to tell me what's going on?" she said casually.

Kendrick gave Stuntz a dirty look. Stuntz was unmoved. The President spoke. "Actually, they crashed this party," he said smiling. "I asked them to stay because of some new information we just got from Algeria. Stewart?"

Woods cleared his throat with some difficulty. "Excuse me," he said. "We have just received a report on the ground in Algeria that this Ismael Nezzar has been seen in Algiers. This morning. He's back home."

St. John was angry. "He knew it would get too hot for him here after killing Stovic's brother."

"We don't know it was him—"

"Of course it was him," she said. "And now he has made it very difficult for us to get him. How did he get out of the States? I personally called Carl and told him to get the FBI to close our exit points to keep Nezzar from getting out of the country. What happened, Carl?" she asked, putting him on the hottest spot in Washington.

"They said they would do it. This man is very elusive."

"What time did you call?" she pressed.

"Why are you cross-examining me?" he asked angrily.

"What time?"

"I don't know, my first chance. About noon."

*"Noon?"* she asked, horrified. She stood back up and got more coffee. "He never should have escaped. He should be in custody. The FBI didn't see the attack coming on the Blue Angel pilot's brother, and they didn't catch him once he acted." She was furious. "That is unacceptable."

"Carl?" the President asked.

"They can't be everywhere, Mr. President."

"They're supposed to be protecting our pilot and his family. Right?"

"Yes, sir, but no one anticipated something might happen to his brother—"

St. John jumped in. "We can still get this terrorist and whoever is inclined to help him."

"How?" Woods asked.

She should give the author of the e-mail credit. It was really his idea, and he could actually make it happen. "I think this terrorist is still after the Navy's Blue Angels. But he has left the country. And why would he do that if he wants the Blue Angels? He certainly isn't afraid."

Stuntz replied gruffly, "Why don't you just tell us?"

"He went overseas because the Blue Angels are going overseas."

"How do you know that?" Stuntz asked.

"They're going to the Paris Air Show, trying to stay alive, trying to avoid the team being canceled for next year due to *'budgetary constraints,'* which has all been approved by the Secretary of Defense."

"You're canceling the Blue Angels?" the President asked, surprised. "That's like canceling Christmas. You can't do that."

Stuntz was steaming. "The *Navy* decided to cut the team out of *its* budget because of additional funding needed for the JSF. I had nothing to do with it."

"What's the point?" the President asked.

"The Blues are going to Paris. The terrorist who wants them dead is Algerian. There is a large Algerian community in Paris—"

"How the *hell* do you know that?" Stuntz laughed, then caught himself, suddenly remembering Brad Walker.

St. John stared him down with an icy glare. "It is well known." She looked back at President Kendrick.

"That's where he will try to strike. I am sure—"

Kendrick was confused. "What are you saying?"

"That's why he has left the country. In my opinion. The Blue Angels have already posted the change on their web site, and the Paris Air Show people have already announced the Blues will fly there on *their* site."

Kendrick nodded, finally getting it. "Well, Howard, I guess it has just been unarguably proved that we need to cancel that show. Keep the Blue Angels home where they'll be safe. Now that we know this lunatic is back in Algeria, they should be able to return—"

"You misunderstand me," St. John interrupted. Everyone in the room stared at her in disbelief. No one interrupted the President. "This is our *chance* to get an emerging terrorist state. A country testing the waters of international terrorism, perhaps for the first time, as a country. We need to make *sure* the Blue Angels go to Paris. We need to send our best people there to protect them, and find the Algerians."

"Just use them as bait? Just hang out our best pilots and jets so we can catch one Algerian nutcase?" Kendrick replied, stung by her intensity.

"He's not a nutcase. This is the Algerian government speaking. They're working through one man. You're the one who wanted to send two carriers into the teeth of Algerian defenses when you thought it would 'make a statement.' And you're not willing to let a few fighter pilots take some risk to achieve the same thing?"

"You don't know what he has in mind! He might blow them up in their hotel!"

"I don't think so. I think it will be during the air show. He will want to make it dramatic."

"In France?" Dirks protested. "You want to put this in the hands of the Frogs?"

"Not entirely. We'll work together. They are as good as we are."

"Ha," Stuntz roared. "I'd never go for this plan unless Americans were in charge of the security—unless the FBI and the Agency had people in place there looking for these Algerians. Maybe then it would be worth the risk."

Kendrick nodded. "This your idea, Sarah?"

She couldn't take complete credit. "Mostly."

"Who else?"

"Someone who works for me."

"Walker?" Stuntz asked.

"No. He and I have discussed it, but no."

"Who then?"

"I'd rather not say. Mr. President, we're onto this man. We know what his objective is and probably when he'll strike. He's the elite of Algerian terrorists. We need to take him out *now*. If we wait, if we cancel the show, we'll lose track of him. He'll disappear and strike with more force later. This is his coming out party. We need to be there waiting for him."

Kendrick considered what had been said. He rubbed his face as he thought. "We need to take every opportunity we have to get at a terror cell. Especially if it is state sponsored, which I'm hearing this may be. Stewart, you need to keep looking at that. But unless I hear a big protest, I say we send our flyers to Paris, and get the son of a bitch that just murdered one of their pilots' brothers."

Stovic turned away from the window and drew the heavy curtains, throwing the room into unnatural dimness. Everyone was sitting in the living room. It wasn't large and didn't have that many seats, so they had brought in chairs from the dining room. They were sitting in what was roughly a circle, staring at each other, looking away, trying to think of something gentle to say, to comfort someone, or witty, to break the somber mood.

Mostly they shared the silence and listened to the ticking of the clock in the hallway. Rat watched Stovic touch his sister-in-law's shoulder. Stovic looked around at his wife and children, his parents, Debbie's parents, and Debbie's sister. They had all come as soon as they heard. Rat sat in the corner by the door. Stovic spoke. "All right. First, and before we do anything else, I want to apologize to everyone. This wouldn't have happened—"

"No," Debbie said, clutching a handkerchief as she sat on the footstool of a fabric-covered chair. "No, Eddie, this was the fault of someone who had a gun. It wasn't you, and even if he was that guy you think—the pilot's brother—it wasn't your fault. You did exactly

what you should have done. We're proud of you, Eddie. Rick was proud of you," she cried. "*God,* he was
proud of you. He was going to go to three air shows
this year. He had them all planned out. We were driving
to two of them. He told everyone he knew that his
brother was a Blue Angel. He wore that jacket you
gave him. . . ." She smiled, but the corners of her
mouth were pulled down by heavy sadness.

"I've got to quit the team. I can't make it to the show
this weekend with the funeral. In ten days we're leaving
for Paris. They can get the pilot from last year—"

His father interrupted him. "I've never seen you quit
before, or run away from someone. Rick wouldn't
have quit."

"Dad, it's for the good of the—"

"We're having the funeral on Friday. You can still get
out of here Friday night and make it to the air show before Saturday. Where is the next one?"

"New Orleans."

"You can make it. You have to decide whether you
want to."

"Dad, I've been putting myself first for so long I've
brought disaster on my family. When did you hear the
funeral is Friday?"

"Just a minute ago. That was the minister on the
phone. Friday at two. He wants to come over here this
afternoon. He said if he's going to talk about Ricky, he
wants to hear all about him from his family. He wants
us to get together here and talk about him for a couple
of hours, tell stories about him, what we loved about
him, what he did that was wonderful. . . ." He couldn't
go on. He pushed his silver-framed glasses up, trying to
ignore the tears running down the sides of his nose.

Stovic nodded. "Good idea. What time?"

"Four."

"Okay." The rest of the family waited for Stovic to

say something, to tell them what to do or what was going to happen next. But he didn't know. He sat down in the cloth chair and asked Debbie if he could hold his brother's baby. He held her close, feeling the smooth innocence of her cheek against his rough, unshaven face. He whispered into her ear, "I'm sorry, Elizabeth, I'm so sorry." She looked at his face with her big eyes, perceiving his distress but not sure what it was about.

"Eddie, I think you'd better go call the head of the Blue Angels and make arrangements to be there Friday night," his father said.

Stovic nodded almost imperceptibly.

"Mr. Stovic?" the FBI agent called from the back door on the other side of the kitchen, looking for the pilot in the group. "Special Agent Savage would like to have a word with you."

Stovic looked at Rat, who nodded. They both got up and went to the back door. Lew Savage and Patricia Branigan were standing in the backyard, where Debbie had just planted some flowers. It was a charming place that looked surreal in the falling mist, just short of rain.

"Yeah?" Stovic said quickly.

"I wanted to let you know that we have security in place. You don't have anything to worry about while you're here." Lew looked at Rat and saw the skepticism. "You got something to say?" he said to Rat.

"Yeah, but not in front of him," Rat said angrily.

"Let's hear it," Lew insisted.

"Okay. You told me in Phoenix that you, you personally, were in charge of Stovic's security, his family's security. That right?"

"I told you I was in overall charge. Another special agent was running the actual protection detail."

"So you never thought maybe Stovic's brother might be a target? It never occurred to you?"

"No, it didn't. You saying it occurred to you? Because if it did, you surely told one of our special agents, right? I mean we're all on the same team, supposedly, although I still don't know what the hell you're doing. So did you think of it?"

"Yeah. I did. But it's like thinking of closing your door when you get in your car to drive. You guys need me to remind you of that too? What about taking off your clothes and your gun when you take a shower?" Rat leaned toward Lew, furious, partially out of guilt. "What about brushing your teeth? Need me to remind you of that too?" Rat leaned back, remembering the people in the house. He spoke quietly. "We tried to stay out of your way. Looks like we should have been in the way. Maybe we could have stopped this. Did you even talk to Rick? Tell him he might be in danger, to watch for unusual situations?"

"No. Did you? I mean you're a friend of the family, right? What the hell did you do?"

Rat stared into Lew's eyes. He saw a man who was angry, probably with himself, certainly with others. "If you can't handle this job, let me know. I'll take care of it."

Lew directed his attention to Stovic. "If you need anything else, I'll be within earshot. Just give me a yell."

Stovic nodded. "Anything else? I need to get back in."

"We'll be set up for the funeral too. Just wanted to let you know not to worry about us."

Stovic turned to go, then turned back. "You getting close to this guy?"

Lew glanced down at the narrow sidewalk leading to the back of the house. "No. Not really. He's left the country. We think it's safe, but we're not taking any more chances."

Stovic turned back to the house. "You know that?" he asked Rat.

"Yeah. He's in Algeria."

"That's good news, right?"

Rat stopped Stovic at the top of the stairs. "I wanted to talk about this later. You've got enough on your mind right now. But I think he went back there to get ready for his next attack. Probably on the Blues."

Stovic was confused. "What do you mean?"

"The Paris Air Show."

"Of course. We've made it easier on him by going to an air show in France."

"Exactly."

"Maybe we shouldn't go."

"Maybe. Or maybe we go over there and get him."

Stovic looked at his brother's backyard, the pretty flowers that looked lonely in the mist, and the house where his brother had lived. "I'm all for that."

"I'm sorry about your brother, Animal. I really—"

Stovic shook his head. "Wasn't your fault, Rat. We all should have thought to tell him what was going on with me. But that's over. Rick is dead because the Algerian killed him. Simple as that."

"They don't know that for sure. . . ."

"You have any doubt about that?"

"No."

"So maybe we'll get a chance to see him in Paris."

Rat nodded and followed Stovic into the house.

Ismael and the other two stood in a room open to the outside; no windows, just a long opening along two of the walls that let in the fresh desert air. They greeted the man they had come to see. Ismael barely caught his name. He spoke softly in a very deep voice. He offered them refreshments like visiting dignitaries. They took coffee. They sat around a low table. The man spoke to Ismael. "So, you have returned safely."

"I'm glad to be home," Ismael replied. He took a drink of the strong coffee. "May I ask you your name?"

The man hesitated. "Chadli."

So it was him. Finally.

"I have heard from Madani that you have not finished your work. Something remains to be done. Is that accurate?"

"It is."

"What else do you have in mind, and what kind of help do you need?"

"May we speak in private?" Ismael asked.

Chadli jerked his head, and the three attendants that had been standing at the doors left the room. "Whatever you want."

Ismael waited until the others were outside. "I don't want information in the wrong hands. I need weapons and some men to help me. That's all."

"What kind of weapons?"

"Stinger missiles."

The man laughed. "We don't have any such missiles. No one does."

"Someone does."

"Who, the United States?"

"There were two hundred Stingers left in Afghanistan after the war against the Russians in the eighties. They were received from the American CIA."

Chadli was unimpressed. "Everyone knows this. But you think some of them somehow made it out of Afghanistan after the war with the Americans? You are just going to carry them back through American customs?"

"The Blue Angels will fly in Paris in ten days."

Chadli looked up quickly from his coffee. "Paris?"

"Yes. At the biggest air show in the world. Hundreds of thousands of people." He let that sink in. "We have friends in Paris, people who would be glad to help us."

"But why not Russian missiles? We have them here. They can do the job."

"They're not as good. We will only have one chance."

"What do you know about Stinger missiles?" the man scoffed.

"I've done some research. If we could buy a new Stinger, we wouldn't be able to use it."

"Why not?"

"New Stingers have GPS built in. If they are used outside of certain specified geographical regions, they will not fire. And you cannot change the geographical regions without a key that is not kept with the missiles. It is unlikely that a new Stinger would work in the United States. Or even Paris."

"Go on."

"Some Stingers were made before GPS."

"The Americans have not forgotten where those missiles went."

"But since the fall of Afghanistan the Americans have been chasing small remnants, not knowing who went where. But I know."

"What do you know?"

"One group of friends was able to get out of Afghanistan early, before the fighting started. They went to Khartoum. I am told they took some of the Stingers with them."

Chadli understood. "Of course. You know them?"

"Not personally, but others . . ."

"Yes. They thought you might ask. You want to go to Khartoum. To ask them."

"Yes. But I must go with others, to ensure I still

look . . . subordinate to them. I am not ready yet to assert myself. Perhaps after Paris."

Chadli nodded. "Of course. You must go to Khartoum. I will speak with Madani and ask him to go there and to take you along. He will not understand. Do you think they will give you Stingers?"

"Perhaps. If I can meet with one man in particular, I think we will have great success. He is very sympathetic."

"Let me know if you need anything else. Money, support, anything."

"I will come see you, alone, when I return from Khartoum."

Sarah St. John went to Brad's desk and leaned over his shoulder until her mouth was near his ear. She whispered, "I want to meet with him."

He tried not to look alarmed. "You told him you'd never ask him to do that."

"I've changed my mind. It's important. Tell him."

He had never met this man. He had only corresponded with him. He didn't know who he was or who he worked for. He only knew what he was to pass on to St. John.

He turned his attention to the intelligence brief he had just received from the CIA. He began reading. He didn't absorb a word on the first page, or the second.

Before dawn on the day of the funeral, Rat went to the church where the funeral was to be. He didn't expect anything to happen at the funeral, but he had stopped trusting the FBI. As he expected, it was covered on all sides with FBI agents. He drove into the parking lot and climbed out conspicuously. A special agent approached him. "Help you?"

"Just wanted to check on your security."

"And who might you be?"

"Friend of the family's. So what do you have? Snipers? Explosive-sniffing dogs? You got a covert team with automatic weapons?"

The special agent was amazed at the questions. "You know, as much as I'd *love* to help you," the man said, "that isn't the kind of thing we usually discuss with people."

"Well, I need to know."

"And why is that?"

Rat pulled a small folding black leather wallet out of his pocket and opened it quickly.

The FBI man read the badge and realized it was an FBI identification with the special indicator that the holder was a member of the FBI's elite Hostage Rescue Team.

"Sorry," the man said. "Nobody told us you were here."

"We're not here. I'm just looking around. Sort of a security backup. Show me what you've got in place."

"Yes, sir," the agent replied, and showed Rat the entire security setup.

Hours later, when the families came out of Debbie's house to drive to the funeral in cars that were driven by friends of the family, Ed Stovic, Lieutenant, U.S. Navy, in his dress blue uniform, was first out the door. He looked into the street and noticed the headlights from numerous cars with Knoxville plates. They made the whole dreary day brighter. He could see the main road a couple of blocks away, and the line of cars snaked its way onto the main road and down past the pond and past the clump of trees, and he couldn't tell how much farther it went. Hundreds of cars. All with their lights on, all with their engines running, all waiting for them to drive to Woodland Hills Baptist Church five miles away, a large brick church tucked into the side of a large hill at the foot of the nearby mountains. All showing their support for him and his brother.

Surprised and humbled, Stovic climbed into the car he had rented. Rat drove. He wore a blue blazer with a black mock turtleneck. Hidden under his blazer was a compact Uzi submachine gun in a special quick-access holster. He didn't expect to use it, but he and Groomer and the rest of the team were ready for whatever came. Karen and the children got in the back. They drove to the church, fifth car back, in complete silence. Stovic was lost in his thoughts. He was two years older than Rick and had always made his brother the brunt of his pranks and early tests of manhood. They were always in competition, and Stovic usually won, mostly because of his years. Stovic would brutalize him in strength sports—wrestling, weightlifting, boxing, or the shot put. But Rick was the faster of the two and more agile. They would go to the park, and Stovic would want them to play football and knock each other down, but Rick would want to play soccer and show his amazing footwork.

Rick had closed the gap, gaining on his older brother every year. He had surpassed him in height three years before, when Rick grew to be six feet two inches tall and Stovic leveled off at six feet.

Stovic knew that in their parents' eyes Rick would always be the favorite, the baby. He remembered their rooms down the hall from each other, away from their parents' room, the corners where they had sat and schemed, the bed frame they had broken when wrestling, the soccer ball on the shelf from the game where Rick had scored the winning goal against another youth team from Tennessee.

He tried to escape all the images of his brother that flooded into his mind. They were wonderful memories that now represented only pain and anguish.

The church had filled with mourners. Knowing they would never get inside the church for the service, many more parked along the street and walked to stand outside the church. The sun was invisible in the confused sky. The last few people that were going to be allowed into the church stepped into the doorway. Organ music could be heard on the speakers that had been set up so those outside could hear the service.

The organ got louder, then stopped. After introductory remarks and some humorous and sad eulogies, the minister spoke in his beautiful Tennessee accent. "This morning we come to honor the passing of Mr. Rick Stovic. His wife and daughter, as well as others from his family, are here to ask for comfort. While I do hope we can give his family some of the comfort they surely need, I deeply regret being here this morning. This is not about the tragic death of a man from cancer or an automobile accident, things we have experienced in the past, but rather the death of one of our family here at the hands of another man, someone who acted with evil intent to take his life.

"In the New Testament, at Matthew chapter five, the forty-fourth verse, we are told to 'love your enemies, bless those who curse you, do good to those who hate you.' It is at times like this that such a verse becomes real. It asks us to do something which is not humanly possible. How can we love our enemies? How can we feel anything but hatred or anger toward someone who has decided to walk hand in hand with evil and take the life of a family man who wanted only to live in peace and raise his family in eastern Tennessee? Only with God's help. And before this service ends this morning, I will ask all of you to join me in praying for the man who did this, someone acting of his own accord, with evil intent. Even though he is our enemy, we will pray for him."

He stopped and took a deep breath. "Don't misunderstand me. We must also do justice. And loving someone, and praying for him, does not mean that we do not find him and bring him to justice. I am confident the killer will be brought to justice.

"But today, let us focus on someone else, Rick Stovic, and his family. Let me tell you what kind of man Rick Stovic was."

The flight was much longer than Ismael had expected. He had grown accustomed to flying on Western airlines and found himself listening to every sound the airliners made as he, Khalida, and Madani flew from Algiers to Cairo, then to Khartoum, Sudan. He had never been to Sudan and had looked forward to traveling to Khartoum ever since Chadli said he would make the arrangements. He had grown tired of Madani, but was willing to have him along, even with his inflated belief in his importance. The French-made jet touched down gently. Customs and immigration were almost nonexistent. Ismael, Madani, and Khalida walked through the checks without being stopped and were directed to an old Russian car, which had TAXI painted on the side with a brush. They climbed in, and the car pulled away from the airport.

As they rode down the boulevard toward the center of Khartoum, Madani said, "You have not been to Khartoum before. Am I right?"

"No. Never."

"What do you think so far?"

"It's fine. I don't know. When do we meet?"

Madani took a bite from a small loaf of bread he had brought with him. He looked at Ismael. "It is one of your faults. This impatience. This idea that everything must be done now. It is what has caused you so much trouble so far."

Ismael was tired of being treated like a small boy. "Either you know, or you don't know."

"We'll go when we're called."

"So you don't know."

Madani shot him a hateful look.

They arrived at the small, dingy hotel where they had been told to stay. They went to the room reserved for them and unpacked their bags, which contained only one change of clothes.

They worked in silence in the gray room, where the paint was peeling from the walls. After some time, with no provocation, Madani turned to Ismael. "And when it comes time to speak, you say *nothing*. Is that understood?"

"Then why am I here?"

"Sympathy. We want them to look into the eyes of the brother of the man who was killed."

"You should have brought my picture."

Madani rushed Ismael, grabbed him, and slammed him against a wall. "Do not speak to me that way! Ever! You have no idea what you're doing or who you're dealing with. You come back to us because your brother was killed. Fine. But it doesn't mean you can say whatever tumbles into your stupid little mind. You keep your mouth shut and do what you're told! Now shut up and prepare to pray toward Mecca," he said as he heard the call from the minaret. "The meeting is this afternoon." He let go of Ismael, who fell back against the wall.

**R**at went to Langley to see Jacobs directly after the funeral. It had been a good funeral. The family had seemed comforted and encouraged. It was a sad thing, but it gave them some comfort, which was as much as you could hope for, he figured.

Jacobs looked as if he'd been waiting for him for three days. He was not pleased. "I've been expecting you."

"Yes, sir. I wanted to be at the funeral."

"Even though I told you in my last e-mail that Nezzar was in Algeria?"

"I'm not assuming anything. He may have someone working with him."

"How did this sorry son of a bitch Algerian get to Stovic's brother without being stopped?"

Rat looked at the floor. He had asked himself the same question hundreds of times. "I knew he had a brother, sir. I knew his brother would be at risk. What I didn't think to do was tell the FBI about that. I assumed they would know the person they were protecting, his weaknesses, his family. I'm sorry, sir."

"It wasn't your fault. Rat. Maybe you should have checked on what they were doing, but hey, that's not your job either. We have to work with them. It's just so damned *typical* of them," he said, fuming. "Give them something to analyze, to send to a lab, and they do pretty well. But to anticipate? To think ahead of evil people?" He shook his head.

"Where is he now?"

Jacobs looked up. "Khartoum."

Rat was surprised. "Why?"

"Don't know."

"The Blue Angels have changed their air show schedule."

"I saw that. So?"

"So they've added a show for ten days from now in Paris."

"The Paris Air Show?"

"And guess where the largest community of Algerians is outside Algeria?"

"You're right," Jacobs exclaimed, considering. "You've operated with the French, as I recall."

"Yes, sir. Many times."

"Could you again?"

"Yes, sir, but I'd like it to be in parallel, not necessarily together. They'd need to know I was there and give me some room. You want me to coordinate with French intelligence?"

"That's up to you. You know some people?"

"Yes, sir. But they'll need to hear from you, or the Director, that I'm coming, with some friends. They'll need to stay clear. If we need to do an op, it may be with them, it may not. I don't know if they'll let us operate like that, but that's what I'm going to do, whether they let me or not."

"Just don't run into them."

"No, sir. I need to get back. I've got a lot of work to do."

"Rat," Jacobs said, "I wouldn't count on the Navy

going through with this air show. Once they find out this murderer may be waiting for them over there, they may just take their ball and go home. It might even come as an order from the SECDEF."

"Don't underestimate them," Rat said. "They may fly in air shows, but they're all fighter pilots. They aren't afraid of much. And if they see the opportunity of rolling up a terrorist network just by flying at an air show in Paris, I don't think you'd be able to stop them."

Ismael and Madani were surprised by the loud knock on the door. Madani nodded at Khalida, who opened the door slowly and saw three people waiting in the hall. As soon as the door was open the three came quickly into the room, speaking to them in low tones. They blindfolded the three Algerians.

Madani was furious. "We are your friends!"

"We decide who our friends are. You bring with you one who has been in America for three years? How do you know he is not with the CIA?"

"His brother was *killed* by the Americans!"

"Come with us." They led the three down the hallway of the hotel and out into the loud streets.

Ismael's blindfold was painfully tight. He saw stars whenever he tried to move his eyes. "Where are you taking us?"

"Silence!"

They drove around the city randomly for twenty minutes, then headed toward the outskirts of Khartoum. The ruts of the dirt road jarred Ismael as he sat painfully on the metal floor of the truck. The brakes finally squeaked, and the truck came to a stop. The back opened, and the Algerians were pulled out into the dust that hovered around the truck where it had stopped.

They were pushed into a building, into a cold, dry room, and their blindfolds were removed.

Ismael squinted at Madani. "Why do we have to be treated like spies?"

Madani ignored him and looked around the room, wondering the same thing but trying to act superior.

Ismael leaned back against a wall with his arms folded. They could hear muffled voices, but no one came for them. Ismael slid down the wall and sat in a crouch with his back against the wall. He picked a piece of concrete off the floor and played with it in his hands. Madani paced. They waited for an hour. Just when Ismael was about to try the door out of annoyance, it opened and a man came in. They assumed it was a guard; the man was as young as Ismael.

The man looked at Ismael, then at Madani and Khalida. "You have come a long way."

"We have. We came for . . . help."

The young man had a dazzling, mischievous smile. "Everyone wants our help!" he said, holding out his hands in mock surprise.

"If you are offended by our request, we could leave," Madani said, trying to determine whether this young man was one of the leaders, someone to whom he should give deference.

"No, no. Not after coming all this way. I will hear your request, although I already know what it is you want." He gestured, "Come with me." He led them out the door into the bright sunshine. He walked along the side of the building toward another building. He stopped and looked at Ismael. He was intrigued. "*You* are the brother."

Ismael nodded.

"The one who just came from America."

Ismael nodded.

"You were successful in your objective, there, in America."

"Some of it."

"And you learned much, I understand."

"I could have done better, but I'm here."

The man smiled again. "Being smart doesn't mean you make all good decisions. It means you learn from your bad ones, and make the best of all of them."

"I had never thought of it like that."

"No, of course you haven't," the man said. He went inside the second building and into a cool room with a low table. "Because all the people you have dealt with are much older, right?"

"Yes."

"They always think they are smarter. But in all their experience and wisdom, they never tell you about all the stupid things they did—and survived—that allowed them to be so old and wise!"

Ismael nodded, amused. He liked this young man, just as he had expected he would from what he had been told.

"And they never tell you about the mistakes they *continue* to make. Many of them are much more stupid than you are, but will never let you see that. It would make them lose power over you. Here," he said, indicating the table. "Let us sit down. Here, with us, everything is based on what you can *do,* or what you have *done,* not how old you are. Would you like some coffee?"

Madani frowned, sure that all this insolent man's comments were directed at him, but he nodded at the offer. "What is your name?" Madani asked.

The young man looked into Madani's face for the first time. Ismael thought he detected a hint of contempt. "I go by Salam."

"Well, Salam," Madani asked, unable to contain his

curiosity any longer, "are you the one that we will be dealing with in presenting our request?"

"Much like Ismael here, I have a very technical mind—electronics, explosives, and weapons come very easily to me. After years of working with such things, I have been put in charge of our weapons. When someone comes to us, like you—which is not uncommon—I am the one who decides. Just me. Not a committee." He frowned slightly. "Generally these requests are not well thought out, and are rejected. So it doesn't take long. What surprises us is that people are willing to travel so far to get nothing. But they come from all over the world to ask things from us. We listen. I listen. And I make good decisions."

"You were able to get out of Afghanistan with your weapons?" Ismael asked.

Salam breathed in audibly and paused. "Not all of them. But most. Most of the important ones, and we've been able to replace the rest. So we are doing well."

"Could you be seen when you brought the weapons here?"

"There was no one watching. Of that we are sure."

Ismael was about to say something but held his tongue. Salam was watching him. "You think I am wrong."

"I said nothing."

"You think we have been observed. Can you not see that we are in a large warehouse? No one can see in. No one comes in without escort, and we know everyone. It is very secure." He still saw a look on Ismael's face that showed disagreement. "What is it that concerns you?"

"Satellites."

Salam smiled. "We track all their satellites. We know where they are and when they will pass overhead. We know what we are doing."

Ismael considered saying nothing, but couldn't resist. "Are you aware of the two launches from Vandenberg in California and Cape Canaveral in Florida within the last six months? Satellites USA 164 and 165. Are you aware of those? They joined the others in the American surveillance system, the Advanced Crystal satellites. The California satellite took up a Sun-synchronous orbit at 97.9 degrees around a thousand kilometers. The second was set at 63.5 degrees about twenty-nine hundred kilometers in an Earth-circular orbit. When put with the radar-imaging satellites launched in October of 2001, they give the Americans an ability to photograph *this area* every hour. Are you aware of that?"

Salam stared at Ismael in disbelief. "How do you know this?"

"I pay a lot of attention to things others don't care about. I find it helps prepare me for what I am doing."

"We knew there were new reconnaissance satellites, and that is why we have moved all our operations indoors."

"The weapons boxes I saw stored in the area between the two buildings?"

"They are just boxes."

"They will look like weapons boxes from the sky. The shape and size is unique."

Salam nodded, smiling. "We were talking about how we got out of Afghanistan. After the World Trade Center . . . attack . . . which we had nothing to do with . . . there were a few weeks before the American bombing started. We knew it was coming and moved our operation here to Khartoum. It has been a good home for us. We are keeping our heads down until the time is right."

A boy brought small cups of coffee for each of them.

"How are things progressing in Algeria?" Salam asked Madani.

"We have made much progress. Islam is finally part of the ruling government, something that has not been the case since before the French."

"So now the problems truly begin." Salam smiled.

Madani was shocked by Salam's irreverence. "Islam is the greatest thing that could happen to a country."

Salam's face instantly changed to show he was deadly serious. "You have misunderstood me. I did not mean that Islam brings problems. It highlights corruption and evil much more clearly than any other sort of government. The country can no longer pretend that it will all work out in the end. It is the light of truth. But before the light shines on a country's activity, no one recognizes how corrupt and evil it is. When the light is on, it is obvious to everyone. It makes people think things are much worse. People prefer living in corruption. I'm sure you have seen that."

Madani nodded enthusiastically. "Forgive me for misunderstanding you."

Salam settled back and breathed deeply. "So. What is it you would like?"

"Stingers," Ismael said before Madani took complete control of the conversation.

"For what?"

"To avenge the death of my brother. The pilot who shot down my brother is a pilot for the American Navy flight demonstration squadron. They fly in air shows. The Blue Angels—"

"I know all this. You killed his brother. You have achieved your revenge."

"I want to get the man who did it."

"How?"

"By shooting him down with a Stinger during an air show."

"In America? You plan on doing this in America?"

"In a few days they will perform in an air show outside the U.S."

"Where?"

"Paris."

"Paris?" Salam raised his eyebrows. That was the first thing he had heard that was encouraging. "That is not much time. How do you plan on doing this?"

Madani pulled a diagram from his shirt. He put it on the small coffee table in front of them. "We have a plan. We have spent many hours on it—"

"With Ismael? Has he been part of the plan?"

"He will be one of the shooters—"

"My question was whether he was part of the planning."

"Yes."

Salam looked at Ismael. "Were you?"

"I helped."

"Then you are comfortable with this plan?"

"Yes." They exchanged a knowing glance.

Salam sat forward and asked, "What is that?" pointing to the document Madani had taken out.

"It is a diagram of Le Bourget airport where the air show will be. It is from their web site and shows the display booth locations, the hangars, and the buildings near the airport. I have drawn in lines of sight for the shooters and the proper time to shoot, calculating the speed of the missiles and the time of flight so they all arrive at the same place at the same time, when the two solos cross right in front of the crowd."

Salam looked at Ismael. "Do they carry flares on their airplanes?"

"I have studied their F/A-18 jets and know where the flares are carried. I looked for signs of them on the jets during air shows and saw no indication. Maybe Paris will be different, but I doubt it. And the Stinger is a very smart missile. It works off a different heat spectrum than the usual flare does."

"How do you know this?" Salam asked, testing.

"Research."

"You are right. The Russians dropped flares all over the place when they were shot at with Stingers. It had no effect. The helicopters were shot out of the sky like wingless elephants. But how would you get them into France?"

"I can do that," Madani said confidently.

"You are sure?"

"Yes. I'm sure. We transport many things to France. In large bulk. It is not a problem. There are many Algerians living in Paris."

"Who will be the other shooters?"

"Two who will go with us from Algeria, and we will be helped by some friends in Paris."

"So you have a plan. Now, why should we help you?"

"For my brother," Ismael said. "For the sake of all those who have had the courage to stand up to the United States in the past and have been killed for trying. For all of us to whom America represents what is decadent and evil and hostile to Islam."

Salam shook his head. "It would be unwise of us to sell our Stingers. We cannot get more. We may have a greater need for them in the future. And if one is used, the Americans will know where it came from."

"Will your Stingers even work?"

"Why wouldn't they work?"

"Because the Stingers you have were the ones given to the mujahideen by the CIA in the eighties to fight the Russians. That was a long time ago. The Stingers have chemical batteries that only keep the missile ready to fire for about ten years. So unless you have found adequate replacements for the batteries, they will not work."

Salam shook his head and smiled in amazement. He spoke to Madani. "This one is very bright," he said, indicating Ismael. "You should make sure you protect him. He is an important part of the future." He looked at Ismael. "We have replaced all the chemical batteries of the Stingers we have, and they are in perfect working order. How many missiles did you want?"

Ismael looked at Madani, who spoke quickly. "Six would be perfect."

Salam laughed. "That is impossible. If we were inclined to sell any, it could not possibly be more than one or two."

"Do you have any Russian missiles?"

"Yes. We have purchased many of them on the black market."

"Perhaps we could have some of those as well."

"They are not as likely to hit the target."

"But they might. And we believe the targets are unarmed. No defenses."

"Then they might be of assistance. Do you have money?"

"Yes. We can pay you."

"In dollars?"

"Of course."

Salam nodded and thought. He rocked slightly back and forth as he decided. "You are confident?"

"Yes."

Salam nodded, and stood up. "Thank you very much for coming all this way."

The Algerians stood. "What is your decision?"

"We have never sold Stingers to anyone. I told you that. They are sure to be tracked here."

"You will not help us?"

"We can help you with Russian missiles. They will

do what you need to have done. You can have six of them, assuming you can pay the market price."

"What is that?"

"Fifty thousand U.S. dollars per missile."

"But they are not as reliable. Not as likely to hit the target."

"You said yourself that your targets are unarmed. Defenseless. They will suffice."

"You will not change your mind?"

"What about my brother?"

"He died in a Russian airplane. His vengeance should be sweeter if you achieve success with a Russian missile."

Ismael was deeply disappointed. "The Stingers would almost assure success." He paused.

"A good plan will succeed with Russian missiles. You must just plan more precisely."

Madani realized they had gotten as much as they were going to get. "Thank you for your generous offer of Russian missiles. We will take them."

Salam stood. "Thank you for coming. And as a gift of friendship, one young man to another, I will let Ismael here," he said, clapping him on the shoulder, "have *one* Stinger missile, as a gift. To do to the Americans what they have done to all of us. For the Tomahawks that the Americans rained down on Khartoum under their President Clinton for no reason at all, killing innocent people. It is time for that debt to be paid."

They prepared to leave.

Salam spoke again, "I would like to speak with Ismael alone. You will be going with us for a few days, so please just wait outside."

Madani asked, "A few days? Where? To do what?"

"For training. We will show you how to use the weapons properly. And how to defend yourself from the attacks that are sure to follow your use of the weapons. You need to be fighters. Please," he motioned. "Wait outside for us."

Madani and Khalida walked outside, unhappy about the relationship that was clearly forming between Ismael and this Salam.

When they were gone, Salam turned to Ismael. "What do you know of these two?"

"I've known them for years. They were involved in many of the attacks in the nineties before the new government came to power."

"As were you."

"Some." Ismael shrugged.

"Do you trust them?"

Ismael considered. "Mostly."

"Do you think they are competent?"

"Somewhat. They are very dedicated. Driven."

"That is good."

"Yes."

Salam paced around the room thinking. He stopped. "If they get all these missiles, can they do this thing?"

"Maybe. It depends on how much help we get in Paris."

"They expect a lot."

"Yes, they do."

"Will you go with them and shoot the missile yourself?"

"Yes. I will."

"I do not have the confidence in them that you have. Maybe they will do it. But I want you to succeed." Salam stepped closer until he was inches away from Ismael. He whispered, "When you get to Paris, do not be predictable. Do not go around with them to meet people. Do only what is necessary for the mission. And if it begins to fall apart, don't panic. There may be others there that can help you. Just you." He paused. "Maybe I will make a trip to Paris myself."

Lew Savage checked with the security detail in Pensacola that was assigned to watch the Stovics' beach house. Everything had been quiet. But now they had assigned additional agents to protect Debbie Stovic and her baby, Mr. and Mrs. Stovic, the parents, Debbie's parents, and anyone else they thought might be exposed.

Still, Lieutenant Ed Stovic, the American icon, was the one who was in the crosshairs. Of that Lew had no doubt. He knocked on the door of the pretty house on the beach as he and Patricia waited on the porch. Karen answered the door. "Mr. Savage, Patricia," she said, remembering their names. "Come on in."

They walked in and looked at the house as if they were considering buying it. They were accustomed to apartments or brownstones, not spacious three-story houses with porches that went all the way around and overlooked the ocean. They were impressed. "Nice house," Patricia said.

"Thanks," Karen replied.

"Is Ed here?"

"Yes. He's about to leave."

"Right. We wanted to talk to him about something . . . to both of you . . . about something important."

"Sure. I think he's on the porch in the back."

They followed her across the polished hardwood floors to the back of the house and out onto the wide porch. Stovic was sitting on the steps with the two children.

"Ed, the FBI are here."

Stovic stood up. "Hey."

Lew put his hands in his pocket awkwardly. "Do you have a second?"

"Yeah. What's up?"

"We need to talk to you about something. I don't know if you want to do this in front of the kids. . . ."

"Is it bad news?" he asked.

"Not really. We want to ask you to do something. Karen, actually. It's something we feel pretty strongly about."

"Go ahead," he said. Karen watched them with guarded curiosity.

Lew was struggling. He took a deep breath. "We think Karen and the kids should be taken into protective custody." He saw the startled looks on their faces and put up his hand. "I don't mean in jail, or anything like that, but sometimes when we feel someone is in real danger, we hide them. We have places that are very safe, unknown to all but a few, and staffed round the clock with very capable agents. I don't think this Ismael character is done. I don't think he'll be satisfied with just taking out your brother—sorry. We—I feel that your family is in danger. And I would just cut my wrists if anything happened to them."

Stovic grimaced. "You told me yourself you believe he left the country."

"We do. But I have no confidence in our ability to keep him out. He must have access to very high-quality fake passports and papers. With those, and his looks being fairly average for any number of groups of people, he could easily slip back into the country undetected. The INS didn't have any record of him coming back into the country when we now know he was here for some time."

Karen watched the children walk down the steps to the sand, looking for something. "That's comforting."

"Exactly. I'm not here to give you comfort, I'm here to put the fear of God into you. I don't trust this Ismael character, or anyone he has working for him, to do the predictable thing. We've been burned bad once, and I don't want it to happen again."

Stovic replied. "We had just talked about Karen coming to Paris. Four or five of the wives are coming to Paris. We've never been to Paris," he said. "Always wanted to go. Planned on going when the *Truman* was on cruise, but having kids makes that tough. We were going to send the kids to their grandparents."

Patricia shook her head vigorously. "Bad idea. She needs to be safe until this whole thing goes away. Safety first. You do want your family safe?"

Stovic was perturbed. "What kind of stupid question is that?"

"Sorry. I strongly recommend, sir, that she allow us to hide her away."

"Where would you take them?"

"That remains to be decided, but even when we do, we probably won't tell you. We don't want anyone accidentally telling the wrong person and it getting into the wrong hands."

Stovic looked at his wife. He could read the disappointment and sadness in her face. How long was this going to go on? How long would they have to change their lives to accommodate this threat? "What do you think?"

She hesitated. She didn't want to sound petty. She looked at him. "I wanted to go to Paris. With you. I'm not really afraid. If anyone is in danger, it's you. And you're not changing what you're doing."

"I want you to be safe. Until all this blows over."

"When will that be? And how will we know?"

"I don't know. At least until after Paris. But I don't

want you in danger. I'm always in danger. This just ups the ante a little. With you, though, and the kids? Why put them through that?"

"We could just put the kids in protection of some kind."

"We can't let the FBI watch over our kids without us, can we? How could we live with ourselves? We wouldn't enjoy our time if we knew our kids were somewhere with a bunch of stuffy FBI agents sitting watching television all day. No, thanks."

"When did you want to do this?" Karen asked.

"Today. This afternoon. We'd like you to leave with us. We have a jet waiting at the naval air station. You don't even have to go to the public airport."

"Would I be able to talk to Ed?"

"I'm afraid not. Not until it's over."

# CHAPTER

## 18

St. John sat straight up in her bed. She was sure she had heard the doorbell. She looked at the clock next to her bed: 10:14 P.M. She felt as if she'd been asleep for hours. She got out of bed and threw on a bathrobe, went down the stairs, and peered through the eyehole in the door. There was someone there, but she couldn't make out who it was. She spoke. "Who is it?"

"Pizza."

She hadn't ordered any pizza. "I didn't order any. You've got the wrong house."

"No, I don't. You asked for me."

She tried to figure out what the man was talking about. She turned on the porch light and saw that he was from Roselli's Pizza of Georgetown. She opened the door slightly to look at him better, without the distortion from the fish-eye lens.

"Step back from the door and let me in, or it's going to start looking real awkward real soon." He gave the door a slight push and she let him in. He closed the door behind him.

"Who are you?" she demanded.

He took off his pizza hat and dropped it onto the chair in the foyer. He put the box with pizza in it on the dining room table to his left. "I told you never to ask me to come see you. It's too obvious."

She suddenly realized whom she was talking to. "Why the pizza disguise?"

"So the guys watching your house wouldn't immediately know who I was."

She frowned. "There aren't any men watching my house."

He handed her a two-by-two-and-a-half-inch LCD screen.

"What's this?"

"It's a detachable screen from my digital camera. I took some low-light photos of the men out there. I thought you'd get a kick out of it."

She picked up the small screen and looked at it.

"Push that small button in the lower right corner."

She did. The screen lit up, showing a picture of two men in a car, with the time and date of thirty minutes before. "Did you take this?"

"Yep. In the street behind your house."

"How many are there?"

"I saw three cars. But I might have missed a few. Hit the button on the lower left."

She did and saw that it allowed her to go from one digital photo to the next. She stared in amazement as one photo after another—each with the time and date on the bottom—proved that her house was being watched carefully. "Who are they?"

"Federal agents, I'm sure."

"They have no right to watch me."

"Sure they do. They might even have a warrant. Walker told me they're onto the fact that he's receiving encrypted e-mails. And they can't break the encryption with the NSA, because no key has been provided and it's a 256k bit encryption which they hate. It would take all the computers they've got about a billion years to read one e-mail. So they are very suspicious. They're sure you're the eventual beneficiary of the communication, wherever it's coming from, and since the encryption is clearly trying to hide something, probably were able to convince some magistrate somewhere that you were worthy of clandestine surveillance. They probably have a worm in your computer, waiting for you to load the encryption device. Then they'd know what keys you're typing as you type them, bypassing the entire encryption problem. They've probably tried on Walker's too, but it's harder on a laptop."

St. John knew he was right. "So now what?"

"So you insisted I come here. Here I am. But you've taken a big chance of showing your entire hand. They'll track me. They'll know it's me me within forty-eight hours."

She handed the LCD screen back to him. He dropped it into his pocket. "I'm sorry."

"It's okay. But tell me what's so important."

"I wanted to talk to you about the Blue Angels. About the discussion we were having through the e-mails. I'm going to do everything I can to make sure they go to Paris. That they participate in the air show, and that we *get* the Algerians that are after them."

He nodded.

"And I want you to go over there. I want you to be part of it. Can you operate freely there?"

"I know some people, but I can't go there without authorization—"

"I'm giving you authorization."

He was afraid she'd forget about the government structure someday. "I need to have that confirmed by those at the Agency or DEVGRU."

"That will happen. And Rat?" she said, calling him by name for the first time.

It amused him. "Yes?"

"If you are able to find the Algerian, I want you to feel free to—"

"To take him out?"

"Yes."

"What about the executive order?"

"One two three three three?"

"Right. The one that says you can't assassinate."

"President Bush suspended that. It's never been reinstated."

He knew that, but wanted her to hear what she was asking him to do. "I can't accept such an order from you. It has to come from the right people, and you're not it."

"You'll get your orders. As clear as you want them."

"But first we have to get the Blues over there. We have to smoke out the Algerians before they try something else."

"Couldn't agree more."

He headed for the door.

"If we get to the Algerians, can you finish it?"

"Guaranteed."

"I'll make sure they go to France. There are some who want to cancel the trip. They say it's too dangerous. But these pilots can handle some danger, can't they?"

"I can't speak for them. I think they appreciate the risk, or at least some of it."

"You should make contact with whoever you know in France."

"Okay," he said.

"Let me know if you need anything at all. We can get it for you."

"I'll be in touch," he said. He picked up his hat, put it on, and walked out of her door with his head down, hiding his face.

\* \* \*

Lew and Patricia flew overnight on American Airlines. They landed at De Gaulle airport and hurried to Le Bourget. They were startled by the furious activity to ready the airfield for the air show that was to begin in ten days. They grabbed a Mercedes taxi into the heart of Paris, to the headquarters of the DST, the Direction de la Surveillance du Territoire. The DST had been created in 1944 to "struggle against activities of espionage and against the activities of alien powers on territories under French sovereignty." It had continued to do just that ever since. Since the seventies it had undergone an evolution to concentrate more on terrorism. The subdirectorate Lew and Patricia were going to, one of the five in the main office in Paris, was the subdirectorate of international terrorism.

The office at 1 rue Nélaton was an imposing five-story marble building overlooking the Seine. It dated from the nineteenth century and had been completely refurbished.

They stepped out of the cab into the warm Paris sunshine and walked through the rotating door into the lobby. They had notified the French that they were coming but had given no indication of why. The French had been annoyed but had agreed to meet them when the word *counterterrorism* was used. They understood it could be a sensitive matter.

What Lew and Patricia didn't want them to know, what made it sensitive in their own minds, was the result of their discussions with those at the CIA and FBI about the Algerian presence in France. Pervasive. Throughout the country, growing, menacing; many adjectives, many superlatives, but all pointing to the conclusion that the Algerian presence in France was a large problem and destined to be larger still, especially now that an Islamic regime had taken over in Algeria. It was thought that the Algerians in Paris would be extremely sympathetic to the new Algerian regime and might take it as a signal, direct or indirect, to assert themselves in France itself. Thus far, the Algerian community in France had been more or less quiet. It was also thought that the French were taking a political approach to the problem by denying its existence in public. The official line in France was that the Algerian community was no problem and did not cause trouble. The actual belief was very different.

They crossed to the reception desk and addressed a young woman in a uniform.

"Bonjour," she said.

"I'm sorry," Lew replied. "Do you speak English?"

"Yes. A little. Do you have an appointment?"

"Yes." Lew pulled a small piece of paper out of his shirt pocket. "We are here to see Mr. François Gigard."

"He is expecting you?"

"Yes." Lew glanced around the lobby at the artwork on the walls and the overall sense of quiet. He appreciated what they had done with the building. He returned his attention to the receptionist, who was on the phone speaking French. She put the receiver down and spoke to Lew. "Please show me your identifications, sign this, and I will give you a visitor's badge. You may go to the third floor, please."

They clipped their badges to the pockets of their jackets and rode the elevator to the third floor. A thin, handsome man wearing glasses greeted them as the elevator doors opened. "Good morning. My name is François Gigard."

"Good morning. Lew Savage. This is Patricia Branigan."

They shook hands. François pointed down the hall. "Would you please come this way? I have a couple of other people waiting to see you." His English was nearly perfect. He had a trace of an accent, but it just made him sound more sophisticated. "We are anxious to hear what you have to say."

They followed him down the hallway, and Lew spoke to him from his right. "I'm sorry we didn't give you more information. It's a little sensitive."

"Here we are." He opened a heavy door and they stepped into a lushly carpeted conference room. An old tapestry hung on the wall. A man and a woman who had been engaged in conversation on the far side of the room stood up as they entered. "May I present Elizabeth d'Agnon and Alain le Fort?"

François introduced the Americans. A tray sat in the middle of the table with hot coffee and pastries. They sat around the table.

"So, I hope you had a good flight. Are you rested?"

"Yep. We're fine. Can I get right to the point?"

François nodded. "Please," he said.

Lew pulled out two thin files and put them on the table. "It is our belief that a terrorist attack is going to occur at the Paris Air Show." The French officers raised their eyebrows and focused quickly on Lew. He continued. "You recall when the Algerians asserted rights to the Mediterranean two hundred miles out from their coast?"

"Of course."

"You remember how they sent out airplanes to challenge one of our intelligence planes, near one of our battle groups, which had sailed within the two-hundred-mile zone?" They nodded. "One of the Algerian jets was shot down. The pilot was killed."

"Everyone knows thees," Elizabeth said in a heavy accent as she knocked the ashes off her Gauloise cigarette into the heavy ashtray.

François sat up with a deep frown on his face. "The shooting down of this Algerian jet was so unnecessary.

We felt at the time that it should not have happened. It was too much."

Lew went right on. "The brother of that pilot is a student at George Washington University. He is studying electrical engineering. He has targeted the Navy pilot who shot his brother down. As luck would have it, he is no longer just an ordinary Navy pilot in a fighter squadron; he is now a member of the Navy's elite Blue Angel flight demonstration squadron. The Blue Angels are scheduled to fly in the Paris Air Show. I'm sure you all know that."

"Yes, of course. They have never before flown in Paris. It has been regarded with great excitement and anticipation by our aviation community. The crowds are expected to be the largest ever. There has been much advertising about their decision to come to this air show."

"You see the problem."

"What do you expect this brother to do? You think he will try to disrupt the show? A bomb in the crowd?" Elizabeth asked.

"I think he's going to try to shoot down one of the Blue Angels."

The French officers looked at each other, trying to disguise their horror at the damage this would do to the Paris Air Show. "How do you know that they have this plan?"

Lew shifted in his chair. "We don't really know. It's what I think, based on a few things."

"Have you placed him at any air show?"

"Yes."

Patricia jumped in. "We think he wants to make a big statement. Now that this Lieutenant is a Blue Angel, he can do both—kill his adversary and show the world America is not invincible."

"But why here? Why Paris?"

"He tried to get weapons in the United States—shoulder-fired surface-to-air missiles. We think he was unsuccessful—"

"You think he can get them here?"

"No, but he can get them into France. He was observed in Algiers last week. It is our belief that he has linked up with some very bad actors in Algeria. You may know them." He pushed two photographs across the table.

Elizabeth studied them, then put them down carefully and slid them back across the table. "We know these men."

"You are the ones who told us about them, and we have been watching them ever since. They left the country with Ismael last week. It is our belief that they went to Khartoum to obtain Stinger missiles."

"Stingers?"

"Yes."

François leaned back in his chair and thought, then spoke to the Americans. "Assume everything you say is true. What is it you believe should be done?"

Patricia spoke. "We've got to find him before the air show begins. And anyone else here who is going to help him. You must have contacts within the Algerian community. If we can get to them before they have a chance to get started, we should be able to prevent the entire incident. We also believe it would be extremely advisable to review the security plan for the air show. If they have Stinger missiles, they can be a mile or more away. Since the Blue Angel airplanes are sometimes two or three miles from the center point of the air show, they could be even farther. We'll need to survey the entire area around the airfield, overlay the Blue Angel footprint where their airplanes actually fly, extend that to the range of a Stinger, and look at all the possible locations from which missiles might be fired."

François said, "Such a missile can be fired from the back of a van. It can be fired by a man standing by himself in a field. From a window. From a car, for that matter. They could be driving around in a Mercedes Vito, open the side door, and fire. We will never find them if they are that mobile. But there is a very simple solution."

Lew waited.

"Cancel the Blue Angels performance."

Lew shook his head. "I don't think that's going to happen. I've tried to convince them of that, but they weren't having any part of it. They don't want to be intimidated."

"A smart man knows when to be intimidated," Elizabeth said.

"Their commanding officer is pretty savvy. And he doesn't scare easily. He said if terrorists succeed in making us change what we do, then they have succeeded in fact. He told us it was *our* job to stop this man on the ground. Not his job to abandon his mission."

François was about to speak, but his thought was cut off by Elizabeth. She stood up and crossed her arms as she leaned against the wall. She took a deep drag from her cigarette and exhaled while she spoke through her uneven teeth. "Why can this not be abandoned or postponed? They have never flown in the Paris Air Show before, but suddenly they have to perform this year? Why? Where does thees pressure come from?"

Lew's face grew red. "I'm not sure. All I know is that we have to stop any attack. We're here to ask for your help. This is your territory. But we can offer you help, including manpower, if you accept it."

François drank his coffee slowly as he thought. He made eye contact with the other French officers, who waited for his decision. He placed his cup down carefully on the saucer and spoke to the Americans. "This will require a lot of work. But I must caution you, it is not only the Americans who can cancel this show. If we are unable to find these men, we will recommend to our government that *they* cancel the show. Until then, though, we must think about how to attack this problem. I believe we will need to create an Emergency Committee—"

"Would the DST run it?" Lew said, hoping so. He had great respect for the DST, which functioned much like a combination of the CIA and FBI within France.

"No. It would be jointly run by the Ministries of the Interior and Defense. It is very complex. Rest assured, though, we know how to do this. We will need to talk to others. We will take the appropriate steps."

"We would like to participate. Actively. I believe you should have already received a communication from the Director of the FBI. It is an official request."

"Yes. We knew you were offering your help. Your manpower. But we didn't know why. Now we do. You are welcome to help. How many people do you have available?"

"One hundred special agents from the FBI."

François raised his eyebrows. "Well. That is a lot of people. Any of them speak French?"

"I kind of doubt it."

"We will put them to good use."

"They would like permission to be armed while they are here."

"Of course. That is not a problem. But you could help us by asking the U.S. Navy, *officially,* to cancel this flight. It seems not to be necessary to me. Too much risk."

"I have, and I will again."

François nodded. Elizabeth pushed away from the wall. He said, "We will need to act quickly and decisively. We have many contacts in the Algerian community. Elizabeth knows all of them." He stood. "This could end very badly. We must find them."

Stovic arrived at the Oceana O' Club exactly on time. Rat was waiting inside at a small elevated table on the far side of several pool tables where aviators played and joked together. Anyone looking at Rat would assume he was a pilot from another squadron. Nothing distinguished him from the other clientele. Rat extended his hand across the small table. "How you doin'?"

Stovic forced a strained smile. "Okay," he said as he sat down on a stool. "We got a visit from the FBI guy with the neck in Pensacola."

"What did he want? You want a beer?"

"Yeah."

"What kind?"

"Anything."

Rat disappeared and returned with two draft beers. "So what about the guy with the neck?"

"They stole my wife and kids."

"Huh?" Rat asked.

"They took them into protective custody of some kind."

"When?"

"Yesterday. Took them to some safe house somewhere. Wouldn't even tell me where."

"So much for a romantic trip to Paris." Rat agreed with what the FBI had done, but it didn't make it easy on his friend. He tried to change the subject. "How's your bouncing going?" The Blues were getting ready to go aboard the *Truman* for their transatlantic journey to Paris. They had to operate under the same rules as everyone else. Navy pilots had to stay in qualification to fly off a carrier. If it had been too long, they had to accumulate a number of landings ashore, on a runway painted and lit to resemble a carrier deck, before they could go back out and land on a carrier. It was the same rule for a new ensign in the squadron or the Air Wing Commander. The practice landings were called *bouncing*.

"Good. These guys are all pros. It's not a problem, just something we have to do. Unfortunately, the only time we could get at Fentress to bounce was this morning at 3:00 A.M. I'm beat."

"Better get some sleep tonight."

Stovic thought of sleep. "I haven't been getting much sleep lately."

"Don't let this thing get to you, Animal."

"Easy to say."

"You'll be completely safe on the carrier, then we'll be in Paris for a few days, and it will be over. I think Paris is where our boy will make his move. There's a large Algerian community in Paris. The 18th Arrondisement."

"The what?"

"Paris is divided into sections. Like small communities. The 18th is where there is a bunch of Algerians. Politically, French security has to pretend the Algerians are no problem, but if you ask them in private, they'll tell you the Algerians are a *big* problem. It'll be easy for Ismael to hide in Paris."

"How do you know all about Paris?"

"I've worked with the French counterterrorism guys. They're very good."

"Exactly. That's what I wanted to talk to you about."

"Why? What's going on?"

"When we go to Paris, I don't know, I want to get this guy, Rat. And I want your help. Cause I can't keep flying all these air shows looking over my shoulder for a small white trail from a missile coming up at me. I'm going to run into Oden or fly into the ground or something. I feel helpless, Rat. He tried to ruin my family and is *set* on killing me. But I can't fight him the way I've been trained—he's not going to get into a jet and come up into the sky and say 'Fight's on.' He's going to do it where he feels he has the advantage. I want to take that advantage away from him."

Rat ran his hand through his hair quickly. "How would you see this happening exactly?"

"I have no idea. You must have connections in the intelligence world. I figured you could locate this guy."

"And if I found him, what?"

"Let me know. I'd take care of this guy with my bare hands. If you find him? Call me. I'll come rip his head off."

Rat didn't say anything. He watched the anguish fighting inside Stovic. Rat thought it was mostly guilt for the death of his brother. But it was aggravated by the elusiveness of his enemy. In spite of Stovic's intent, Rat was sure he had no idea what it was like to kill someone up close while you watched his eyes.

"I don't believe in waiting around. I believe in taking the fight to them."

"Sounds real good in airplanes, Eddie. Works different on the ground. It's not as clean. It can get messy."

"Do you still know people in France?"

"A few."

"Weren't you trained as a sniper?"

"What does that have to do with it?"

"You wouldn't even have to get close to him. If you found him, you could set up a long way away. They'd never know what hit him."

"They'd know what hit him, all right. Sniper fire is fairly obvious, especially with the round that I shoot." Rat tapped softly on the side of his glass with his fingers. "Let me give this some thought. Maybe we can work something out. We do know that he's left the country."

Stovic stared at him, amazed. "Seriously? It's safe here now?"

"I don't know about safe. He may have other people working for him. But after . . . your brother . . . he fled the country the next morning. Through Miami."

"So Paris isn't just an idea. He's going somewhere."

Rat nodded. "That's how I see it. But he isn't in Paris right now."

"How do you know?"

"I just do."

"Where is he?"

Rat glanced around. "He left Algeria on an airplane headed east."

Stovic frowned. "To where?"

"Khartoum."

"For what?"

"Stingers."

Ismael bent over, gasping for breath. He had always thought of himself as being in good shape, but nothing had prepared him for the burning sensation in his lungs and the waves of nausea that were flowing through his body. He had expected the training to consist of an explanation of how to use the weapon, how to pull the trigger, not running with an AK-47 across pits and climbing walls.

There was no electricity and no running water, but no one complained. Ever since the War on Terrorism, training bases were mobile and inside—in buildings or warehouses—and almost always in cities, where the risk of getting bombed or being attacked by American Special Forces was much lower. The problem was it allowed many more people the opportunity to sell you out for the right amount of money.

They had been in this camp for two days already. Ismael was sore and tired. They kept them up eighteen hours a day, and other than stopping for prayers, they trained all day. The classroom was a welcome respite from the rigors of the obstacle course and running that the instructors preferred.

Ismael held the AK-47 down below him as he bent

over. He glanced over at Madani and Khalida, who were in worse shape than he was. No one wanted to speak and use up precious air. Their instructor stood next to them. "Come to the classroom. It is time to learn about antiaircraft missiles."

Finally, Ismael thought. He stood up straight, gasping for breath, held his assault rifle in one hand, and put his other hand on his hip to give his lungs their full ability to fill with air. They walked to the "classroom," a low open area in a corner of the cavernous hangar.

They sat on benches and waited while the instructor went behind a curtain. He reemerged carrying two boxes. They were heavy but not so heavy he couldn't handle them by himself. He opened one box, pulled out a device, and looked at the three of them. "This," he said in his accented Arabic, "is a Stinger missile."

The Boss handled all the radio communications of the tightly stacked six-plane formation approaching the *Harry S. Truman*. The other five Blue Angels were stepped closely behind him, down and to his left. They were more conscious of their formation when flying in front of other Navy pilots than they were flying for hundreds of thousands of civilians. The harshest and most valued critics were their fellow naval aviators.

*"Gulf Bravo, this is Blue Angel One, flight of six Foxtrot 18s five miles for the break. See you,"* Boss transmitted.

*"Roger, Blue Angel One. Cleared for the break. You're number one in the pattern."*

All the other squadrons had already flown aboard. Unlike the carrier's other squadrons, the Blues knew they were just passengers, just riding the ship like a ferry. But if the truth were known, they were all excited to be there. There was nothing like flying a jet fighter aboard a moving aircraft carrier. It was something they held in common with only a few people in the world. It could be described, photographed, filmed, and written about, but nothing was the same as experiencing the force of a catapult shot or an arrested landing. It was a fraternity.

The Blue Angels were flying thirty-six inches apart at three hundred fifty knots as they approached the stern of the *Truman* at eight hundred feet, the break altitude for all visual carrier approaches. Hundreds crowded on the bow of the carrier deck among the planes parked there, inches apart, away from the landing area. Numerous others stood on Vultures Row behind the flag bridge or on the signal bridge, all hoping for something different. Every one of them had seen hundreds of F/A-18 landings, but none of them had seen a Blue Angel land on a carrier, let alone all six come into the break at once. Everyone hoped they would do something different, not just cruise into the break and turn downwind like every other airplane that came aboard every day. This was the Blues. They *owed* it to the world to live on the edge of aviation risk, to dazzle with their precision and make the difficult look routine. At the very least, they had to do something different. Those on the carrier smiled up at the sparkling blue jets. Everyone noticed that the formation was opposite the normal formation approaching the break. The second and third planes were always to the right of the lead, so that when the lead broke to the left and turned downwind, they could follow easily. If the wingmen were to the lead's left, as the Blues had it, the lead couldn't break left. They had something up their sleeve.

The carrier steamed at a leisurely fifteen knots into the wind. The fifteen knots of wind blowing over the ocean gave them the thirty knots of wind down the deck they needed to land the jets.

The Blue Angels passed the bow of the carrier. The Boss looked down to his left and, with a clear nod to number two, pushed his stick to the right and started a right-hand roll. He kept rolling until he was completely upside down, and he kept rolling a full two hundred seventy degrees, leaving him directly below the other Blues and in a hard left-hand turn relative to them and the ship. Number two followed the Boss in the dramatic, beautiful, and illegal "tuck-under break" and executed it perfectly, following the Boss at a perfect four-second interval. The other four planes followed precisely, giving those on the carrier a beautiful show of grace and precision.

Stovic was last, and kept exactly the same spacing between his airplane and the other Blues as they turned downwind. He lowered his landing gear and flaps, ensured his tailhook was down, and continued his left turn into the groove. He watched the meatball on the left side of the carrier—the landing lens that showed him where his airplane was on the glide slope. He landed hard in the middle of the deck, grabbed a two wire, and felt the familiar tug of the arresting gear stop him even though his throttles were full forward and the engines were pulling as hard as they could. He reduced throttle, raised his tailhook, folded his wings, and taxied off the landing area.

He was thrilled to be back aboard the carrier. He had completed two Mediterranean cruises on this ship, and it felt more like home to him than his own house did, particularly his new house in Pensacola, where he had spent a total of thirty days since buying it. As he taxied forward carefully at the direction of the yellow shirt, he thought of the empty house and his wife and children being kept somewhere by the FBI. It gave him no comfort at all.

Stovic opened his canopy and climbed down to the

deck. "Welcome back to the *Truman,* sir," the plane captain said grinning.

"Great to be here. Thanks for looking out for our jets."

"To be honest, sir, we're pretty excited to have the Blue Angels aboard here at all."

"We are looking forward to being in Paris, I must admit. And going to sea for a week can't be that bad, can it?"

A Lieutenant approached Stovic standing by his airplane and extended his hand. Stovic took it and spoke first. "Morning. Ed Stovic."

"John Kresner. Let me show you down to the ready room. We'll store your gear, then show you to your stateroom."

"Thanks. What's the movie for tonight?"

Rat strolled casually through the 18th Arrondisement, looking lost. He wore a Jacksonville Jaguars baseball cap and carried an Eyewitness guide to Paris in his hand. He looked like a goofy American tourist. He stopped to examine an old building before turning and walking into his hotel and up the three flights of stairs to his room, which overlooked the main street in the area. He checked his watch, looked around the hallway that surrounded the steel-cage-enclosed elevator, and went into his room.

He closed the door without turning on the light and crossed to the window. He removed his hat and tossed it on the bed. The curtains were old and dusty. He pushed them aside to peer out the window. The street below was full of pedestrians. He could hear North African music. He looked for releases on the window, which had old glass that distorted the images outside. He raised the window and stepped back from the opening. The music and noise flooded into his room. He watched the people on the street through his high-powered low-light binoculars. There was a soft knock at the door.

Rat looked at the bank of monitors in the long trunk sitting on his single bed. He saw who his visitor was. He closed the trunk and crossed to the door. "Who is it?"

"Air France. With your other luggage."

Rat opened the door to see a large man with thick eyebrows carrying a large trunk. "Come on in," he said.

"We apologize for losing your luggage, sir," the man said slightly loudly in English with a heavy French accent.

Rat closed the door behind him as the man set the trunk down in the middle of the floor. He spoke quietly. "Did you have any trouble?"

The man glanced around the room and up at the ceiling. "No. Do you have the money?"

"Yes. Let's have the keys."

The man handed him some keys dangling from a small key ring. "Help yourself."

Rat knelt down in front of the trunk, unlocked it, and lifted the top back. It was tightly packed with foam rubber. Under the foam was a large silver case with a handle. Rat lifted the case out and crossed to the bed. The case had two latches on the ends and two on the side by the handle. He opened all four latches and threw open the case. The blue metal barrel of the rifle looked sinister in the low light. The enormous scope sat in its own foam cutout above the rifle itself. Rat took the pieces out and quickly assembled the Barrett semiautomatic .50 caliber sniper rifle. He held it, felt its balance, slid the scope into place, and turned on the night vision. He clicked off the scope and placed the rifle gently on the bed, with the flash suppressor resting on the pillow.

Rat nodded and went back to the trunk. He pulled out several small cases and inspected the contents of each one. He turned to the man. "It's all here. Any trouble?"

"Not much. Let me know if you need anything else."

Rat took a wad of hundred-dollar bills out of his pocket and handed it to the man. "Here. Count it."

"No need," the man replied, stuffing the wad into his pocket.

Rat took a 9-millimeter Beretta handgun out of its case, checked the bullets in the clip, and rammed the clip into the handle. He pulled the slide back to chamber a round, ensured the safety was on, and slid the Beretta into his belt. "Pleasure doing business with you."

"Likewise."

The large man in the Air France uniform let himself out the door. He said loudly as he left, for those who might be listening, "Let me know if you have any other problems, sir. Air France will make sure you are taken care of."

"Thanks," Rat said, shutting the door behind him. He took out a small cell phone, one of several he had with him, and dialed. It was a digital phone with an encrypted signal that had been sent to him by an old friend.

A man answered. "Oui, allo?"

"Jean," Rat said.

"Oui?" he replied.

"It's Rat."

He switched to English. "Ah, you have arrived."

"Yes."

"Anyone else know you're here?"

"No. Did you tell anyone?"

"Only those you specified. So don't do anything stupid."

"Never. Any scent yet of these guys?"

"Nothing really. We have one man who is Algerian. He heard of some men needing someone for a short time. Some kind of warehouse work. He answered, and we haven't heard from him, which means they haven't let him go since talking to him. They are protecting themselves by never letting him out of their sight. If he has stumbled into them and is able to break free, we may get some intelligence from him, but I am not expecting it."

"Good. I've got a couple of things in the works. Probably be a large American presence here in time, but I'm it right now. Let me know if you need me."

"Yes, of course." Jean Marcel hung up.

Ed Stovic walked into the ready room of the VFA-37, the Ragin' Bulls, the squadron he had left a few months before to become a Blue Angel, and tossed his helmet bag on the ready-room chair. It was as if he'd never left. He glanced over at his chair, the one in which he had been sitting watching a movie when the word came that they wanted him on the *Today* show. He had swollen up so big with pride he could hardly get out of the chair. He had tried not to smile or look as if it mattered, but right then he knew his life was going to change. As he looked at the chair now, he wished he could have that moment back and do it over again. He would choose the inconspicuous life. The standard, anonymous life of a family man who complained about going to sea too much. He wished he had the whole flight back, the whole shoot-down, everything. He had learned too much about himself, things he wished he hadn't discovered.

The pilots who had just flown aboard were filling out their maintenance sheets and talking excitedly as the *Truman* plowed through the Atlantic heading due east. The Blue Angels stood out like flamingos. Their flight suits were royal blue with yellow stripes and had their names and airplane numbers embroidered on their left breast. They looked their usual spit-polish-all-American perfect. The other F/A-18 pilots had the standard Navy pilot look—olive green Nomex flight suits, black or dark brown scuffed flight boots, various patches representing their squadron, and a blue T-shirt representing their squadron's color underneath the flight suit. The Blue Angels felt at home in spite of their obviousness. Every one of them—except Hoop, the Marine—had spent years at sea. The Ragin' Bulls continued to steal glances at their guests.

The commanding officer of the Ragin' Bulls was still Commander Pete Bruno. He was excited to have the Blues as part of his ready room for the week. The Boss, who'd been talking with him since they first entered the ready room, finally said, "I'd like to talk to you about something specific when we get a chance."

Bruno glanced at the flight schedule for the rest of the day and determined he was not flying again until the night launch. "Sure. Anytime. My next brief is at 1700. What's it about?" he asked.

"I may need to . . . borrow some things from your squadron."

Bruno was surprised. "Like what?"

"I was trying to get something requisitioned before we left. They didn't have time to fill it. They said they'd try to get them aboard ship, but frankly, I don't believe they will."

By now Bruno was confused. "What are you talking about?"

The Boss spoke softly. "Flares."

"Pencil flares? Survival jacket flares?"

"No. For the airplanes."

Bruno screwed up his face. "What the hell would you need flares for?"

"We've got a pretty focused threat we have to be ready for. We need to load the blue jets with flares for the Paris Air Show."

"You're shitting me."

"No, I'm not."

The maintenance chief grabbed Bruno's arm and asked for his decision on a detail of plane maintenance as another airplane slammed onto the steel deck above their heads, catching a three wire and pulling it out loudly through the deck from the landing gear machine just a few feet away from the Ragin' Bulls ready room. Bruno gave him an answer and returned his attention to the Boss. "Why don't you just cancel the show?"

"Not happening."

"Anything else?"

"They're shutting the Blues down after this season."

"*What?*"

"This is our last season."

"*Who* made that decision?"

"The same people who will be in Paris to see the first air show demonstration of the Joint Strike Fighter— the plane that just ate the entire Blue Angels budget, without even a belch."

Bruno nodded with complete understanding. "I'll make sure you get the flares."

Bruno looked over his shoulder at the squadron duty officer sitting at his desk in the middle of the ready room. "Hey, Washboard!" he yelled to him. Washboard was so called because he was fifteen or more pounds overweight, mostly in his belly. It was a reference to the washboard abs that no doubt existed somewhere underneath his layer of insulation.

"Yes, sir?"

"Got the movie list? Captain McMahon of the Blue Angels will be selecting our movie for tonight."

"Got it right here," he said as he handed the list to the Boss.

Ismael had expected to arrive in Paris full of confidence and anxious to complete his task. Many of the instructors in Khartoum were convinced that the Blue Angels flying at the Paris Air Show was a trap. They found it very curious that the Blue Angels had changed their schedule after he had become known to them, to fly in a place where they had never flown before, a place that was known to have the largest Algerian community outside of Algeria.

They told Ismael that Western intelligence would be waiting for him. Any misstep would result in his death and the failure of the entire operation.

When Ismael arrived in Paris by airplane from Athens, he went straight to the room that had been pre-arranged for him with an Algerian family. It was over their restaurant, a crowded, noisy restaurant with hundreds of Algerians walking in and out all day and deep into the night.

The night they arrived in Paris, Madani introduced Ismael to someone he had talked about on the way to France—Hafiz. He described him as clever and wise and impossible to fool. It was quite a shock when Ismael first saw him. He clearly slept on the street. His hair was matted and hung in a haphazard style. He had a wispy beard and cold eyes.

Madani had seen the look on Ismael's face. "He is our eyes and ears. Nothing gets by him. He is also able to look like anything he wants, even a professional football player if he is cleaned up. And he was born here." His French was perfect, and he had no North African accent.

Ismael hadn't gone out since their arrival. He had taken Salam's warning to heart. He took all his meals downstairs, hunched over a table facing a wall. He didn't want to meet anyone or see anyone or be seen. He knew the Americans were looking for him.

Madani knocked on Ismael's door.

"Oui?"

"It's me."

Ismael pulled the door open, and Madani closed it behind them. "How are you doing?" Madani asked, quickly surveying the room.

"Well," Ismael responded.

"Come with me."

They walked down the back stairs of the building to a busy street in the middle of the Algerian quarter. Men smoked in small groups crouched on the sidewalk or on small stools. Ismael and Madani headed straight for the Metro stop and descended the stairs. They took the Metro all the way to the end of the line. They walked through a quiet neighborhood to a small building that had a steel garage door that was padlocked. Madani knocked gently on the door three times, then walked around the block to an identical door in the back of the long building. He again knocked three times. He could hear a door being opened from the inside next to the garage door. A boy not more than twelve years old emerged, looked at the two men, nodded, and backed into the dark doorway, gesturing for them to follow him. Madani went in. Ismael looked up and down the dark street and followed him.

The boy closed the door, threw the bolt closed, and padlocked it. They followed him up a steep stairway to a set of offices above the small warehouse. Ismael looked down as they climbed and noticed two delivery trucks, the kind that could pass for a baker's truck, or a plumber's truck or work vans. They reached the top of the stairs and were ushered into a brightly lit office with two desks. Two men sat in chairs; the others either sat on the edge of the desks or leaned against the wall. They had obviously been waiting. The tallest of the group stood and embraced Madani. Madani introduced Ismael, and the other man introduced the rest of the group to both of them.

Madani spoke to the tall man. "Have they arrived?"

"Yes. You have our money?"

Madani removed an envelope from inside his leather jacket. He handed it to the man, who counted out thousands of French francs. The man nodded and placed them in his own jacket pocket. "Do you want to inspect them?"

"Of course."

"Downstairs in the two vans. Two boxes in each van. Take your choice."

Madani turned quickly and headed down the stairs. Ismael followed closely behind him, and the others behind him. Their footsteps echoed loudly on the stairs. The tall man walked quickly to the back of one of the vans and pulled the door open. It rolled up and disappeared into the top of the van. He climbed into the back of it and pulled the handle on a large box, dragging it to the door. It was roughly made but solid. It had several hinges on one side and four latches on the other with a large lock in the center. He unlocked the lid and pushed it back. Between the lid and the weapon was a perfectly flat head of foam. He pulled it up and exposed the olive drab SA-7, Strela-2 Russian-made surface-to-air missile. Madani quickly pulled it out of its box. He placed it on his shoulder, threw two switches, and stimulated the electric battery, which started with a high-pitched whine. He stepped back from the van and looked through the eyepiece. The missile launcher was four feet long, eighteen inches of which was in front of the shoulder. A viewfinder rotated up in front of his eye. He looked through it into the darkest part of the garage and waited for the battery to activate the seekerhead. He began aiming at various things around the warehouse, like the warm engine of the van in which the missile had been transported. He attached small headphones to his ears and listened carefully. He heard a faint, hesitant growl in the missile seekerhead. He looked up toward the office from which they had just come, toward another man standing at the top of the stairs smoking a cigarette. The surface-to-air missile growled hungrily at the cigarette. Madani smiled. He reached up and flipped the switch, turning the missile off. He took it off his shoulder and rested it on the base of the truck again as he stared down the barrel of the weapon. "Flashlight," he demanded of the others. A man produced a Mini Maglight. He turned it on and shone it down the barrel. He could see the missile sitting exactly where it belonged inside the firing tube. He turned the missile around and looked at the exhaust section, noting that the paint was intact. This too had never been used before. "Perfect," he said. "I must examine all of them."

He opened the other three boxes in order and conducted the same evaluation of each of them. "The Stinger?"

The tall man motioned to a metal cabinet at the end of the room where the smoke had drifted from his cigarette. Madani, Khalida, and Ismael opened the cabinet and pulled out the distinctive aluminum box. They watched Ismael's face as they opened the box to reveal a beautiful American Stinger missile that looked as if it had been manufactured that day. Ismael's heart jumped. Madani took it from the case and handed it to him. He rested it comfortably on his shoulder.

"Turn it on," Madani ordered.

Ismael threw the switches by feel. His hours of practice on the Belgian Stinger training device in Khartoum made him completely comfortable with the actual missile. The low hum of solid-state electronics and their displays was audible to Ismael but not the others. He looked through the eyepiece and its sighting reticle. The display was crystal clear and intuitive. He envisioned a Blue Angel airplane above him, a thousand feet away in his sights. He took his finger away from the trigger, turned off the missile, and placed it gently back in its container. "Perfect," he announced.

Madani nodded and looked at the tall man. "You have posted guards?"

"Of course."

"You have enough weapons to defend yourself in case someone tries to break in?"

"More than enough."

"Do you have our weapons?"

"In the back storage room."

"Excellent. Get them." The man hurried away. Madani saw Khalida touching the Stinger, running his hand along its smooth tube, trying to read the English writing along the sides. The man returned and put several weapons on the table. Two other men placed more automatic rifles and hand grenades there. Madani said to the tall man, "I do not need to emphasize the confidentiality that we seek, do I?"

"Of course not."

"If someone were to learn about this, it would be very bad for us all," he said softly.

"I understand."

"Especially for you." Madani picked up one of the AK-47s and placed the banana clip into the weapon. He pulled back the slide and let it slam home, loudly placing a bullet in the chamber.

"Yes. We understand."

"Good. We will be in touch. Do nothing until you hear from me. We will be back to pick up the trucks—" Madani stopped. He looked up the stairs at one of the warehousemen. "Who is he?"

"One of ours."

"He was listening."

"Of course. They are all listening."

Madani stared at the man, who was obviously afraid. "Come here!" he yelled.

The man came down the steep stairs and stood in front of Madani.

Ismael watched.

"What is your name?"

"Omar."

Madani spoke to the tall man without taking his eyes off Omar. "How long have you known this man?"

"Just shortly. We needed another man. I asked around, and he offered."

"How do you know he is not an informant?"

"He has not left here once since arriving. He has had no chance to inform. Why do you antagonize him?" The tall man frowned.

"He was listening. With bright eyes, trying to remember what he was hearing."

"How do you know this?" the tall man protested.

"Why did you offer to work here?"

Omar spoke. "I needed the money."

"How much are you being paid?"

Omar hesitated. He had never asked. "I don't know. I never asked."

"You did this for money, and you don't know how much you are being paid?"

"I'm sure it will be fair. He is a fair man."

Madani saw the fear in Omar's eyes. "Go back upstairs. Now!" Madani yelled. "And stop listening! From now on you don't even look at me!"

Omar turned obediently and hurried toward the stairs.

Shots from Madani's AK-47 rang out and echoed around the small warehouse. The man fell into the stairs, mortally wounded. "He was a spy," Madani announced.

The tall man ran to the fallen man and saw he was beyond help. He turned toward Madani in fury. "You knew nothing about him!"

"Neither did you!" Madani replied. "Get him upstairs. Put him in the freezer." He removed the clip from the AK, pulled the slide back, caught the remaining bullet, and replaced it in the magazine. He placed them carefully on the table. "We will be back."

The tall man nodded reluctantly as two of his other men dragged Omar up the stairs.

Madani, Ismael, and Khalida left the small warehouse and walked slowly back toward the subway station. It was dark and quiet in the neighborhood. There were no sounds except a distant noise from cars and one loud motorcycle. As they approached a deep recessed doorway one block from the warehouse, Ismael heard a whispered voice in Arabic.

"You are alone," it said.

Madani heard Hafiz as clearly as Ismael did, and made no acknowledgment. But they all knew now they had gone in and out of the warehouse without being followed. This Hafiz was showing himself to be very resourceful and valuable, Ismael thought, feeling more secure than he had since their arrival in Paris.

Stovic hurried down the ladder from the 03 level to the VFA-37 ordnance shop on the 02 level aboard the *Harry S. Truman*. He could feel the ship moving under his feet, the reassuring gentle motion of a giant. As an officer in the Ragin' Bulls he had been the ordnance division officer, in charge of the ordnancemen—those in charge of weapons and missiles. Now with the Blues, the Boss had given him the responsibility of going back to the same people to find the flares they needed. Stovic knew it was his burden anyway. He was sure the other pilots felt the same way. They wouldn't need flares if it weren't for him.

Tension had been building ever since the FBI had met with the team in Arizona, ever since they sat in the Boss's room with the noisy air conditioner and learned that a killer was after them, but it wasn't really *them*, it was him. They had all tried to pretend it didn't matter. But he knew, and they knew, it did matter. He could read the conflict in their eyes; the solidarity and brotherhood and steadfastness but also the doubts, the insecurity, and the obvious answer—Stovic could just step down. Or disappear. But they all knew it would be unmanly to ask him to. The better thing would be if he just recognized what they all knew. But he wasn't quitting now. Not when he had a chance to get the man who had killed his brother.

He opened the door to the ordnance shop and looked around. He spoke to one of the men. "Petty Officer Wilson, where's your division O?"

Wilson looked up quickly, recognizing the voice. "Hey, Lieutenant Stovic. How have you been?"

"Great, thanks. You have a division O?"

The men looked at him with amusement. Wilson spoke. "Sure, but I've never seen him down here."

"One of those."

"Yes, sir. One of those. Anything we can do for you, sir?"

"I'm in the market for some flares. Skipper has already authorized it, I'm told."

"We've got enough flares for an Italian soccer match," Wilson said. "I'll load them aboard your airplane myself."

"Thanks. I'll put our guys in touch with you."

"Yes, sir. Happy to help." Wilson stopped him. "Can I ask you something, sir?"

"Sure," Stovic replied.

"Which kind of flares do you want?"

Stovic smiled. "I guess I figured we only had one kind. I don't recall us having a lot of options when I was the division officer."

"There are about five types, sir, and we only have one or two. Do you know which ones you need?"

"I guess I don't."

"What's the threat?" he asked.

Stovic didn't really want to say, but he had to. "Handheld SAMs. Not sure which ones, so probably need to cover Russian and . . . American made."

Wilson looked perplexed. "American made?"

"Stinger."

"Ouch," he said. "That makes it harder."

"I'll say. But frankly, I didn't think about which flare we'd need. Where's the secret supplement that shows the flare types by threat?"

"It's in the safe."

"Would you get the Gunner to give me a call? We need to pull that out and see if we've got the right ones. We're playing catch-up right now, and I'm not sure we've got enough time if you guys don't have them."

"We'll turn the ship upside down, sir. We'll find the right ones for you. They've got to be on board somewhere."

"Thanks." Stovic took out a piece of paper and wrote a number. "Here's the phone number of my stateroom. If you could get him to call me right away, we can start finding out how big a problem we have."

"Will do, sir."

Stovic turned and rushed up the ladder toward the ready room.

The other four men had left at odd intervals over the last fifteen minutes. They had gotten their brief from Rat and knew what they had to do. Rat put on his windbreaker against the fresh rain that was falling and stepped out of his Paris hotel into the 18th Arrondisement. He assumed Ismael would at least pass through the district at some point; it was inconceivable they would use all imported help. He had memorized Ismael's photos. He had long ago distributed copies to his team. They all knew exactly what to look for, including likely disguises, facial hair, haircuts, bleach, all the ways of changing one's appearance.

He waited outside the Metro for two of his men. His expert eyes searched the faces of all the people streaming out of the Metro stairway behind him. He wore wool slacks, Italian shoes, a black mock turtleneck with a sport coat, and designer glasses. He looked like a sophisticated European businessman.

He saw his two men come out of the subway but did not acknowledge them. He turned and walked up the sidewalk like a man going to an appointment at a local restaurant, an adventurous restaurant off the beaten path that had been recommended to him by the CEO of an Albanian shipping company. The sounds and smells were distinctive and placed him back in North Africa, where he had been so many times. On the other side of the street was Robby with his now closely cut hair and the gait and accent of an Ethiopian. Behind him was one of Robby's squad, a short, squat Argentinean-American who spoke French with the distinctive accent of a Spaniard.

No one who wasn't with them could possibly know

they were conducting a sweep of the street, looking for Ismael or any hint of him. Rat walked with steady determination, looking around only once in awhile, as if walking through a neighborhood that didn't interest him very much. Robby and his man were still across the street, behind him.

They were now in the heart of the 18th Arrondisement. The lights were dimmer and less reliable. The establishments were peeling and in disrepair.

He walked by a man squatting on the sidewalk and stepped around him. The man looked up at him and made eye contact, then quickly averted his eyes. Rat felt it but continued walking, trying not to look back at the man. He raised his hand to his glasses, marking the man on the sidewalk.

Robby looked from across the street and took a quick photo with the digital camera hidden in the plastic shopping bag dangling from his left hand.

The captain stopped the enormous carrier in the glassy Atlantic Ocean. One of the ship's motor whaleboats was quickly lowered into the water with its white canvas cover. It would be the center point for the air show. All the people on the carrier who weren't on watch and could otherwise be spared had been given exactly one hour off and invited to the flight deck to observe something that had never before occurred—a Blue Angel air show in the middle of the ocean for a private audience. The six blue jets were catapulted off the deck, and three thousand men and women hurried onto the flight deck behind them. The sun was brilliant and high in the sky. The ocean was dark blue, slightly darker than the jets coming from the right of the carrier, the direction the bow was pointing.

The pilots in the diamond formation crossed from right to left in their first pass. The sailors and officers of the *Truman* smiled and cheered as the air show got under way. The announcer, #7, Lieutenant McKnight, was on the 5MC, the PA system built into the flight deck at every corner. It was the loudest PA system imaginable, designed to be heard over jet noise and through sound-protective helmets. It was usually used by the Air Boss to yell at someone: "Get out of the catwalk!" or "Heads up on the flight deck, props and jets are turning!" They had turned the 5MC down slightly so that Knight's announcements didn't deafen the audience. Knight stood on the flight deck in uniform. He stared at the crowd through his aviator sunglasses with his back to the ocean. Directly behind him the motor whaleboat kept its position as the center point of the show. The admin officer stood behind him with a handheld radio, keeping Knight on time to the second.

With his head unmoving, never looking for the Blue Angels in the air, Knight began his narration in exactly the same way he always did: "Goooood afternoon, ladies and gentlemen!"

Stovic hovered three miles away and watched the diamond formation approach the carrier from its bow, to the right of the officers and sailors standing on the flight deck. He began playing the tape of the air show in his mind. It allowed him to go through each step as if he had done it a thousand times, and he could concentrate on the smallest details; it gave him comfort and pushed everything else out of his mind.

He spotted Oden five miles away as he began to position himself for the takeoff "dirty roll." Stovic waited, then began his descent toward the water. Their normal altitude—twenty-five to fifty feet over the runway—was raised to a hundred feet so they wouldn't be below the crowd. The carrier deck itself stood seventy-five feet above the water.

Stovic simulated streaking down the runway on his

own takeoff, then as he reached the aft end of the carrier did his first maneuver of every air show. He pulled back hard on the stick and rocketed up away from the ocean. The moist air condensed into white vapor on top of his wings and spilled off behind him. He pulled away from the earth and watched the carrier recede in his rearview mirror.

On their next pass Stovic turned quickly toward the deck of the carrier. He spotted the motor whaleboat at the center point and judged that they would pass almost directly over the top of the boat. He picked up Oden, now head-on to him on the horizon. He aimed directly at Oden and waited until they were less than a half mile apart, when he took a very minor offset from Oden to ensure they had sufficient distance to avoid hitting. He kept his throttles completely forward, just short of afterburner, giving his jet sufficient power to push him to six hundred knots. They closed quickly, and he heard Oden's familiar transmission: "Hit it!"

Stovic threw the stick to the right. He went into a ninety-degree angle of bank—a knife-edge pass—at exactly the same time Oden did. They passed exactly parallel to each other directly over the center point. It was as close to perfect as such a pass could ever come. He heard the call, and he leveled his wings and pulled up as the Blue Angel diamond came back around to perform its next maneuver in front of the *Truman* crew.

For Stovic it was a glorious day, the reunification of everything he loved in the Navy. He was able to fly his jet off a carrier with his friends in a private air show in front of his family. As he rolled over on his back and looked at the ocean, he pulled the G forces once again that kept him coming back, and headed toward the ocean. He fought the thought that began to intrude in his conscious mind, that perhaps this would be the last time he would ever finish an air show with the Blues.

* * *

The Emergency Committee had been formed, and several members from each of the seemingly endless and overlapping French security and military organizations were now present at the first coordination meeting. The large conference room in the Ministry of Defense was humming. Most of the people knew each other and enjoyed getting together. They greeted the American FBI special agents and spoke to them in French or occasional English, but never enough for Lew and Patricia to get a good feel for what was going on. Present were representatives of the gendarmery—the French police—and their counterterrorism strike team, the GIGN—Groupe d'Intervention de la Gendarmerie Nationale. Also, represented by a tall dark officer, the Police Nationale and their equivalent group, the GIPN, Group d'Intervention de la Police Nationale. François and Elizabeth were there for the DST, and to the surprise of many, also represented was the equivalent for intelligence outside the country, the DGSE—Direction Général de la Sécurité Extérieur.

François was trying to translate and explain, but Lew and Patricia were lost. François leaned over and said to Lew quietly, "The biggest question everyone has is whether these Algerians are after only the Americans. If they are, then the consensus is to simply ask—or tell—them not to fly. But there is a building consensus that Algerians with surface-to-air missiles in Paris are dangerous no matter what. We may *think* they're after the Blue Angels, but what if they change their mind? What if the Blue Angels decide not to fly, so they decide to shoot at someone else? This is unacceptable. So this debate now goes on, as to whether," he struggled for the English, "whether to cancel the entire air show. If we do, we are giving in. But if we don't, they may create quite a disaster. So we find ourselves where you did when you got here. Trying to move forward with very good decisions and try to keep everything as close to normal as possible."

Lew nodded. He was impressed. But he also realized they didn't have any magic answers.

"We are going to concentrate our initial efforts on the Algerian community in Paris. We expect it to be a rich area for information."

Lew tried to turn his head to look at him, to thank him for including the FBI, and to thank him for translating some of the conversation. But he couldn't turn his head at all. He felt terrible, and the pain medication hadn't cut the edge off the nearly unbearable pain that he was usually able to control. It was all he needed, he thought. For his neck to start taking over his life again just when he needed to be doing a million other things. He took a deep breath against the pain and fought back a grimace. "I hope you're right."

Ismael and Madani walked into the back room of an apartment above a discount camera store. What could not be seen from the street was the substantial security that protected the nondescript apartment. Members of the security detail were placed in various positions around the block. And there was the ever-present Hafiz, posing as a street beggar, kneeling on the sidewalk watching passersby, the same man who had looked Rat in the eye twelve hours before.

The early morning meeting was as unusual as it was important. It was the first time Ismael had been to this apartment; he felt privileged to be in the planning session. There were four others he had never seen before. They greeted Madani and Khalida warmly, and everyone gathered around the table. Ismael crossed to the table and stood between two of the men he had only just been introduced to. He was shocked to see what sat on the table—a scale model of the airport that covered the entire table. The runways crossed in the middle in an odd shape, with the tower and passenger terminal clear on one side. Even the roads leading to the airport were obvious on the model. Buildings stood two or three inches up from the base; every building was shown out to three miles.

"Where did you get this?" Ismael exclaimed, his eyes trying to take in the entire model at once.

Madani glanced at him but didn't respond. "Before we discuss the plan, you said you had something to report, Hafiz."

Hafiz glanced around anxiously. His life was that of an informant. His nervousness manifested his constant discomfort and insecurity. "Someone is here. They are looking for us."

"French?"

He shrugged. "Of course. They are doing their usual search. They have their agents out looking, but we know most of them and are quite sure they are not close."

"Someone else?"

Hafiz nodded. His eyes were wider than usual. "He is different. American."

Madani nodded and looked at Ismael, who was growing concerned. "So the Americans have arrived. FBI, no doubt."

"I don't think so, but maybe."

"CIA?"

"This one is . . . different. An intelligence operative of some kind. He looks dangerous. I am . . ." He was about to tell the others that he was afraid of this American, but he knew he would get not sympathy but ridicule for having such fears.

"You had an idea?" Madani interrupted his thoughts.

"Yes. But I do not feel free to discuss it," he said, moving his hands awkwardly as he glanced at Ismael.

"He is one of us. Speak freely."

"I do not speak in front of anyone I do not know. I have never worked with him."

"It is all right. It was his brother that was killed by the Americans."

Hafiz quickly understood. "I think you should allow me to take care of this in my own way, to cause the circles to . . . overlap."

"You can do this?"

"I am confident."

"Then do it."

Ismael was confused. "Do what?"

Madani looked at him. "It does not concern you. He uses information as a weapon. He is very effective."

Ismael was put off. "Tell me the plan for the airport."

Madani nodded. "It will be difficult, but it can be done. Here is what we will do." He pointed to places at the airport. "We will have five independent shooters. We will not talk with each other after the night before. We pick up our missiles in our vans, drive independently to our positions, and fire at the same time. You," he said to Ismael, "have given us a chart that shows exactly when that will be, and it is based on when the four American jets take off. Start your watches then. As you can see from the time marked, it is at that time we shoot. It's not based on the clock but the air show. It's up to each of you to get there, get in position, and fire. They may change the time of the air show, they may change everything. But once those four airplanes take off together, start counting." He took a deep breath, envisioning the event. "We will shoot the two solos as they approach the crowd. If we succeed, the Americans will crash in fire into thousands of spectators for the whole world to see." He stopped and lay the pointer down on the model. "Any questions?"

"Yes, sir?" Sarah St. John asked as she stepped into the family quarters of the White House, a place where she was rarely invited. The Secret Service agent looked at her quickly and looked away.

"Hi, Sarah. How are you?"

"Fine, sir," she said. She nodded at the First Lady, who looked at her with some content that St. John didn't immediately translate. "Good evening," she said to her.

"Hello," the First Lady replied. They both stood up from the beautifully set dinner table.

"I'm sorry. I'm interrupting your dinner. My timing is horrible. I just received your message and came right away."

"No problem. We were just finishing," President Kendrick replied, glancing at his wife. "Come in, come in."

The First Lady disappeared into the family room two rooms away. "Sit down," Kendrick said pointing to the dinner table. Two men had removed the dishes and the tablecloth.

St. John sat. "What can I do for you?"

Kendrick looked at her and frowned. "I was answering your message. You said you had something to tell me."

"Oh, of course. Sorry."

"So what is it?" Kendrick asked, clearly intent on going on to something else quickly.

She reached into the pocket of her suit coat and handed him the digital camera screen Rat had left with her. "Here."

He took the small LCD screen and looked at it. "What is this?"

"Turn it on." She reached over and showed him the button.

The first picture came on. Two men sitting in a car in front of her house. The camera angle showed the men and the house. He recognized the house immediately. He had been there several times. "What's this?"

"Look at the others. That button . . . there."

He went through the photos, then looked at her. "When were these taken?"

"Just the other night."

"Who are these men?"

"I'm not sure exactly, but I am confident that they've been placed there by Howard. He doesn't trust me. He has tapped my phones, followed me, and taken illegal steps to—"

Kendrick tossed the screen over to her. "Why is it you two can't be on the same team? Why this lack of trust? He thinks you're running some private intelligence operation." He paused. "Are you?"

She sat silently for too long.

Kendrick leaned forward. "What is going on?" he asked quietly. "I haven't raised it, but it's time. Tell me about the encrypted e-mails Walker gets and gives to you. Who is sending them?"

"It's not what you think. I get some information from friends in the government that is probably unorthodox. I'm a believer in raw intelligence." Her eyes grew intense. "That's why I don't completely trust the CIA, or the DIA, or the NSA, or much of anyone else. They always have their own agendas. I don't try to get *everything*, and I do listen to the intelligence agencies." She leaned forward. "But haven't you ever wondered what they're doing that even you and I don't know about? Because they don't want us to know, and because it allows them to build their own little empires? Well, I do have a few . . . friends in certain places that give me information. Straight information. *Direct* information. It's the best stuff out there. And I use that information. And we're better off because of it. My friends are very well placed. Nothing major happens that they don't know about."

He pointed at the small screen on the table in front of her. "One of your friends?"

"Yes, sir."

Kendrick stared at her. She had never felt this scrutiny from him. It was usually directed at others. It was unsettling. He asked her, "How much confidence do you have in your friends?"

"A lot."

"Who is it?"

"I promised him I wouldn't reveal it. There's nothing wrong or illegal about it, but it might be contrary to the chain of command."

Kendrick waited, letting her consider the implications of not telling him. "Who?"

"It's a Navy SEAL, a member of DEVGRU who is TAD to the Agency, working with the SAS. A Lieutenant."

"Kent Rathman."

She was stunned. "How did you know?"

"Stuntz told me. Those guys he photographed also photographed him in his pizza outfit. Once they knew who it was, they backed off."

She looked down at the carpet, feeling small. "I'm sorry. I shouldn't have thought I could do this well. I just wanted good information, not just the things some agency *wanted* me to know."

Kendrick gave a small, ironic smile. "Perhaps you should let me know what your friends say, when it seems important to you."

Her relief showed immediately in her face. "I'd be happy to, sir."

The six Blue Angel pilots sat in their jets on the deck of the *Truman,* surrounded by numerous Navy planes painted flat gray, waiting for the first launch of the morning. The Blues were to be the first airplanes off the carrier. The day was chilly, which gladdened the hearts of the aviators. Planes flew better in colder air—more "lifties," as they said. Lieutenant Ed Stovic lined up behind the No. 2 catapult in Blue Angel #6. The Boss was on the No. 1 catapult in front of him and to his right, with Oden right behind the Jet Blast Deflector—the JBD—for cat one. The other three Blues were on the other bow cat, number two, and the two waist cats, three and four.

Everything was ready. They waited for the clock to hit 0600, when the Boss would be thrown down the catapult and into the sky, with number two following four or five seconds behind him. The team was excited. The other members of the traveling Blue Angels team were aboard the COD, the Carrier Onboard Delivery plane—the Greyhound, as it was called—to fly directly to Le Bourget. Most of the other normal Blue Angels supplies had been flown by C-17 cargo plane from Pensacola to Paris. The usual transport for the Blue Angels, their C-130—Fat Albert—had been left at home.

The catapult officer stood on the deck between the two Blue Angel F/A-18s. Although he wouldn't admit it, he was excited about launching the Blue Angels. He usually stayed inside the glass bubble buried in the deck and launched from its warmth with a cup of coffee in hand. But when the Blue Angels were around, everybody raised their game to a different level.

Stovic had been in this position hundreds of times before. He sat on the catapult with all the hot jet engines screaming around him. Steam swirled through the turbulent air over the flight deck. The bow of the carrier moved down toward the ocean two hundred feet in front of him, stopped, then headed back up toward the horizon. Thirty knots of wind raced down the flight deck forcing the men and women on the deck to lean forward fifteen degrees to avoid being blown over. It was the most exciting place on earth. He loved sitting there on top of the largest warship ever built, piercing the Atlantic as they headed east.

Against all the grayness of the carrier, the ocean, the sky, and the Navy gray airplanes all around, the Blue Angel planes stood out with their high-gloss royal blue and yellow paint schemes. Unlike everyone else in naval aviation, they *wanted* to be seen.

Stovic's attention was drawn toward the Boss as the JBD, with its large steel deflectors, was raised up behind his jet to deflect his jet exhaust skyward instead of into Oden sitting right behind him. He could hear and feel the Boss's engines as they went to military power, then afterburner. The catapult officer pointed toward the bow and rotated his hand above his head to tell the Boss to keep his engine at its highest power. He looked at everyone involved and received a thumbs-up from each of them. He looked back at the Boss, received a sharp salute, returned it, and watched the bow of the ship. He leaned forward hard in a near crouch with his left hand extended, like a fencer piercing his target, and watched the bow of the carrier move back up. At exactly the right moment he leaned forward and touched the deck with his left hand. The petty officer on the side, watching him like a hawk, pushed the button and the catapult fired. The Boss's Hornet raced down the catapult track, taking it to one hundred forty knots—one hundred fifty-nine miles per hour—in just over two seconds. The huge ship shuddered slightly as the catapult piston slammed into the water-break at the end of its stroke. Steam rose out of the catapult track as the Boss raised his landing gear and accelerated over the water away from the carrier in a right-hand clearing turn.

The same sequence was repeated for Blue Angel #2, and the yellow shirt motioned to Stovic to taxi forward. He released his parking brake and taxied toward the catapult, steering the nose of the Hornet with the rudder pedals. The double nosewheel straddled the slots in the deck where the shuttle ran. The yellow shirt straddled the slot and motioned Stovic forward. The steam rose up between his legs and engulfed him, almost rendering him invisible. A young sailor ran up to Stovic's aircraft on the side and held up the weight board that showed the weight of the Hornet. It was correct. Stovic gave him a thumbs-up, and the sailor showed the weight to the catapult officer and to the petty officer sitting inside the bubble, who would set the catapult for the right weight.

As Stovic approached the shuttle he lowered his launch bar. The yellow shirt brought his hands together slowly, and Stovic moved into position. His launch bar dropped across the shuttle, and a petty officer scurried under the nose of the Hornet to attach the holdback bar. As the quality assurance people scrambled around the jet to ensure he didn't have any leaks or other obvious problems, Stovic ran through his cockpit checks. He checked his caution and warning lights, circuit breakers, and engine instruments. Everything was on line and working. He looked up at the catapult officer, who was waiting for him.

Stovic was struck with how safe he felt. Flying off carriers might be among the most difficult and dangerous flying there was, but at least no one could get to him there. There was no Ismael under the bow in a rowboat with a shoulder-fired missile. There was no Ismael flying toward the carrier in a Cessna loaded with explosives, or aiming a rifle at him from some stationary position nearby. The entire battle group was designed to keep the carrier's planes secure and ready to strike out. Anyone trying to approach the battle group to do the Air Wing harm, or Stovic, as he saw it, or his stereo, as they had often joked in the staterooms, would have to come through a multilayered defense of fighters, surface-to-air-missile–firing destroyers and cruisers, and guns before ultimately facing the enemy it sought—a Navy F/A-18, one of the most difficult fighters in the world to attack successfully. It was a good feeling to have that kind of protection and security. It was how the entire system of naval aviation was designed. To protect the tip of the spear.

But the Blues were different. They were exposed. As soon as they launched off the carrier and headed east to Paris, they would fly out from under the umbrella. All this protection would be left hundreds of miles behind. No cruisers, no surface-to-air missiles to defeat his enemies, no guns to stop low-flying missiles, no electronic warfare black boxes operated by specialists, no Air Wing or other armed aircraft to help. Just the unarmed shiny blue jets in their "Hey! Over HERE!" paint scheme, exposed before the whole world to convey the nature of naval aviation and the skill and precision it required. It was like a President in an armored limousine, surrounded by Secret Service, stopping along a motorcade and stepping into the crowd with a big smile and a distinctive hat.

The catapult officer turned two fingers over his head as he slid his right hand forward, facing Stovic on the right side of the plane. Stovic felt the pull of the shuttle against the launch bar on the nose gear of the Hornet, ready to pull it off the deck. He checked his flight controls, took a deep breath, said a prayer, gave the catapult a crisp Blue Angel salute, and put his head back against the headrest. The catapult fired, and his Hornet flew down the catapult track and off the deck.

As soon as the acceleration stopped, Stovic raised his

landing gear and flaps and did his clearing turn. He climbed to five hundred feet and leveled off.

He waited until seven miles, pulled up to six thousand feet, and came back over the carrier to rendezvous. They were flying in a tight formation—not as tight as they would at an air show but much tighter than any other group of F-18s might even think of flying.

"*Strike, Blue Angel One, flight of six, departing,*" the Boss said in his always casual voice.

"*Roger that, Blue Angel One. Your vector is 084 for three hundred twenty miles. Stay button eight until transferred to Le Havre control.*"

"*Roger that. Switching button eight.*"

"*Have a good flight. Go Navy.*"

"*Roger. Switching.*"

The Blue Angels turned east and waded into the crowd.

The two Frenchmen wore the clothes of truck drivers. One, Gerard, forty-five, had gray stubbly hair. The younger one, Alain, who looked more English than French, was small and thin. Both looked hard and unshaven. They concentrated on Hafiz in the dark corner of the dingy café. The night was pleasant, and most of the café's clientele were sitting outside on the sidewalk, within easy sight of the Frenchmen and directly behind Hafiz. Gerard spoke first. "Several men have just come here from Algeria. Probably this week," he said in French.

Hafiz looked like someone who might have insects crawling on him, like someone who had been living on the street for months. Over time he had established some credibility with French security, but they regarded him mostly with skepticism. The one thing he had going for him was that his information to them had always been perfect. Elizabeth had been leaning on them to develop some intelligence. She had nearly ripped them in half with their lack of any leads on the whereabouts of the Algerian everyone knew was in Paris. They didn't like this Hafiz character, but they had to start taking some risks.

Hafiz waited for the rest of the information, but there wasn't any. "That's it? Men who got here within the last week?" he replied in his own perfect French. He feigned disgust. He had to work it just right to dribble out the information he wanted them to have. If it was too easy they would be suspicious of the information. If he sold it well, French security would rush off and do exactly the wrong thing. "*Hundreds* of men each week come here from Algeria. Some stay, some—"

"These are not just *men*," Gerard spat. "If *you* do not know, then you know nothing, and we shouldn't be paying you one centime!"

"I know *everything* of importance. If I don't know about them, then your information of their importance is wrong," Hafiz said. He looked over his shoulder, calculating the exact amount of time to look, then turned back. "There is *something* happening. I can't really tell what it is. I just watch. I tell you what I see. And something is happening."

"What have you seen?" Gerard asked, trying to control his excitement.

"A lot of activity."

"What kind of activity? I need specifics."

"I just tell you what I see—"

"So what have you seen, for God's sake?" Alain asked.

"Several men that I do not recognize. I have not seen them before. Their clothes tell me that they are here directly from Algeria. Lots of activity and . . . security."

"What you mean, 'security'?"

"Many eyes," Hafiz said.

"Eyes?"

"People watching. You know, the kind who are looking out for someone else. There is always some of that. But now? It's everywhere. They have probably seen you."

"Let me worry about that. Tell me what else you have seen."

"I have seen them taking weapons—guns and other things—into one place."

The officers' eyes got big. "What kinds of weapons?"

"Hard to say. Sitting on the street, you can't walk up to them and say, 'What's in that long skinny box that's so heavy?' "

"Long boxes?"

"And assault rifles. Some right out in the open, right from trucks into a hotel. Then I watch where the lights come on."

"You think it's where they're storing their weapons?"

"Oh, I doubt it's a storage place. Too small. Too public. But there are a lot of weapons in that place. What I don't know is what they are going to do." He hesitated and appeared to think about what he was saying. He groped in his clothes for a cigarette stub. He looked at the ashtrays on the other tables in the café and was about to get up to snag a promising cigarette butt two tables away when Gerard disgustedly gave him one of his own cigarettes. Hafiz lit it with a book of matches he produced from an unexpected pocket inside his clothing. "Maybe what they're going to do is something I would approve of. Maybe I shouldn't be telling you about them. Unless you're going to make it worth my while."

"We have been paying you. And we already agreed to pay you more if you provided *useful* information instead of some of the dung we get from you. So far your information is something you would read on a bathroom wall. It is worthless."

"I have found probably the very thing you're looking for. What I don't have is the money you should pay me to find out where this all is."

"How much money did you want?"

Hafiz nodded. "This is what you're looking for, isn't it? I can see it in your eyes," the Algerian said as he leaned forward within a few inches of Gerard's face.

"You smell like a pig."

"If you want information from people who smell nice and go to the opera, you should be asking *them* your questions. I'm sure they would be—"

"How much?"

"One hundred thousand francs."

The officer stood up to leave the coffee shop. "Never mind."

"You did not have in mind to pay for this valuable information? This could get me killed!"

"I'll give you ten thousand francs."

"That's not even close—"

"Ten thousand francs. That's all you're ever going to get. Tell us or don't, but that's what I've got." Gerard took ten colorful French notes out of his pocket, each worth one thousand Francs, and slid them across the table. "And once I hear what you have to say, if I don't like it, I'll take my money back. If the information is good, and we get who we're looking for, I'll give you another twenty thousand francs."

Hafiz knew that was as good as it was going to get. He took the money greedily and slid his soiled hand holding the money deep into the folds of his clothing. He relished the idea of the chubby, middle-aged Frenchman trying to take the money back from him. He loved being in disguise—looking stupid, unkempt, dirty, and desperate. He was none of those things. His eyes darted around to the mirrors in the café to look at as many people as he could, to evaluate the risks. "You can't tell anyone where you got this information," he said soberly. "If they find out, they will kill me."

"Why would I care about that?"

"Because there are more of them than just what I'm going to tell you now. You may get some of them, but if you want all of them, you'll still need me."

"Tell us what you have."

Hafiz glanced around and began speaking in a whisper. "I followed one of them to a hotel. I even went upstairs as if I was drunk and lost, looking for a corner to sleep in, and watched what room they went into. I'll tell you the hotel and the room. But first, I must caution you, they have been very clever. They are using a cover. An American—"

"An American?"

"I think. I have not heard him speak. He is American looking, trying to pose as a tourist. I have it from other sources that certain weapons have already been delivered to him, and he is some sort of weapons specialist for them, maybe a specialist in Stinger missiles? Aren't they American?"

The Frenchmen looked at each other. Very possible, but they were still skeptical. "Where?"

"The Hotel d'Afrique du Nord."

"Yes."

"Fourth floor."

"What room?"

"The one facing the street."

Gerard studied his face. He said softly, "If you're lying to us, I will personally track you down and rip off your balls with pliers."

"You think I'm stupid? You think I would take

money from the DST and lie to you? My life would be worth nothing."

Gerard stood. "I couldn't have said it better myself. I'll be in touch."

Stovic sat in his hotel with his feet up on the beautiful antique French settee. Bean was studying the bidet in the bathroom. He came back to the seating area of the large, high-ceilinged room and looked around. "This is just awesome. I can't believe we're in Paris."

"Wish we could do this every year," Stovic replied.

"Have you forgotten this is the last year?"

Stovic shook his head. "When the Admirals see us they'll want to keep the Blues going. They'll be begging us to come back again next year."

"Right, I'm sure. That is so not happening. If someone wants to live in that fantasy world they can, but not me. I'm just here to enjoy Paris, fly the air show, and at the end of the year try to get some more shore duty before I go back to the big gray boat," Bean replied. "What are you thinking about doing tonight?"

Stovic thought of Rat. "Dunno. I thought I'd try Karen again."

"Call her? I didn't think you could."

"I can't. But I have a Hotmail account she can reach from anywhere. She can do e-mails, but they censor them to make sure she doesn't tell me where she is. It's weird." Stovic opened his laptop and leaned over to examine the wall outlets. He compared the outlets to the various power adapters spread out on his bed, picked up the one with two widely set thick prongs, plugged his computer in, then selected another oddly shaped adapter for the phone line connection. He quickly inserted the international number for his Internet service provider and dialed in to check his e-mail. He was surprised to find an e-mail from Rat. The return address was entirely numerical, an address Rat had told him to watch for. Nine numbers. He knew the e-mail would not be signed, nor would it be addressed to him individually. It would just convey information. Rat said that such precautions were not really necessary for their communication, but it had become a habit. He said he had hundreds of e-mail addresses that used different servers in different countries. He used one for only a short time before switching to another. Stovic opened the e-mail from Rat, but only after checking his inbox to see if his last few e-mails to Karen had been answered. They hadn't. No response at all. Even the e-mails he had sent his children had gone unanswered.

He scanned down the rest of the e-mails, deleted the news bulletins from various sources, and by the end he had three from Rat. The third was important. Stovic read it carefully. "Have arrived. Am at the hotel. Will call when have more information."

He quickly hit reply and confirmed that he was at his destination and awaited a call. He wasn't going anywhere until he received that call. It was time to go on the offensive. "I think I'll just stay here, Bean. I need to get some rest."

"Okay," Bean said, heading for the door. "You sure you're okay? I mean you've got a lot of things on your mind."

"I'm fine. We all have things on our minds, don't we?"

"Not like you."

"I'm fine."

"See all the security around this hotel? I feel like the President must feel. He goes nowhere without a couple of hundred of his closest friends around him carrying weapons of mass destruction. I feel like getting a machine gun somewhere just so I fit in."

"Get me one too. May as well have a machine gun to sleep with. Did they say whether we can go out? Are we like under house arrest?"

"No. They said as long as we don't wear our uniforms, and check with them on whether where we're going is safe, they think it's okay. They know we came here in part to enjoy Paris."

"Who are we supposed to tell?"

"I don't know. Ask Andrea. She was taking notes."

Lew and Patricia waited in the operations building for the airplane to land. It had been flying all night. Getting a hundred FBI agents on such short notice had been much harder than Lew had thought it would be. But it was Paris. And even the most hardened agent could be talked into a weekend in Paris without too much difficulty.

The Air Force transport taxied toward them. Lew and Patricia stepped into the cool morning air. It was still dark. The airplane shut down, the ramp was lowered, and a hundred sleepy, grumpy FBI special agents walked out of the back.

Lew knew most of them. "Let's go over to the operations building," he told them. "There's an auditorium set aside by the Emergency Committee."

They grabbed the coffee that was lined up on a table, filed in to the auditorium, and waited for Lew to fill them in.

"Thank you for coming. Although this isn't the best

situation for organization and cooperation, we need all
the help we can get. . . ."

Rat didn't call, and Karen didn't respond. Stovic went to
bed. The next day dawned clear and warm. The Blues
had been given one time slot to check landmarks and
practice. It was in the middle of the air show but on an
otherwise quiet day with no other flight demonstrations
scheduled. They were hurried out to the airport by police escort in their usual caravan, blue lights flashing.
The gendarmes were well aware of the danger and had
been told to keep an eye out for anyone who might try
to attack the caravan. It was appreciated that a few
well-placed RPGs—Rocket-Propelled Grenades—could
wreak as much destruction on the Blue Angels' caravan
as surface-to-air missiles could on their airplanes. Such
an attack was thought to be unlikely. Not dramatic
enough. No crowd to watch. No fiery airplane crash.
The Blue Angels took little solace from such assurances,
but even they had to acknowledge that the French as-
sessment was almost certainly right, and that it was a
possibility, but remote.
    They arrived at the airport without incident and went
to the briefing room. Their standard briefing require-
ments had been met. The videotape machines were set
up in the middle of a large table, and an array of food
was there, far superior to what they were accustomed to.
There were French pastries and high-quality espresso
and other coffees. There were crackers, fruit, and cheese
spread out as on a movie set.
    They sat at the table in their usual places and began
the brief. The photographs of the airport were placed
before them, the weather brief, the air show schedule,
and the French aviation administration cautions about
certain objects nearby. It was comfortable, ordinary,
and exciting. The pilots tried to go about the brief with

their usual studied casualness, but each of them was thrilled to be flying in the Paris Air Show. The show was legendary. The biggest and most important air show of the world, and their one and only opportunity to impress the Admirals who had cut them out of the Navy.

The Boss began the brief, and when he was done, he went on, "As you know, we're especially concerned with security. The two Americans you have met have been working with the French to make sure the security is as tight as it can possibly be. But these people might strike, or at least try, today. We must be alert. We've made the decision to go forward with the air show in spite of these threats, as I think we should. The United States Navy does not respond to threats.

"If, in fact, they get a missile off, if the security cannot spot them in time, we will have to break the air show open and take individual evasive action. We have gone over the escape routes for each airplane from each maneuver. Do each of you have them down?"

The pilots nodded confidently.

"We brought flares from VFA-37. They'll be loaded on our jets today and on the day of the show as well. We don't know what they'll be firing, but they've got to be either Russian SA-7s or SA-14s; I suppose there's an off chance they could have a Stinger too. The flares should be effective no matter which missile it is. We had to scramble to get them, but we've got the latest flares around.

"Animal, Oden, you guys are the ones with the best ability to eyeball the horizon. It may be up to you. If you see something, get on the radio right away. We'll scatter like scalded cats. And if anybody hears a missile's airborne, everyone pop flares, get on the deck, as low as you can, and get as far away as you can. We'll regroup later. Fuel will not be an issue. We may have to land at De Gaulle, our alternate field. Everybody have the info on De Gaulle?"

They nodded.

He finished the brief, then jumped up. "Let's go fly."

The storefront was guarded by lookouts in every direction three blocks deep. Ismael and the others gathered for the last time.

The Algerians were comfortable except for Ismael, who was brooding. They stood around the model of the airport again, this time with their firing positions marked. Madani spoke to the others. "Tomorrow night we pick up the weapons at the warehouse, and the embarrassment of the United States is the following day. Is everyone clear? Is everyone ready?" Madani looked at the others. His eyes passed over Ismael, then returned. "What is the matter with you?"

Ismael looked up quickly. "No one here has seen *one* of their air shows except me. Why did you not allow us to observe the practice, make sure our firing positions give us good lines of sight to the airplanes?"

Madani was furious that Ismael would confront him in front of the others. "You have planned other missions?" he asked pointedly.

Ismael shook his head.

"You have participated then in other missions? You have done something, I hope, that makes you have such knowledge and skill to question me."

Ismael had had enough. "I am the one who made this all happen. You are helping *me*."

Madani looked at Ismael with a fury in his eyes that none of the others had seen before and threw the small stick he had been using as a pointer onto the three-dimensional map. "Did it occur to you that your stupidity is what has made this risky? That because you did not ask for help in America you now have the

Americans looking all over the world for us? The security here is more than anywhere I have ever seen. They are *waiting* for us." He moved around to the other side of the table, next to Ismael, so he could speak directly to his face. "We would have succeeded easily if not for you. Not only succeeded, but escaped to return to our homes. We will still succeed, but we have little chance of making it home. Now we will show them we are not afraid. We will go straight into their tightest security and succeed. They are not safe anywhere. We are capable and smarter than they think. But it is only because of *you* that the security is as tight as it is and we are likely to die in this mission. So do not question me!"

He took a deep breath before continuing. "As for looking at our shooting positions, have you not thought of what *they* will be doing? Do you think they don't know what our target is? They will do the same analysis we have done of where to place ourselves. And today, this afternoon, during the practice flight, did it not occur to you that they might expect us to check out positions and get ready, and that they would be there in force?"

"I know all that."

"And you still question my decision?"

"I am . . . sorry," he said, not meaning a word of it.

Khalida came to Madani's defense. "When the French security police see your missile and come running toward you, will you die with honor, or will you cry and beg them not to hurt you?"

"They will not take me. I will fire at them as soon as I see them."

"You will, will you?" Khalida asked.

Ismael stared into his face inches away. "Yes, I will. Will you?"

Madani turned to Hafiz, who was smoking in the corner, disinterested in the details of the planning, more interested in bemused watching of the others in the room. "What of you? You said you thought you had made progress. What is happening?"

"I don't know," Hafiz said. "I thought . . . I don't know. Maybe tonight, maybe tomorrow night."

"We need that distraction."

Hafiz bowed in such a way that it could be interpreted as respect or contempt.

Madani decided to let it pass. "Tomorrow at midnight. Stay out of sight and out of touch until then."

Rat watched from the darkness of their Peugeot van as Stovic stepped out of the Police Nationale car. The French police had balked when he told them he was going out. They had initially said he couldn't go anywhere. He had insisted, and they agreed, but only if they took him.

Rat almost hadn't invited him. He certainly didn't need him, but he knew Stovic was growing more and more frustrated by his inability to face the threat that surrounded him. "Let's go," Rat said to Groomer, who started the van. They pulled up next to Stovic at the curb, and one of the other men slid the door back.

Rat climbed out and spoke to the edgy policemen in French. Stovic had no idea what he said, but it satisfied them and they left smiling.

"Rat!" he said, extending his hand. "How the hell are you?"

"Okay, so far," Rat replied. "Come on. Get in the van."

Stovic looked at the banks of electronic equipment in the van. There were small television screens, radio dials, other things he couldn't identify at all, and wiry men operating all of it. "Who the hell are these people?"

"Don't worry about it. They're with me."

"They your employees?" Stovic asked with concern.

"Yeah. Minimum wage guys."

"Did you find him?" Stovic asked.

"We're getting closer. I just don't know if we'll have time. I have a lot of friends here, and they've been helping me. But these are some elusive mothers—"

"Rat," one of the men at the console said, "check this out."

Rat turned and looked quickly at the screen. It was a small but clear image of some men walking carefully up some stairs with small machine pistols. "Holy shit," Rat said, giving the screen his full attention. He slid over and looked at the other screens. "They're at the hotel! Somebody set us up." His head spun one direction, then the other.

"What?" Stovic asked, concerned.

"These cameras are in my hotel. My room, the stairs, in the back—which is what that is," he said pointing.

Rat spoke to the driver. "That's the GIGN. The big boys. Only they're being *used*. Boy are *they* going to be pissed." He thought for a minute. "Take us over there. Whoever set this up won't be able to resist watching."

The driver looked at the GPS navigation screen. The van's position was overlaid on a Paris map. He selected the hotel's location, and the computer showed him the most direct route back. The driver turned down an alley between two stone buildings and went back in the direction from which it had come.

"Go to the front of the hotel," Rat ordered. He slipped the thumb safety off on the Para Ordnance handgun in the holster on his belt. The others checked weapons Stovic had never seen. He noticed they were all wearing black trousers and rubber-soled shoes with lightweight black sweaters. They could pass for normal clothes if they had to, but they also reflected no light.

"What are we doing?"

"A lot of information is being traded in Paris these days. Somebody has bought some bad stuff, and they're about to find that out. Somebody told them about my room and is going to be very happy to see the French counterterrorism boys go in there to take care of me. I should have figured it was them. Somebody was in my room yesterday—"

"How do you know that?"

"Sensors." He looked at Stovic. "I have motion detectors. They not only show someone was there, but where in the room they were. A maid has a particular pattern. Others would look different. And these sensors have memories. Yesterday they were different. Turn here!" he yelled to the driver, who had driven by the street. "Back up!"

The driver apologized, backed up in the deserted street, and turned right up a hill toward Rat's hotel.

Rat watched the screen. "That's the GIGN all right. I think that's Jean Marcel. *Damn* it." He turned to the man next to him. "Give me their frequencies. Set the encryption codes." The man complied. Rat listened on several radio frequencies until he heard them. He nodded, then spoke into a small boom mike attached to an earpiece. "Jean! That's my hotel room!"

Rat watched as the French officer stopped. "Rat? Is that you?"

"Yes."

"Are you here?"

"No. I'm remote. But I can see you. I've got some cameras there. You bought some bad information. Stay there. I think whoever set this up will be watching. Give me a minute to find him."

Marcel was disgusted. He told his men to stand in place. "One minute," he said.

When the hotel was half a block away, they slowed even more as they headed up the street. Rat looked through the tinted window out the left side of the van and saw a man sitting on the sidewalk leaning against a doorpost with a bottle in a brown bag.

"Stop," Rat whispered to the driver. "*There's* that sack-of-shit we marked," he said. "Groomer, come with me. Bring your tool." Rat grabbed a black silk scarf out of his pocket as he opened the door quietly. He wrapped it around each hand as he walked swiftly across the street. The man was trying hard not to look to his right, where he sensed a van had stopped and someone had gotten out. If he was to maintain his drunken state, he couldn't be looking around, and Rat knew it.

Rat was on him in two seconds. He threw the scarf over the man's head, wrapped it tightly around the man's neck, and pulled him up off the sidewalk. The man grabbed for the scarf and tried to yell, but both attempts were useless. The scarf had cut off his air, and Rat was too big and strong. Groomer slammed his brass knuckles into the man's solar plexus, knocking all the wind out of him.

Rat pulled the scarf over his shoulder until the man's head hung over his right shoulder and his legs flailed in vain behind him. He walked back to the van carrying the man, with Groomer right behind him.

Rat went around to the back of the van where others had prepared a place for their visitor. It was separated from the rest of the van by a curtain. Rat moved the curtain aside, pulled the man off his shoulder, and threw him on the deck of the van. Groomer followed Rat into the back of the van. As the door was closed quietly, the van pulled away from the curb.

Stovic breathed heavily as he watched the entire thing. He had no idea what was going on and no idea how to help. He wondered whether he should ask to be let out of the van and go back to his hotel, but he was too fascinated, and too determined to do something himself. He couldn't just let others do things for him.

He leaned toward the curtain and listened. He heard struggling. He heard low tones, insistent, in a language that was clearly not English. He listened for the distinctive sounds of French, but it sounded different. He couldn't tell if it was Rat's voice or Groomer's. It was frightening to Stovic just to hear the tone. He couldn't imagine the terror of the man to whom it was being directed.

He heard Rat's voice loudly from behind the curtain. "To the shop!"

Stovic turned and watched the driver nod and take the next corner. They drove in complete silence as the others in the van watched the French walk slowly into Rat's room, having lost their motivation.

The van pulled up in front of an automotive repair shop with a steel door. One of the men jumped out and opened the door. The van pulled in, and the man pulled the steel door closed behind them. Groomer came out from behind the curtain with the man whose head was now covered with a thick black canvas bag. The drawstring was pulled tightly around his neck. His hands were bound behind him, and Groomer was pushing him ahead by raising and lowering the man's hands behind his back.

Stovic got out of the way. The man was filthy and smelly. He reeked of alcohol. Stovic couldn't imagine why Rat had grabbed some homeless alcoholic, but he was sure Rat knew what he was doing; more sure now than he had ever been.

The van disappeared, and the rest of the men came into the dark auto shop next to Rat, who was standing over the homeless man on the concrete floor. One of them turned on a lamp, the kind that hooked on the inside of the hood of a car.

Rat turned and looked at those around him. "Okay, Animal," he said to Stovic. "You wanted to be part of this." He pulled a small knife out of his pocket, a Smith and Wesson HRT. Stovic had never seen anything like it. The blade wasn't any longer than two or three inches, but it was curved and serrated, and there was a small handle with a large loop at the base of the blade. Rat slid his index finger through the loop, making the razor-sharp blade an extension of his hand and impossible to get out of his possession. He cut through the plastic cuffs binding the man's hands and turned him over. "Come on, Animal, get over here."

Stovic hadn't moved, but now inched his way toward Rat.

"Pin his arm," Rat said looking at him. He could see Stovic's revulsion and fear.

Stovic knelt down on the hard concrete and held the man's arm. One of the others got on the other side and put his knee directly on the meat of the man's upper arm, causing him to cry out.

"*Kneel* on his arm!" Rat said to Stovic harshly.

Stovic reluctantly put his thick knee on the man's arm as the other man had done. He knew from wrestling that the ulnar nerve ran through that very area. Prolonged pressure could cause permanent nerve damage. Stovic's breath came faster as the man began to cry out in pain. One of the other men pinned the man's legs to the concrete.

Rat spoke in a low tone near the man's face. The blade passed close enough to the man that he could feel it cutting the hood. Rat didn't need to cut the hood; he wanted the man to sense the blade and its sharpness without first seeing it.

The man's face was full of terror and pain. He spoke in French as he begged for an explanation.

Stovic watched with amazement as Rat answered

him in French, then switched to another language, one
Stovic didn't recognize but guessed was Arabic. How
did Rat know how to speak Arabic?

Rat leaned close to the man and asked him a question. There was no answer as the man tried to turn his
head away. Rat suddenly stuck the curved point of the
knife into Hafiz's nose, a full inch up into a nostril.
Hafiz froze at the feeling of steel inside his nose. "So,"
Rat said in Arabic, "you told the GIGN about us."

"I don't know what you are talking about!" Hafiz
protested.

Rat leaned on the knife harder, and put his knee in
the man's gut. "You thought that would be funny? Get
us going after each other? Well, you are stupid. You
saw me on the street. You could tell I'm not stupid,
right?"

"I never saw you!"

"You liar! I saw you! Our eyes met, liar! You deny
it?"

"I don't remember," Hafiz said desperately.

"Where is Ismael?"

"I don't know him. They're breaking my arms!"

"You won't be needing them. You don't know anyone named Ismael?"

"Yes, but no one who has done anything," he said
trying to control the terror in his heart.

"Ismael Nezzar. From Algeria. The one who has
come to shoot down the Blue Angels. *That* Ismael."

Hafiz was shocked. "The what? The blue what?"

Rat quickly pulled the knife outward, slicing
through the side of Hafiz's nose from the inside. Blood
spurted down his face and onto the concrete as Hafiz
screamed. "Where is Ismael Nezzar? The brother of
that worthless Algerian pilot?"

Hafiz felt the blood running down the side of his
face. He tried to move his hand to feel his nose, but his

numb arms were still immobilized. "I don't know anyone!" he cried.

"That's too bad for you. Now I am going to have to
cut off your nose. Do you know how hard it is to look
normal without a nose? Just a big cavity in the middle
of your face? You know how easy it will be for others
to identify you when you have no nose?" Rat put his
blade against the bottom of Hafiz's nose and began to
apply pressure.

"I don't know where he is!"

"You have seen him?"

"Yes. He is here. I don't know where he is! I don't
know!"

"When did you last see him?"

"A few days ago. He was with men I don't know."

"The one thing that disappoints me," Rat said quietly, continuing in Arabic, "is that you would lie to me.
After all this, for you to lie makes it unlikely that I will
find it worth my time to keep you alive. We have *seen*
you together," Rat lied. "I am sorry—"

"No! Wait! I saw him yesterday, but I don't know
where he is. They have scattered."

"They who?"

"All the ones. The ones who came here together. All
of them."

"How many?"

"Four or five. I'm not sure."

"How many missiles do they have?"

Hafiz hesitated. "I don't know, they didn't—"

"Liar!" Rat screamed with a frighteningly red face as
he quickly flashed his blade against the man's head and
sliced his ear. Hafiz screamed. "You must tell me the
truth. I know when you don't." He put the knife tip
against the middle of Hafiz's lower eyelid, just hard
enough for him to feel the steel against his eyeball.
"How many missiles?"

"I think four, but maybe five."

"Are they to shoot on Sunday?"

"Yes, Sunday. My arms ... could they move ... they will be ruined." He started to panic.

"They're not moving until we're done. If your arms are ruined, it is your fault, not mine. How many shooters?"

"Four or five. I don't know. I haven't been in the planning."

"Russian missiles?"

"Yes."

"Any Stingers?"

He hesitated. "No. They tried. They couldn't."

"Where are the missiles?"

"They wouldn't take me. Somewhere out north."

"Where did you see Ismael yesterday?"

"At a restaurant."

"Did they have any maps? Any charts, mock-ups? Did you see any of the planning?"

"There is a model," Hafiz said, knowing that if he told them of it he might live to see it.

"Of what?"

"Le Bourget."

"Where?"

"I can show you."

Rat decided instantly. He pulled Hafiz up to his feet by his hair. The blood ran down his chest from his nose and ear.

One of the other Americans grabbed a rag and some duct tape from a table and taped the rag around the middle of his head to stop the bleeding. Rat took the black silk scarf out of his pocket and put it over Hafiz's eyes. Rat said to him, "If I don't like the looks of where we're going, I will simply drive my knife into your heart and drop you on the sidewalk. You understand?"

Hafiz nodded.

Rat nodded to two of the men, who bound Hafiz's hands behind him and led him to the van.

Stovic stood staring at the Americans in shock. He had never seen anything so horrifying. He didn't want any part of it, yet he knew at a deep level that it was all for him, to defend him, to "help" him. Especially Rat. It was like a cat killing a bird and laying it at his feet to please him.

The man who had been on Hafiz's other arm said to Rat, "Could be a trap. He might be taking us into a beehive."

Rat nodded. "We're getting about eighty percent truth from him. But I don't think he'd make up the model. And he knows if we get to wherever we're going and there isn't one there, he's finished."

"What if there's a roomful of mad Algerians with AKs?"

Rat nodded as he wiped the blade of his knife and slipped it back inside the hard plastic case hanging from a chain around his neck. "Chance we have to take." He looked at Stovic. "Let's get to the van."

Stovic followed him. "Did you have to cut him up?"

Rat hesitated, then looked at his friend. "You said you wanted to kill Ismael yourself. With your bare hands, I think you said. I don't think you appreciate what that means. I think you're starting to, though. Maybe you'll still get the chance tonight. But only if this guy gives us more. We don't have anything else to go on." He turned to Stovic as the van started. "We can drop you off if you want. This could get very ugly."

Stovic shook his head.

"All right."

The van drove slowly to the Algerian section. They went back near the hotel where they had picked up Hafiz, and he directed them to a busy street three blocks away. He pointed to the second floor of the building. "Up there," he said, finally being allowed to look out the windshield without his blindfold.

Rat looked around and didn't like what he saw at all. Everything was wrong. Too many people, second floor, only one obvious ingress and egress, and walking into an unknown situation. "Groomer, drive around the block slowly. Let's see what we've got."

The van drove slowly. They didn't see any obvious security. "Groomer, stay here with Root. You others, and you, Animal, come with me. We'll be back in five minutes. If we're not, start driving. Stay in touch on the radio," he said pointing to the miniature receiver he had in his ear.

Rat slid the door of the van open gently, stepped down casually, with Hafiz, three others, and Stovic, and walked directly to the inside stairway running up next to the storefront.

They went to a door, and Hafiz tried it. It was locked. Rat didn't even hesitate. He kicked in the door and pushed Hafiz inside with the rag taped around his face. The room was empty except for the model of Le Bourget. Rat couldn't believe his eyes. He turned to Hafiz and struck him on the nose. "You liar!" he said in Arabic. "You said they didn't tell you anything. No one would let you see this model unless you were one of them! On the inside." His face was full of rage. "Animal!" he said to Stovic. "Put him on the deck. I'm going to finish this."

Stovic hesitated, then grabbed Hafiz and threw him to the floor. The other two grabbed him and pinned him down. Hafiz's eyes were full of horror. "No!"

Rat struck him in the face and tore off the tape protecting his nose. "Shut up!" He took out his razor-sharp knife, slipped his finger through the hole, and cut off Hafiz's shirt with one rapid movement. He pulled it away from Hafiz's chest, which was heaving with his breathing. Hafiz strained to get away from this inevitable disaster.

Rat looked at his watch. He went on in Arabic. "I don't have time to toy with you. Either you tell me right now what I want to know, or you're going to die a slow death." He took the knife and ran it quickly down the length of Hafiz's chest, cutting just deep enough to cause the blood to well out of the line and begin to run.

Hafiz took in a deep breath and held it.

"I know where every one of your arteries is. I will start out slowly now, in the hope you tell me what I need to know. If you don't, I will leave you here with just enough cuts so that you will die in about ten minutes. And even if you get to a hospital, they won't be able to sew you up. There won't be enough *thread*. You understand?" he said.

"What do you want to know?"

"Where is Ismael?"

"I don't know!"

"Yes, you do," he said, as he pulled the blade down in another cut from his neck to his belt, two inches from the first cut and parallel to it. "Where is he right now? I have to talk to him."

"I don't know! They all left me and went other places! They didn't tell me where they were going. I have no way of reaching them!"

"That's too bad," Rat said, "because that's the only information that would have kept you alive. Feel this right here? That's your carotid artery. If I cut that, which I might, you would die in a minute. And this? That's your jugular. One minute. Tops. For now, though, I just want to let out a little more blood—"

"No!" Hafiz screamed.

Rat slammed the butt of his hand into Hafiz's nose, breaking it. "Shut up! If you make any more noise, I'll drive this knife into your brain! You understand?"

Hafiz nodded and began to cry. "I don't know where they are. I don't know," he sobbed.

Rat cut another stripe on his chest.

Stovic was sickened. He had seen fights, he had seen broken bones in wrestling matches, but he had never seen anyone being cut with a knife again and again, bleeding and sobbing. He swallowed the bile in his mouth, trying to fight the nausea that was welling up. "We need to go."

Rat heard him and nodded. He raised up on one knee. He looked at Hafiz bleeding on the floor, losing strength. He took his machine pistol from the man to his right and wiped the blade on Hafiz's cheek, then the other side of the blade. He leaned over to Hafiz and said into his face, "Tell Ismael, be *sure* you tell him, that whatever happens here in Paris, whatever comes of all this, I will track him down and break his neck like a chicken. Right where the skull attaches to the spine. Right . . . there," he said, reaching behind Hafiz and touching his neck just below his skull. "C-1. Snap. And make sure he knows that if he thinks he can hide in Algeria, or Khartoum, or anywhere else in the world, he's wrong. I will find him. Personally. And . . . snap. You tell him that. And if he comes out into the daylight here in Paris, if he even looks up into the sky, I'll be there, and I'll see him, and I'll be on him like stink on shit. And . . . snap. You be sure. You can even snap your fingers, like this. The sound will remind you. And you tell him my name is Rat. R-A-T. Got that?"

The miniature receiver in his ear crackled to life. "Rat, we got some men coming up the stairs with machine pistols. Looks like GIGN to me. Get out of there."

"Roger," Rat said. He looked at the others. "We've got company. Out we—"

He didn't even have time to get it out before the lead

French commando kicked in the same door Rat had kicked in and nearly fell forward from using too much force on an already broken door frame. Two others came in right behind him, yelling and aiming their weapons at the four Americans. *"Arretez!"* the first one yelled.

Rat started to rise slowly to his feet, holding his weapon up so they could see it. They saw it all right, and fired. The first soldier's bullets hit Rat in the chest three times before he could say a word.

The French commandos closed on Rat and pointed their weapons at him lying on the floor. Rat released the weapon from his fingers. He fought for breath, then sat up slowly. He looked around. The French were yelling at him. He put up his hand to show he meant no harm. He waited, then saw the French officer enter. Just as he had hoped. Rat spoke softly in French. "Marcel, tell them I'm okay."

Stovic was frozen, not wanting to end like Rat.

The French officer crossed quickly to Rat and squatted. "Rat, what are you doing here?"

"You knew I was in Paris."

"Yes, but not *here*."

Rat pointed to Hafiz lying next to him on the floor. "Asking him a few questions."

Marcel gave him a hand and helped him up. "You have a vest?"

"Or I'd be dead."

"I am sorry. They saw you were armed—"

"Shit!" he said, fighting for breath. Some cartilage had been damaged. He could feel it. "Let's get on with things. We have a long night ahead of us."

"What do you have in mind?"

He spoke English. "Put the cuffs on me."

"What? Why?"

"Do it."

Marcel spoke quickly to one of his men, who put plastic cuffs on Rat. Marcel led him out of the room and down the stairs. "So what's this about?"

"Take that guy in. He's the only lead we've got. Start interrogating him, then let him know you have no idea how this lunatic American was able to get away with this. Apologize, then release him. Unless I miss my bet, he'll lead us to them. Can you get me out?"

"Of course."

Lew paced back and forth. Stovic and Rat sat at the same conference room table where Lew and Patricia had first met François and Elizabeth. Rat continually rubbed his chest where the three shots had hit his bulletproof vest like a sledgehammer. He knew he would have bruises the size of his fist in the morning, but at least he was alive. Stovic was in shock. He should have been in bed, not rolling around on the floor while Rat cut up some Algerian and nearly got killed by French counterterrorism forces. He sat with a dry mouth and a stunned look.

Elizabeth and François came in with dark faces. She spoke across the table to Rat with a tone of recognition. "What are you doing here?"

"Tourist."

"Who are you working for?"

Rat pointed to Stovic sitting next to him. "For my old Academy friend here. He felt like he needed some protection. I came to help out."

"Are you with the Agency?"

"Agency for International Development? No. They don't pay enough."

"You know what I mean."

"No, I wouldn't trust those guys as far as I could throw them."

"You were torturing a Frenchman, about to *kill* him, in possession of an illegal knife and an automatic weapon. You could go to prison for many years."

Rat was unimpressed. "Since you *shot* me three times, let's just call it even."

"We are *not* going to just call it even unless you tell us who you were working for!"

Lew interrupted. "Your commandos broke in and attacked an American's hotel room based on a hot tip from that Algerian. What made you think some Algerian was gonna help you out?"

"We have had success in such things many times in the past and have been accurate," Elizabeth answered coldly.

"From the same guy?" Lew asked.

"No, of course not. It is always someone different. It's just money."

"Did you not think maybe this guy might be working for our targets? Didn't you wonder how this guy came out of the blue and came to find you just to tell you all this great information?"

"Of course we thought about it. We wanted to check it out."

"Didn't you put the hotel under surveillance?"

"Yes. We did."

Lew was not impressed. "I'm starting to get worried here. I've got a bunch of Americans exposed here, dangling in the water like worms on hooks. I sure would like to hear how you're going to make all this come out okay."

"We are doing our best." François looked at Rat. "Are you with the CIA?"

"I don't answer those kinds of questions."

"Where did you get the weapons? Did you bring them with you, or did someone inside France provide them?"

"They were in my carry-on bags on Air France."

"We should put you in prison."

"Well, before you do that, let's talk about putting in prison the shit-for-brains who put together the operation you guys just pulled."

The Frenchman was not amused. "You said you checked in yesterday. But you registered three days ago as Benjamin Sutton from South Africa."

"I *am* Benjamin Sutton from South Africa," he said suddenly with a remarkably precise South African accent.

The Frenchman frowned and tried to reevaluate what he "knew" to be true.

"My company requires that I travel as an American," Rat continued in his South African accent. "South Africa is still not appreciated as it should be in the commercial world."

The Frenchman looked at Lew. "Don't you know him? Haven't you seen him before?"

"I thought I had," Lew said staring at Rat.

"You don't know anything," Rat said to all of them. "I am a rare book collector looking for manuscripts from the French Revolution."

"Enough," the Frenchman said.

"What's your plan?" Lew asked, trying to be respectful but failing.

Elizabeth leaped to her feet. "You have no idea what we've done. You think all we did was storm this man's room?" she asked, pointing to Rat. "We've done twenty raids so far tonight. We have people all over Paris. We've rounded up every suspicious Algerian and many who are not suspicious at all. Maybe we have one or more of those who came here to harm this pilot.

Maybe not. We are doing the best we can with the information we have—"

Lew replied, "I'm betting they left their beggar around just for us to play with. They're nowhere near the Algerian section now. They're with their weapons somewhere else. You will never find them. So now we have to get them in the act, before they actually shoot. You've made it ten times as hard." He breathed out audibly, expressing his anger and frustration.

Rat stood up. "I've got other things to do."

"You're not going anywhere," Elizabeth said.

"Wrong," Rat said. "Come on, Animal," he called to Stovic as he walked out of the conference room. He stopped at the door and looked at Elizabeth. "What did you do with the beggar?"

"The man you cut up?"

"Yeah. Him."

"We have him in custody. A doctor is attending to him. Then we will interrogate him."

Rat stopped, his face showing concern. "He doesn't need a doctor. None of those cuts is deeper than two millimeters. He needs to go find the enemy. They need to *see* him, he needs to tell them that some out-of-control American cowboy was the one who attacked him. Tell him you're sorry, you had nothing to do with the nut-case American. He was out of control and is in custody. Then let him go. See if he leads you anywhere."

"You are *not* free to go," she said. "We still have more questions for you."

"Sorry," he said, shaking his head in regret. "I am *completely* out of time. Ask Marcel about me. He'll answer your questions."

"Of the GIGN?" Elizabeth asked, surprised.

"Him." He walked out with Stovic, who jogged ahead to catch him in the hallway.

"Do you know what you're doing?"

"Yes."

"I thought you said they knew you were coming."

"They do. Not the bureaucrats, not the office pukes."

"Shouldn't they know who you are?" Stovic asked, pointing over his shoulder.

Rat stopped. "Let's go to your hotel room."

Rat knocked gently on the door, a continuous rapping that Andrea had come to recognize. No one just *kept* knocking. Only Rat. She looked through the peephole and confirmed it was him. She opened the door. "What are you doing here?" she asked as her eyes adjusted to the light in the hall.

"Morning. Time to rise and shine," he said walking right by her.

"Come on in," she said to his back. She looked at her watch. "It's two in the *morning*! What are you doing here?"

"Can I use your computer again?"

She rolled her eyes and turned on the laptop on the antique desk by the window. She turned on the lamp by the bed. She sat where she had thrown the covers back. "How long have you been in Paris?"

He sat down at the desk and waited while her laptop booted up. "Couple of days."

"You promised me a dinner along the Seine. You said you knew just the place."

"I do." The computer was ready. He inserted a mini CD and called up the encryption software.

"I think you only like me for my computer."

"How'd you know?" he asked as he began typing. "Just your computer. Well, there is one other thing."

"What?" she asked.

"Your . . . smile. I love your smile too."

She shook her head. "Why do you keep rubbing your chest?"

"Had a little event tonight."

She threw the covers back and began feeling his chest. "You get shot?"

"Yeah."

She pulled his shirt off, helped him with his kevlar vest, and examined his chest. "Any trouble breathing?"

"Little."

She went to the closet and pulled out a stethoscope. She listened to his lungs. They sounded clear. She felt his ribs. He winced as he typed. "You may have cracked the cartilage in your sternum."

"I know."

"Want some Motrin?"

"Sure."

She went to her bag to get the medicine, then to the bathroom for a glass of water. "Here."

He took it quickly without looking away from the screen.

"What's so important?"

"Can't talk about it. Trying to finish our job here."

He continued working furiously on the computer keyboard. This was the critical time. This was when people lost their nerve, particularly politicians. He typed his encrypted e-mail to St. John, telling her to hold the line, keep the air show on, not to cancel it simply because they hadn't caught all the Algerians. He was sure Ismael and the others were confident they could pull it off now. They had gotten the weapons and people into Paris, they had avoided capture so far, and would certainly be confident now of their success. But Rat knew the closer they got to their objective, the narrower their options became. They would have to put themselves in place and ultimately show themselves.

That's when they became predictable. He knew Washington would want to pull the plug. Much better a non-event than a disaster. In his experience, too many politicians couldn't take the heat. They'd rather leave the noose a little loose than risk stimulating an event that resulted in deaths. Rat felt differently. If you didn't take chances to catch terrorists, they simply raised the ante next time. He tried every argument he could think of that Sarah St. John could use. He read it quickly, checked the spelling, and hit "send." He ejected the encryption disk and turned the computer off. "See you," he said, pulling his shirt on slowly.

"Anything else I can do?"

"No. I got to keep moving. Maybe we'll do the river tomorrow night. After the air show."

"It's a date."

He walked quietly out of her room and down to Stovic's room. The Police Nationale who were guarding the rooms recognized him and nodded.

Rat knocked gently, and Stovic opened his door. He knew he had to get Stovic's mind off himself. He looked in the mirror at the bruises forming on his chest. "I feel like I've been tackled by six of those fatboy NFL linemen."

"Where'd you go?"

"Had to stop by my good friend's room."

"Andrea?"

"Yeah."

"What in the world for?"

"See if she was all right."

"You didn't . . ."

"Give me a break. No. I just needed to use her computer for a second."

"For what?"

"Had to send an e-mail."

"Anyone I know?"

"No." Rat got serious. "Sorry we didn't get Ismael tonight. We're actually getting close."

"Did you really have to cut that guy up?" Stovic asked, still affected by the picture of the writhing, bleeding man under his knee.

"He'll be okay. He won't know that for a while, but he'll just have some scars. I stayed away from the arteries."

"You do this stuff a lot?"

"Can't talk about what I used to do."

"The French think you work for the CIA."

"That's the French for you. Does it matter?" Rat asked, looking at him over the bottle of water he had picked up and started drinking.

"I don't know."

"Don't worry about it. You can just stay in your warm existence, and others will go out there and do the dirty work for you."

Stovic was stung. "What is *that* supposed to mean?"

"You pilots," Rat smiled. "Big heroes. Big huge fights in the sky, missiles, always know who your enemy is, no ambiguity. No gray areas. And no blood. If you kill somebody, they just sort of disappear. That's not what war is. When people die, they die unhappy. They bleed to death, or their bodies come apart.

"You may kill somebody, but even if you drop a bomb, all *you* see is the blue sky. If you kill someone inadvertently, you don't have to see the little girl with her legs blown off. You just say, 'Gee, sorry, inadvertent. Didn't *mean* to kill her. Let's go to the O' Club!'

"There are a lot of people out there who do some pretty dirty work you'll never hear about. And it's only because of them that you can go to the O' Club and get shit-faced and tell the girls what heroes you are."

Stovic put his hands on his hips. "What's this all about?"

"You're a *pilot*. You have no *idea* how the world really works. Not the way it works today, anyway. It's only because this Ismael guy has crossed the line to go after an actual military target that you're even aware of his existence. Most of these assholes like to kill women and children and blow themselves into tomorrow. They never actually *fight* anyone."

Stovic looked at Rat with a peevish face. "Are you going to tell me *you* understand how carrier battle groups operate, and airborne rules of engagement? You going to tell me flying is just pretty boy shit, and all the real work is done by you SEALs, or whatever the hell you are now?"

Rat chose his words carefully. "Look. What you do is important. I'm just telling you that today, most of the defense of the United States is done where you don't see it. And now that you've seen just a little of it, you're shocked. We're in transition," he said, looking for something else to drink. "The world used to fight with armies, and uniforms, and rules. Since World War I, pilots have been the heroes. They get all the medals. The battle was where we wanted it to be. Not anymore. Ever since the World Trade Center, when the War on Terrorism got going, we started seeing that things were going to be different. Snake-eaters like me *are* the front lines, because there aren't any front lines. And it's dirty, and ugly. And we're wrong now and then, just like pilots are. But we're where the fight is."

Stovic ignored him. "You can't just torture people."

Rat frowned. "Why not?"

"It's illegal and . . . immoral."

"So if he knows where the guy is that's going to try to shoot you down, you won't let me cut him up a little?"

"I don't know." Stovic changed the subject. "Where'd you come up with that South African stuff?"

Rat smiled. "When people start asking questions, I give them answers that don't compute. Gives them time to think about what was said. They tend to get distracted."

"All because they think you're working for some company?"

Rat smiled. "They don't believe that for a second. Not a millisecond."

"Who *do* they think you're working for?"

"They're not sure."

"So how is it you're here talking to me instead of in some French jail?"

"They know I'm an American counterterrorism operative—or used to be—and they have no idea who I'm working for right now. And they're afraid if they piss me off, they might piss off the wrong people and end up picking their feet in Poughkeepsie, as Gene Hackman would say."

"What?"

"*French Connection.* You know."

"Never saw it."

"Well, *our* French connection isn't that hot. These guys are *not* on the trail of your shooter, and unless things change, he's going to be there waiting for you tomorrow."

"So now what?" Stovic asked, chilled by Rat's last thought.

"So he'll assume you have flares. What do we make of that?"

Stovic frowned. "It'll just be a little harder, I guess."

Rat shook his head vigorously and stood up. He crossed to the cabinet where some bottles of water stood by crystal glasses. He looked around for ice, and finding none, poured the warm water into a glass. "If you were going to shoot an airplane, and you knew he had flares, would you do anything differently?"

"No. You get yourself into a firing position—and fire. If he has flares, maybe they help him, maybe they don't. You don't do anything differently."

"What if you're on the ground?"

"I don't know."

Rat answered his own question. "You'd make sure they can't *see* you. You'd surprise them."

"How?"

"Think!"

"From underneath, and directly behind. They don't even know you've fired at them, so they don't know to drop flares."

"Exactly. And your flight is a shooter's dream. Totally predictable and can be timed down to probably a couple of seconds. He'll put himself directly under your flight path. He just has to pick what part of the show to do it in." He cleared off the coffee table and grabbed the hotel stationery and pen. "When is the best time to do that, in your air show routine? To do the most damage, get a lot of others, especially the crowd, if that's possible. But you guys never really fly right at the crowd, do you. It's all from one side."

"There's one time," Stovic realized as he said it. "It's kind of late in the show. We come in together—the two solos—flying right at the crowd. Then when we cross over the center point, we break in opposite directions. It looks like we're going to hit each other."

"Right in front of the crowd?"

Stovic nodded.

"Heading toward the crowd?"

He nodded again.

"What if you got hit right before the break?"

"If it went out of control right away, there'd be some risk of crashing into the crowd. Full-on."

"Shit, Animal. That's it! When exactly is it during the show? Draw it for me."

Stovic got on his knees and drew on the stationery on the coffee table. "You want the whole air show?"

"No, just the part right before this, and some way to know when this happens."

Stovic nodded. He drew a picture from directly above the field and showed the airplanes' line of flight.

Rat studied it. "That's where he'll be. Right along this line."

"So what do we do?"

"I'll be there waiting for him," he answered as he looked at his watch. "It's 0300. You'd better get some sleep. I need to make some phone calls." He walked toward the door, then stopped. "There's a lot of security around, but it's not perfect." He reached behind him under his polo shirt and produced a small but thick semiautomatic handgun. He crossed back and handed it to Stovic. "Here. Take this. Odds of you having to use it are low. You did qualify expert in pistol, didn't you?"

Stovic nodded.

"Good. This is a Glock 9 millimeter. Great gun. Very reliable. There's a round in the chamber and lots more in the clip. If some lunatic runs out of the crowd and points something at you? Just pull that out, squeeze off a round, and get the hell out of there."

"Come on," Stovic protested. "Don't get dramatic on me."

"Just a precaution. Carry it in your flight suit. Never know when you'll need it."

Stovic rolled his eyes, lifted his shirt, and stuck the cold, plastic-feeling handgun into his belt against his skin. "Be careful."

"Count on it. I'll be on your frequency during the air show. If I see anything, I'll yell it out. If you hear my voice, something bad is happening and you should take evasive action. If there's nothing, you won't hear me at all."

"Okay."

Rat walked to the door.

"Thanks, Rat. I appreciate what you've done so far."

"It's not over yet. We've got to get you through the weekend."

"Where are you going now? Back to look at Andrea's computer?"

"Nope. No time for that. Unless I miss my guess, our good friend with the carved-up chest should be about ready to do something stupid. I'll be in touch."

Karen woke in the middle of the night. She slipped on a bathrobe and walked out to the family room of the large cabin. Two FBI agents were playing cards with just a desk light. "Hi," she said, surprising them. They jumped up.

"Everything okay?" Kate asked. "You okay? Kids?"

"Fine, fine. I just couldn't sleep."

The other agent, a tall black man who looked intimidating, glanced at his watch. "It's only one in the morning. You sure you're okay? Did you hear something?"

"No, I didn't hear anything." She walked to the huge windows that looked out over the Colorado mountains. The moon reflected off the snowcapped peaks. "I want to call Ed. Is that okay? I know what hotel he's staying at in Paris. Just one call."

"Sorry," Kate replied. "Can't. Against the rules. No communication at all, except e-mail that can't be traced."

Karen nodded. She knew that would be the answer. "All because of one person." She looked at them. "Kind of amazing how much trouble one person can cause."

"You have no idea."

"Actually, I do. He has almost ruined my family. He's trying to kill my husband, he's already killed my brother-in-law, . . . you think he's trying to kill me or the kids. . . ."

"No, we don't think that," Kate said. "We're just being overcautious."

"The air show is tomorrow. I want to be there for him."

"I don't think that would be a good idea," the man said, suddenly concerned that she might try to go anyway. "Definitely not a good idea. The risk is probably over after this weekend. If nothing happens, you can go back home. We're just afraid this guy has plans we haven't anticipated. He surprised us in Tennessee."

She couldn't argue with that.

"We don't want that to happen again. I'm sure you don't either."

"How many people are here to protect us?"

"Why?"

"Just curious."

"Enough."

"What could really happen?" she asked, crossing her arms.

Kate replied, "You don't really want us to go into that, do you? After Tennessee?"

"No. It's okay." She headed back to her bedroom. "You sure I can't call him?"

"We're sure."

Hafiz staggered into the dingy room in the basement of the tobacco shop. His shirt was filled with blood, his face looked as if he'd been in a terrible fight, and he felt dizzy. He couldn't believe the French had let him go. They seemed to be so furious at that American lunatic that they had failed to realize who they had in custody, the one who had given them the false information that led to the raid on the hotel aimed at the very American who had taken him within an inch of his life. It had been the most frightening experience of his life. He knew he couldn't stay in Paris. He had to leave with Madani and the others when they fled. Why wait, he asked himself? Why not just get out now?

His room had been completely dismantled. It was never much to look at, but now it was a complete disaster. His minimal clothes, disguises, and food dishes were strewn all over. The GIGN had been there.

Hafiz went to the bathroom and looked at himself in the mirror. Blood was crusted all around his broken and cut nose. It still didn't look as bad as it felt. The smashed cartilage was throbbing in pain. He opened the shirt the French doctor had given him and looked at his chest. He would be scarred for life with five cuts from his neck to his waist, all perfectly straight and parallel. They were dark with blood, but most of the active bleeding had stopped. The doctor had begun to sew a couple of them but had inexplicably stopped. Hafiz had been given a new shirt and dropped in the Algerian quarter with apologies for the American psychopath they were now interrogating.

But now what? What do to? Madani had given him a cell phone and a number he could call only once. It was to be used only in an absolute emergency. Hafiz had to warn them. He knew the French would be watching his every move, but they couldn't trace a phone call from a phone they didn't know he had.

He turned off the light, stood on the bed, and painfully removed the light fixture from the ceiling. He pulled the fixture entirely from its suspension, then dug at the plaster around it. Finally it was hanging from its wires, and a small ziplock bag showed through the hole in the ceiling. He pulled it through carefully, stepped off the bed, and took the small phone out of the bag. He turned on the power, waited for a good signal, and dialed the number Madani had given him.

Groomer was a block away in the van, waiting for the signal to come on. The French had found the cell phone earlier that evening when they were searching the room. They knew these old buildings and knew which rooms had crawl spaces above the ceilings. They had copied the phone's identification information and put it back. Groomer had simply copied down the information when the French had triumphantly radioed it in to their superiors.

Hafiz gently fingered his nose to feel its deformation as he waited for the phone to connect.

Groomer and the French caught the signal at the same time. They both wanted only one thing—the recipient—the one on the other end of the call.

Madani looked at the ringing phone on the seat next to him in the truck. It could only be bad news. Some emergency. He picked it up. "What," he asked.

"It's me," Hafiz said.

"What's the matter with your voice?"

"I was attacked by an American. He is the one I put the French onto. He is after us. He is after Ismael—"

"Don't use names, you idiot!"

"He cut my nose and broke it, then carved my chest up. The French broke into our planning room—"

"What were you doing there?" Madani asked furiously.

"The American *tortured* me until I took him there—"

"You should have let him torture you to death!"

"There is nothing on the model."

"We must change our plans now."

"The French are everywhere. They broke into that room anyway! They knew where to come. And they broke into my apartment. They are arresting every Algerian who has done anything. They are interrogating everyone, probably keeping them in custody until after the air show—"

"Shut up!" Madani screamed. "Don't say anything!"

"You said this is secure—"

"Nothing is secure!"

"The American said he is going to be waiting for you. He knows everything, and will be there—"

"You must disappear and never contact me again!" Madani said as he ended the call abruptly.

Hafiz looked at the phone, angry at the way he had been treated, angry that he was never paid for any of his work for this Madani, angry that he had been the one tortured and scarred for life. He threw the phone on the bed, grabbed a plastic net shopping bag, found his passport, and headed for the train station. He opened the door and found two French counterterrorist agents waiting for him. They grabbed his arms, went into the room, found the phone, checked the last number dialed, and dragged him into their car.

Groomer had the ID of the receiving phone. That was all he needed. The CIA had perfected the technique of triggering a cell phone to make a low-level transmission without showing its owner it was doing anything. As long as the battery was in the phone, it could be used as a constant locator signal.

Groomer looked at the strobe from the second phone, stored it in the computer from their current location, and began driving to get a triangulation strobe from another place. He transmitted to Rat on their encrypted signal. "We've got the ID on the second."

"Roger. When you get close, we may want to let the GIGN handle the takedown."

"I'll keep in touch. We're rolling. Out."

Ismael had slept in the back of his van in an industrial section of Paris, blending in easily with the other work trucks around the neighborhood. He drove directly to the warehouse. He drove by once, went to the end of the road, turned around, and drove by the back of the warehouse. He drove by twice more before committing himself. He stopped in front of the warehouse door, turned off his lights, and waited.

The gray steel door rolled up, and Ismael quickly pulled his van into the garage, almost hitting the bottom of the door as it retracted. The men operating the door lowered it as soon as the van was inside. Ismael turned off the engine and hopped out of the van. Several men were working on the weapons. A table was against the stairway with dozens of handguns, assault rifles, and grenades.

Two men opened the doors to another van that was already there and grabbed the Stinger case. Ismael surveyed the warehouse, looking for anything odd, anything out of place. No one said a word. He watched the men open the Stinger box. They carefully removed the Stinger and showed it to him. He nodded, and they put it back in the case.

Guards stood at the far end of the warehouse by the other door, ready to raise it by the rolling chain gearing at a moment's notice. Everyone waited anxiously for Ismael to be done and gone. The other four vehicles would be behind him in a rigid, preplanned order. Everything was on a schedule. They had only allowed ten minutes for him to be there. Any time more than that and the schedule would be off. No one believed that a few seconds lag in the schedule was a problem, but if someone noticed too many vehicles going in or out of the warehouse in the middle of the night, one random call to law enforcement might send the entire scheme crashing to the ground. That was why Ismael was first. The best missile, the best position for shooting, and the designated shooter.

They loaded his missile into the van and closed the doors. He crossed to the table, chose an AK-47, a handgun, ammunition, and two grenades. He placed them on the rubber floor of the modified van and climbed into the driver's seat. He started the truck and drove toward the other door of the warehouse. The thin blue smoke from his exhaust left a haze in the warehouse. As he approached, the door rolled up in front of him, and he drove out into the dark Paris morning. He and the other shooters were to drive around the city all day, mostly in the suburbs and the auto-routes, breaking no traffic laws and stopping nowhere in particular. They were to draw no attention to themselves at all; no stops except to refuel.

He was to refuel before dawn and once more around noon. That would take them right up to the air show— or at least the time in the air show when the Blue Angels flew. Le Bourget was in a wide-open area north of central Paris. Those who were anxious to get there would take public transportation. There would be a lot of traffic, but the place that had been chosen for Ismael to shoot from was far off the path of anyone heading toward Le Bourget.

Ismael pulled away from the warehouse quickly as the door rolled down behind him. He turned the radio to an Arabic station.

Groomer and the others in the van watched carefully as they quietly stimulated the cell phone of their target. They didn't have any idea who their target was, but Hafiz had reported to him. That was good enough. The signals were strong and excellent for direction finding. Groomer had gotten several hits but was becoming convinced that whoever had the cell phone was moving. The positions were not correlating with each other.

They drove toward the general area of the signals. *"Rat, you up?"* Groomer transmitted on his digital encrypted radio.

*"Go ahead,"* Rat responded through the tiny earpiece.

*"We're getting a good trace. I think it's mobile."*

*"Is it the lead?"*

*"We think so. It's who our spy-boy called."*

*"Pick me up."*

*"Where are you?"*

*"At our friend's hotel."*

*"Too far off our path."*

*"Pick me up!"*

*"Roger,"* Groomer said, perturbed as he wheeled away from their mark to get Rat. He raced through the deserted Paris streets watching for police. Fifteen minutes later they pulled up in front of the Blue Angels' hotel. It was ringed with security. They regarded the van skeptically. Groomer watched several fingers slide slowly down to triggers. "Easy," he ordered to no one in particular. Rat stepped out from the dark and in front of the van. They stopped, threw open the sliding

door, and he jumped in. Groomer sped off back toward the cell phone they were tracking.

"You still getting a good signal?" Rat asked.

"Yeah. . . . We're getting away from it, but we've got a good signal."

"Let's go get him," Rat said sitting at a console. They drove for nearly twenty minutes. Rat studied the screens in the van, the cameras, the electronics monitoring, and the communications equipment hooked up to Washington.

They followed the signal and turned down a poorly lit street in the suburbs of Paris. A van turned down an alley in front of them. Groomer drove by the alley. He saw the taillights of a small panel truck turn onto the parallel street a block away.

"Shit, we're right on top of him!" Rat said. The others in the van sat up taller, focusing on their prey.

"He see us?"

"Don't know," Groomer said. "We're the only two people even awake out here. We're kind of obvious."

Rat picked up one of his cell phones and dialed a number. A man answered. Rat replied in French. "We're on the leader," he said.

"Where are you?"

Rat gave him coordinates off a map he pulled out of a case between the seats in the front.

"We have him. Stay behind, and we'll see where he goes. We may need your help."

Rat looked at Groomer as he checked his weapons. "Stay out of sight, and track his signal to see where he goes."

They stayed a mile away from the other van, following him through the suburbs.

"Where the hell is he going?"

"He's waiting. He's just staying on the move until it's time." He glanced at the clock on the dash. It was nearly 5:30 A.M. Rat leaned over to look through the windshield at the sky. It was showing the first signs of dawn.

"He's stopped," the man next to Rat said.

"Get there," Rat said. "Everyone get ready." Everyone except Groomer reached for a weapon and readied to jump out of the van.

As they turned the corner, Groomer slowed suddenly. "Here they come," he said, looking in his side mirror. He pulled over to the curb to give way to the flashing blue lights behind him. There were three French vehicles, the front one of which looked like an armored personnel carrier. They drove silently, with only their lights on to warn other traffic.

"That you, Jean?"

"Yes. They're headed for a warehouse in the middle of the block. Stay behind the armored car and be ready to help if we hit a large group of them. We're going in."

"Will do."

Rat looked at the others. "Put on your jackets."

They all slipped on dark blue nylon jackets with FBI stenciled unmistakably on the front and back in yellow.

"Hold on," Groomer said. "More of them."

Three other French vehicles came down the road from the other direction. They could see more lights reflecting off the damp buildings a block away, on the other side of the buildings in front of them.

"Here we go," Groomer said. He turned the corner just in time to see the armored car turn hard and run directly into the steel door of what appeared to be one of many small, quiet warehouses along the row. The steel door gave way and the APC stopped in the mouth of the building. Several French police in body armor and helmets ran out the back of the APC with automatic weapons, yelling at the top of their lungs.

Madani couldn't believe it. He was to be the last one

to retrieve his missile. He had driven around the neighborhood for three hours. There was *no one* around. It had been clear, yet here were the French breaking down the door and no doubt waiting on the other side of the other door. They were doomed, and he knew it.

He looked up the stairs to the men working there and screamed in Arabic, "There is no way out! We must fight!"

"What for?" the man asked. "We should surrender! They don't have anything on us, maybe arms charges!"

Rat and the others in their FBI jackets scrambled out of the van.

Inside the garage, Madani ran to the back of his truck and opened the case for the Russian shoulder-fired missile he had just put there. He flipped the switch turning the missile on as he lifted it to his shoulder. The reticle lit up, and he aimed it at the APC. Several of the Frenchmen saw him lift it to his shoulder and began firing their automatic weapons at him as they yelled for him to put it down.

Madani heard a good growl from the missile as it locked onto the heat from the APC's engine. He pulled the trigger, and the missile flew out of the tube directly to the APC and smashed into the front of the vehicle. It hit with tremendous energy but didn't explode. It was too close. The warhead had to travel two hundred yards before it would arm. The missile lay on the concrete floor hissing and going in circles, its guidance and flight abilities crippled by the jarring impact with the APC.

The French expected the warhead to explode any moment and ducked.

Madani grabbed his AK-47 off the seat of the truck and began firing at the French. When he couldn't see them, he jumped into the driver's seat and started the engine of his truck. Two French gendarmes stood and began firing. Two of the warehousemen at the top of the stairs came out and began firing at them as Madani drove madly toward the door at the other end of the small warehouse. He didn't even slow, and smashed through the door. His van ran into the French security truck waiting just outside the door. The French gendarmes fired into the front seat, hitting Madani several times in the chest and neck within two seconds. He slumped forward, dead.

The gun battle continued inside the warehouse until the Lieutenant of the GIGN ordered the French to stop firing. They stopped instantly, leaving only the distinctive sound of the AKs that the Algerians were using. The Lieutenant estimated four to five men in the warehouse. He had twenty. He spoke through a microphone that was attached to the APC. "There is nowhere to go. If you stop now, you will not be killed. Put down your weapons, and we will not harm you."

One wide-eyed Algerian threw his gun down and walked down the steps. "Don't shoot! I had nothing to do with any of this." He hurried down the steps toward the Lieutenant.

The head warehouseman leaned over the railing and shot the Algerian in the back. "Traitor!" he yelled in Arabic as the man fell the last few steps.

The French fired again and hit the leader, who fell into the railing, then back. Two other Algerians waited on the floor in the office at the top of the stairs. They lay face down, with their weapons several feet away. "No more!" they yelled in Arabic, then, *"Arretez! Arretez!"* Stop! Stop!

The French officer, Lieutenant Jean Marcel, moved the dead man's body off the stairs and stood at the bottom. Rat walked in carefully, ensuring that the French saw him and his FBI jacket. He crossed to Marcel. "Nice work. How many topside?"

"I think two," Marcel replied. "Let's go."

He and Rat hurried up the stairs, weapons drawn. Two other gendarmes went up behind them, covering them. Marcel went into the office and looked for a trap. "Get up!" he yelled in French. "Get up!"

They rose.

"Come out of there, and walk toward me with your hands up. How many of you are there?"

"Just us."

The two behind Rat and Marcel went around them and grabbed the two Algerians. They threw them to the ground and bound their hands behind them, then dragged them down the stairs and walked to the back of the APC. More French commandos scurried around the garage looking for other men and weapons. It was quiet.

Rat and Groomer motioned for the others to stay where they were. They walked to the Lieutenant, who was herding the two Algerians into the APC. The French Lieutenant looked at them as they came closer.

"They have a lot of weapons," Marcel said.

"And we probably missed most of the missile shooters. They were running through here while we were following this driver around. Damn it!" Rat cursed. He began to fume.

Marcel squinted at him. "Why an FBI jacket?"

"Just a little camouflage. Keeps you from getting shot. Even in France."

"So you got out of the headquarters building. I thought you'd talk your way out of it. Why didn't you tell them you had been in touch with me?"

"They wouldn't understand. I don't trust anyone except operators."

Jean nodded. "You really cut that other guy up."

"He'll be fine. No real damage."

Jean regarded the two scared Algerians who were being led into the APC. "Let's have a talk with these two. Your Arabic still good?"

"Not bad."

Jean slipped into the APC and sat across from the two Algerians. Rat sat next to him. Jean removed his helmet and rubbed the top of his head. He picked up his machine pistol and pointed it casually at one of the Algerians. "What's your name?"

The man hesitated. "Assad."

Jean didn't care if he was telling the truth about his name. He moved forward on his seat so he could look the Algerian in the eye. "Where did you get that missile?"

"We didn't get them anywhere."

"Why was it in your warehouse?"

"The man who got it asked us to store his truck. That is all. We don't know anything about missiles."

Marcel looked at him sadly. With no warning he leaned forward quickly; his right arm flew out and jammed the barrel of his machine pistol into the man's side, instantly breaking one of his ribs. A sharp, searing pain shot through the man's chest. "I had hoped you would be truthful. I was wrong, so now I'm going to have to ask you more directly. Do you know how many ribs you have?"

The man shook his head. His face was sweating from pain.

"I am going to break every one of your ribs in order, bottom to top, until you tell me what I want to know." He waited until the man looked up at him through the pain. "You are helping a terrorist. We don't like terrorists in France. We like order, and civility, and decency. Not terrorism." He looked at the other Algerian. "You are next. After I break his last rib, I will start with yours. First on the left side, down here," he said, indicating on his own rib cage, then that of the man with a broken rib. "Then working up. Then over here, on the right." He rammed his machine pistol forward again unexpectedly and felt the snap of the first man's next rib.

"Aaaahggh," he cried, looking at the Lieutenant as if he were crazy.

"Do you know how hard it is to breathe if all your ribs are broken? It may be impossible. I don't know. I've never made it to the last rib. People have always told me what I wanted to know. But I am sure it's hard to breathe. It *has* to be, doesn't it? I mean your rib cage expands—"

"What do you want to know?" the man asked pleadingly.

"Who is the dead man?"

"I don't know. Algerian."

"He was here to shoot down the Blue Angels, yes?"

"I don't know! He just wanted a place."

"To keep missiles, and you didn't ask what they were for?" The Lieutenant shook his head and shot the machine pistol forward again.

"Yes, an airplane! To shoot down an airplane!"

"An American airplane."

"Yes, I think so."

"How many missiles did you see?"

"I don't rememb—"

The Lieutenant's hand feinted a move forward and the man jerked. "Five! Five missiles total! Just five."

"Where are they now? There weren't any missiles in your warehouse."

"They all came. He was the last."

"Four others?"

"Yes."

"Did they come together?"

"No. Thirty minutes apart."

"Starting when?"

"At 3:30 A.M. The first."

"And was that Ismael Nezzar? The brother of the Algerian pilot who was shot down?" He pulled out Nezzar's passport photo and showed it to him.

The man's widening eyes told the lieutenant he had found him. "I don't know."

The machine pistol rammed forward but this time upward into the man's jaw, breaking it instantly. The Lieutenant leaned forward so the man could feel his hot breath on his throbbing face. "You *lied* to me again. I told you not to do that. I thought I could rely on you. But now I think I'm going to have to break your spine instead. I'll leave you in the sewer for the rats to chew. You won't be able to move anything because your neck will be broken. How long do you think you would last?" He let the man consider the question for a minute. "Tell me, I need to know, would you rather be face up in the gutter so you can see what is coming? Or face down, so the vomit spills out of your mouth?"

The man was beyond pain, verging on incoherence. He nodded, as the tears streamed down his face. He nodded again.

"What kind of van is Nezzar in?"

"Blummimm."

The lieutenant frowned. "I can't understand you very well. Here," he said, adjusting the man's jaw to increase the pain.

"Mrmrmrmrmrm!" the man screamed. "Blummimmm!"

"What?"

The other man couldn't stand to see his friend in such agony. "Plumbing! He is in a plumbing van!"

"What color?"

"Black."

"And the others?"

He told the Lieutenant the times and types of vans of all the shooters.

"One last question. What kinds of missiles did they have? Were they all like the one that your former friend shot at me? Russian SA-7s?"

The second man shook his head in complete fear. "No. Four were, but one was different."

"What was the different one?"

"American."

"Stinger?"

"I heard that name, but I don't know. They treated it differently. It was special somehow. It arrived differently."

"How did it arrive?"

"On a truck. A standard French delivery truck."

"Algerian driver?"

"No, he spoke Arabic, but he wasn't from North Africa."

"Thank you. You have been helpful. Perhaps we should discuss a future relationship."

"I don't know what you mean."

The Lieutenant moved down on the bench seat to look directly into the second man's eyes. "You were the only one to survive a violent shoot-out with the French counterterrorism forces in this warehouse. You're a hero. You can return to your community and tell them how evil we are, and I could make sure neither you nor anyone you care about is ever harmed or in need for anything."

"But I am not the only survivor," he said, looking at his boss.

The Lieutenant gazed at the other man holding his jaw and his ribs. "I'm afraid he didn't make it. It was very unfortunate—he charged us as we came into the warehouse, and he fell down the steps."

He understood the chilling implications of what the French Lieutenant was saying. "I don't know."

"Think about it. I'll be in touch with you." The Lieutenant told one of the other GIGN men, "Take care of these two," and hurried out of the APC. Rat followed him. He walked out into the street and looked at his men tearing up the warehouse. He took a deep breath. "We're done here," he said to Rat in English.

"This won't be easy, but we're closing in on them."

"A black plumbing van and three other blue Peugeot vans, unmarked. We'll find them."

"Good work." Rat watched the activity. The French counterterrorist group knew what it was doing. "I'm heading to the airport anyway, in case anyone escapes or we don't have them all. I want to be there during the air show."

The lieutenant nodded. "Can't hurt."

"Let me know if you get them all."

"You still have that same cell phone number?"

Rat nodded.

"I'll call you."

Stovic awoke with his stomach in turmoil. He skipped his usual morning run and ordered "café Americain and deux croissants" from room service, which appeared at his door in five minutes. As he devoured the second croissant there was a knock on the door. His heart jumped as he stood in the middle of the room in his boxer shorts. He felt completely defenseless. The knock came again. He went to the door and opened it, and it was Bean. "Hey," Stovic said as he stepped away from the door and let him in.

Bean was already in his Blue Angel flight suit, looking perfect. "Nice of you to get up." He looked around the messy room. "You going to the air show in your boxers?"

"Yeah. The new look—Blue Angel boxers—except they aren't blue."

Bean studied Stovic's face. He noticed the dark circles under his eyes and the generally disheveled appearance. He hadn't shaved. "You doing okay? You and I need to talk about anything? Cause you don't look so good. What did you do last night?"

"If I told you you wouldn't believe it."

"Try me."

"Nah. It was just a dream anyway."

"We've got the new flares loaded on all the planes."

"That was my job!" Stovic said, concerned.

"They called you, you were nowhere to be found. The Boss almost sent out the whole gendarme force to find you. I told him it was okay, you went to see Rat, and you'd be back, no problem. He told me to report to him when you returned. I guess you didn't see me sitting in the hall when you came back."

"You were sitting in the hallway?"

"Yeah. Trying to stay awake, which I didn't do. I was sleeping like a baby, but you guys were so loud, and the gendarmes were so concerned, I woke right up. Reported to the Boss and went back to bed. Anyway, we got the new flares. The ones that are supposed to work against a Stinger."

"Hallelujah," Stovic said, a great weight lifting from his shoulders. He felt for the first time as if he might make it through the air show unscathed. "How much time do we have?"

"Caravan leaves in one hour. You need to get your ass in gear."

"Roger that." He turned toward the bathroom. "Hey, Bean, thanks for sticking by me. I know you were sort of out there by yourself."

"No, I wasn't. You'd be there if it was one of us. You really think we'd walk away from one of our own?"

"I know it was talked about."

"We're all behind you, Animal. All of us. No exceptions. You've got to know that."

"Thanks, Bean."

"Let's just hope we're all making the right decision."


Ismael turned off the heat in the van. He was tired, and his eyes were beginning to feel raw. In spite of his intention to get plenty of rest the night before, he had been unable to sleep. He was more anxious than he expected as he drove through the deserted streets of northern Paris, then onto the auto-routes, then off.

He pulled into an all-night gas station, one of the few he had seen, and stopped next to a pump. He turned off the engine and leaned his head back against the headrest. Coffee, he thought. He needed coffee—the largest cup he could find. He sat up, rubbed his bearded face, and looked around for anything unusual before getting out of the van. He climbed out and put his prepaid, anonymous gas card into the slot in the pump. He placed the nozzle into the neck of the filler tube.

"So, brother," he heard a voice say from directly behind him. One foot behind him, so close that the mere existence of the voice gave him chills. He turned slowly, expecting the worst. He looked into the face of the man who had spoken and recognized him instantly. He was thrilled to see him but petrified at the same time. Ismael replied, "What are you doing here?"

"Looking out for you."

"What for?"

"Your friends, they mean well, but I have known of Madani for a very long time. He is not smart. His entire plan here was weak, and now he has paid the price."

"What do you mean?"

"After you left the warehouse, he led them to it. He was being followed. The French broke in, Madani was killed, and others were captured."

"That is impossible! That warehouse was known to *no one*!" Ismael said.

"They now undoubtedly have a description of your van and are looking all over for you. They are rolling up Madani's entire operation."

Ismael replaced the nozzle on the pump and the cap on the van. He stood looking at Salam. "How do you know all this?"

"I have had the warehouse watched day and night. They saw what just happened."

"And how did you know where the warehouse was?"

"Ismael," he said in a tone of disappointment, a how-could-you-doubt-me tone, "who do you think delivered the Stinger missile?"

Ismael's mind raced. "What now?"

"You will be dead in thirty minutes unless we get rid of that van. I am just around the corner. You will follow me, move everything of importance into another van I have for you. You must change everything."

"What about the missile?"

"Leave it in the van."

"What of Madani? He needs to know where I will be—"

"He is *dead*! And the others will be within the hour. You are the only one left. You will get your chance. Come quickly." He signaled with his hand, and a man about Ismael's height and age climbed into the plumbing van with a grin, gunned the motor, and rolled out of the gas station into the dark French morning.

Rat's team gathered in the apartment they had rented for the week next to Le Bourget. Rat had been horrified at how easy it had been to rent an apartment for a week that had a view of Le Bourget and a balcony. Anyone else could have rented an apartment in the same building. They would never be seen until they stepped onto the balcony with a missile.

The sliding door was open letting in the cool morning air. It was still dark. There were twenty men, most dressed in casual civilian clothes, but some were in camouflage and others in flight suits and security uniforms.

Rat brought everyone up to date on the latest developments. They all had their assignments. He laid out the map of the airport and showed them the large tree he had chosen. It was tall enough so that he could see in several directions for a long way and wasn't so full of foliage that he couldn't see out.

Robby asked, "French know where you're going to be?"

"Yeah. They know where each of us is going to be."

Robby shook his head. "You're taking that .50-caliber up in that tree? You'll need a damned crane to get it up there."

"It's already there. Groomer built me a duck blind. He carried the Barrett up there. Don't worry, I've got some other surprises too. You all set?"

They all nodded. One spoke. "Don't you think they'll get the rest of them? I mean you said that guy was singing. He told them about all the trucks."

"He did. I hope they find them all. Makes our job really easy. Maybe we'll be there just to watch a great air show. But we will be there. I never assume I've got it *all* figured out. That's when you get blindsided."

"Fair enough."

"You going to keep everybody up on our discrete freq?"

"Yeah. Everybody got the comm plan?"

They nodded.

"I'm going to have a lot of comm coming in, so I may not hear you. We're encrypted, so feel free to use my name. I've got a good view of pretty much the whole area, so if you need to call in my fire, do it. If it's too dangerous, I'll decide. If you need me, call me. If we need more help, the GIGN is here. I'll be in touch with Marcel, but I don't want to get in his way unless we need to." He looked around the room. They were getting restless.

Groomer had noticed the sky was getting lighter in the east. "You sure you want to be in a tree shooting a

.50 cal? The signature is enormous. You shoot once, they'll all know where you are."

Rat nodded. "If I were afraid of being seen, I wouldn't be up there at all. But you've built a good blind and cleared shooting lines of sight to most areas. That's all I need. And this will all happen in a few seconds, when they are ready to shoot. We'll be hard-pressed to see them before then, but when they get ready to shoot, we'd better be ready to fire. When that happens, I don't think their shooters will put down their missiles to try to get me. They may have others who are there to take care of people like me, but they'll never reach me. My .50 cal has a lot more range than whatever they have."

Groomer wasn't so sure. "They may have snipers too, or RPGs, all kinds of things."

Rat nodded. He had considered that. "It's possible. There's always some risk." He stood. "It's time," Rat said. They all stood. "Everybody got their assignments?"

They nodded.

"Let's go."

The Emergency Committee at the Le Bourget command center had notified the governments of France and the United States. In spite of its best efforts and in spite of being close, they had not found everyone in the Algerian cell that was intent on shooting down the Blue Angels or at least disrupting the air show. It was their recommendation that they cancel the Blue Angels, and the heated discussion now ongoing was about whether to cancel the entire air show.

In Washington, the news had been received by all the members of the national security team. The reactions had been mixed. It was late at night, past midnight when they were awakened and warned of the impending disaster and the recommendation to cancel. They all thought of Sarah St. John, the one who had pushed it, the one who had *insisted* that this was the way to eliminate the growing Algerian threat, which almost certainly had the Algerian government behind it. They were tempted to rub her nose in it.

But the more St. John heard about Ismael Nezzar and his relationship with the murderous band that had fought a vicious civil war for control of the government, and the subtle way he'd walked away from that just to attend an American university, the more sure she was that he'd been sent to the United States to be here in case he was needed. The fact that his brother was involved in the event that caused him to be called on to act simply made his resurgence sweeter. She wasn't at all surprised he was still at large on the eve of the air show. She had expected him to be.

She was fully dressed, and her driver was waiting. The President wanted everyone at the White House ASAP. She climbed into the limo. Brad Walker was sitting in the back waiting for her. They nodded to each other as the driver accelerated away from her Virginia home. The driver was thrilled to be driving in Washington without traffic. It made for a fifteen-minute trip instead of her usual forty-five minutes.

Walker handed her the latest intelligence reports, with Rat's latest e-mail on the top. She looked at Walker surprised, then at the driver, whose eyes were on the road. She read by a small laserlike spotlight on a gooseneck suspended over her right shoulder as they drove through the gate to the White House. They climbed out, walked inside, and he headed to her office while she turned to go to the situation room to meet with the other members of the national security team. She knew she would be on the receiving end of this.

She was the last one there. A staffer closed the door

behind her, and she took her seat. Hot coffee was in the pot in the middle of the table. She poured herself some.

President Kendrick looked tired and annoyed. "Well," he began, "our worst case scenario is here. We have our Navy flight demonstration squadron in Paris ready to perform, and we know the terrorists are definitely in Paris. Sarah, I think you said you wanted to lure them there, to give us a chance to get them. Well, half of that has happened." He looked directly at her, and she returned his gaze, nodding.

He went on. "We have received a recommendation from what is called the"—he looked down at his notes—"Emergency Committee, and thus from the French government. They say that they have identified many if not most of the terrorists from Algeria and may get them all tonight. But as of now they do not have them all, and they know for a fact that the terrorists have surface-to-air missiles, possibly including Stingers. They suggest that we cancel the Blue Angels. They are so concerned, in fact, that they are considering canceling the entire flight demonstration portion of the air show. They don't see the benefit in having them fly. That's their recommendation.

"So here we are in the middle of the night debating an air show. I frankly don't want to be here, and I don't want to be discussing this. This looks like an easy decision to me."

Stuntz jumped in at his first opportunity. He finally had his chance to torpedo his only rival. "I couldn't agree more," he said. "This whole thing is ridiculous. We have ways of getting to terrorists. We have counterterrorism teams. We have wonderful cooperation with the French counterterrorism people. We know where these people are—Paris—and we should leave it to the right people to get them. The Blue Angels are not a counterterrorism team, and frankly, using them as 'bait' was misguided and dangerous. I was against—"

"We know, Howard."

"I don't want to go on, Mr. President. I think we should just shut this thing down now."

Others spoke, generally in support of Stuntz.

Finally St. John spoke. "You are all forgetting two things. First, there is another airplane flying at this air show." They frowned. "The Joint Strike Fighter. It was agreed to let the Navy push the JSF into the air show agenda to increase sales to other countries who are less enthusiastic to cut the cost per airplane below the target level. Your department signed off on that, Howard. They're there for a purpose. No one has ever thought that maybe the terrorists from Algeria could target the JSF. But they could. How would that look? So are you going to cancel that flight as well?"

Stuntz was thrown off, but not for long. "Sure. We'll give a private demo to whoever wants them."

"So getting the JSF, all the logistics, all the support, getting all the Admirals and VIPs to Paris, that was all for naught?" she asked.

"At this point, apparently so. Better than getting the plane shot down."

"So you had considered it."

"Sure," he said.

"In any case," St. John went on, "as you can see from the most recent intelligence reports, so far this operation using U.S. and French security and intelligence has been a success. They have indeed found the Algerians, they found their headquarters, they found their storage facility, and they know the identity and contents of the vans that are part of the conspiracy. They have captured members of the cell and have obtained very useful intelligence from them. I expect their warn-

ing is just an attempt to ensure we understand the risk
we will be taking if we keep the air show on schedule.

"I believe that, with our help, they will find the rest
of the terrorists, including Nezzar, before the air show
starts. I think it would be counterproductive to cancel
it now. That would allow the terrorists to melt back
into the city and escape, able to strike later, when
we're far less well prepared to deal with it." She
looked around the room with a pleading look on her
face. "You all know how hard it is to get anywhere
near a terrorist cell like this. When you get this close,
you have to finish it. Yes, there is some risk. But it's
*worth* it. We have to stop them. If we let these Algerians slip away now—which they almost certainly will
do if their target goes away—we'll lose them. We can't
do that.

"The Blue Angels are military men. They are trained
and expected to take risks. This risk is for the benefit of
the country. We need to find *any* terrorist. It won't get
easier to find these men if we walk away from this. Do
we really shy away from this challenge because we
know they're still coming at us? I say go right at them.
We will *win*."

"The Blue Angels are *unarmed*, Sarah," Stuntz said.

She shook her head. "They have flares, and we have
a lot of people in place who are very well armed. This is
not an unequal fight. We will get these terrorists. We
must. We can't let them escape."

President Kendrick waited for the others to speak.
No one did. "Sorry, Sarah. I think in this situation,
with such a large threat—I mean what if they shot an
American jet into the crowd? It could kill thousands if
not tens of thousands of people! We simply can't risk
that. Sorry, but I think it's time to pull the plug. They
should keep looking for the terrorists and do what they
can, but I don't see the point in giving these Algerians a

big juicy target." He turned to Stuntz. "Pull the plug on the JSF *and* the Blue Angels."

Stuntz nodded.

They adjourned, and St. John joined back up with Walker, who had been waiting in her office. "Let's go," she said harshly as she walked quickly down the hall-way. They went to her limo and got in. As she settled in and the driver started, she closed the glass. She turned slightly toward Walker. "Is sending one of those encrypted e-mails hard?"

"No. Nothing to it."

"I want to send one to Admiral Hooker as well. What if he doesn't have the software?"

"I can imbed the software in the e-mail you want to send to him, as well as the execution file to make it all operate right. Sounds like you have somebody else in mind too."

"Mr. Rathman."

"He's got to be chasing people around over there. Think he can get an e-mail?"

"He can get these e-mails on his phone."

Walker was surprised. "So what's the plan?"

"I want to give them some instructions. Contingency instructions, in case things don't work the way everyone seems to think they will go." She stared at the brightly lit Washington Monument in the dark night. "Do you have your laptop with you?"

"Sure."

"Let's start drafting."


The Police Nationale had people on nearly every street and corner in Paris. They weren't looking for pedestrians anymore. They had specific vehicles they were looking for, if their information was accurate. Their orders were clear, and they expected any encounter to end violently.

Anouar, the man who had replaced Ismael, also had clear orders. He was to drive around Paris cautiously. Other than at traffic lights he was not to stop at all. He would continue driving through the morning, and as 2:00 P.M. approached, he was to drive to Le Bourget airport, wait until the Blue Angels were overhead and broke up in their fleur-de-lis maneuver, one of the last things they would do, turn on the Stinger, on which he had received training, and at the right moment, open the rear doors, step out, and fire.

Anouar had never been to Paris before but had a good map and was confident he could complete his mission. Salam had never shown so much confidence in him before. He had never even been trusted to take on a mission outside the country, let alone one where he was to operate by himself. And to take on the Americans was a demonstration of trust in him that he had never expected. It could only mean good things for his future with Salam.

He was tired but excited. The van drove nicely, and no one paid any attention to him at all. He had found a very long street, a four-lane road that went for ten kilometers without any major turns. Rather than get lost in some of the difficult areas of Paris, he had decided to drive up and down on the boulevard, one way, then the other, until it was time, then out to the airport. No way to get lost.

He turned and drove back the other way, checking the fuel and engine instruments. Everything was perfect.

The French operator of the Mini-Mart had been up all night. He looked up from *Le Monde* and saw the black plumbing van make another U-turn along the quiet boulevard. The man frowned. Was that the third U-turn? Fourth? And what is a plumbing van doing out on a Sunday morning at 6:00 A.M.? Something not quite right about it. He picked up the phone. His call went to the Paris police, who quickly routed the call to the national police. They had been waiting for such a call. They asked for the description and location of the van. It was all they needed.

It was twenty minutes before they could get there, but they quickly spotted the black plumbing van driving at exactly the speed limit on the wide boulevard. Two police cars and a van were routed ahead of the van by several blocks. They turned onto the boulevard heading in the same direction and watched the van behind them in their mirrors. Two police vehicles and another van full of men approached from the rear. One was sent ahead to stop it.

The Police Peugeot turned on its blue lights and closed to thirty feet behind the van.

Anouar saw the blue lights reflecting in his mirror. He nearly panicked. He had done *nothing* to bring attention to himself. This must just be a routine traffic stop. If he stayed cool, nothing would happen. He would show them his papers, and all would be well.

He pulled over to the side of the road and came to a gentle stop. The police car stopped behind him, and suddenly a second car shot around him and pulled in front of him, pointing in toward the curb, blocking his way. His heart began to beat furiously. He was running out of options. He glanced at the assault rifle on the floor beside him. It was ready to fire, but he knew that if he had to use it, his chances of escape were nil.

The man wearing the blue uniform of the Police Nationale approached his window. Anouar lowered it with the handle, taking a good long time. The sun was near the horizon, and it was easy to see. The policeman looked at him carefully and spoke to him in French. "Driver's license."

Anouar didn't speak French. He said in Arabic,

"What do you want? I don't speak French. I need to go."

Suddenly a second gendarme stuck his head in front of the first and yelled at him in Arabic. "Keep your hands on the wheel! What is your name?"

He was shocked to hear Arabic. He had expected to be able to use the lack of communication as his reason for not giving them any information. "Yes, yes," he said, putting his hands on the wheel. He inched his heel over toward the accelerator as his foot held the brake.

"Give me your license!"

Anouar put his hand up, showing it was empty, and began reaching slowly for the papers in his pocket. He handed his Uzbek driver's license to the gendarme.

"What are you doing, driving up and down the boulevard? Where are you going?"

"I am looking for the building where I am supposed to work this morning. I cannot find it."

"What is the number?"

He tried to remember some numbers he had seen on the road and choose one somewhere in the middle. If he gave him a number that was nowhere on the road, they would know he was lying. "One three four zero."

"What work?"

"Install a new water heater. Their water heater broke Friday, and they are desperate. Sunday costs three times what this would cost during the week. They didn't care. They said come Sunday morning."

The policeman had a grizzled face and a mean disposition. "At five in the morning?"

"It is not five," he said, trying to smile.

"No, but you have been driving up and down this road since five have you not?"

"Yes. I didn't want to be late."

"Get out of the van," the policeman said suddenly, pulling on the door handle. It was locked.

"What are you doing?" Anouar cried. "Leave me alone!"

"Out!"

Anouar froze. He didn't know what to do. If he reached for his weapon he would be too slow, and it was too confined to point an AK-47 at the policeman. He rammed his foot onto the accelerator and let out the clutch at the same time. The van shot forward, slamming into the small car in front of him. He drove it to the left, pushing its nose away from the curb as the tires on his van smoked under the torque of the engine and the resistance of the police car. He broke free and drove up onto the curb, around the police car, and down the boulevard.

The two policemen ran back to their car as the police van raced around them. They got on the radio. Several more cars raced to the scene but were minutes away. The two in front of Anouar's plumbing van pulled across the boulevard, blocking the two lanes between them and the racing van. The four men got out of their cars with machine guns and shotguns.

Anouar saw them and saw that his way was blocked ahead and behind. He had only one chance. He drove up on the grassy median, between two large trees, and into the oncoming lanes. Traffic was light, and no cars were in his way.

The four national police who were waiting for him ran across the median and pointed their weapons at him. Anouar saw them, ensured he was pointed straight down the road, and leaned over below the dash. Bullets crashed through the windshield, scattering glass all over his neck and hair. He could hear shotgun blasts slamming into the fender and hood and felt the van jerk to the right as his right front tire was shot out. He felt the bullets and pellets hitting the van to his right, then behind him. He sat up, corrected his line, and continued down the road into the traffic. It was difficult to hold the van straight with a blown tire in the front, but he could do it with effort. At an intersection he crossed back over to the right side of the road, but by now the police van was right behind him.

A red light lit up on his indicator panel. The engine temperature was getting dangerously high. One of the bullets must have pierced a hose. He cursed and looked for a road to turn down. He had to find another vehicle. The blue van was right behind him.

He slowed to turn. It was the chance the police had been waiting for. The van skidded to a halt, and a man in the front jumped out with a semiautomatic shotgun. He pumped shell after shell low into the van, aiming for the wheels, the tires, the brake lines, the exhaust system, the transmission—anything that would stop the van. Shot after shot sent hundreds of pellets into the van and the pavement below as the crippled van tried to negotiate the sharp turn without turning over.

The left rear wheel suddenly gave way and folded over, coming completely off the axle. Sparks shot out as the metal scraped along the asphalt and the van ground to a halt.

Anouar grabbed the AK-47 and jumped out. He headed for an alleyway as bullets cracked into the stone buildings on either side of him. He looked over his shoulder and saw eight or nine men pursuing him with automatic weapons. He reached the corner, shifted the AK to his left hand, and began returning fire in the full automatic mode. He had two clips for his AK, one that was loaded and a second taped to the first. When the first was empty, he needed only to pull it out, turn it over, and insert the second.

He aimed at the running men and was hit by dozens of 9-millimeter bullets. He spun around the corner of the building and fell to the ground mortally wounded.

The police came to the corner of the alley, covered each other carefully, entered the darkness, and found Anouar lying in a pool of blood.

"Should we get an ambulance?"

"No," said the Arabic-speaking policeman. "He is finished."

"Guy!" another yelled from the back of the van.

He turned.

"Come see this! It looks like a shoulder-fired missile. The writing is in English!"

The French continued to arrest every known Algerian troublemaker and even many of whom they were simply suspicious while they scoured the city for the remaining vans from the Algerian team. There were loud complaints of mistreatment and brutality. As the time approached, the security noose closed around the entire city. Security was everywhere, in a depth and thoroughness that impressed the Americans. At its center, as the Blue Angels readied to head to Le Bourget, French Police Nationale surrounded the Americans, two to each Blue Angel, like personal body guards or the Secret Service. They had machine guns and vests and were deadly earnest.

The entire street and circling driveway in front of the hotel were lined with armed Police Nationale, some in regular uniform, many in much more serious gear, with automatic weapons and obvious bulletproof vests. The route to Le Bourget had been revised since the journey on Friday.

The Blue Angels gathered in the lobby in their royal blue flight suits with their khaki caps pulled down to their eyebrows. The time for their show had been moved up. Several other performers had canceled when they learned what had caused so much additional security. Without prior notice, the Emergency Committee changed the order of the air show participants, and the Blues were now scheduled to fly at 10:00 A.M.

Outside the lobby of the hotel the Peugeots waited in a line. They were different models and colors than on Friday. They had been inspected for problems and bombs and had been watched every second since.

The Boss checked to make sure everyone was ready, checked his watch, and nodded to the lead policeman, who was treating the American pilots like heads of state. He didn't want anyone to even get close to them.

Animal climbed into the black Peugeot where Oden was waiting. Neither spoke. The line began to move, and the French police led the way as the caravan snaked through the narrow streets, feeling exposed and vulnerable. The sirens screamed and the lights flashed as they made their way toward the freeway on their way to Le Bourget.

Oden looked over at Stovic, who was staring out the window to the side. "You ready?"

"Sure," Stovic replied quickly.

"I'll keep my eyes peeled for us, Animal. I'll make sure nothing happens to us."

Stovic sensed a certain camaraderie from Oden that he hadn't often felt before. Maybe he just felt sorry for his friend. Stovic replied, "If they actually get a shot off, you'll probably see it before me. It'll probably come from behind me. Just yell flares, and I'll dump my whole load. We'll light up the air show like it's Christmas."

"Shit, Animal. We can't do that," he said.

"Why not?"

"Because then the spectators will love it, and they'll want us to do the flare thing at *all* our shows."

Stovic forced a smile. "If you wanted to get an airplane with a shoulder-fired missile, is there any doubt in your mind you could get the missile off?"

"No." Oden knew he could. He knew the Algerian could too if he was determined and careful. But he still hoped that with the security in place, there would be enough notice to keep him from succeeding.

The Blue Angels wheeled onto the airfield through the main access road but turned off before reaching the terminal. The lead police vehicle led them down an unmarked road toward the operations building at the airfield. The air show was well under way.

The Blue Angels filed into the briefing room. A large mahogany table dominated the conference room, and snacks and pastries lay on a side table against the paneled wall. It was such a beautiful room the Blue Angels found themselves speaking in subdued tones. What was usually an enjoyable time, if not exactly full of levity, was tempered by the two FBI agents sitting in on the brief; not VIPs interested in the Blue Angels, not local dignitaries the Navy was trying to impress, but two federal officers trying to keep them from getting killed, Lew and Patricia, who felt like small dogs trapped on a freeway, dashing around and not accomplishing much, with disaster always just around the corner.

Several Blue Angels drew coffee from the urn and sat in their usual places. They were doing their best to make it feel like another ordinary air show. Routine. They were all very aware of the swirl of security around them and the anxiety that dominated everyone's thinking, but they tried to pretend it wasn't there.

Exactly on time the Boss began the brief. He worked very hard to stay normal. With so much attention being paid to security, with the subtle way security concerns were dominating the thinking of his pilots, he knew he had to conduct a brief that refocused them on

the flight before them. If they continued to be distracted, they might risk more from an accident than
from any terrorist. "Good morning," he began.

"Good morning, Boss," they replied in unison, leaning over the most recent aerial photo of the airport,
which they had memorized, seeing all the landmarks
and their orientation to the runway.

"It's a beautiful day for flying. We're scheduled for a
1000 takeoff. Earlier than usual, but not unusual for us
in winter training. Just think of this as our first flight in
El Centro."

The pilots smiled, remembering the beautiful days of
desert flying and the quaint concerns about precision
flying and Mexican food.

The Boss continued the brief. "Okay. We're parked
in reverse order for a remote reverse walk-down. We'll
crank 'em up on eight, nine, and eighteen, take off
checks in the chocks.

"It'll be a left ninety out of the chocks and go wingman clear of the parking.

"Take the runway for the covered wagon. When
Bean's ready we'll go sixteen, comm two. We'll be
cleared for takeoff with a wind check. Check parking
brake is off.

"Maneuvers for the diamond. We'll go a diamond
burner loop with a right turn out, followed by Oden's
dirty roll on takeoff and Animal's low-transition, high
performance climb to split-S."

The Boss then began to run them through the entire
routine with the same calls as if they were actually flying.
The pilots leaned back. Most closed their eyes and
fell into a sort of trancelike state. The Boss assumed
the same croaky singsong voice he used on the radio.
"Power, burners . . . ready . . . now, power . . . set,
gear. Up . . . we . . . go . . . a lit-tle . . . more . . . pull . . .

burners ready . . . now . . . easing the pull . . . easing
the power . . . easing more power . . . boards . . . smoke
off . . . now. Come . . . uz . . . a . . . pull. . . ."

With their eyes still closed, the pilots moved their
hands as if they were holding the sticks in their jets,
moving them back and forth as if they were flying
through each maneuver, visualizing it as the Boss
talked them through it. One maneuver after the other
for the entire air show.

Stovic kept his eyes closed, flying his F/A-18 in his
mind, closer than he had ever come to Oden on the
passes, smoother than he had ever felt on the pull-ups
and turns. It was a ballet, all the way to the break,
when the Blue Angels were about to land. . . .

The door opened loudly, breaking the atmosphere
and the rule against interrupting the brief. The Boss
stopped in the middle of a sentence and looked angrily
at the intruder. It was Admiral Hooker. He knew no
one was to intrude on the brief, but there was something he had to say. "Boss, sorry. Sorry guys," he said to
the rest of the team, raising a hand in apology. Hooker
was in his dress blues and looked handsome but
drained. His face didn't have the usual tennis-tan-all-is-
well look. "I am really sorry to interrupt your brief. I
know how sacred a time it is. But this is important."

The Boss sat back, looked around the table, and put
his hand up to indicate the brief was on hold. "What is
it, Admiral?"

"I've received word from Washington. Frankly, I'm
glad. I was up all night imagining how horrible this
could be if these terrorists got through. If they actually
shot down one of you . . . it would be catastrophic.
More catastrophic to the Navy than losing the Blue
Angels would be. Sorry." He walked slowly behind
three of the Blue Angels who weren't looking at him.
"It was my idea for you to come over here." He smiled

ironically. "And that is the very thing that probably put you in the greatest danger. We were closing in on this maniac in the States, I'm told. Well, Washington, from the highest authority, has told us to cancel the air show. Not only the Blues, but also the JSF, which was to fly right before you. The whole reason we came over here," he said with an annoying smile full of relief.

The Blue Angels looked at each other. They tried not to show the contempt they were feeling for this pretty Admiral and his burning conscience. They were willing to take the risk, but now they weren't going to be allowed.

"Just like that?"

"Yes. I'm sorry. It isn't worth the risk."

"We've been living with this risk, Admiral. We think it *is* worth the risk. We're willing to do it. It wouldn't be fair to the team to bring us all this way when we know the risk. Has something changed? If anything, it's gotten better. We've been told the French have taken care of most of the risk. I say we go forward." He looked at the other pilots sitting around the table. He knew them well enough. They didn't need to say anything. "Now if you'll excuse us, we need to continue briefing."

"It isn't that simple, Boss. This is an order. From Washington."

"From whom, exactly?"

"SECDEF," Hooker replied. The Secretary of Defense.

The door flew open, and François and Elizabeth burst into the room. "Excuse us, but we wanted to inform you right away," she said, looking at the Americans sitting along the walls of the room and the Blues sitting alone at the table. She ignored Lew's skeptical stare. "We have broken up the ring of terrorists that was after you," Elizabeth announced triumphantly. "We have captured or killed them all. The last one, this

Ismael, who started all this, was sighted in a plumbing van. He fought and was killed. His Stinger missile was captured intact." She smiled with closed lips, a smug, self-important smile, which showed that she had not discussed with François who was going to make the announcement and had done it herself before he could say anything.

The Boss sat back, showing the relief all the Blues felt. "Thank you." He looked at Admiral Hooker. "Well. We were briefing, Admiral. Would you like to join us? There's a seat right over there."

Admiral Hooker got it right away. He nodded, his face showing color again, and walked to the door. "Perhaps after I go tell the people who are here with the JSF. They would want to know. Maybe we can still kill both birds with one stone." His smile faded. "Bad analogy. Sorry. Anyway, please forgive me for interrupting, Boss. You've got work to do."

Lew walked over and extended his hand to Elizabeth. She took it triumphantly.

He spoke softly, so the others couldn't hear. "You sure you got them *all*?"

"Yes. We believe we have," she said a little less firmly.

Lew heard the equivocation. "Are you *sure*?" Lew pressed.

François replied. "We found their warehouse and got there at the same time as their leader."

"I *know* that. But what about Ismael?"

"They arrived to pick up their missiles," François said, ignoring him, "and ended up in a gun battle with several of them. Two—actually one—was captured and described the vans and trucks the others had. Over this morning we have located every van and every missile. We have captured all the shooters."

The Boss had been eavesdropping. "Even the one who had it out for Animal here?"

"Yes, sir. He had changed his appearance somewhat, grown his hair out, grown a beard, but it's him—"

"And you found all the missiles?" Lew pressed.

"Every one."

"You believe him?" Stovic asked, focused.

"We had our best interrogator on it. He is quite confident."

"One of them had a Stinger—"

François jumped in. "We got the Stinger. It was in this Ismael Nezzar's van—a plumbing van. There was an exchange of gunfire, but we got the Stinger. And in that exchange of bullets, this Ismael, this terrorist from Algeria, was killed, I am proud to tell you. You won't hear about it on the news—we don't like giving them their sought-after martyr status."

Lew was uneasy. "Did you identify the body?"

"He has been identified."

"By who?"

"By one of our best officers."

Lew stood. "Take me to his body. I sat across the table from him. I've stared at his photo every day for weeks. I want to ID him myself."

"It is not necessary—"

"Take me to him!" Lew yelled.

François hesitated. "You do not think we are capable of identifying a terrorist?"

Lew wasn't going to play games. "No. I don't."

"And why is that?"

"I don't feel like arguing with you, *Francis*. Just take me to his damned body. Is his face intact?"

François reddened, then nodded. He looked at Elizabeth, then motioned with his head for her to take Lew to the body. She was furious at the way it had been handled, not recognizing any of it as the payback for stealing François's thunder. She stormed off with Lew behind her. Patricia stayed where she was.

The Boss sat back and drank some water. "We okay to keep briefing, Admiral?" he asked Hooker.

"Of course. The risk has been taken care of. I will communicate to Washington. The JSF will still go first. Fly a great air show. Make us proud!" Hooker smiled as he hurried off to make sure the JSF team could stay on schedule.

The Boss looked at the overhead photo and got himself back in the correct mind-set. "Lining up for the diamond flyby." The Blue Angel pilots returned to their meditative positions. "Coming . . . left . . . a lit-tle . . . more . . . pull. . . ."

Rat had been in place for three hours. He had chosen the perfect tree in the early morning before daylight. He had donned his gillie suit and aimed his long-range .50-caliber sniper rifle in the direction where he expected the threat to appear. He had taken the last water and food he would consume before assuming his current position. He had stopped moving.

The small cell phone earpiece in his left ear came alive. His French phone was on auto answer after one silent ring. "Yes," he whispered.

"Rat?" Jean said.

"Oui."

"We got them."

"Ismael?"

"Yes. Including his Stinger. It was a plumbing van, as our new friend told us."

Rat was surprised. "Congratulations," he whispered. "Were you involved?"

"No, it was the Police Nationale. The GIPN."

Rat frowned. "You have confidence in them?"

"Yes. They are excellent."

"But you didn't see Ismael. You weren't there."

"No."

"How do we know it was him?"

"Who else would it be?"

"I have no idea. Who identified him?"

"Someone from the DST."

"He wasn't destroyed in the fight?"

"No. He was shot several times, but his face was intact."

"So we're sure?"

"Yes. We are staying in place, but the DST have told our government and yours that the threat has been eliminated."

"Stinger?"

"I told you. Intact. In the van. You can come down out of your tree and enjoy the air show."

"Thanks," Rat said, still whispering. He cut off the connection. The relief he felt was immediate and complete. He knew he would pay with stiffness for the stillness he had maintained for some time now. It would be nice to stand on the ground and move around.

He sat up and looked through the sight lines he had established out of the tree, toward the building straight away from the runways, the route Stovic would take when he approached with Oden, the line to his right, toward the runway itself, the line directly behind him toward the crowd, the buildings, and the operations center. He had a good spot. There wasn't one better anywhere nearby. And now he wouldn't need it. He sighed and smiled as he started packing his gear. He put away two of the miniature radios, then stopped.

Ismael let himself be caught in a van? True, they probably weren't in contact with each other; they wouldn't want their comm tracked. That was the error made by their spy, the one who was now looking for some bandages and antiseptic. So of course Ismael could have been caught. The French knew what to look for, and he didn't know they were after him.

But Ismael was clever. Things with him weren't always what they appeared to be. Rat was still convinced Ismael had contacted the FBI on purpose. He settled back down into his perch with his sniper rifle and huge scope under leaflike camouflage. He put his right eye back to the scope. It wouldn't hurt anything to stay where he was. If nothing else came of it, fine. He listened to the other radio earpiece. The security forces were passing the word. The terrorists had been caught. Some were laughing, some were celebrating the good teamwork of the Emergency Committee that had brought everyone together and successfully stopped a known terrorist threat. They were crowing quietly and patting themselves on the back. Even the FBI's channel was full of self-congratulation. There had been reports among the French that some of the FBI's special agents had magically shown up to support the attack on the terrorists' weapons garage. The men there unmistakably had their FBI jackets on and were American. They knew more than they let on was the conclusion and had appropriately stayed out of the way to let the French take the lead. They had gotten a lot of credit for that too.

Rat looked through his scope again. He picked up his scan where he had left off—any place for a shooter to hide. Everything was amazingly quiet. He looked over the top of the rifle. Nothing out of the ordinary or out of place. He shifted his weight. He put his face against the stock of the rifle again and looked through the scope, moving it slowly, waiting for nothing.

Stovic and the other Blue Angels stood in a line shoulder to shoulder in front of their polished blue jets. They were five minutes away from starting their walk down the line in front of their aircraft to begin their air show. Stovic glanced over at the stands and into the VIP section. He had never seen more Admirals in one place in his life. Directly in front of them was the Admirals' baby, the Joint Strike Fighter, the one that had been selected in 2001 in a flyoff between Boeing and Lockheed. The Lockheed design had won the contracts for some four thousand airplanes. This was the winner, the one selected to replace the aging attack planes of the Navy, Air Force, and Marine Corps. It had just finished its flawless air show routine, sure to inspire interest from other countries that were sitting on the fence. It had landed triumphantly and taxied to its position in front of the stands.

The Boss spoke the command to begin marching, exactly as he had at every show and every practice, quietly but unmistakably. *"Atten-hut!"*

"For-ward, *har.*"

The Blue Angels marched down the tarmac with their shoulders touching. As they reached each jet, a pilot executed a smart right turn and marched to his airplane. Stovic was first. He climbed up into his cockpit. His crew chief followed him up the ladder, helped him strap in, and handed him his helmet. He caught himself looking around at the buildings, the crowd, the runways, the perimeter of the airfield; anything different, out of the ordinary, threatening, shining, anything. He knew they had found Ismael and the others but found his relief incomplete. He saw nothing out of the ordinary. The blueness of the sky seemed brighter than he remembered it when they had arrived for their brief under a smothering police escort. The 9-millimeter Glock in his pocket felt silly. He was sure the other Blues had noticed the bulge, which made him feel even more stupid.

On command, the Blue Angels lowered their
canopies and turned on the radios. Stovic lowered his
gold-mirrored visor in front of his eyes and positioned
his lip mike until it touched his lips. No oxygen mask
for the Blue Angels. No G-suit. Just their blue flight suit
and the straps for the parachute over their shoulders
and lap, and they were ready.

Lew thought the Police Nationale car was a joke. It
was so small he could fit a six-pack of them into his
garage. Riding in the backseat was torture. His brace,
belly, and attitude were all in the way. He didn't even
try to put on the shoulder harness. It would take a con-
tortionist to get his arm to where the seat belt rested behind his left shoulder. They motored through the
streets of Paris at a leisurely clip, no lights, no siren;
just driving along. He was furious. "Can we hurry it
along a bit?" he asked.

Elizabeth turned and glared at him. "You want us to
use lights and siren?"

"Yes!" he replied.

"To see a dead body? He isn't going anywhere," she
quipped.

Lew held his tongue for the remainder of the fifteen-
minute ride. The car finally pulled up in front of yet another stunning marble building built two hundred
years ago and beautifully maintained. But this one
housed the Paris morgue in the basement.

Lew was sweating profusely as he hurried to keep up
with Elizabeth. She was angry, and her dislike of Lew
was showing. She didn't care if his neck hurt or even if
it stopped him completely. She was insulted that he insisted on seeing the body of a man already identified by
the French.

The basement of the building was cold and clammy,
but nothing stopped Lew's sweating. Part of his sweat

was from the exertion that had taxed his ability to endure the pain of his not-quite-healed cervical spine. The other part was from the haunting fear that they were being outmaneuvered while the hands on his watch approached 10:00 A.M.

They walked quickly into the reception area, which was brightly lit and clean. A Frenchman in a white coat greeted them, unhappy that they were there. Whenever anyone visited the morgue who didn't work there, it was always bad news. Either they were there to identify someone who shouldn't be dead, or they were there because they thought the dead person was other than who he had been identified to be. Always bad news, always trouble. He hated visitors.

Elizabeth nearly yelled. "We need to see a body. He was brought in here this morning. Arab. Several bullet wounds."

"I have a few of those."

"This one would have been about . . ." She dug in her purse for the information she had been given on her cell phone on the way over. "Here he is, decedent number six-six-five."

The man nodded as he examined the number on the piece of paper she had read from. "Your ID?"

Elizabeth gave it to him. He looked at it and gave it back.

"What about him?"

Lew hadn't understood anything either of them had said, but could tell the man was expecting something else before access would be granted. "Look, dumbass, we need to see this body now!" he yelled.

The man looked at Elizabeth again. "And who is this loud person?"

"American. FBI."

"Tell him I need to see his identification."

"He needs to see your identification."

"To see a dead person? This is *bullshit*!" Lew roared. He pulled his FBI identification out and showed it to the man. "There! Where's *your* ID as the person in charge of dead people?" he roared, hoping the man didn't speak English.

"What is the matter with him?" he asked Elizabeth.

"He is an angry American."

The man nodded, gave Lew a condescending look, and led them to a refrigerated room full of small stainless steel doors. He opened the door corresponding to six-six-five and rolled the man out. He lifted the cover and showed the face to them.

Lew walked around so he was looking at the man as if he was standing up. There was a bullet hole just over the left ear that had distorted the shape of the head, but not so much that there was any doubt. Lew's heart went cold. "Shit! It's not him!" he said, his mind spinning to the various possible places Ismael could be now. "It's not him!" he yelled. "We've got to get back. Get on your phone." He pulled out his radio and tried to call the other FBI agents, but his radio wouldn't work in the basement. "Can you get out?"

She tried her radio. Nothing. She looked at him with a pained, embarrassed look. "Are you *positive*?"

"Yes! I'm positive!"

"We've got to get back to the airport! Now!"

The Blue Angel diamond pulled up into their loop. White smoke streamed behind them as the Admirals and the enormous crowd followed their trajectory in the sparkling blue sky. Stovic's heart pounded as he waited at the end of the runway. He listened to the boss, "*A . . . lit-tle . . . less . . . poooower . . . ,*" as the Blue Angel diamond pulled over the top on their backs, looking for all the world like four airplanes welded together three thousand feet above the ground. "*Speed breaks . . . now.*"

Oden lifted off and kept his landing gear down. He maintained the minimum speed necessary to stay airborne, pulled his nose up slightly, and rolled the airplane over on its back with its landing gear sticking up away from the ground like a dead bug. He kept rolling back over in a fluid motion that brought it around again so that the landing gear was only twenty feet off the ground. It was a scary roll to watch as the airplane completely lost lift twice when its wings were perpendicular to the ground. Since he was at minimal airspeed and altitude, any miscalculation would bring the Hornet slamming down into the runway. But Oden had perfected the roll. His execution this time was no different as he cleaned up his aircraft, raised his gear and flaps, and threw his throttles full forward to race off to his reference point for the pass with Animal.

Stovic jammed his throttles outward and forward into full afterburner. He released the brakes and leaned slightly forward as his Hornet raced down the runway. He kicked in a little right rudder and made a mental note that the crosswind was slightly stronger than briefed. He held his Hornet on the deck a little longer than usual . . . one hundred forty, one fifty . . . he pulled the nose up sharply but just until he was ten feet off the ground and pushed the nose back level quickly. He pulled up the landing gear and flaps. The perfectly tuned hydraulics whirred the flaps up and carried the gear into the belly of the plane.

As he approached midpoint, where the large white semi tractor-trailer was parked, he passed through two hundred knots and continued to accelerate. The runway at Le Bourget was long—by the time he reached the end he was at four hundred knots.

Stovic lowered the nose of the Hornet just slightly, then jerked viciously back on the stick. The Hornet pivoted around its center point and the roaring tailpipes rotated downward, sending afterburner exhaust onto the runway, then the dirt at the end of the runway just inches over the threshold lights, with such violence that the crowd gasped, thinking the back of his airplane had hit the ground. As the crowd looked on in horror, Stovic rocketed out of the dust cloud up into the sky in a demonstration of raw power and acceleration. He unloaded the Gs on the airplane and climbed up at a forty-five–degree angle. The airplane held four hundred fifty knots as he pulled away from the ground without losing any airspeed, defying gravity as long as he chose to.

\* \* \*

Ismael felt for the button on the outside of his digital watch. Although the sound of the Hornets going into afterburner was slightly delayed in getting to him because of the distance, he knew it was close enough to start his stopwatch. He knew the show so well he could point to where Stovic was going to be at any moment. He didn't have to look. He had been dropped off in a Dumpster, a big blue one with French writing that prohibited its use by anyone except Le Corporation Aeronautique de Lyon, which, conveniently, did not exist. It had been placed at the end of a line of booths that extended all the way past the end of the runway, parallel to it. He had been driven through the security line as if it weren't even there. Salam himself hadn't actually driven through, of course, but rather one of the many people Salam was using, without names or explanations.

When he had first seen Salam, Ismael had immediately known it had been inevitable. When he learned of the existence of an entire alternative plan, organization, and weapons, of which he had been completely unaware, his beliefs had been confirmed. Salam had been completely right about Madani. Eager but untested. Likely to make a critical or fatal mistake. Now it was different altogether.

Ismael's small protective steel cave had grown hot and stuffy. He was running out of oxygen. He illuminated his watch. He removed the flashlight from his pocket and checked the Stinger. He flipped the switch to turn on the electronics and run a self-contained electronic test, a BIT test, as the Americans called it—Built-In Test—required every time the missile was powered up. He began to breathe harder as the moment approached. He grimaced as the missile went through its checks, slower than he had ever remembered them going before, taking at least ten times longer than usual.

But everything was checking out beautifully as the blue and gold jets screamed overhead, vibrating his dumpster with their thunderous presence.

Rat listened on the radio to every syllable of the Blue Angels' flight. He knew he might be the only one able to warn them if he saw a missile fired from behind them. In his other ear was the radio for the Police Nationale, the gendarmes, the GIGN, and the GIPN. Some units had been given their own discrete frequency, but everyone was to monitor the general frequency as well. Rat understood the French and could tell that although the general sense of completion was dominating their work, they were still going through the motions.

*"Check the truck parked behind a building in a parking lot. It is idle, but there are people inside, or at least one person. Request assistance. One kilometer due west of the end of the runway. By the tire store."*

Rat moved, aimed his rifle slightly south, and focused on the truck a thousand yards away from his position. He had seen the truck before. It was a good shooting position. Even with hundreds of gendarmes, Police Nationale, and FBI now swarming all over the area, it was too large an area to cover all possible shooting positions with any effectiveness. He focused on the truck and could detect movement in the driver's seat.

The operations center had become nearly silent. Quiet confidence and self-congratulation had replaced panic and disappointment.

That changed quickly. Elizabeth and Lew had finally reached a place where they could transmit. They shouted the news on different frequencies to different people. Everyone participating in security heard about it at the same time. The dead man wasn't Ismael. Lew was sure.

The security forces all around the airport suddenly knew they'd been had. They tried to avoid panic as they went to maximum alert and protection. They ran toward anything suspicious. Police cars flew around the perimeter. Gendarmes were stopping everyone with anything that could contain a missile. Le Bourget had become an intense, frenzied place filled with radio communication and last-minute attempts to avoid a disaster that they didn't understand.

One group of Police Nationale men raced toward a van off the airport, while another group suddenly began transmitting on the radio from the southwest section of the grid. Their position was marked on the large computer screen in the front of the operations room. *"Suspected launch tube projecting out of a bush. We are closing in."*

*"Need assistance?"*

*"Negative,"* they replied in French.

The FBI agents were on a separate radio frequency. Lew had a horrible feeling that no matter what they did, they would never anticipate what was about to happen. They had been outmaneuvered, but he couldn't imagine who was behind it. They had gotten all the Algerians. So was Ismael operating by himself? Could be, but Lew doubted it. And if not, who was helping him?

Lew looked up as the radio speaker in the front of the room broadcast the voice of a French officer followed by the unmistakable sound of gunfire. Lew leaned toward the interpreter, who looked grave. "They were approaching a construction site. They saw a man dragging a body away from a portable toilet. Inside the toilet was a missile launcher. They closed and"—he waited for

more information—"he fired on them. They fired and
he is down. The top of the toilet is hinged—he was going to stand on the seat and fire from inside the toilet.
Quite clever, but he will not be shooting anyone. There
must be others. Everyone is looking. . . ."

Lew nodded, still listening to the FBI channel. They
had no idea of the scope of the threat, the origin of the
threat, or its composition. They had nothing. He
turned to Patricia. "Why the *hell* don't they just declare
victory and land their damn planes?"

"Because no one has told them about these sightings!
They don't even know this is happening. Last thing
they heard the French had gotten Ismael. They have no
idea!"

Lew ran to the front of the room. "Where's a radio I
can use to talk to the Blue Angels?"

A small thin man looked at him and replied in good
English, "We are forbidden to be on that frequency."

"I didn't ask you for your stupid opinion! Where is a
radio I can use to talk to them?"

François saw the commotion. "What is the matter?"

"We need to warn the Blue Angels."

François glanced at the wall clock. "They will be
done soon!"

"Bullshit!" Lew yelled. "Where's the radio?"

"Right there," Francois pointed.

Lew grabbed the handset and listened. The frequency was quiet. *"Boss, this is Special Agent Lew Savage. They didn't get Ismael. Do you read me?"*

*"Affirmative,"* the Boss replied.

*"We've seen a couple of shooters. There may be
more. Suggest you call it a day and land immediately."*

*"Thanks for the info. Coming around for the line
abreast loop."*

*"Hoop. Link. Beeeeaaaner!"*

"Up . . . we . . . go . . . a . . . lit-tle . . . more . . .
power . . ."

Lew slammed the radio handset back into its cradle
and ran back to Patricia. "Let's get outside. We're not
doing much good here."

Rat clenched his jaw. What a group grope this had
turned into. Not only had they not gotten their target,
they had believed they had until their noses were
rubbed in it. Rat had to admit that Lew was the kind of
person that could rub people the wrong way, but he'd
been right this time. Now they were fighting an enemy
they didn't know, with weapons they couldn't identify,
and a setup and network they knew nothing about.
They were going to have very few chances to stop this.
And it might all come down to him. He had given the
French his location. They had reluctantly allowed him
to stay there, to participate, but only with the understanding that he wouldn't shoot anyone without their
specific direction. He had immediately agreed to that
condition since he had no intention of following it. No
sense in arguing about it since it was beyond consideration. He'd take the chance of being wrong. If he shot
someone who didn't deserve to be shot, then they could
talk to him.

Stovic pulled the nose of his plane through the horizon
and relaxed the G as he leveled out at two hundred feet
above the ground. He had heard the exchange between
Lew and the Boss. As he feared. The threat was still
there, maybe even worse than it had been.

But the Boss hadn't called anything off. They were
going to finish the show. He lined up for the knife-edge
pass opposite Oden. They were to do it at two hundred
feet so others could see it. He hoped Oden took it

down much lower. The lower they went now, the safer from being seen by someone with a missile standing on the ground, their view of the runway mostly blocked by hangars and static display aircraft.

He leveled his wings and pointed directly at Oden. He smiled. Oden was at fifty feet, or even lower. He had heard the Boss. Stovic stole a quick look at the trailer at center point. He tried to see whether there was anything else out of order in his quick scan of the horizon and the ground, but saw nothing.

*"Hit it!"*

They rolled into their knife-edge pass and shot past each other thirty feet apart. Stovic leveled his wings, pulled into a hard left turn behind the crowd, and streaked out to the east of Le Bourget. He held his throttles to the stops and glanced around again for signs of missiles or trouble. Rat had promised not to say a word on the frequency during the air show unless there was a missile in the air. That assumed Rat was in place to see it. Now the FBI had jumped onto their frequency and thrown a cold glass of water into their faces. Stovic glanced around and moved his finger to the button on the stick that would release his flares. One touch, and flares would be released in a timed program.

Stovic pulled around to the northeast of the airfield, continued to accelerate, and steadied at fifty feet off the ground, below the level of most of the hangars, which hid his presence from the crowd. Low, fast, and unexpected. It didn't really matter who they were or what their flying experience was, "the sneak," as his next maneuver was called, gave the crowd the unexpected sensation of having jet noise rammed down their senses. It never failed to evoke ducking by the crowd, cries of shock and concern, then exclamations of joy. He pulled around and pointed his Hornet at the crowd.

* * *

Inside the operations center, the noise of the single Hornet racing directly overhead was equally unexpected. The gendarmes and GIGN commandos buckled their knees and leaned over to avoid the sudden scream of the plane. They strained over the noise of Stovic's jet to hear the radio reports from the gendarmes in the northern sector, who transmitted in a burst of energy, *"We have what appears to be a launching tube sticking out of a bush in the back of a house. We are investigating."*

*"Say your coordinates! Do you require backup?"*

*"Negative,"* they replied.

The police proceeded cautiously toward the wall. The top of the tube was barely noticeable above the wall, projecting out of the bush only an inch or two at the most. There was no movement at all.

They could hear the Blue Angels thundering over the crowd behind them. There was a gate into the patio. The lead policeman tried the handle. It was unlocked. He glanced at his partner, who nodded. He pulled gently on the gate door until it began to squeak. They both jumped back and placed their backs against the wall, waiting. One indicated he was going to call for backup, surround the house, and come in from the front. His partner nodded. Suddenly the air broke as gunfire erupted from behind the wall in the patio next to the one they were investigating. Both were shot before they even knew what was happening. The sound of the assault rifle was drowned in the noise of the Blue Angel diamond passing overhead for its next maneuver. A man jumped down from his platform, out of the gate next door, and pulled the two dead policeman through the squeaky gate into the area where the fake missile launcher had been placed in the hope of luring police. The man returned to his platform behind the wall and activated his Russian missile.

The radio calls to the dead gendarmes went into their radios, into their earpieces, and pleaded for them to check in, but there was no response.

Stovic looked up and spotted Oden dirtying up his airplane so they could do their next maneuver, the clean and dirty loop; Oden would begin his loop with his landing gear, flaps, and tailhook down, while Stovic came in below him, flew directly underneath him, and performed a clean loop at much higher speed and higher altitude, returning back to the same spot at the same time as Oden, after which they flew off together.

Stovic watched Oden ahead of him, two hundred knots slower. He was flying a flawless routine, as were the other Blue Angels. He wondered whether the threat of death from a source other than your own mistake focused your mind even better on the task at hand.

Stovic bunted the nose of his Hornet down just slightly to pass under Oden's dirty Hornet. He flew sharply underneath Oden.

*"Hit it."*

They pulled the noses of their airplanes up. They began loops, Oden a slow dangerous loop with his landing gear down, Stovic a fast sleek loop in a circle outside Oden.

Rat watched through his rifle scope as the gendarmes silently surrounded the van in the parking lot. They came around a wall and pulled open the side door. They screamed at the single occupant to raise his arms and lie down on the floor. He was completely stunned by their intrusion and reached for something. One of the French soldiers struck him in the side of the face with the butt of his machine pistol. The three men went into the van and looked around. It was full of electronics gear and screens. They headed it toward a command center. *"We have found a radio van,"* a proud gendarme said.

*"Anyone there other than the one man?"*

The head of the French detail looked at the man really for the first time. He was surprised to see a young man in his thirties, clearly French. *"No."*

*"Who is he?"*

The gendarme took his wallet. *"He is French,"* he transmitted.

*"What is he doing there?"*

*"He has a private investigator's license."* The gendarme threw the wallet back on the man's bleeding face and gave a jerk of his head to the other two. They dashed out into the sunlight and back around the wall.

Stovic and Oden rendezvoused three miles west of the airfield. They were to fly directly at the crowd, roll two hundred seventy degrees, and pull in opposite directions. It was a visually complex and stunning maneuver, always one of the crowd favorites. It looked to the crowd as if they were pulling into each other and were sure to collide. But what the crowd couldn't see was that although they were in formation, one of the Hornets was two airplane-lengths behind the other.

Stovic's right hand began sweating on the stick as they approached the portion of the air show that Rat had warned him about. The 9-millimeter Glock was heavy against his chest in the pocket of his flight suit. The G forces built as they came around. The Gs were comforting, representing acceleration and movement. The more G forces he was pulling, the more he was moving, turning in the sky, the harder he would be to hit.

Stovic was in front. He lowered the nose of his F/A-18 and leveled out toward the center point, pointed directly down the runway.

Rat sat with his eye hard against the scope, waiting to see if the work van a thousand meters away would throw its doors open. There was no movement. The single man he had seen hadn't emerged from the van for several minutes. It was the position of the van that made Rat concentrate on it. It was strategically positioned. As soon as the back doors opened, the man would have a perfect shot at the tailpipes of the F/A-18 solos as they screamed back toward the stands, toward the spectators.

Rat heard them first, then glanced up and saw them coming toward him, heading for the center point of the air show at five hundred knots. This was it. He could hear the frantic efforts of the French and the FBI trying at the very last minute to find the shooters, looking everywhere.

Rat put the microphone for the UHF radio near his mouth, the one he could use to talk to Stovic, who was above him.

Just behind the Admirals, Lew and Patricia looked around frantically for anything out of the ordinary. Patricia saw him first. Out of the corner of her eye she noticed movement on the roof of the operations building. She immediately assumed it was another security officer, since it was the roof of the building from which the entire security operation was being run.

She screamed, "Lew!"

He turned and saw the head of the man immediately. "What the hell?" he asked. He was about to reach for his radio when they saw the man stand and lift a long shoulder-tube launcher onto his shoulder.

"He's got a missile!"

Lew and Patricia reached for the guns on their hips as the man they were watching casually looked through the sight and lowered the missile tube to the level of Oden and Stovic racing directly toward him.

"No!" Lew screamed.

Several spectators saw them pull out their sidearms and began screaming. The panic quickly spread through the crowd, which began to realize they were at the center of an unfolding catastrophe.

Rat continued to stare through his scope. He listened to Lew and Patricia call for backup and announce the first live shooter. *Here we go,* Rat said to himself. Kill or be killed. He thought of turning and finding the shooter back near the stands, but those there should be able to handle him. Shooting into the stands or the operations building could be done, but it was risky at this distance, almost two thousand yards. He studied the van and saw the slightest movement, almost a shudder. He squinted to make sure he wasn't missing anything. No doors were moving, nothing seemed out of the ordinary, yet there was that slight move, as if someone heavy had walked from one side of the van to the other. Then he noticed the small patch of gray, barely visible to him, on top of the van. He realized it was changing size.

The roof of the truck began retracting, rolling back toward the cab like the security doors in front of so many shops in Paris. The small motor hummed as the top steadily retracted. After a few seconds the top of the truck was completely gone, and the man inside stared into the bright sky. He could hear the approaching jets. They were coming from behind him, perfectly on schedule. He turned on his missile.

Lew stared at the two solo jets screaming toward him. They sounded like a giant ripping cardboard. Patricia transmitted on the radio, triggering the microphone with her left hand as she reached around to her right hip for her handgun. *"We've got a shooter on the roof of the operations center!"* Lew transmitted.

Patricia was faster getting out her gun and aimed at the small target fifty yards away, a difficult shot with a handgun. Only the man's head was visible with a small portion of the launch tube. Patricia wasn't waiting for anything. She fired at the man, missing him widely with her first shot. She kept firing. The man looked at her as he saw the dust fly from the top of the building where her shots hit. He crouched as low as he could and kept the infrared reticle of his Russian-made SA-7 on the approaching jets.

Patricia was still on the radio as she continued to fire. Lew fired as the spectators around them crushed down and tried to get away from a situation they did not understand. Lew and Patricia fired again and again, missing the shooter. The man was nearly ready to shoot when a bullet from Patricia's gun clubbed him on the top of his head and drove him down to the top of the building. His missile tube clanged down next to him.

*"Warn the Blue Angels!"* Lew screamed into the radio. *"They have to break off!"*

Ismael illuminated his digital watch again. The time had come. He stood quickly and thrust his shoulder against the lid, which flipped completely over. The lock that deterred anyone from using the Dumpster was still there. The rest of the plastic cover had been cut to allow a quick tearing away. He stood to his full height with his shoulders and head outside the Dumpster. He squinted and listened for the jets. He blinked to force his eyes to adjust more quickly to the brightness. He raised the Stinger to his shoulder. He placed the sight in front of his eye and searched for the Hornets, which should be just off to his right, racing toward the crowd from his right to his left. Ismael aimed carefully, putting the two Hornets in his sight, and waited.

* * *

Rat realized the van had a retractable roof. There was only one reason someone would have a retractable roof on a van and park it there today—to shoot down the Blue Angels. Rat wasn't going to wait. He put his crosshairs on the center of the back of the van and fired.

The enormous bullet tore through the back of the steel door and raced down the centerline of the van. The man inside, sitting comfortably in a plastic chair attached to the floor at the proper angle, was stunned to hear the bang of the bullet tear through the door and slam into the wall of the van three inches to the left of his head.

He never heard the second bullet.

Rat had a clip of .50-caliber bullets in his semiautomatic Barrett sniper gun. Some snipers didn't think the gun was accurate enough to be a true sniper rifle—and there wasn't sufficiently high-grade ammunition to get small enough groupings on bench shots with the rifle, but Rat loved it for the mass of the bullet, its range, and the fact that it was semiautomatic. And it was accurate enough. He had never missed a target. His second shot was lower, aimed down toward whatever was supporting whoever was looking out the roof of the van as the two Blue Angel solos flew over. Rat's second bullet tore a hole in the door and the man sitting behind it instantly. The Russian SA-14 missile clattered to the floor of the van as the man bled onto the floor.

Rat watched the Blues fly over, then saw a hissing trail of angry white smoke come from behind a wall.

*"Missile away!"* Rat yelled over his radio. He quickly controlled his breathing again, released half his air, and aimed at the wall fifteen hundred yards away where the missile had been launched. He fired quickly. His bullet tore through the wall, sending a cinder chip

into the eye of the Sudanese shooter and the bullet into his shoulder. He fell in pain as his missile climbed furiously. *"Missile airborne!"* Rat yelled again as he picked up what looked like a shotgun with an enormous barrel. He aimed up at the Blue Angels, who were now past him, and fired.

The flare flew out of the barrel toward the two solos. It quickly deployed at one hundred feet and started burning.

*"Flares! Break away!"* the Boss yelled over the radio.

The four Blue Angels in the diamond couldn't see the missile. They pumped flares out the back of their jets in case it was headed for them and broke out of their tight formation to head to the four corners of the compass and the safety of the ground. They accelerated downward, leveling out as low as was safe as they fled the airspace over Le Bourget, except for the Boss, who pulled up and stayed high watching the missile fly toward the two solos. *"Oden, it's at your six! Break right!"*

*"Break!"* Oden said. *"Get lower!"*

*"You got the missile?"* Stovic asked, desperately looking himself.

*"Negative!"*

Their flares dropped beautifully, following the computer-programmed timing for the release to achieve maximum deception as they broke in opposite directions, forcing the missile to follow one or the other. But they were too low for their flares to operate effectively. They bounced on the concrete below them and hissed and burned hot on the ground like nuclear fireflies. The missile was already ahead of Rat's flare. It flew over the Blue Angels' flares toward the four hot exhausts in front of it.

Oden and Stovic were turning as hard as they could in opposite directions to get their exhausts away from the missile. They each had one wing straight up in the air and the other straight down toward the ground. They grunted against the Gs as they gained a better angle on the pursuing missile. The missile chose Oden's jet and turned right to follow the moving heat source.

Ismael watched the missile chase the two fighters and their furious turning to avoid it. Number six was turning hard and in seconds would be pointed directly at him. The Stinger was the only shoulder-fired weapon in the world that could shoot down a jet from head on. The seeker-head was that good. The hungry missile rested on his shoulder, waiting for the American jet to finish its turn and head directly for him.

The first Stinger followed Oden. It drank in the heat of the exhaust, recognizing the range of the infrared spectrum that represented an engine. The closer it got, the more sure the missile was it had the right target. The oscillations of its flight path lessened and it focused on the center of the heat source. The missile flew right up the tailpipe and exploded in the back of Oden's jet. The hydraulic flight control lines for the tail were severed and the horizontal stabilizer went hard down, forcing the nose of the jet down toward the ground. Oden jerked the stick back, fighting the sudden loss of control, but felt no response. He pulled his ejection handle the instant before the Hornet hit the ground, burst into flames, and skidded toward the hangar filled with sales booths for aircraft engines.

  Stovic saw the flash of the missile impact in Oden's jet and relaxed his pull. He was heading down the runway away from the center point. He flew as low as he could safely fly. The small wings under the engine nacelles of his Hornet were no more than five feet off the ground. He tried to get even lower, hugging the ground for cover and making the lines of sight impossible for other shooters.

Ismael looked up to see one of their SA-7s chase a flare instead of a high-flying Hornet. He then watched Stovic turn #6 directly toward him. He watched flares drop out of the Hornet and pop against the runway as they lay there burning, completely ineffective, and behind the Hornet where they wouldn't do any good even if they were floating carelessly through the air.

He looked on in alarm as he realized Stovic was flying directly at him so low that his airplane would hit the Dumpster if he continued at the same altitude. He raised his Stinger to fire.

Stovic looked for obstacles at the end of the runway. He still had two thousand feet before he reached the end. He had bled off a good deal of airspeed with his hard turn and had stayed out of afterburner. But now he needed speed to escape. He slammed the throttles outward and forward to pump raw gas into the exhaust of the two powerful engines, the afterburners, and felt them kick the airplane forward, accelerating even faster.

He looked through the windscreen and saw the Dumpster directly in front of him, past the end of the runway at the end of the line of booths. A man was standing in it, a missile launcher on his shoulder aimed directly at Stovic. If he continued on, he would fly directly into the missile, but if he pulled up it would make the shot even easier. He moved the stick slightly until his screaming Hornet was headed directly at the man aiming at him. He knew without a doubt who was standing in the Dumpster.

* * *

Ismael watched in alarm as he realized Stovic had seen him. He now had to shoot at the jet coming directly at him, a small target with a lot of speed. He didn't know if the Stinger missile was up to it. He couldn't wait until the jet was past him, when he might have a clear shot at the exhaust. He knew what Stovic was doing. It was like an air show, like his first maneuver where he would fly low along the runway, then pull up hard and streak into the sky. Stovic was going to pull up and put his exhaust, or his tailpipes, right into the Dumpster. He was going to fry Ismael like a sausage on a spit.

Ismael closed his left eye and concentrated on the sight picture of his weapon with his other eye. The missile growled hungrily. He curled his finger around the trigger.

Rat saw him. He sighted down the barrel, put his scope on the target, and saw a man standing in a Dumpster about to fire at Stovic. He didn't have time to linger on the target, to check the wind, to confirm the distance, to ensure his bullet would hit in a four-inch circle. He simply had to fire and guess at the details.

The next .50-caliber bullet had already been chambered automatically by the Barrett and was ready. Rat put the crosshairs on the man's chest and fired.

The supersonic bullet raced to Ismael before the Algerian could even tell himself to pull the trigger. He knew he had a few seconds to perfect his shot at the Blue Angel, but he hadn't accounted for Rat seeing him from two thousand yards away with a cannon for a rifle.

The bullet nicked the top of the Dumpster just enough to disfigure the bullet before it hit Ismael. It was tumbling, trying to go end over end, but before it had a chance, it entered Ismael's chest, opening a hole through him and driving him back into the wall of the Dumpster. The Stinger fell from his hand as he crumpled inside the waste container.

Stovic raced toward the Dumpster in full afterburner. He waited for the missile to come up after him, but the man had disappeared. Stovic continued ahead, unsure of what had happened, expecting the man to stand back up. He flew as close to it as he could, then pulled up hard as he reached it, throwing his afterburning exhaust directly into the steel container as if it were a runway light at El Centro. He shot breath out of his lungs and grabbed another mouthful to hold as he automatically flexed every muscle in his upper body to trap blood to stay conscious. The ground disappeared and all he could see was sky.

Salam was in a black Mercedes van parked along the curb in the road outside the fence. He had wanted to be there when Ismael fired his Stinger into the mouth of the arrogant American. He didn't know what had happened. Ismael was in place, then suddenly he dropped like a stone. Sniper, Salam realized grimly. Someone centrally placed. He hadn't expected that. He envisioned Special Forces with their machine pistols racing to get Ismael after the fact. Ismael's Stinger never fired.

Salam checked his own Stinger, readied himself, and slid the side door of the van open. He stepped outside and looked up. Before anyone had a chance to see him, he raised his missile toward Stovic's jet and fired. He tossed the Stinger launcher on the ground and jumped back into the Mercedes.

Stovic held the stick back. He strained as he climbed and hit the button on his stick to deploy his last flares. They dropped out the back, but the missile had chosen its target. It hit his Hornet in the belly between the two engines. The warhead on the Stinger penetrated the thin skin of the jet and pierced the fuel tank between the engines. It exploded, sending hot steel fragments through both engines, which were spinning furiously, and into the fuel tank rich with fumes.

The engines began to come apart, and a flame shot up out of the back of the stricken Hornet.

*"You're hit!"* the Boss called from above. *"Eject! Eject!"*

Stovic looked at his instruments. The caution and warning panel was lit up like a scoreboard. He knew he wasn't going to make it. He still had three hundred fifty knots on the airplane and control. He continued up, trading his airspeed for more altitude. He decided to continue over on his back into a half Cuban Eight and try to land the Hornet on the runway heading the other direction. He pulled gently, just enough to keep going, and found himself on his back directly over the end of the runway at Le Bourget almost out of airspeed with a raging fire in the middle of the Hornet right behind his ejection seat. His engines were both full of steel fragments and were steadily coming apart, generating very little thrust. He knew he should shut off the engines and deploy the fire retardant through the fire handles. But he needed the hydraulic power and electrical power the engines gave him to keep flying.

He had no idea what had happened. The man with the missile had been shot. Rat probably got him. So where did the missile come from that got him? He was furious, but he had to focus on his airplane to have any hope of getting it on the ground. He wanted to roll level and head down to land at the other end of the runway, throw down his tailhook, and grab the arresting wire. He looked up at the ground through his canopy and saw a figure behind him dropping a launching tube and climbing into a van.

*Over my dead body,* Stovic thought. He checked his altitude, saw that he had enough, and pulled hard. The nose of the Hornet sliced through the horizon and headed down toward the ground. He saw the runway pass through his windscreen, and he completed a small loop with his nose pointing down at the field. He shut down one of his engines and pressed the fire extinguisher button for that engine.

*"Animal, eject! Eject!"* Boss yelled.

Stovic pulled the nose through until he was pointed directly at Salam. He could see that the man was looking over his shoulder at the shrieking, burning Hornet that was headed straight for him. He seemed to realize his predicament. He threw the van door open again and came out firing an AK-47 at the jet.

To Stovic it looked like a fast series of lights without any noise or effect. He knew every flash represented a bullet leaving the weapon aimed at him, but it didn't register. He didn't care. He was at five hundred feet. He looked at his airspeed and compared it to his altitude. He was approaching the edge of the envelope—the last chance he would have to successfully eject and live to tell about it. If he waited, the airplane's descent rate would trump the rocket motor in the ejection seat, and his ejection would end with him smacking into the ground without a parachute. Stovic saw more flashes from the barrel of the assault rifle and suddenly wished the 20-millimeter Gatling gun in the nose of the Hornet were loaded. But he had no weapons other than himself.

He flew down the path of the bullets and trimmed the Hornet's controls quickly so it would continue straight into the man firing at him. He waited until he was one hundred feet off the ground and reached between his legs. He grabbed the loop attached to the ejection seat and leaned back to make sure his spine was straight. He put his left hand on the wrist of his right hand and pulled with all the strength he had.

The canopy was instantly blown off, his seat motor fired, and he was blasted up the rail by the rocket motor on his ejection seat. He flew into the sky as the shiny blue Hornet with two dead engines and a raging fire in its back slammed into the ground ten feet from Salam. It exploded in a concussive conflagration. The metal and fire tore through Salam instantly, completely destroying him.

But Stovic had waited too long. His descent rate was too high. The barometer in the seat knew it was too low and pushed him out of the seat by inflating a bladder behind his back. The passing airstream jerked the parachute out of its pack, and the ballistic spreader fired sending the canopy into its instantaneous imitation of an airborne jellyfish racing for the surface.

The canopy caught the air once, and Stovic hit the ground right in the middle of the burning Hornet he had just abandoned. He reached for the Koch fittings of his parachute to get away from it and run out of the fire.

Rat threw his Barrett to the side and jerked a rope that ran down the trunk of the tree. It came free and he slid down it in two seconds. He ran toward Stovic's jet. He saw the Hornet hit and the single small, futile puff of the parachute before it was engulfed in the flames. *"Ed!"* he screamed as he ran as fast as he could.

The French crash trucks and crews sped toward the scene, leaving half of them to deal with Oden's Hornet, still burning out of control. Sirens tore through the air from every direction. Security helicopters with GIGN forces lifted off with some fear of additional Stinger missiles but determined to close the perimeter and catch anyone fleeing or any other hopeful shooters who still had weapons.

Stovic felt his parachute come free as he fell to the ground and felt the flames rolling up around his back. He held his breath and fought to stand without putting down his hands. He jumped toward the only daylight he could see, his quickest path out of sure death. He broke into clear air but still held his breath as he looked for cool ground. He saw intact grass to his left and threw himself down on it, trying to extinguish the flames he could feel on his flesh.

He rolled and rolled as the crash crew arrived. A French fireman shot carbon dioxide over him and suppressed the remaining flames as they encouraged him to walk quickly away from the burning airplane, out of the range of a possible explosion. His lungs burned from holding his breath, and he exhaled, exhausted and beaten. He was grateful for the coldness of the carbon dioxide around him. He gasped for air. They stopped moving, and he leaned over as the fire crews surrounded him. He looked at his hands and wrists and saw that the fire had done its damage—skin hung limply from the back of both hands.

The crash crews were talking to him emphatically in French, insisting he do something. Finally one of the firemen said in English, "Down. Lie down!"

Stovic shook his head.

Rat broke through the circle of firemen and gasped for breath. "Eddie! You okay?"

"I think I got burned."

Rat looked at his hands. "You'd better let them put something on those. They're going to hurt like hell in about thirty seconds."

"Did I burn my face?"

Rat looked at him and shook his head, quickly looking around for any other trouble. "No. Just a little on your neck. Won't matter."

Stovic nodded as the shock started to wear off and the burns on his hands began talking to him. He started feeling light-headed and weak. He sat on the ground, then rolled over on his back and stared up at the blue sky.

The fire crew slid him carefully onto a stretcher and backed the ambulance up to load him in. They wrapped his hands and put a cold damp compress on his neck as they placed him carefully in the ambulance. Rat spoke in French to the rescue crews. The EMT asked Rat to see if Stovic wanted anything for the pain. Stovic declined.

The Boss was frantic. *"Rat, is Animal okay?"*

*"Yeah,"* Rat transmitted. *"Few burns, but he'll be okay."*

Rat began to climb into the ambulance but was held out. He spoke softly in French. They stepped aside and let him in as they closed the doors and rolled toward the hospital with the lights and siren blazing.

Rat waited until they were on the pavement of the runway, then sat on the fold-down seat. He watched Stovic stare. "You okay?"

Stovic tried to shrug. He pointed toward his chest with one of his bandaged hands.

Rat looked at his chest, confused.

Stovic pointed again. Rat leaned over and looked at the bulge in his lower left chest. It looked as if several of his ribs had been broken and were protruding. He reached down and touched it gently and felt the hard steel of a gun barrel. He nodded, unzipped the flight suit pocket, and withdrew the Glock. The EMT raised his eyebrows as Rat shoved the Glock into his belt.

"Rat, what happened? I thought you got them all."

"We did. But they didn't get Ismael, and there was a

whole second team in place. A backup team. They got off a few shots, and unfortunately a couple of them got through."

"How's Oden?" he asked, afraid of the answer.

"They took him away in an ambulance. But I saw him step in. He's fine."

Stovic took the first deep breath he had allowed himself in a while. They rode in silence for a mile or so. "Rat."

Rat came out of his thoughts, back into the ambulance. He moved his chin up, a "yeah" on his face.

"You know how to get in touch with Karen?"

Rat reached into a pocket and pulled out a miniature cell phone. He dialed a long number, obviously international, listened until it started ringing, and held the phone up against Stovic's ear.

"What?" a gruff voice answered.

"Is Karen there?"

"Who wants to know?"

"Ed Stovic."

"Never heard of him."

Ed looked up at Rat, who took the phone. "Who is this?"

"Who is this?"

"Rat."

"What are you doing calling here?"

"It's over. Put her on."

"How do I know—"

"Put her on!"

There was a pause of ten seconds, then Karen came on the phone. "Hello?" she asked expectantly.

Rat put the receiver back up to Stovic's ear. "Hello?"

"Ed?!"

"Karen."

"Ed! Are you okay?"

"Yeah. I'm fine. It's over. We thought we got them

all, but there were a few left. They got Oden and me.
We busted our jets."

"How? That doesn't matter, are you hurt at all?"

"Got a little sunburn on the back of my hands, but
I'll be fine. Just need some vitamin E."

"Did you crash?"

"Yeah. Look, is there any way you can come over? I
know this isn't how we planned it, coming to Paris. We
were going to go out to dinner and drink wine and look
at art and walk along the Seine—"

"I'll be there—"

"and go to the Eiffel Tower and Notre Dame and sit
at the cafés—"

"I'll leave this afternoon. I can't wait to see you!"

"I'll share half my hospital meal with you, and we'll
drink wine if they'll let us, but I don't think we'll get to
do—"

She could sense from his voice that he wasn't doing
as well as he had said. She could sense a desperation, or
fear, something serious in his tone. "I don't care. You
know that. I just want to be with you. The Seine and
the cafés and the walks are all there. We can talk about
all the things we'll see. I'll read to you from every tour
book I can find."

"When you get here, Karen, we need to talk."

"Anything you want."

"We'll talk about lots of things, but I want to talk
about what your dreams are." He paused. "I don't
know enough about them."

"I'd like that."

"I love you," he said, and they hung up. He closed
his eyes and handed the phone to Rat.

Rat accessed the web and typed in a short message,
then hit "send."

Stovic opened his eyes. "Who was that?" he asked,
looking at the phone.

Rat smiled. "Had to report to someone who thinks I work for her."

"Do you?"

Rat slipped the phone into an invisible pocket. "I'm just a private citizen with a new security company to run. Remember?"

St. John excused herself from the situation room. She was shaken. She had watched the burning hulks of the Blue Angel jets as they lay on the ground at Le Bourget. She and the others had received word that the pilots were slightly injured but would be okay, but the bill of what she had set in motion lay in front of her. It was worse than she had hoped, but no one had been killed.

President Kendrick stepped out of the other door and called to her in the hallway, "Sarah?"

She stopped and turned around. "Yes, Mr. President? Sorry, I was just sneaking to the ladies' room."

"Can I talk to you for a second?"

"Yes, sir," she said.

He walked up to her. "One thing I've been trying to figure out," he said.

"Yes, sir?"

"Stuntz told the Blue Angels to pull the plug. Right?"

"Yes, sir."

"But they flew anyway. How did that happen? I mean, by the time we got to this room, they were airborne."

"Yes. I saw that."

"Do you have any idea how they flew in spite of the Secretary's order?"

"I think everyone understood that the cancellation was based on the fact that we hadn't found all the terrorists. As I understand it, they did find all of them, or thought they did. So since the reason was gone, they launched."

"Who gave them the go-ahead?"

"Maybe you should ask Mr. Stuntz."

"I get the feeling he doesn't know."

"I assume it was Admiral Hooker, the Admiral at the Pentagon who is in charge of the Blue Angels." She paused. "The same one who told them they'd been canceled for next year."

Kendrick processed what he was hearing. "So they thought they had gotten them all, but in fact there was a second team we hadn't even expected. So they flew, and although it was at high cost, we got all of them too."

"I think that's exactly right."

"This whole thing has made Stuntz look like he doesn't know what's going on in his own house. Was that part of what you were trying to achieve?"

"Always after the truth, Mr. President." She smiled.

Kendrick turned to go back in, then had another thought. "Seems to me you were a little closer to reality through this. More in tune with the risks that are out there."

St. John waited.

"If the opportunity ever arose, would you consider becoming the Secretary of Defense?"

From
*Secret Justice*
by James W. Huston,
available now in hardcover.

The SEALs ensured their weapons were ready. Most carried H&K MP5Ns like Rat, a small submachine gun that only weighed six and a half pounds. The favored of the SEALs; were reliable, accurate, and their 9 Millimeter round was subsonic—they could use sound suppressors. But this time Rat removed the sound suppressor. Noise was a weapon against those who weren't ready for it. It would add to their confusion.

Rat raised his hand. The others lined up behind him. He lifted the lever to the door and walked in slowly with his submachine gun on his hip and began speaking loudly in Arabic, "I am Major Wassoud of the Sudanese Army. Who is in charge here? Who told those men to stop our Army patrol?" Rat's heart was pounding as he looked around the room. He immediately recognized Duar.

Rat's Sudanese desert camouflage uniform was perfect. He wore the shoulder badge of an officer of the southern security detail. The two men at the table looked at him in fury. Duar immediately suspected something. But Rat's boldness gave him just enough time get all the SAS team members into the room that were coming. They picked their targets quickly and pointed their weapons directly at them. The men in the room with Duar and Lahoud were reluctant to reach for their own weapons. Rat paused, then pointed his weapon at Duar and yelled in Arabic, "American special forces! Lay down your weapons!"

Three of the men behind Duar quickly raised their AK-47s toward Rat and were immediately gunned down. The room erupted in pandemonium. Everyone fought to stand up and bring their automatic weapons to bear on the intruders. Several began firing but were hit by American fire before they could even get their assault rifles to their shoulders. The sound of automatic weapons fire was deafening as muzzle flashes illuminated every corner of the room. The Americans trained for just such an event every day. They fired over a thousand rounds of live ammunition every day of every week. They trained in the kill house every week, where they would practice putting a three round cluster in the chest of one attacker and quickly go on to the next. Duar and Lahoud's men were up and running around inside the room, looking for cover, falling to the floor to fire, falling to the floor dead; blood was flying, bullets chipped the floor and walls, and men screamed in fear and agony.

Groomer ran to Acacia and pulled him away from the wall. Lahoud saw the look in Acacia's eye. He knew he had been betrayed. He stood and pulled a handgun out of the folds of his robe to shoot Acacia. Groomer fired quickly and the short square man dropped in a heap.

Duar bolted toward the back of the room with two of his men covering his move. Rat saw him go through a door, that led outside through a small hallway. Two of his men were waiting outside at the other end of that hallway. "Banger, coming your way."

"Roger."

Suddenly bullets zipped by Rat's head as he moved left. The American next to him took two bullets in the face and spun to the floor. Rat turned to the assailant. The beast that lived inside him, his anger, raised its ugly head. He knew if he wasn't careful it could consume him, completely override his judgment. It could burn white hot. Rat fought it and tried to stay calm. He raised his weapon to kill the man who had just shot the American. The man threw down his AK-47 and held up his hands. He had a slight wound on his shoulder, but was otherwise fine. As Rat hesitated another man fired at him. Rat turned slightly and blew open his belly. Bullets flew wildly into the wall and out the top of the building as the man fell to the floor still clutching the trigger of his weapon.

Rat glanced at the downed American who was clearly dead. *"Damn it!"* he yelled. The firing died down, the clicky sounds of the AKs vanished, replaced by the deeper chop of the American weapons. The fight was over in less than a minute. Men lay dead and moaning around the room. The one he had spared sat in the corner with his superficial wounds. Three of the Americans rushed around the room disarming everyone and ensuring that there was no additional threat.

"Everyone okay?" Rat asked.

The others responded by number, through twelve, with number nine silent.

"Somebody get over here and keep an eye on this live one. He shot Nubs in the face, then threw his gun down. Banger, you get Duar? He charged out the back of the room." Rat asked.

"Didn't come out this way, sir," Banger replied.

Rat frowned and looked at Groomer who had put Acacia on the floor near the door. Groomer grabbed one of the other men. "Stay with him. Nobody touches him at all."

He nodded.

Groomer stood and followed Rat toward the door. Rat approached cautiously, confused by where the man could have gone. He kept his weapon trained in front of him. Groomer was right behind him and to his left. "What we got here, Groomer? Where'd the son of a bitch go?"

"Must be between us and the door, right?"

"Must be a soft wall here somewhere."

"Or floor." Rat stopped. "I don't like this. They can hear us. Might shoot through a wall. Robby!"

Robby ran to where they were.

"Give me the ULF."

He took the device out of his backpack and Rat held it to the walls, then the floor. There was some ambiguity about what was behind them, some space, or odd construction, but no people. No stairways, no ladders, no obvious escapes. "What the hell," he muttered to no one in particular. He turned the device off and handed it back to Robby. "I think I'll ask one of his men where he is."

Groomer stopped and started backing out of the hallway. "And what if he doesn't want to tell us?"

"I'll encourage him. Stay here by the hallway entrance in case he or someone else comes back. If he left in a tunnel, he may have more men there."

"Roger that," Groomer replied. He turned his back on the main room.

Rat re-entered the main hall with its stucco walls and exposed beams. It was a well-constructed building. Rat wondered what it had been, and why it was abandoned. He looked at the dead men on the floor. He was completely unmoved. He had no sympathy for terrorists. They were sub-human to him. The bodies lay all over, bright red blood pooling around each of their bodies and going dark when exposed to the air for a few seconds. Each man had fallen in his own haphazard way. Several still had open-eyed surprised looks on their faces. The Americans stepped around them, making sure they were dead. Robby, one of the two black team members, was videotaping the entire scene with a miniature digital video camera. Robby's rating of radioman only scratched the surface of his vast capabilities. He was a technology wizard.

"You call in the helos?" Rat asked him.

Robby nodded. "Fifteen minutes."

Rat checked his watch and considered whether he had time. "Toad, take six men and check every inch within a hundred yards of this building. That asshole has an escape tunnel or some way out of here. Find out where he came out. If you find anything, any sign of life, let me know."

Toad, a first class petty officer but at fine TAD to the CIA like several of the others, nodded, grabbed five men and hurried outside.

"All right, where's that live one?" Rat asked, stepping over a dead terrorist. "And where's Acacia?" He came upon Nubs. "*Damn* it," he said, stooping to examine his man. He pulled the desert scarf up. Nubs' face was ruined. The two AK-47 bullets had entered just above the lower jaw on the left side of his face. The exit wounds in the back of his head were massive. Death had been instantaneous. "I'm going to rip somebody's head off," Rat said marching to the only living terrorist in the room. He fought the building fury he felt, the white anger that occasionally got him in trouble.

Acacia stood and followed Rat to the corner.

Rat looked at the man sitting on the floor. He stood over him, waiting for the man to look up at him.

Rat glanced at the wooden table strewn with papers. "Somebody get all these papers. We'll let intel take a look at those out on the ship." He turned to Acacia and spoke in Arabic. "So, you're him."

Acacia looked him in the eyes. "Speak English. I don't want him," he said indicating the surviving terrorist, "to understand." He continued in English. "What are you going to do with him?"

"I came to get Duar. You know where he is?"

"No."

"He was here, wasn't he?"

Acacia flared angrily. "I wouldn't have sent the signal if he wasn't. I am not stupid."

"So where is he now?"

"I don't know." He looked around the room at the dead men. "If he is not dead, you must have let him escape. But he cannot have gone far."

Rat regarded the prisoner. "He may know where Duar is. I'm not leaving without him, even if we have to burn this building down to find him. I think I'll ask him a few questions."

"And after you ask him questions?"

"I'll take him out to the ship with us so the pros can interrogate him. Banger, find me a bucket of liquid. Water, anything, coffee, goat's milk, whatever. And two good-sized cups. Must be a kitchen around somewhere."

"You gonna water-board this guy?" Banger asked, his eyes getting bigger.

"If he makes me," Rat replied.

Banger left the room.

Rat turned back to Acacia. "We've only got a few minutes."

"Everyone was supposed to be killed except Duar," Acacia argued.

"Doesn't work that way. You don't go into it and plan on killing everyone. You just do what's necessary. He surrendered. Can't shoot him in cold blood."

"*I* can," Acacia said, looking at the man.

Rat stared at him. "Don't worry, he'll be put away for so long he'll forget all about you."

"No he won't. He will get the word out. I betrayed them and he knows it."

Rat didn't reply.

Acacia spoke quietly. "After you're done with your questioning just turn your back for one minute. You can be furious with me afterward." He paused.

"Sorry," Rat replied. "Can't do that."

"Then you may have to stop me."

"I probably can do that."

The Jordanian's anger was starting to show on his face. "You are more interested in protecting him than me?"

"I just play by the rules I'm given. I don't execute prisoners. Sometimes I'd like to. Like now. But I'm not going to."

Acacia turned his back and walked away.

"Bring him over here," Rat said loudly.

The terrorist was brought to him.

Rat spoke to him in Arabic. "What's your name," he asked.

The man said nothing.

Rat slapped him in the face with his open hand. He yelled, "What's your name?"

The man's eyes flamed with anger, he spat, "Mazmin."

Rat looked at him intently and spoke softly. "I'm going ask you some questions, and you are going to answer. Do you understand?"

Mazmin was emboldened. "I will not answer any questions."

Rat replied quickly, "You may *think* you're not going to answer, but I guarantee you that you that you will."

Mazmin shook his head.

Rat asked, "Where is Wahamed Duar? Your boss?"

Mazmin shook his head again, growing firmer with every passing second that he wasn't shot.

Acacia stood two steps behind Rat, fuming, fingering the trigger guard on the 9 MM semi-automatic handgun in his pocket.

Rat stared at Mazmin.

Banger came back into the room carrying a large, heavy animal trough full of water. He set it down carefully as some sloshed over the side and darkened the concrete floor.

"Banger, help me with this table. We've got to make a water-board out of it, and we're down to ten minutes before the helos arrive. Turn it over and rip the legs off."

They flipped the table over, laying it on the floor with the legs sticking up. Each gave a few sharp blows with the heels of their hands splintering the legs off quickly.

"Turn the table over, and put the legs under one end. I need some incline." He looked up. "Groomer. I need you to hold his head. Get a shirt or something off one of the dead guys."

Groomer threw the sling of his weapon over his head to free his hands and rushed to help. They slid the four table legs under one end of the table, pointing the shattered ends toward the center of the table. It raised one end of the table higher than the other end by the thickness of the square legs, about four inches.

"Think that's enough?" Rat asked.

"Beats the hell out of me," Groomer said.

"Put him on the table."

Two other SEALs grabbed Mazmin and threw him down on the table on his back. They held his arms while another SEAL came and held his legs. Mazmin's eyes grew in fear. He began yelling in Arabic, "You can't do this to me!"

"Shut up," Groomer said, "whatever the hell you're saying." He grabbed his head and pulled him down to the lower end of the table. Groomer kneeled on the floor and folded up a shirt lengthwise. He placed it across Mazmin's eyes and forehead. He rolled up the excess on the sides of his head so the shirt stretched tight. Groomer leaned down with all his weight, pinning Mazmin's head to the table. His mouth and nose were still exposed. He struggled to get free, but it was hopeless.

Rat dragged the water closer to the table and took the two cups in his hands. Mazmin's chest was heaving from his heavy breathing. He knew something bad was about to happen.

Rat leaned over so his mouth was right next to Mazmin's ear. "Where is Duar?"

"I don't know any Duar."

Rat lifted the dripping cup of water four inches above Mazmin's face and poured a quick stream into his nose. Mazmin blew it out, afraid of more.

"Where is Duar?" Rat asked, with the image of Nub's shattered face vivid in his mind and the white anger fighting to return.

"Don't know—"

Rat poured quickly while Mazmin's mouth was open. Water went into his mouth and nose, but he was ready for it. He closed his mouth and stopped breathing.

Rat continued to pour water from the cup into his nose in a constant stream. As he poured, he filled the other cup. As soon as the first cup was nearly empty, he began pouring from the second cup, one continuous stream of water. As the second cup emptied, the first was re-filled and ready to be poured behind the second. Again and again, one cup, then the other, an endless stream of water. "You have to breathe sometime, and when you do, all you're going to get into your lungs is water. And unless you tell me what I want to know, you're never going to get another breath of air. Think about that," he said as he continued to pour.

Over a minute passed, but Mazmin couldn't stand his burning lungs any more. He gasped for breath but there wasn't any air; he sucked the water right into his lungs. Rat kept pouring.

Mazmin tried desperately to breath, but all he got was water, in and out, and again, nothing but water. He tried to cry out, but the water wouldn't even let him form a scream. There was no air to pass through his vocal chords. His body strained against the men holding his arms and legs as he fought for breath. He was drowning and he knew it.

Mazmin tried to beg for mercy. Rat stopped water flow. "Where is Duar?"

Mazmin's chest heaved as he breathed deeply again and again, grateful for the air. "I don't know."

"Bullshit!" Rat said as he dipped his cups back into the water. He began pouring and Mazmin began yelling then snapped his mouth again and held his breath.

Groomer tightened his grip on the fabric, putting extra weight on his head, driving it into the hard wooden table.

Mazmin's lungs were burning from not having enough air. He wouldn't be able to hold his breath for long. He tried to get a quick breath through his nose, but choked on it. The water went into his lungs and stomach. His stomach fought the intrusion and he began to throw up, sending food up against the water. Rat didn't stop. He knew he was within a minute of breaking. He had seen many men on the waterboard. They all broke.

The water washed away the vomit and ran back

down into his lungs. Mazmin couldn't stand anymore. He was on the verge of passing out. He couldn't even tell them he was about to die. He tried to nod his head. If they didn't stop he'd be dead in thirty seconds.

Rat watched Mazmin carefully. He stopped the water. "Where is Duar?"

Mazmin spit the water out and blew it out of his nose, furious and fearful. He began crying. "If I tell you, you stop this!"

"If I believe you."

"In a well! Perhaps three hundred meters to the south."

Rat turned on his encrypted UHF radio. "Banger, check for a well three hundred meters to the south. Duar may be there."

"Roger. Copy. On our way."

Rat dipped his cups back into the water and filled them. He looked down at Mazmin. He knew he had heard the cups. He was confident that the sound alone was too horrible for him to handle right now. "Who does Duar report to?"

"Nobody. He ran everything."

"How did he communicate with others?"

"I don't know."

Rat poured a small stream of water onto Mazmin's face.

The man screamed. "I don't know! I did things for him. I was not with him. I don't know how he communicated with anybody."

Rat wasn't buying it. He began pouring water into the man's nose and mouth again. Mazmin tried to scream, but again it was muffled by the constant presence of water. He fought it, but it was no use. He inhaled again and sucked water into his lungs, completely filling them with what felt like an ocean of water.

Mazmin suddenly went unconscious and sagged as

his mouth hung open. Rat stopped pouring. He looked at Groomer.

Rat stood up. "That's enough for him. Turn him over."

They rolled him over on his stomach. Rat pressed his back between his shoulder blades. The water gushed out of his lungs, running down the table and onto the floor. He raised the man's arms behind him and nearly touched his elbows. He repeated the motion two or three times until he heard Mazmin gasp for air.

Rat looked at the SEALs who had been holding Mazmin's arms and legs. "Hold him here. I'm going to go find that well. Groomer, come with me." Then loudly in Arabic, "And if I don't find Duar, I'm going to come back here and stab *him* in the eye."

He was interrupted by the receiver in his ear. "We've got what may be a well. Small building. Nobody in there."

Rat lowered his night vision device and walked carefully through the room and into the darkness. Groomer was right behind him. "Maybe he's in the well itself. I'm on my way."

He broke into a trot. "We've only got three minutes. Robby, you up?"

"Here." the techno-wizard replied into his earpiece.

"Check in with the helos. Get an updated ETA."

"Wilco."

He found the small building. The others were waiting outside for him waiting for his instructions. He looked at Groomer.

"It's a well all right. Two flat doors on top of it that are folded closed. The well is probably underneath those doors."

Rat walked directly inside the building. His men covered the entrance and all sides from the outside. Rat stooped down and studied the two doors over the well opening. They had handles. He was tempted to just grab one of the doors and fling it open. He looked at Groomer. "Could be booby trapped."

*"ETA five minutes,"* Robby transmitted.

"Roger," Rat replied. He glanced at his watch. Rat could hear himself breathing. "Give me some line, or wire. He stuck out his hand, and felt nylon cord being placed in his open palm. He carefully wrapped the line around one of the handles that was attached to the door over the well and retreated back to the outside.

He handed the line to Groomer. "When I say, pull on this and get on the ground."

Groomer took it and nodded.

Rat kneeled down next to Groomer with his submachine gun pointed at the well. He took a breath and nodded to Groomer.

Groomer gave a huge pull and lay flat on the ground. The door flapped opened immediately and slammed over. Suddenly, bullets rang out in the well house. Rat couldn't tell where they were coming from, then realized the bullets were flying into the roof of the well house. They were coming from inside the well. Someone was definitely in the well, and he had been surprised.

"He's got to be standing on something, or suspended by something," Groomer said.

Rat crawled back into the well house on his belly as the bullets continued streaming out of the well. He examined the top of the well from the side; a rope was tied to the hinge of the opposite door. He slid back outside as the harmless firing stopped.

Rat turned to Groomer. "He's on a rope. How the hell do we get this guy out of there without killing him?"

Groomer nodded. "We need to get our rope underneath his. But he'll see it. We need to distract him. I'll pull open the other door. Give me one second. That's all I need. Let me put some black cammo on this rope. When I'm ready, fire some bursts right over the mouth of the well. I'll slip our rope under his. Then I'll just pull his ass up out of there."

"First I'll drop something heavy into the well. He doesn't know we want him alive. He'll think it's a grenade. He'll try to look down before he looks up and tries to get out. That's when I'll fire. He'll feel trapped." Rat transmitted, "*Everybody away from the south side of the well house. I'll be firing directly across the mouth of the well. Anybody see a rock, or piece of rubble anywhere? I need something that weighs a couple of pounds that will sound like a grenade hitting the water.*"

Robby answered. "*Drop a real grenade. Just don't arm it.*"

"*Good idea,*" Rat replied. He took one of the grenades out of the pocket of his vest. He nodded at Groomer.

Groomer tied the rope to the second handle, backed away slightly and pulled the second door wide open. The firing started again, slamming harmlessly into the ceiling. Duar was in too far to aim with any angle out of the well.

Rat lay directly next to the opening. Groomer moved up with his now blackened, rope, and nodded at Rat. Rat tossed the grenade into the opening. He heard it click against the wall of the well, then clunk into something. He heard the man curse. He had hit him in the head with the grenade which then tumbled past him into the water below with a loud splash. Rat started firing.

With amazing speed Groomer slid his hand underneath the rope down in the well. He pulled it around and walked back out of the well house. The line was perhaps twenty feet long. He held both ends. "You, and you," he said. "Give me a hand here. We've got to pull this asshole out of this well like he's been shot out of a cannon. Heave on this line when I say." He moved the rope over his shoulder and the other two got behind him and did likewise.

Rat moved in to the well house and gave Groomer the sign.

"Go!" Groomer yelled as he started pulling with all his might. They ran away from the well house; the line rapidly pulled Duar up. Rat watched as his head and the barrel of an AK-47 reached the top of the opening. Rat moved behind the terrorist.

As soon as his head passed the lip of the well Duar started shooting, the bullets slamming harmlessly into the ceiling. Rat waited until the barrel of his weapon began to clear the well's edge.

Rat grabbed the barrel of the assault rifle. The man tried to turn around, but had nothing to push off from. He was standing on a loop of rope that was unstable.

Rat pulled the rifle back hard, making sure it didn't point at him. He struck the man's wrist sharply causing the man to cry out and release the rifle. Rat tossed it away and grabbed the man by the throat, pulling him backward out of the well.

The man was as big as Rat and struggled. Rat put him in a choke hold, cutting off his air. The man pulled at Rat's arm, but had no hope of breaking the grip.

Groomer felt the rope go slack and ran back into the well house. He took the man's legs and pulled him the rest of the way out of the well. As the man tried to kick him, Groomer reached up and punched him in the groin. Rat released his grip and the man moaned in pain.

Groomer grabbed his legs again and turned him over on the floor. He pulled plastic hand ties out of his pocket and bound the man's hands together. He pulled out a flashlight and shone it in the man's face. "It's him. Sure as hell," Groomer smiled.

Rat and Groomer stood up and pulled Duar to his feet. Rat looked up to see the approaching CH-53s the Air Force was bringing in to pull them out. "Let's get him out to the carrier."

# Listen to

# BALANCE of POWER

## By

# JAMES W. HUSTON

ISBN: 0-694-52515-4
Price: $9.99/$14.95 Can.
3 hours/2 cassettes
Performed by Michael Paul Valley

**Available wherever books are sold or call 1-800-331-3761 to order.**

HarperAudio
www.harperaudio.com

JHA 0503